RESURGENCE
IN MEMORIAM
BOOK II

EVELYN GRIMALD STONE

Tarney Brae Creative Endeavours

*For all of you who were told you were stars, when really you
were goddesses*

CONTENTS

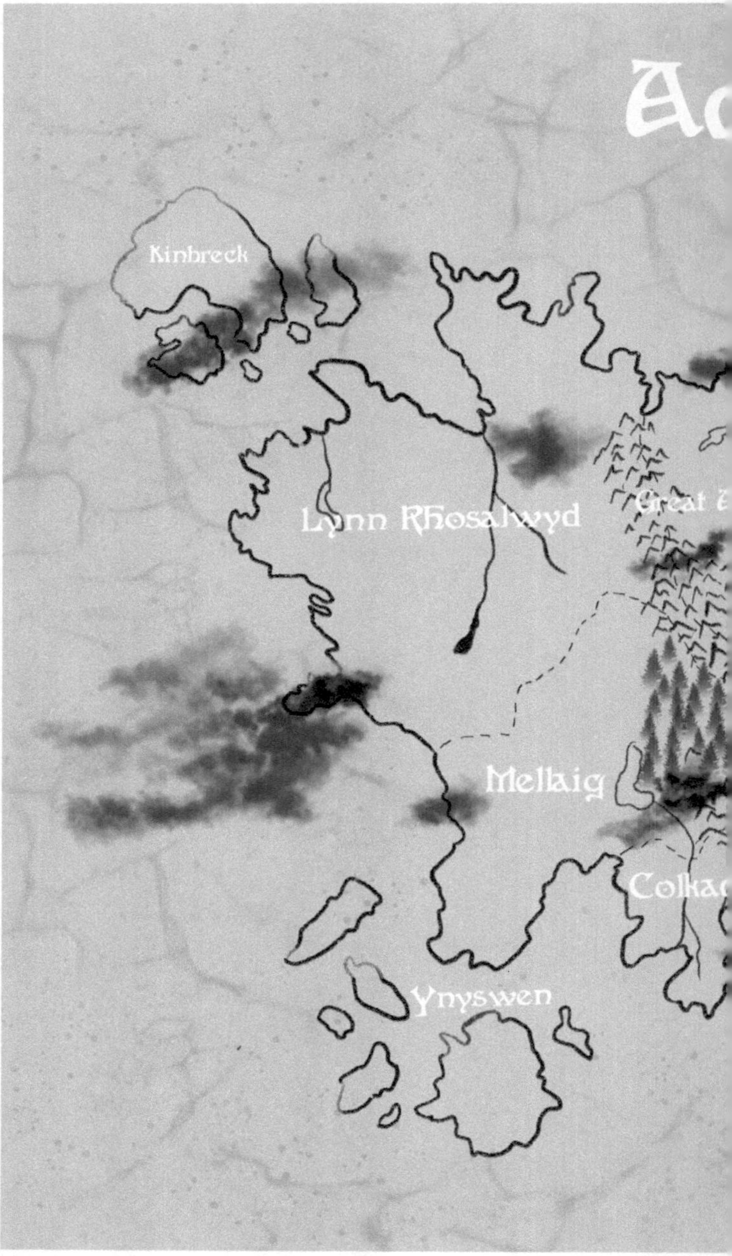

Kinbreck
Lynn Rhosalwyd
Great
Mellaig
Colkac
Ynyswen
Ac

or
Ynysfawr
Altier
Baldarskiel
igsmuir
Melkirk
ontys
unnaig
Balmalyne
Cortaesi

CHAPTER 1

Flickers of light were all that kept her sane in this impenetrable darkness. She knew darkness well, had created it, had fought it, had even loved it for a while, and this was different. This was not the darkness of a plain beneath an impersonal sky. This was not the shadow of midnight, the clutch of shade in the hours before dawn. This was not the grasp of the void, nor of the living space between stars, the guardians of the sky.

This was the darkness of beneath. Of spaces below the earth where no light had ever touched, save now for the flickers she managed to produce. This was worse than darkness. This was the place where she would surely die.

A slight scraping came from the other side of the wall, and the stone melted away, revealing a woman wreathed in earthen silk, her form wrapped in flowers. Beyond her, a reddish light gleamed, unnatural and hot.

"You live still," the goddess said, sounding surprised.

Astraea scoffed. "You think to subdue *me*? To reduce me to, what, a whimpering mule of a creature, simply because you cut off my connection to the sky?"

The goddess smiled, the movement bringing a bloom of life into the depths of this cavern. Lavender and corn flowers twined around Astraea's feet. She shook them off with poorly restrained fury. "Dear star, no, I expect a great deal from you. You, who cut yourself off from the sky willingly, only your foolish guardian by your side. Oh, no, I expect much from you!"

"Casimir is not foolish," Astraea snapped, curling her lip into a snarl.

"He fell in love with you, did he not?"

Astraea lowered her gaze, saying nothing.

"Oh, do get on with it, Sister." A second woman, born of living flames and molten rock, peered into the prison. She sneered at Astraea, brushing a strand of fiery hair from her face, a spark landing on one of the blooming flowers. "The vessel is almost ready."

The earth goddess sighed. "Impatient as always," she murmured. Then, to Astraea, "Come. It is time."

"Time for what?" She had no chance of escape, not now she'd been captured and separated from the sky. Her light was so weak down here, and even the darkness was wrong, draining rather than invigorating, refusing to let her shine properly. No, these two goddesses had done well in their capture of her. She'd let her guard down, thinking the void an infallible barrier between her and the realm of the gods.

Astraea fully expected to die here, but she would turn nova first if it meant taking these two with her.

The earthen goddess reached forwards, and with a gesture, spires of rock pushed Astraea forwards so that she stumbled on cracked and bleeding feet. "No need to be so pushy," she said on a laugh. The goddess of fire eyed her warily.

"This way," the earth goddess said, gesturing. Scraping together the last dregs of her dignity, Astraea straightened her shoulders, tossed her hair back, and lifted her chin. She walked forwards, delicate, graceful, the very image of what a goddess should be. There was, after all, a reason that the humans had so preferred her over these forgotten fools.

The main chamber was little more than a small platform extended over a pool of magma, churning and bubbling with eager abandon. The light coming from this pool was harsh to Astraea's eyes after the oppressive deep of her earthen prison. It was not harsh enough to miss the figure that lay on a pedestal, featureless and plain.

A human?

They drew closer, and Astraea's stomach clenched.

Not a human. A being crafted from stone and clay, fused with fire. A godling. Empty of life.

"Do you see my daughter there?" the earth goddess asked. "Is she not beautiful?"

Astraea could only swallow, the words she might have used to taunt her captors stuck in her throat. The fire goddess stepped forwards and drew a gentle hand down the figure's face and arm, the stone steaming as she did.

"Sister!" the earth goddess scolded. "Now look what you've done. She is burned."

"She will have both your earth and my fire in her. It is only fair that she show it," the fire goddess said. She looked fondly at the creature, the godling who now bled. Then, she turned to Astraea and the expression on her features struck the star with terror.

"It has been many long ages since the gods created new life. Your kind, star, was the last, and the Walkers Between that we spawned between us both," the earth goddess said, resting a hand as firm as stone on Astraea's shoulder. She had seen the Walkers, what humans called voidlings, recently, and knew that they held little of their divine parents in them, their natures more like the greedy stars.

She would admit then, in that moment, that she had been greedy. Desperate for things that made her feel wanted. Needed. Worshipped.

Casimir would think her the fool for wanting such things, though he would never say as much out loud.

"My daughter here is a true god," the earth goddess continued. "Formed from the divine spark of both my sister and myself, for with what *you* did, there was not enough of us to do it alone. We will bestow our powers upon her, the last of us, and she will right the wrongs you caused."

Astraea lifted her chin. She refused to beg, not when these had already condemned her. The fire goddess clicked her tongue, a bit of flame leaping off her hand.

"Do you not care that you have, through your selfish actions, brought about the death of the two greatest among us?" the fire asked. Astraea sneered.

"You would not die if you didn't do things like creating life," she spat. "Just release me, let things continue on as they are."

The earth mother's hand on her shoulder grew heavy, the weight of countless layers of granite bearing down on her. Astraea cried out and fell to her knees. She gathered her light inside, pulling it tight, the pressure nearly unbearable.

"If we do that, then the world, and all three realms you forced into being, will be doomed to languish. We are interdependent, and you would have us starve. No," the earth goddess said. "This is the only way."

Astraea said nothing, gritting her teeth against

the pressure building inside her, her light begging to be released even in its weakened state. The fire goddess took one look at her and laughed. "Yes, go nova little star, you will only help us on our way."

The pressure tipped past the point of being bearable and Astraea gasped, her light escaping. No, not escaping. Being called forth, pulled from her and screaming in the process. Leaving her for the godling that lay so empty on the pedestal.

"Our power, too," the earth goddess said, and before Astraea's vision went black, she saw stone and flora and fire and magma streaming into the godling. Then she saw nothing at all, and knew it was her end.

CHAPTER 2

I woke with a scream. Every part of me was being torn to pieces as I struggled to hold on to my magic, onto the three different worlds in which I stood, weaving them together. It was suffocating, draining, and surely would be my death. Alone, afraid, unsure, I would fulfil my destiny and die.

Only, I wasn't dead.

No. I cradled my head in my arms and brought my knees close to my chest. Around me, the nearly lifeless rock hummed with energy, offering it to me. There was a small fire not far away that crackled merrily, the flames leaning in my direction, as if warming me and me alone.

"Ast—Are you alright?"

Reality crashed upon me like a wave, dimming my magic with disappointment and shock.

Casimir crouched by my side, his hands hovering over me but not touching. I wanted to lean into his touch, take comfort from him, but I couldn't. Not when I wasn't who he truly wanted.

Not when I wasn't Astraea.

I'd learned, in those moments before I pulled the doors to the realm of the gods open and cast the void into its own realm, that I wasn't Astraea, Chosen One of the Star that Fell, destined to push back the jealous void, that most people thought. Nor was I a star that Casimir had loved, who had pretended for centuries that she was the Chosen One, each time basking in the love and devotion of a desperate people before pushing the void away until next time. I was none of those things, instead a goddess born of the last of the earth and fire, with a star's stolen magic inside me. Astraea's stolen magic.

And Casimir—solemn, beautiful Casimir with a heart so loyal and true—who was not a Void Runner, but the star's guardian, born of the darkness between stars. He who had followed her from the heavens into exile, loving her all the while, through each incarnation as the Chosen One. He had been both horrified and devastated at my pronouncement that I wasn't his star.

I wasn't Astraea.

I had no memories before my waking with burns on my face, not because I had a head injury as I'd initially thought, but because I was new. I had failed at my supposed destiny, not because I lacked the power, but because my destiny wasn't to destroy the void, to push it back, it was to contain it.

I had done so, locking one of my few friends, Devereux, into its new, vast realm.

Now, here I was, with no name and no certain future, no love and no idea what I was meant to do next. Casimir and I had camped tersely on the beach of Ynysfawr, the boat already taken back across by Tali, the wandering poet who had borne witness to the truth.

To most of it, at least.

I was exhausted, Casimir was uncertain, and the weight of unsaid words lay between us like iron fetters.

"I'm fine," I said at last, when I was certain of my voice. "Just a bad dream."

A memory was no dream, and yet I wished it to be anything but true.

Casimir retreated and sat beside the fire. It was so strange to have a fire merely for warmth and light, and not as some protection against the void and the voidlings. But there was no wall of black over the strip of ocean between Ynysfawr and the mainland of Baldarskiel. Just water and stars, all glowing with predawn light. Casimir didn't even seem to notice the coming dawn, his expression transfixed by the flames.

He had always been handsome, with fine features, sharp eyes, and those shadows at the tips of his fingers, along his neck, in his white hair. But now that he'd given up the pretence of being human, he was more beautiful than handsome. His features were smooth, polished, like marble. The shadows on his skin were more numerous now and twined in impossibly intricate patterns that were too difficult to follow for long. His eyes, too, had changed. They were harder. Warier. Sadder.

"How do you know you're not her?" he asked me again, perhaps the third time he'd done so. Each time, the words were quieter, more desperate.

"A memory came to me," I said, just as I'd answered before. And it was true, even if the memory was one of Lady Earth, the queen of the gods, planted in the crater where the doorway to the realms now lay. Lady Earth. My mother.

"What of?" Casimir asked, as if he could perhaps explain away anything, as if he could make me into who he wanted.

"Cas," I said, shaking my head. "Don't do this to yourself."

Don't do this to me.

"Please," he begged.

"I'm not her," I said. "I know, because a memory came to me, of being imbued with a star's light. I wasn't ever a star. Only me, whoever that is."

A goddess with no name.

He wiped his eyes with fierce motions, but more tears took the place of the ones he dashed away.

"Gods, this isn't fair," he said. I flinched. "After last time...it was so bad. So many people died fighting the voidlings, for her. We fought. Empty night, we fought like we'd never done before. Then we went our separate ways."

He laughed darkly. "I should have stayed with her. Then maybe I could be with her now. Maybe I could help her."

"We'll find her," I said, though I believed it to be a lie. I had only vague recollections of before, of those moments before I was given over to the mortals who called this realm home, broken and burned and bruised. Empty.

Casimir scoffed at me. "Face the truth, Astr—" He shook his head. "Astraea was a beautiful creature, so lively, vibrant, so bright she could outshine any other star. But she never had the confidence that should have been her right. She doubted. So fiercely that it almost doused her light entirely. Then she fell, and here, where people loved her for protecting them from the void, she felt whole. She was again the star I fell in love with."

I said nothing, knowing that Astraea had been the one to bring forth the void to begin with. She had caused so much suffering and pain, all for the worship of people who pushed aside the gods for her.

"She would have come before now," Casimir said, more softly. "Before the void grew as much as it did, before the voidling incursions, before all of it. She would have come and pushed it back, just like she had done so many times before. Because she needed to know that she was loved, so that she might shine as brilliantly as she could. It wasn't something she could give up. Not even..."

"Not even for what?" For the lives of the people she professed to save? For the forgiveness of the gods?

"Not even for me," Casimir breathed. He looked up at me with those tears of his catching the firelight, and I wanted to recoil in horror at his pain. Instead, I stayed perfectly still, what little crumbs of my magic that remained after sealing off the void coming to life with alarm.

"Casimir," I whispered. "No, you can't think—"

"I was so damn relieved when I learned that you had truly lost your memory, that it wasn't some game like all the ones we'd played before." He threw a rock into the fire and the coals hissed. "I was so relieved that you seemed to care, seemed to truly and actually care about the people affected by the void. I thought that maybe this would be the last time, that maybe we could just go on and live our lives afterwards without a care to what other people thought."

And then I'd destroyed his hopes by revealing that I wasn't her.

"She's dead," he said. "I recognise her light, and you wielded it. It was why I didn't question why you looked so different, why you acted so differently. I thought you were bored with your previous facades, wanted something new. Something real."

In a flash, he reached up and brushed his fingers along the burns on my left cheek. I sucked in a breath, but remained still. Oh, gods, how I'd longed for him to touch me, but not like this. Not with such grief in his eyes.

"I don't know how you managed to be bestowed with her light, or the darkness of a guardian, but you were. You had both. I thought it was my darkness, since we'd been so close for so long." He scoffed and lowered his hand from my face. "Empty night, what was I thinking?"

"I'm sorry," I murmured. "I know how much you wanted me to be her. I...I wish I was. I wish I could say that this was all a mistake, that I was her, but I'm not."

"And you're certain?" A low, dark question.

I lifted my gaze to where the last of the stars were winking out into the dawn light. They seemed so far away. Casimir had been outcast from his fellow stars and their guardians for centuries, and he had always been okay with it, because he had Astraea. Now, he had me and the memory of a love that he thought was real.

For my part, it was.

I couldn't possibly tell him that, though. Not now.

"I'm certain," I said.

He took a deep breath, not meeting my gaze. Then, in a fluid motion, he stood and started kicking rocks and sand over the fire. "Come, we have a long way to go, and I want to get started before it's too late in the day to make much progress. Tali should have made it back to the horses by now, and maybe she has Dancer with her, too. And Whisper."

I pressed a hand to my side, where the connection I'd had with my beloved voidling, a shadow tiger cub I rescued from the Baldarskiel Council of Nobles, had been. He had taken some of my magic into him while defending me against a unicorn voidling, and in return, he and I could feel each other's emotions. Ever since I'd returned the void to its own realm, an antechamber to the realm of the gods, that connection had been silent. I didn't even know if Dancer was alright. And Whisper, a wolf-like voidling we'd rescued from Hunters, she, too, was likely gone.

"Can you swim?" Casimir asked. The familiarity of confession we'd had only moments before was now gone.

"I don't know," I answered. I had never done it before, and being made of earth and fire, didn't know how well I would fare. If my magic were recovered, I would create a landbridge between the island and the mainland, but it would be at least another day or two before I could manage such a thing.

"I'll be there to help you," Casimir promised. His eyes were closed as he made the vow, and I had a feeling that he was referring to more than swimming. As if a guardian without a cause, without someone to keep, was nothing at all.

I stood, brushing off my skirts. They were shining, jewels mixed in with fabric, a gift from the void for returning it to its position between the worlds. It would be heavy in the water, but I could sell the jewels if need be on the way back towards Altier. I had no other clothes besides.

"Cas—"

"You need a name."

I faltered. "What?"

"A name. I certainly cannot go around calling you Astraea." His voice broke on her name.

"We *will* find her," I promised, a vow of my own. "Whether it is only to put her to rest, or to restore her to the sky, we will find her."

Casimir's throat worked. He blinked back what few tears remained. The expression he fixed on me was hard, hiding his pain. "What sort of name do you want?"

I frowned and turned my head, a harsh laugh held back between my teeth. Here we were, discussing his lost—probably dead—lover, and he wanted to know what sort of name I wanted? Everyone dealt with grief differently, but this felt harsh. Still, I recognised that he needed a distraction, so I offered him one.

"I sealed the void into its own realm, between this

one and the realm of the gods," I said. "But there is a doorway. And it is not impenetrable."

He sucked in a breath and stumbled backwards, his boots squelching in the rising tide. "Empty night," he breathed, eyes flicking towards the broken temple and the crater that had burned until yesterday. "Are you saying that the gods can now get out?"

I nodded. "Devereux warned me that they will want to be released after so long trapped in their realm, separated by the void."

"The gods were not pushed aside for nothing," Casimir said. His throat worked. "Astr—damn it! I must have *something* to call you other than her name!"

Ah. Suddenly, I understood. I could not furnish a reply, though, for though I had searched what little knowledge I had, no name sprang to mind. I wasn't sure my mother had even given me a name. Plucking one from thin air seemed impossible, also, for I knew nothing of these things.

"Calanthe," Casimir said, not looking at me. "It means flower in an ancient tongue, long forgotten by these humans."

Calanthe. I tested the name out on my tongue, the long vowel at the end dropping off into a whisper. A name that meant flower, one that had been long forgotten. It suited perfectly, and yet I wished that it had been presented to me with a little more ceremony. I wished that he had looked at me as he said it.

"Calanthe it is." I tried to smile. "Thank you."

Casimir gave a slight bow of his head. Then, as if he hadn't named me at all, he said, "The gods would probably look at Astraea and decry her for her selfishness, pushing them aside and taking the worship of humans for her own. And I will freely admit that she was desperate for that affirmation, that attention. But what she did, in pushing the gods aside, was not merely for her own gain. The gods are not all kind, benevolent creatures. Some, like Lady Earth and Father Sky, are more temperate than most, but even they can be fickle. Demanding. They, and all the others, are arrogant, lowering humans in the world so that they depend on them, so that they need the gods, even while the gods are free to do as they wish. They can be cruel, Astr—Calanthe."

As my mother had been when she drained a star's light to give to me.

"All I know is that Devereux spoke to me from his place in the void, telling me that the gods would not be confined for long. They will have to travel through their realm, and that of the void, before they can reach the doorway here, but they will come. And the world is not prepared for it."

Casimir cursed, kicking at the rising tide and clenching his fists. "You cannot seal the doorway?"

I shook my head. "No."

I had no magic left, and even if I were full of power, I didn't know how to seal the door. Breaching the realms had been instinctual, as had making the door. Sealing it was something else entirely.

"Fine. They we'll just have to prepare the world for the return of the gods."

"How?" Was it even possible to do such a thing?

Casimir finally looked at me, something sad about his mien. "You will have to continue pretending," he murmured. "The people will listen to the star reborn, the one who dispelled the void. They won't listen to a..."

"Pretender?" I hadn't been pretending, before, when I'd acted as Astraea, the Chosen One. I simply hadn't known better. Now I did.

Casimir turned away from me. "Come. Let's swim before the tide becomes too high and the current is swift. You'll need to leave the dress here; it's too heavy to swim in."

"I have no other clothes." I started undoing the laces at the back, the silvery fabric slick between my fingers, catching on the burned skin of my left hand.

"We'll find you something," Casimir promised. He glanced at me and froze. Then, in two swift steps, he was behind me, his fingers brushing against mine as I struggled to undo the laces. "Here." A quiet breath.

Slowly, agonisingly, he undid the laces on my dress, his fingers brushing against my bare skin. Sparks travelled up my spine, making me shudder. I closed my eyes, heart beating in my ear. Every breath was a torment. Every touch a shard of joy. Then, he was stepping away, the dress slipping from my shoulders with ease.

Without a backwards glance, Casimir walked away from me and into the sea, as if he couldn't stand to be so close to me. Whereas I stood on the beach, naked and trembling, unsure how I could ever be parted from him.

I followed, the frigid water shocking my senses as thoroughly as had his touch. He started swimming, parting the water with ease, and I could do nothing but struggle along behind, as if I was now tethered to this broken man who wanted none of me.

Who I needed to help prepare the world for a catastrophe of my own making. Who I needed to help save the people who thought themselves free.

Who had named me, and then walked away.

Gods, I was a fool.

How was I to have known, though? For moon cycles, I had thought that I was Astraea, that I was the Chosen One. Casimir, too, thought it. So our attraction and love had grown. Now, things were different, and I couldn't help that I was still in love with him. For all that he had wanted me to leave things as they were, to not fix the problem of the void and instead leave with him, be with him, and leave the humans to their lives. I couldn't, and now look at the situation we were in.

A wave struck me in the face and I spluttered, coughing. My arms were weak and though I was paddling as best I could, my progress was slow and ungainly. I felt more like I was sinking than swimming. Casimir heard me coughing and turned, slicing through the water like a fish.

"Slow, broad strokes," he advised, tone gentle. "Try to match the movement of your arms and legs, so they're in sync. Good. Yes. Look, we're almost there."

I wanted to curse him and his swimming, but focused my energy on breathing and moving. Finally, after swallowing more than one mouthful of seawater, my eyes stinging from salty waves, I crawled out onto the rocky shore, my hands and knees stinging from the sharp points.

"Lady Star, you have returned." A reverent voice, gruff and thick with emotion. I started, jumping to my feet and swaying. Then, "Get her a cloak, now!"

Within seconds, a fur-lined cloak was draped over my dripping form. I blinked more water out of my eyes and looked up at the person—people—who were gathered on the shore. Hunters. Led by the one who had captured us on our journey to Ynysfawr, intending to torture us, or worse.

Ilar.

As one, every Hunter fell to their knees before me, prostrating themselves on the ground, their eyes filled with awe. Ilar spoke, barely able to form words, his voice was trembling so. "You have saved us all,

Lady Star. Forever more, we are yours to command, your obedient servants, bound to you heart and soul."

I opened my mouth to tell them that I wasn't the star, that it had all been a mistake, then Casimir was behind me, his hand pressed against my back, only the cloak a barrier between us. His breath tickled my ear. "Lie to them, Calanthe," he said. "You cannot tell them the truth. Not with the gods at our back."

I squeezed my eyes closed and nodded. Then, summoning every ounce of energy I had, I straightened my shoulders, lifted my chin, and smiled.

"Thank you, my beloved people. It is good to stand before you in truth, as I truly am. As a star, not merely the Chosen One."

Inside, my earth magic roared to life, the spark of fire I held blazing, both screaming with rage at the lie I told. I pushed it down, down, down, and became, once more, Astraea.

CHAPTER 3

Despite Casimir's anxiousness to be on our way, Ilar insisted that we join him by a fire while we dried, and someone found me clothes to wear. In minutes, I was presented with a coarse shirt and fur-lined hose, a woollen shawl draped over my shoulders and cinched with a belt. Combined with the cloak and the fire, I soon stopped shivering.

"After you, ah, left us," Ilar started, handing over a waterskin to Casimir, who drank swiftly, then shoved the skin at me. The Hunter rubbed the back of his neck. "Well, after you left us, we had a discussion and realised the error of our ways. How we weren't following the Path of the Star, but our own greed while we kept the voidlings at bay. We vowed to do better, even rode after you in the hopes that we could apologise. Perhaps lend our assistance against the void. Only, yesterday, the world shattered and was remade and the void was gone. Your doing?"

I nodded. What had it felt like when the void vanished? At the epicentre, I had felt every moment of the realms being torn asunder and then repaired, but what had happened everywhere else on Adhor? Had the earth heaved as it did beneath my feet? Had the sky wrenched apart? Or was it, as Ilar said, a shattering?

"The true Star indeed," the Hunter breathed, once again bowing to me. I hunched my shoulders, uncomfortable with the admiration in his eyes and the false truth on his lips. "We waited for you to return to us, as we knew you would, for the void could not defeat the true Star. Now, we await your command. Shall we take the world? Remake it to follow the true Path of the Star, instead of whatever nonsense the Temple preaches? Shall we make the fools in Altier bend their knees to you, send emissaries to far-off lands, calling them to acknowledge what you've done?"

I clutched the cloak tighter as Ilar's hungry gaze bore into me. Casimir, too, watched me, impossibly still, gaze penetrating and desperate. As if he watched to see if I would do what Astraea would do, or if I were truly different. Even now, he hoped I was wrong about not being her.

"No," I said simply. "I want no accolades, no worship."

"Then..." Ilar looked disappointed, as if unsure what to do with himself now that he'd pledged his sword and people to a leader who wanted no glory. "What do you wish of us?"

"We must..." I closed my eyes. The crackle of the fire heightened as my magic reached for it, restoring by degrees. If I wanted, I knew I could call the flame to me and watch it dance. I did not, instead just drawing on its energy to revitalise me. The earth beneath my feet offered its own fortification, not wanting to be outdone. "We must warn the people."

"Warn them?" Ilar was incredulous. "Against what? Surely the void isn't returning."

"No, the void now is its own land, its own realm, and it can no more encroach here than we can encroach there." Devereux was king there, and he would have to tame the void, hopefully before the gods tore it apart in their eagerness to cross it and reach this plane of existence. "There is still danger, though. The gods, once kept back by the void, now have a door into this realm."

"A door." The Hunter now stared at me with something else in his gaze. A hard, reluctant look.

"The creation of such was inevitable," I said. "It was the only way to seal away the void. But it also opened up the realm of the gods. And they are eager to return."

Ilar smiled. "Surely that is a good thing! Lady Earth and Father Sky and—"

"Foolish man," Casimir snarled. "Have you and your kind forgotten all the stories? The cruelties of the gods delivered upon those people who displeased them. Who defied them. Lady Earth was benevolent, yes, but she could be fickle, leaving crops to blight just as easily as she would allow them to flourish. And Father Sky? From whom all storms are born? How many storms have destroyed settlements since the void came? Few, and even those were not borne of a god's wrath. And they are the kindest of the lot."

"Casimir." I reached out and put a hand on his arm. Instantly, he recoiled, eyes wide, terrified. His breath caught; he seemed to fold in on himself. He settled to his knees beside me and studied the fire.

Ilar had a hand on his belt-knife, his eyes narrowed. "You said, 'you and your kind.' I'll have you know that the world has no more need for Void Runners. You'll not defy the Star again or—"

"Ilar," I said, shaking my head. "Casimir is my most loyal advisor, a true friend. He is more than you think, and if I hear of you insulting him again, then I'll leave you and your people here without a second thought."

The Hunter sneered. "Is he your lover, then?"

"That's none of—"

"I love her with all my heart and soul," Casimir said easily. I gaped at him before managing to snap my mouth shut. Why would he say such a thing? "Where she goes, I will follow."

Was he talking about Astraea, only making it seem like he was talking about me? Surely that was it, because he wouldn't even look at me, instead staring firmly at Ilar. The gruff Hunter swallowed, tightening his grip on his belt-knife, before relaxing and ducking his head in a nod.

"Of course, Lady Star," he murmured. "My apologies. If you say that the gods are dangerous, then they are dangerous. You saved us from the void, after all. You will save us from the gods."

I wasn't sure I could do that. I had been created by my mother for the express purpose of righting the wrong that Astraea had set into place by bringing forth the void in the beginning. It had been my destiny, though not in the way I initially thought. Now, though, the future lay before me, undetermined. Vast. Regardless, it was now my responsibility to help the innocent people who would be in the way of the gods, for it was I that had opened the door to them.

"We must warn people," I said, trying to sound sure rather than afraid.

"If we are to fight the gods, we will need an army," Ilar said. "My Hunters, capable as they were against voidlings, number only about a hundred. Gods are something more."

An army? I glanced at Casimir, alarmed. His jaw was set, though, and he nodded.

Stars above, what had I brought upon this world?

"The Void Runners, I think, will follow you." Casimir still didn't look directly at me. "And more, if you can convince the queen of the necessity."

Queen Raya, her husband Istar, and daughter Beatrice were not likely to be fond of me, given that I had left Altier after defying them over and over. They had sent me, Devereux, and Casimir to Ynysfawr in the hopes that either I would not return, or that I would push back the void and Devereux would somehow claim my heart and my influence for his own. Well, now the void was gone entirely, as was the crown prince. The royal family would not openly defy me, but I doubted very much that they would be pleased to see me again.

I longed for Dancer, the tiger's midnight fur impossibly soft and comforting. I reached again for the spot in my side where our connection had manifested, but there was nothing there. No feeling, no twinge of power, no heartbeat. It was as though he'd vanished.

"What of the wandering poet?" Casimir asked, breaking me from my thoughts. I flushed; of all the time for him to be watching me, solemn and unfathomable, it had to be when I was feeling vulnerable. Lonely, even. "She and the two voidlings left Ynysfawr before we did."

Ilar wrinkled his nose. "We've had scouts riding the hills, looking for any trace of the void. All we found were a few places where void pools had been. A trunk of a tree still dark as night, a bog shrouded in shadow, that sort of thing. But we haven't seen any other living souls but birds. The animals fled this area months ago. We would have noticed your poet and two voidlings."

Something in me cracked at that news. I'd hoped to find Tali alive and well, with Dancer and Whisper at her side. Instead, it seemed as though they had vanished with the void. Had I, in my terrible use of power, killed them? Or just pulled them in with the void? Were they now trapped, just as Devereux was trapped?

It seemed a cruel fate, to me. And one that I would not have wanted for them.

"We should get moving," I said at last, standing and pulling the cloak tightly around me. I wanted to wallow, to languish there while staring into the fire, but that would do no one any good. Ilar scrambled to his feet and bowed to me again before hurrying off to inform his people that we were leaving. Those with horses started packing saddle bags while others doused fires and wrapped supplies into bundles. The clanking of knives and swords and makeshift armour was surprisingly loud.

Casimir rose and started to kick dirt over our own small fire. I reached towards the flames instead, and they leapt to my fingers, swirling there a moment before vanishing into my skin, feeding that spark of magic I yet bore. Casimir flinched.

"You still have your magic," he whispered. He wanted to know if I still had *her* magic.

"Only the earth and the fire. Whatever light and shadow I bore was used in the forging of the door." There was nothing of her left in me, not anymore.

"I'm sorry about Dancer. And Tali. I know you two were growing close. It would be good for you to have a friend out here," he said, already straightening his armour and the cloak he'd been given. A swift glance at me. "There are dark times ahead, I fear, and you will need all the friends you can find."

"And are we not friends any longer?" I asked. Casimir sucked in a breath.

"Is that ever what we were?"

Before I could ask him what he meant, what he could possibly mean when, even if his love for me was a pretence, he could be so cold as to never meet my gaze, Ilar rose up on a large draft horse. "Lady Star! A scout sent to Ynysfawr found the door you spoke of, said it seemed stable. For now. He brought back a dress of jewels, which I assume is yours. We will bear it for you until you have need of it."

I didn't mind if the dress stayed on that beach to be buried by the tide, but it was valuable and could fund our needs for some time. So I just nodded and murmured my thanks. Then, shaking my head in refusal at the offer of a horse, I started walking back across Baldarskiel towards Altier, the only place in this vast world that I had known.

I wondered what else was out there, in the world. If maybe there were some quiet corner I might call my own when all of this was finally over. I didn't think it would end easily, or well. So I set my eyes forwards and marched.

*

A week came and went with ease. Travelling at the Hunters' pace was slower than the trek I'd followed the first time, being on horseback and moving as swiftly as possible. We were instead bound by the slowest members of the group, walking from dawn until midday, when we stopped for a meal and a rest, then again until nightfall. The night held few terrors now that the void was gone, but still a watch was kept. And, as Ilar had said, no animals save birds and fish remained in the area, though signs of life were creeping onwards, despite the approach of winter.

It was a desolate journey, yet it was calming and relaxing in its own way. I talked with the Hunters, learning what it was that had driven them to this path. Some had joined out of desperation for food. Others joined so they could provide their family with some modicum of protection against the void. Few did it out of devotion to the Star, though they all claimed it now. I ignored their bows and muttered prayers, instead doing what I could to help set up and break down camp each night.

I learned to cook soup over a fire. I learned to skin a fish. I learned how to tie knots and sew a patch. I learned songs sung over a campfire. I learned things I'd never thought I would know. Normal things. Human things.

Casimir, too, seemed to relax some in the presence of others. He listened to stories told over dinner with a quiet interest. He helped with the horses. He caught fish from streams. He lent a hand to those who were tired or weak or injured from fights with voidlings in the past. He carried firewood, fetched water, and generally made himself useful. At night, our bedrolls lay beside one another, and he seemed content with that, even going so far as to smile at me once or twice, my new name a whisper on his tongue.

For a week, I felt almost normal.

Then, we stopped for the night at a rise that felt familiar. Dread settled in my gut as the sun drew lower, and when it finally came time to sleep, I tossed and turned until the earth beneath me was trembling with my anxiety and the fire in my blood sang. I gave up on sleep entirely and snuck past the embers of a fire, several sleeping forms, and a scout whose back was turned. I scrambled down the hill, grass making the trek slippery enough that I slid the last ten feet.

When my hands caught my fall, my magic recoiled. The ground here was tainted with blood.

Dancer's blood. There was enough of the void still remaining in that place to evoke memories of shadow and desperation. The call of the void that had captured Devereux. This was where he had vanished, the only remaining evidence a scab on the trunk of a tree that would never show light, and the taint in the ground from Dancer's blood.

"I wondered if you would come here."

I whirled and found myself looking at a figment of my imagination. "Devereux?" I reached out tentatively and my fingers met solid flesh.

He smiled. "Hello again."

Devereux stood before me, an impossibility. He was just as he had been when I saw him last in the void, more mist and shadow than man, but it was him. His eyes glowed brightly, the colour of embers, and a crown made of wisps rested on his head. He wore simple clothes, had a single knife at his belt, a single ring on his left hand, none of the finery of the Crown Prince of Baldarskiel adorning him. He looked the better for it.

"How are you here?" I breathed, even as I moved forwards and was engulfed in a hug. His arms were strong, sure, and immediately a burden was lifted from my shoulders.

"This place is a tear in the veil between realms. There are a few of them, even with the doorway. I've learned that they can be opened at certain times of day, and that I can step through. It's not easy, and something of me is left behind, but I can remain for a time." Devereux held me away from him and studied me, tucking a strand of hair behind my ear. "It is good to see you again, Astraea."

"Calanthe." It was maybe the first time I'd smiled while saying my new name. "My name is Calanthe."

Devereux grinned at me. "It suits you perfectly. Strong and beautiful."

I rolled my eyes, but I was smiling. "And what of you? Are you taming the void as its new king?"

His smile faltered. "There is a great deal of magic here, more than I've ever seen, and the creatures who use it have little compunction about morality. The voidlings were only a few of the beings that call this place home, and not all are fond of having a new king."

"You're alright, aren't you?"

He smiled again, this time softer. "I'm alright. For the first time, I think I'm doing some good."

I was so pleased for him; living under the oppressive thumb of his family had drained such life out of him, made him desperate and alone. To hear that he'd found his place in the world was good, much needed good.

Then, his smile faded. "I would love to talk with you until the dawn, Calanthe, but I came here to warn you. These tears in the veil are not numerous, but they are dangerous. Power—life—sacrificed here will draw the attention of some of the beings who live beyond the veil."

"The gods?" Surely they couldn't have broken through already?

"Not yet." Devereux shook his head. "And these tears are too small for gods to step through. But there are beings who would not hesitate to bargain with those who would offer them power. I've placed restrictions, as much as I can, but be wary. Do not wish at a crossroads. Do not ask for help from the midnight wood. Do not offer your name freely. And do not bargain with anything you cannot bear to lose."

"I promise," I said. "And I will pass on the message."

Devereux once more reached for me, brushing his hand across my cheek. "You have a battle ahead of you, my dear. One that will shake all the realms. If anyone can withstand it, though, I think it might be you."

I laughed weakly, the sound a tremor in my joyful facade. "Take care of yourself, Devereux. And if you have need of me, you have only to ask."

"Goodbye, Calanthe," Devereux murmured, pressing a kiss to my forehead. Then, he started to fade away.

"Wait!" I snagged his sleeve. "Have you...Tali and Dancer and Whisper haven't been seen since I separated the realms."

Devereux hissed through his teeth. "I haven't seen them, but the void is vast. If they're here, I'll find them. Dancer and Whisper will keep Tali safe until I do."

"Thank you." I released his sleeve. "Your Majesty."

Devereux tossed his head back and gave a wicked laugh, then was gone in a breath of wind. I leaned against a nearby tree, wrapping my arms around my waist. Another friend, just out of reach. I was glad for him, truly, but I also wished that he were here at my side.

"Goodbye, Devereux," I breathed, then made my way back to camp. Casimir was waiting for me, mouth drawn into a worried frown. He reached for me, hesitating at the last moment.

"I was worried about you," he said as I settled back into my bedroll.

"I'm alright." I pulled the blankets to my shoulders and wiped tears from my eyes. Casimir studied me, more openly than he'd done since the night on the beach. After a minute, he nodded and lay back down, propping his head in his hand.

"Sleep," he said. "I'll watch over you."

I slept, and I believed him.

CHAPTER 4

"I saw Devereux last night," I said as we packed up the camp. Casimir froze, something in him impossibly still. Another reminder that he wasn't the human he had pretended to be.

"Why didn't you tell me?" It was a breath, but I could still hear the hurt. I wanted to reach out and reassure him, touch his arm and let him know that I was still here. Instead, I rolled the bedroll and secured it with the leather ties, attaching it to the sack I had been given by the Hunters.

Rather than answer the question, I relayed what Devereux had said, repeating the warning twice before Casimir nodded. He looked down at the remains of our fire, dirt kicked over the divot in the ground. As before, I'd taken the energy of the flames into me, as well as the remaining energy from the other fires in the camp. I was not so open with my magic before the others, but a whisper of flame as I passed by was hardly registered.

"We'll have to pass the information along. Interactions with the...well, they're not exactly voidlings now, are they?" Casimir shook his head. "Whatever they are, they're dangerous."

"I'm sorry."

"For what?" The words were soft, sad.

"For not telling you about Devereux last night. For not taking you with me when I left. I know you worry, and...I'm sorry." There was so much emotion in me, a tight knot that interlaced with my magic and my past, such as it was. I didn't know how to articulate it, only to acknowledge that Casimir was hurting, and some of it was my fault.

"I understand. You needed time to yourself. You've just discovered a truth about yourself that would have broken most people. If you aren't...her... then who are you? If I were you, I would be tearing down the sky until I got my answers. Instead, you are determined to go back to the world and protect it from the gods. This world doesn't deserve you."

"It's my fault that the gods can now move through the realms," I muttered. Casimir moved so swiftly that I barely registered the movement. He caught my chin in my hands, lifting until I looked him in the eyes, until I saw the fury blazing there.

"Never think that this is your fault," he snarled. The shadows that lived in his eyes blazed, proof of the blackness between the stars, from whence he came.

"But I—"

"You did what she could not." Abruptly, he lowered his hand. Agony filled his eyes, replacing that rage, that life. "You returned the void to its place in the realms. You bound it to its own space, letting the energy between realms flow freely, even if it meant opening the world to the gods once again.. You saved the people from the fear and desperation that lived in the void as it tried to protect its magic from a greedy, hungry world. You did that. Not her."

"Casimir." I caught my fingers on the edge of his sleeve. "If it's not my fault, nor is it yours."

He huffed a breath of laughter, cruel and aching. "I followed her from the heavens. I bore witness to all the things that she did in bringing forth the void, in pushing it back in endless cycles. I was there. I helped. All because—"

He broke off as Ilar approached, the Hunter running his fingers through his beard with an anxious expression. "Our scouts have returned."

He'd been sending scouts ahead every dawn, returning by the time that the camp was packed and we were ready to go. Each day, the news had been the same: the land before us was empty, and all was safe.

"What is it?" Casimir demanded, hand already at his sword.

"There's an abandoned village up ahead. Or rather, it was abandoned."

"Surely that's a good thing," I said. "People returning home?"

Ilar shook his head. "This village was raided months back by bandits and farmers looking to recover losses when their livestock was attacked by voidlings. I remember, because me and mine got here too late. It was a massacre, farmers turning on farmers, families slaughtered in desperation at escaping the void with something to fund their refuge in Altier. This was one of the reasons we...ah...you know."

The Hunter shrugged his shoulders expansively, likely referring to the activities they'd been performing when I first stumbled across them. Extortion to fight the voidlings. Tormenting false Chosen Ones. They were considered worse than bandits by some, and saviours by others. And now they answered to me.

"What did the scouts find?" I asked, still confused. "Someone rebuilding the village? Surely even if it was as bad as you claim, someone would still want to come home and...what it is, Ilar?"

"They're not Kielians."

I looked at Casimir for explanation, the word unfamiliar. "Those from Baldarskiel," he murmured, filling in the gaps in my knowledge.

Ilar nodded, still wincing. "Best we can tell, they're from Craigsmuir."

"The nearest neighbours to Baldarskiel," Casimir explained to me, highlighting my ignorance once again. He frowned. "How did they get so far inland so quickly? They would have had to sail along the coast immediately after the void fell to come this far."

"Aye," Ilar said. "The scouts think they must be heading to Ynysfawr, to see what's happening. That they're stopping here to resupply, or to test the waters and see how Baldarskiel is faring, now that it's open to the world again."

For so long, Baldarskiel had been bound behind a ring of void, the darkness here so much more vast than anywhere else on Adhor. The other lands were plagued by void pools, but nothing so large or expansive as that which surrounded Baldarskiel, due to its proximity to Ynysfawr, the site where Astraea had first fallen, and first drawn the void into being. It was one of the few things I knew about the lands beyond.

"What do we do?" I turned to Casimir, who was so much more knowledgeable about such things. I had no notion of strategy or politics or any of it, simply because I'd never been taught. Since emerging at Starfall Meadow, I'd been schooled in using my magic, in fighting the void, and not much else. Yet here I was, trying to raise an army to fight a war.

Was it arrogance? Or folly?

He shook his head. Then, to Ilar, "How many of them are there?"

"The scouts say no more than twenty. We could fight them and win, with little loss of life. Less, if you take the lead, Lady Star." Ilar bowed slightly to me. I winced. I had little desire to kill anyone.

"We should confront them," Casimir said slowly. Ilar nodded and started to turn away. "*Not* to fight them."

"Not fight?" The Hunter was aghast.

"If they've come to see Ynysfawr, then there's no need. We have the Star with us." Casimir nodded to me. "They can help in our war against the gods. Or do you think only Baldarskiel will be affected?"

Stars and stones. He wanted me to persuade these people from Craigsmuir to fight on our side. How was I meant to do that? I gaped at the former Void Runner, but he provided me with no answers.

"Get her a horse," Casimir said. "It will be better if she is seen to lead."

Ilar bowed perfunctorily, then scurried off, already spreading the news of what we were to do. I rounded on Casimir.

"Are you insane?" I hissed. "I have no idea how to talk to these people! I can't convince them to fight against the gods! And they'll never believe that I am the Star; I have none of her light left."

"It would be better if you still had Dancer," Casimir said. I felt a pang for my missing friend, but now was hardly the time to give in to grief. I opened my mouth to continue arguing, but he shook his head. "Listen to me, Calanthe. You can do this. You had people believing you were the Chosen One long before you could summon the Star's light. You are compassionate and kind and good. People listen to you. Use that."

Then, without another glance, he walked away, muttering about a horse.

Gods, he was infuriating.

Within ten minutes, Ilar had returned with his own horse, massive and imposing, as well as two young men barely out of their youth, bearing pieces of armour and a sword. Casimir followed, a band of plain metal in his hands. I was soon kitted out in a breastplate that barely fit, greaves that were too loose, even over my boots, a pair of boiled leather bracers, and a sword belt that had to be wrapped around me twice. The sword was the finest in the camp, and I desperately hoped that I wouldn't need to wield it, as anyone who saw me do so would be instantly aware I was useless with weaponry. Then, Casimir handed me the metal band.

"From a grain barrel. You'll have to use your fire to make it fit. It's the closest I could find to a crown," he said, and it sounded like an apology. I nearly threw the band away. He pushed it back towards me, fingers wrapping around my own. That familiar spark jumped between our skin. I wanted to close my eyes and lean into it, but instead I just stared.

"I'm no queen," I whispered.

"I fear that to fight the gods, you will have to become more than a queen," Casimir said, just as quietly. Then, he pressed his forehead to mine, hair falling into his face so that it hid us from view for a precious second. "Just do it, Astraea. Please."

I recoiled at the sound of the name that was not mine, realising a moment later that he only called me that because of the witnesses surrounding us. I forced a smile and nodded. Casimir stepped back as I willed fire to my hands, to the metal ring. It flared cherry red with only a little effort, the magic in my blood singing happily. Even as I called forth the flames, the earth in my bones also clamoured for attention. As I reshaped the band clumsily, flowers bloomed around my feet. I finished as swiftly as possible, the metal feeling cool in my hand even as it glowed. I pulled back the heat, the fire, until it was a band of iron as dark as night.

I jammed the circlet on my head, shocked at the fact that it fit me perfectly, then whirled to Casimir to ask if he was happy. I froze. The Hunters were gathered in neat lines, each with a solemn expression on their face, hands braced on knives and axes and swords and hammers. They stared at me as if I meant something, as if I gave them something to believe in.

My heart beat erratically in my chest. I knew they

were waiting for me to say something. Anything. They were depending on me.

"I..." My words got stuck in my throat. I coughed. "Before, the thought of fighting the gods felt like a dream. Now, with you standing beside me, it feels like a hope."

They were the only words I could find, and I begged silently that it would be enough. As one, they clapped arms to their chests and bowed. Casimir hesitated only a moment before he did the same. My stomach dropped and my throat felt tight. I hadn't wanted this. I didn't need people bowing to me. But how else was I to lead them?

A moment later and the Hunters stood, ready to march. Ilar helped me into the saddle of the massive horse, and I was pleased that Casimir and the Hunter both climbed into saddles as well. I tightened my hands on the reins, my legs already protesting at the strange position. With a nod from Ilar, we started forwards.

The village was only a half hour march from where we had camped. Part of me was worried that they were so close, but mostly I was relieved that it would soon be over.

I saw the fringes of the village and nearly drew the horse up short. There were buildings—barns and homes and the like—scattered about the hills, some obviously belonging to farms that had abandoned fields and gardens, others closer together like family

homesteads. They were all, without a single excep-
tion, in tatters. Some were tinged with soot, more
solidly built out of stone and therefore somewhat
intact. Others were little more than charcoal on the
ground, a beam or two giving the general shape of the
house. I saw items strewn across the ground, scattered for the wind to take as it wished: scraps of
fabric, ruined leather, bits of furniture too broken
to use.

Ilar was right. This village had been razed.

A shiver crept down my spine as I wondered how
many of these broken buildings held bodies buried
beneath them. How many spirits of the dead
wandered here. The horses nickered and tossed their
heads, Casimir's even stamping and shying away from
the ruins of a stone wall.

There was no sign of the people from Craigsmuir.

A twang shattered the silence, a whistle splitting
the air. It was so swift that I didn't understand what
had happened until my shoulder was pierced, pain
blossoming through the burn scars that I bore. I let
out a cry, which was soon drowned by the shouts of
warriors leaping from behind broken buildings,
weapons raised.

Casimir let out a curse, wheeling his horse close
enough to mine that he could pluck me from the
saddle with a strength I'd not expected. I tried to
protest, but he was already curving his body over
me, shadows dancing on his skin. Ilar roared from

somewhere nearby, and the Hunters sprang into battle.

"No!" I shouted, but it was too late. The Hunters had seen me shot with an arrow and they were furious.

Their opponents were well dressed in a silver and blue uniform, each with sleeves of mail or leather and weapons that gleamed with care. I glimpsed only a few scraps of features, but I did see an embroidered dragon on most of the tunics. The Hunters, by comparison, were ragtag and reckless, their fighting frenzied rather than practised.

"We're leaving," Casimir snarled, drawing his sword awkwardly, arms still wrapped around me. "The Hunters can find us."

"No," I repeated, struggling enough to push him back. Before he could stop me, I threw myself from the saddle. I landed badly, my uninjured right shoulder taking most of the fall and sending reverberations through my bones. The earth beneath me rippled at my pain, energy flowing into me from the few living things still in the soil. I pushed myself to my feet mere moments before the blade of an axe collided with the ground where I'd fallen.

Casimir roared, dismounting and standing in front of me, sword drawn and eyes full of darkness. I could see the shadows etched into his skin spreading, taking control. If I didn't do something, now, then he would become the guardian to the star, a creature born of the space between, the dark emptiness of the heavens. The humans here wouldn't stand a chance.

Closing my eyes, I reached deep into the earth, summoning the roots of trees that had been burned down, or fell long ago. Their trunks were gone, but the roots remembered what it was to feel life, to touch the sky, and they were happy to obey my command. They shot through the ground with resounding cracks, sometimes splitting stone as they rose. Vines and grasses that had claimed the fallen village grew as well, twining around the feet of attackers on both sides, holding them firm. The roots wrapped around weapons and tore them free. The stones that had been displaced rose from the ground in terrible tremors, forming a waist-high wall between warriors.

There were screams from the Craigsmuirians as they struggled and tried to free themselves. I held up my hands, flowers wrapping around my fingers and into my hair.

"Enough!" I said, my words amplified by a ripple in the earth. Everyone fell silent. The Hunters were slowly freed from the vines, and they all retreated until they stood behind me. Casimir was at my injured shoulder, breathing heavily. Ilar stood at my right, axe held in a white-knuckled grip.

"Who leads here?" I asked. A woman not five feet from me—the one who had attacked—lifted her chin. She had skin so dark it was almost blue, a shaven head, and eyes that glistened like ambers. For a moment, I thought I was looking at a void-touched being, like Devereux. No, she was fully human, with a confidence that could cow kings. A silver band wrapped around either arm, the sign of command most likely.

"Who are you?" she hissed in a sharp accent, fingers flexing for a weapon that was no longer there.

"All in due time," I said. "Tell me, what is your name?"

"Kina," she said. "Captain Kina, of the ship *Windborn*." Her jaw tensed and she glared at me. "Of Craigsmuir."

"Captain," I said, inclining my head, all too conscious of the circlet I wore. "What is a captain of Craigsmuir doing here in Baldarskiel? We are far from Altier, so it cannot be a diplomatic mission. And Ynysfawr is farther along the coast. You have no need to stop here, in this place. To attack us."

Kina lifted her chin higher, holding her shoulders back. "I have no need to answer to you, fiend. Either kill me and mine or let us go. I will answer no questions."

Somehow, I hadn't counted on animosity. I had thought—foolishly—that we would be able to talk, that I could lay out the details of the situation and they would join with us willingly. That they would see and believe the gods were coming, and all were in danger. It was painfully obvious to me that I knew nothing of politics, nothing of leadership.

My shoulder throbbed. I brought my fingers up and winced as I realised the arrow was still there. When I lowered my hands, though, Kina's eyes went wide. Had she been free to move, she likely would have been backing away. As it was, her arms fell to her sides and she swayed, only held up by my vines.

She started murmuring, a sing-song chant, in a language I didn't understand. The longer she spoke, though, the more the words sounded familiar. When I realised what she was doing, I nearly recoiled in horror. She was *praying*. To *me*.

"Stop," I said, holding out my hand. That was a mistake. I could see something glistening on the tips of my fingers, shining in the weak morning light. Others of her people saw as well and those that could fell to their knees.

I turned to Casimir, hand in front of me. He took a single step back, his sword clattering to the ground.

"Gold blood," he said. "Empty night."

Ilar made a motion with his hand, sketching a circle in the air before kissing his fingers. He didn't take his eyes from mine. "You're not a star, my lady."

I swallowed, true fear rising in my throat.

Ilar fell to his knees before me, reaching for my hand, now dripping with gold blood. He had awe in his expression, and I trembled. "You're no star. You're a *god*."

CHAPTER 5

Oh, gods. They knew what I was. I turned to Casimir, who was still staring at me, deathly pale, as though I'd mortally wounded him. Ilar was on his knees, muttering under his breath. Kina prayed in her own language, one I was beginning to understand in full. Some godly power, perhaps? I took a step back, away from all those standing near me. The earth trembled at my distress.

"Don't run," Casimir breathed, hand stretching towards me. He looked almost desperate, some of his colour returning in a feverish flush. I hesitated, ready to throw myself back at a moment's notice. He took a single step forwards. "*Please.*"

I closed my eyes, counted to three, then nodded. "I'm not going anywhere."

Ilar looked up at me. "Why didn't you tell me?"

Casimir's hand threaded through mine, heedless of the blood still streaked there. My shoulder throbbed, but I didn't dare move it. Didn't dare draw more attention to myself. "She didn't know before, when we met you on the way to Ynysfawr."

"So it *was* you," Kina breathed. "You destroyed the void, did what the Chosen Ones could not."

I gave the smallest nod. The words tumbled from my mouth in a blur, all truth, and yet they felt like lies. "I...I banished the void to its own realm. I didn't know what I was until then. Until I...used my power to rend the world into three. Mortal, immortal, and godly. The world we see, the void between, and the realm of the gods."

"You could have said on the shore." A choked, desperate sound reverberated in Ilar's throat, even as he tried to smile.

"You were expecting the Star," Casimir said, squeezing my fingers. "She didn't have any memories of before the burns, and we all assumed she was the Chosen One, or the Star reincarnated."

"She is so much more than that," Kina said. She rose from her knees and bowed deeply to me. "You are the hope for our future. One of the lost gods, returned."

"No!" I recoiled. "I am not them. I was never bound beyond the void. I..."

I would have to tell Casimir the truth. I would have to tell him who I was, what I was. He would know that I'd lied to him, that I'd held back information so central to my being that it would only mean I didn't trust him. But he was still there, still holding my hand, still looking at me as though I existed. And for all my aching heart, I didn't want him to stop looking at me. To stop seeing me.

"I don't remember anything before I was burned," I said, shaking my head. My shoulder twinged, a sharp remonstrance. "I think...I think I was made, and sent here, to fix the void. But there were consequences to that."

It was close enough to the truth that it rang sincere. Hopefully, Casimir wouldn't look too closely, wouldn't ask questions.

"You saved us all," Kina insisted. "The void beyond Baldarskiel was growing, with voidlings amassing on our lands. We couldn't get through to beg for more Void Runners...and then the world trembled and the void vanished. You *saved us*."

Casimir squeezed my fingers harder, just as my breath was beginning to hitch, my heart pounding in my ears. "There are consequences, always. Ast...*Calanthe* saved this world from the void, perhaps, but in doing so, the gods can now make their way here. And they are hungry for blood."

It was a simple explanation, a basic one that didn't highlight the nuances of the desires the gods would have for human devotion and sacrifice and flesh and more. An explanation that didn't lay any of the blame at Astraea's feet. It would have to suffice, though; I feared if I opened my mouth to say any more, that the entirety of my knowledge would spill at my feet and the entire world—Casimir included—would turn aside from me with ease.

"Calanthe," Ilar whispered. "Your name?"

"Astraea was the Star," I said. "She deserves her own legacy. One of light, not bloodshed as mine will surely be."

Casimir's breath hitched.

Kina frowned. "How could you bring about bloodshed?" Then, narrowing her eyes, she looked at the Hunters gathered around me, the ill-fitting armour I wore, the arrow in my shoulder. "You mean to fight the gods."

I nodded. "I cannot have them desecrating this world in their desperation and desires for what was lost. There are innocents here."

"The Hunters stand with you, Lady Calanthe, to whatever end." Ilar clasped his hand to his chest. The other Hunters did the same, letting out a roar as they did. A battle cry in support of me. All I could think was that I was hardly fit to lead an army. I turned to Kina.

"I know you came to Baldarskiel to learn of what happened to the void. If you leave now, then I will do my best to ensure that you and your people are safe. I...cannot promise anything, but I will try." Already, my vines and tree roots were retreating, dropping weapons and releasing captured limbs. The warriors of Craigsmuir picked up the discarded weapons and rubbed their arms and legs, murmuring between each other. Some, I noted with disquiet, plucked the wild-flowers that had grown over the ground and tucked them into pockets or folds of clothing, handling the flowers with reverence.

Kina turned to them. She spoke in her own tongue, but as though the prayer had unlocked the words in my mind, I could understand. "She is a god. She has saved us from the void, and proposes to stand between us mortals and the destructive power of gods long forgotten."

"The lost gods would never harm us!" one of her people said, more aged than the others, with a flaxen beard and wrinkles around his eyes. "There are stories of their favours still told around our firesides."

"Just as there are stories of their *dis*favours, Tiko. Or don't you remember the warnings given to you as a child?" This from a woman of Tiko's age, her hair streaked with grey, her shoulders strong.

"All we have of the lost gods is stories," Kina said firmly. She pointed at me. "But *she* stands here before us now. She saved us from the void. And she says that the return of the gods would be dangerous. She will fight those who wish us harm. I will fight them with her."

More people to stand at my side and face poten-tial slaughter. I didn't even know if it was possible to fight the gods. Did they hold similar powers to my own? Mine came from Lady Earth, and possibly her sister, The Eternal Flame. Did that mean I was stronger than the others? Or weaker? Would everyone I lead into battle die?

Things I should have thought of before undertaking this impossible task. My stomach knotted itself.

"We fight with you, Lady Calanthe," Kina said, and her people murmured agreement. I probably should have given them a speech, a few words of comfort, but all I could do was smile weakly.

"Thank you," I murmured.

Afterwards, it felt like chaos. I was led to a boulder and immediately swarmed by two Hunter healers and one from Kina's crew, as well as the Captain and Ilar, who were still peppering me with questions. Casimir never let go of my hand, even when the healers had to cut away the arrow from my shoulder. Between the pain of that, and the sting of the poultice that was lathered all over my wound, I stopped listening to the words being spoken at me and let the world fade away. I closed my eyes, feeling my heart beating in my chest. For a brief moment, I thought I felt a second beat there.

Dancer.

When I opened my eyes, though, Dancer was nowhere to be seen. Only Casimir remained, and one healer from the Hunters, who stared at me with awe.

"Calanthe?" Casimir asked. I hummed in response. "Do you feel any pain?"

"Some," I admitted. "But it's diminishing."

Casimir stroked my hand. "Look at your shoulder."

I did, and my stomach dropped out from beneath me. My breaths became shallow and I was certain I was going to faint. My shoulder, which had been bleeding freely when they removed the arrow, now looked as though it had been injured weeks before. All that I saw were my burns, long since scarred, and an angry patch of red. A welt, if that.

"Stay with me," Casimir said firmly, letting go of my hand and cupping my face. "Breathe."

"What's happening to me?" I whimpered. I hadn't ever been able to heal before. I'd struggled to recover from exhaustion, magic sickness, the weakness of my body after waking after the battle at Starfall Meadow. Now I bled gold? I healed within minutes?

"Whatever you did at Ynysfawr must have catalysed a change in you. Your godly nature is taking over." Casimir said, still holding my face. Still looking at me. "It's alright, Calanthe. You're still here. I'm still here. We'll figure this out."

I wanted to believe him. I wanted it so badly, enough that I almost let myself dream that we would figure it out. But the truth was, he was only here until we discovered what became of Astraea. Once he was reunited with his Star, I would be nothing but an afterthought. *And if she were dead?* a small, mean part of me whispered in my ear. I shook that thought off. She wasn't dead. If she were, then...well, Casimir would eventually go his own way.

Why would he stay here with me, when he'd thought I was her, only to discover that I was anything but?

No, I would have to learn to stand on my own. So I stretched my shoulder—still sore, at least—and smiled politely at Casimir. "I'm sure we will," I lied.

He frowned and let go of my hand, a slow release. Before I could even ask, someone brought me a damp cloth and wiped the blood from my fingers. The Craigsmuir healer, a girl more than woman, her hair a shock of blonde, eyes bright blue, entire frame eager. Everyone around me was eager, I realised. All looking at me as if I held all the answers, the hope for the future.

I knew very little at all.

"What do we do now, Lady Calanthe?" Kina asked. "I can set sail in a day, back to Craigsmuir, to raise an army for your cause. They will follow."

The healer held the cloth with my blood on it, and I realised that the captain meant to keep it as a token, proof that a god walked among them again. I wrinkled my nose at the macabre thing, but knew that it was likely all that would persuade others. And, as much as I didn't want it, we needed others.

"Go," I said. "With all haste."

Kina bowed, tucking the token into her belt. She turned to the healer. "Stay with the Lady, Rietta. You and Lionel will have to advocate for our people when you reach Baldarskiel. It has been long since we've had anyone in the court of the Defenders Against the Void. Make certain they haven't forgotten about us."

Defenders Against the Void? I'd known that Baldarskiel was the central force in the fight against the void, as it had been surrounded by the shadows, but that title sounded ceremonial, like something that Beatrice would have given to solidify the impression of power. I wondered what the royal family was doing now, given that the void had vanished.

I wondered more how they would react when I returned to Baldarskiel with the beginnings of an army, and no Crown Prince.

Ilar and Casimir were given instructions on how to contact Kina by messenger bird, a method of communication not used in Baldarskiel since the void sprang up due to the birds being attacked by voidlings. Apparently, it was still used freely in other lands. I wished I'd had a history lesson before being sent off to the void, one that had more to do with the people of Adhor than my role in facing the void. Then again, I hadn't exactly expected to survive my encounter with the void, and what good would history have done against that enemy?

Within an hour, the Craigsmuir warriors were gone, each one having stopped to introduce themselves to me, their heads bowed. I tried to keep each name in my mind, but knew I would soon forget. My heart still pounded and I still felt weak, despite the diminished pain in my shoulder. Using that amount of magic after Ynysfawr had taken a toll, one that I would likely pay later when I slept like the dead.

When all was said and done, it was late afternoon by the time the Hunters were prepared to move again. No one wanted to remain in the razed village, and now they were eager to press on towards Altier, even if it meant travelling later in the evening. For my part, I wanted to move, not stand around talking any more. Standing still would force me to face truths I didn't want to face.

What I was.

What I would have to do.

That look of desperation in Casimir's eyes as he'd stared at my wound.

So I walked, refusing the horse offered to me. The earth beneath my feet whispered to me in words I could barely hear, a lulling sound that seemed to replenish my energy even as it soothed my pulse into a steady rhythm.

We travelled late into the evening, eating dried meats and plants as we walked. Rietta and Lionel, the two youths Kina ordered to remain behind, stayed near me, but never ventured close enough to speak. Once, I caught them staring as I knelt by a stream and washed my face, but they quickly turned away when I looked. Casimir, too, remained close at hand, hovering almost annoyingly close, as if ready to tend to my every whim. Only, he never actually spoke to me, wavering between watching me with open interest and studying the landscape around us. The Hunters, too, with whom I'd developed a reasonable camaraderie, seemed distant. Aloof. Or perhaps they were just afraid.

After all, I was now a god.

By the time we stopped for the night, setting up camp with quick and hurried movements, I was in a foul mood. My shoulder, while healed to a nice pink, still throbbed, as if my body held on to the memory of pain if not the actual injury. I was both hungry and too distressed to eat, my meals throughout the day little more than handfuls. Yet the thought of going to the large cauldron, around which several handfuls of people were gathered while they waited for an extra evening meal, made my skin itch. So I just unrolled my bed by a fire on the outskirts of the camp, lay down, and willed myself to sleep.

"Why didn't you tell me?" Casimir sat beside me, too close to ignore. The plants on the ground started leaning towards him, as I longed to do, clover sprouting and climbing through the earth even as I watched. I bit down on the urge for closeness, my magic retreating.

"About being a god?" I asked, rolling onto my back and staring up at the vast sky. Stars speckled the heavens, glowing regally, shining through the spaces of blackness between. I wondered if they knew where Astraea was, or if they even bothered to watch this world at all.

"Surely you figured it out at Ynysfawr," Casimir said. He didn't sound angry, only sad, and I had to remind myself that he had lost the only person he loved, only to have me serve as a living reminder that I was not her. "When you walked through the realms, when you used your power to bind the door into place."

I sighed. "Would you have wanted me to tell you? When I told you that I wasn't Astraea, that I was someone else, though I didn't know who, would it have helped if I'd said I was a god?"

A heartbeat. Two. Three. Then, "It would not have helped. Stars above, I don't know why I didn't see it before. No mortal could have the power to bind the realms."

I said nothing, keeping my eyes on the stars twinkling brightly above me. I didn't have the words to describe my feelings, only that they were somewhere between resignation and hurt and sadness and determination. I would never be what Casimir had hoped I was, and I would never be the thing that the humans wished of me. I was not ready for abject admiration, nor for worship. I just wanted to be me, whoever that was.

I still didn't know.

"I'm sorry for not telling you," I said at last. "I'm not sure I really understand it all myself. Where I came from. How. I just..."

"I understand." Casimir shifted on his bedroll. I flicked my eyes to him long enough to watch him stretch out beside me, eyes looking at me instead of the stars. I swallowed and turned back to the sky. "I meant what I said before, Calanthe. I will be here for you."

A guardian in truth, then.

"Thank you. We'll find her, Cas," I replied. His breath caught.

"I don't know what you mean."

Liar.

"Astraea. We'll find her. And we'll make everything right."

Silence.

"Calanthe, we won't find her."

I twisted onto my side, propping my head in my hands. Casimir was staring at me, eyes shadowed and expression carefully blank. I waited. His expression broke, and he squeezed his eyes shut, pressing the heels of his palms to his eyes. "I let her leave, last time. We argued, and I just let her leave. I thought that we would meet again, as we always had in the cycle against the void. I thought that she delayed in dealing with it for so long because she was still upset with me. I thought...I thought that when you came, that you were her, and that meant you...that she forgave me. That we would be okay. Only, you aren't her, and she's gone, and I failed."

"You didn't fail, Casimir," I breathed. He swallowed, still with eyes shut, tears dripping down his cheeks and reflecting the fire we shared.

"I was her guardian. Born to protect her, to keep her safe, to watch over her. I was the blackness between stars, bound to her for all time. And I let her die."

"You don't know that she's dead. And she walked away. She *walked away*."

"I should have followed."

I sat up, the fire crackling angrily, tongues of flame licking at the sky. "No. Someone walks away like that, without giving you a chance for communication, for apologies on either side, that is not on you. She could have reached out any time in the last, what, fifty years? She chose to leave you, Cas. That is not your fault."

I could tell he didn't believe me. He still had tears streaming down his face, but his eyes were empty again, shaded from me. He was closed off, and I knew that I would get no more from him that night. I also knew that until he acknowledged that Astraea had a part in her fate, that it wasn't entirely his fault, he would bear the weight of his guilt like a shroud. I could do nothing but be there. Support him. Love him, even if he didn't love me back. Even if he never could.

I lay back down and reached out to take his hand. He flinched at first, but threaded his fingers through mine with such force that I felt like a lifeline.

"I'll be here for you, too, Cas," I murmured, my words snatched away by the fire, carried to the distant heavens. He tightened his grip on my fingers, a simple squeeze, and it was enough.

CHAPTER 6

I don't know what I expected from my return to Altier, but it was not fanfare. As the Hunters and I approached the outskirts of the city, having passed several smaller villages on the way, cheers broke out amongst the people. They gathered along the roads, in front of houses and stores, and as we drew closer to the city itself, the number of onlookers made it so that they had to press in impossibly close, some sticking their heads out of windows and waving scraps of cloth as they cheered.

Ilar and Casimir had insisted that I ride the massive horse into town, wearing the iron band that had become my crown. Casimir rode at my side, his Void Runner armour polished of dirt and grime, making it impossible to mistake. The leader of the Hunters rode at my other side, followed by the two Craigsmuirians, both seated on a single horse. The other Hunters came straggling behind, hardly as organised as a true army and yet daunting in the grim looks on their face, the hollows in their cheeks. They followed me willingly, their god.

The thought of their blind devotion still twisted my stomach.

"How did they know we were returning?" I asked, having to raise my voice so Casimir could hear over the shouting of the crowd.

"Someone must have run on ahead from the villages. We did stop for food along the way."

"Void Slayer!" Voices chanted. "Star Blessed!"

Uneasiness tightened my throat.

"It's her! The Burned One!" a young girl screamed, running into the cobbled street before me, flowers bundled in her hand. The horse snorted and tossed its head, but the girl was hardly deterred. She reached up as high as she could, holding the flowers to me, eyes gleaming with joy. I leaned over and took the bundle, more afraid for her safety than concerned with the gift she bore.

Casimir eyed me, his brows furrowed. I tried to smile, but the bouquet of flowers trembled in my hands. My magic reached for the plucked blooms and recoiled. They'd lost their connection to the earth and so I could not make them grow. I tried to hold on to my calm, to any grip of reality in the moment, but the spark of fire in me started to rise. If I could not grow the flowers, then surely they would burn.

"Calanthe," Ilar said, drawing my attention long enough for me to break my magic's hold on my mind. I pushed the spark of flame down far enough that it wouldn't hurt anyone in this crowded city. "Are you well?"

"Perfectly," I lied, plastering a smile on my features. I looked to the girl, who was still standing there, expression awed. "Thank you for the flowers."

She bowed deeply then ran, her face lit with a blush.

"Come, we should get to the palace," Casimir said, drawing his horse near. I didn't want to go to the palace, that place bound in by a stone wall and most of the memories I had, but it was necessary. We'd decided it the night before over a fire, all the people counselling me illuminated by flame. The palace was the only place I could gather an army with ease, the only place where my voice would be heard loudly enough to spread across Baldarskiel and into the lands beyond. Yes, I returned without Devereux, the crown prince, but Casimir had argued that the queen and king would hardly refuse me.

I had saved everyone from the void, after all.

The cheering of the people began to make my head pound. I tried to smile, tried to look at everyone and acknowledge them, but the noise grew too much. By the time we reached the palace gates, it was all I could do to stay on the horse, my hands white-knuckling the reins. Then, in a rush, everything grew silent.

The gates were shut.

Guards stood at the entrance, polearms held at their shoulders. They eyed me and the Hunters, taking note of the crowd behind me. They said nothing, made no move, and yet it was obvious that I would not be allowed to pass.

"They won't let the star in!" a man's voice shouted from behind us. People that had been screaming for me only moments before now started murmuring angrily, pressing closer to the Hunters, to me, to the gates.

"Tate," Casimir barked, making one of the guards jerk. "What is the meaning of this? Why are we barred entrance?"

The guard tightened his grip on the polearm, looking between me, Casimir, Ilar, and the gathering of people behind us. I didn't turn around to look. I already knew that it looked like I was bringing an army to the palace, and in a way, I was. Only, the army wasn't for them. Tate worked his mouth, but no sound came out. He was terrified, I realised.

Of me?

Or those I had brought with me?

I dismounted from the horse, hardly a graceful motion. The ground beneath my feet felt blissfully solid after being on horseback. In my relief, I lost hold of the grip on my magic for a moment. Flowers bloomed at my feet, wrapping around my legs. The guards took a step backwards, Tate making a strangled sound in his throat. Immediately, I pulled back on my magic and the flowers disappeared.

They were truly terrified of me.

"Guardsman," I said, tempering my tone to be gentle, as though I were talking to the horse. "May I ask why the way is barred? I am returning here after defeating the void. Have I done something wrong? Is that why I'm kept away?"

Tate looked away, but the other guard, an older, harder man with a scar through his left eye, cleared his throat. "Lady Astraea—"

"Calanthe," Ilar hissed. "This is the *goddess* Calanthe."

I waved a hand at Ilar, silencing him. "Please, continue," I said to the guard. "I will not harm you."

"Begging your pardon, ah, Lady, but that's not what we were told."

"What?" Casimir snarled, suddenly at my shoulder, his hand on his sword. "Who spouted such lies?"

"Her Majesty said that now you've defeated the void, you would come to conquer Altier, and all of Baldarskiel beyond, so that you could..." The guard trailed off, looking to the crowd of people behind us, all citizens of Altier, all silent and waiting with bated breath. "She claimed you would destroy those who lost faith with the star during the time of the void, as was told by the Temple long ago. Those who did not follow the tenets of your rulings would be hunted down and killed. The world would be remade."

Casimir let out a feral sound, like Dancer on the hunt. My heart yearned for my lost companion for a brief moment, enough to make my breath hitch. "The *absurdity* of—"

"Sir," I said, cutting my guardian off, "I truly mean you no harm. I have little care or knowledge of the tenets of the Temple's religion. I do not wish to destroy, or to remake the world in my image, or any of that. I wish only to return to where I had lived before venturing to Ynysfawr. I'm tired, haven't had a proper bath in weeks, and wish for a decent meal. If the queen does not wish me to return, however, I'm sure that I can find reasonable accommodations elsewhere."

The guards looked at each other, faltering. Murmuring started up behind me, people offering me their homes, their meals, even when they said it would hardly be fitting for the Fallen Star. They did not yet believe that I wasn't her. I rubbed my chest. Would I forever be having to explain that I wasn't Astraea, that I was my own person?

My own person? Ha! A being formed but moons ago, a goddess, staring down immortality. I barely even knew who I was myself.

"Do you swear that you mean no harm?" Tate asked, looking me in the eye.

I reached for the knife at my belt, and before he

could do more than flinch, brought the blade across my palm. Golden drops of blood fell to the ground, hissing as they met stone. "I swear by my blood upon the earth that I mean you no harm unless you harm me or mine."

"Goddess," a voice murmured. The word spread like wildfire through the gathered crowd. The Hunters gathered closer, puffing up with pride as they stood by me. Casimir took my injured hand and twined my fingers with his. There was a mild sting as he pressed against the cut, but it faded as the injury did.

Tate and the other guard grew pale, eyes fixed on the blood I'd spilled on the ground.

"Well?" Casimir asked, voice a low rumble.

In an instant, the two men sprang into action, unlocking the gate and ushering us through. As we passed, they bowed, low and deep. I turned my face away.

The Hunters remained in the courtyard, as we didn't want it to seem like I was invading. I brought Casimir, Ilar, and the two Craigsmuirians, Rietta and Lionel, and even that felt like both too much and not enough.

I'd thought that returning to Altier would be at least familiar, even if it didn't feel much like home, but no matter how I tried, entering the palace felt more like entering an entirely new world than anything else. The stones were worn, weary, barely whispering to me through my magic. The servants ducked their heads and hid as we passed. There were no guards in the corridors, perhaps expecting that the two at the gate would be enough. The hallways echoed and wind whistled through the tiny arrowslit windows.

"The throne room," Casimir suggested, tugging me along. Ilar kept by the young healer Rietta, looking wary, while Lionel jumped at every sound. I tried to look confident, for their sakes, but the closer we drew to the throne room, the more my self-assurance waned. I wished for Dancer, for the feel of his fur against my fingers, the tacit comfort that he offered. I wished for Devereux, his easy smile and irreverent attitude. Instead, I tightened my grip on Casimir's hand and tried to smile at him as he returned the touch.

"What would you have us do, *Your Majesty?*" A voice rang through the corridor just outside the throne room. There was a single guard stationed there, young and obviously inexperienced. She jumped and pointed a knife at us as we approached, then relaxed as she saw Casimir's armour.

"Your people are now useless. Redundant." Queen Raya's voice was sharp, angry, yet perfectly smooth. "All I'm doing is offering you a new position in this new world."

"One without any say at all!" the other speaker scoffed.

"Open the door," Casimir murmured to the guard. She stiffened for a moment, casting a glance behind her. When there was no answer forthcoming from the throne room, only more angry words, she did as Casimir asked.

The door swung open with a *thud*, striking the stone wall. I strode through without hesitation, knowing my role in matters, my people at my back. What I found gave me pause.

The throne room was full of people, more so than I had ever seen in the space. The Council of Nobles sat at the long table, looking rather the worse for wear, their clothes wrinkled and eyes surrounded by dark circles. Queen Raya stood on her dais before the throne, hands clenched into fists, chin raised. She, too, looked less than her usual perfect, though she looked considerably better than her Council. Her husband, King Consort Istar, sat in the corner, fiddling with the frayed edges of his tunic, eyes casting about nervously. Beatrice, the High Priestess of the Temple of the Fallen Star—and Devereux's sister—stood beside her mother's throne, wearing her finest gown, threaded with Fallen Star gems and gold and silver embroidery. Crowding the rest of the room were a number of people, some wearing fine clothes and others in the ivory and black armour of the Void Runners.

From the divisions between the Council and the

Void Runners, it would appear that I had returned in the midst of a standoff.

The queen was the first to break the silence that followed my entry into the throne room. "Lady Astraea! You've...you've returned."

"The *goddess* Calanthe has indeed returned after defeating the void," Ilar said, a hint of a sneer in his voice. The queen stiffened. Beatrice stepped forwards, a mocking smile painted across her features.

"A goddess? Goodman, this is no goddess. She was the Chosen One, whose task has now been fulfilled. Not your—"

"Look at her blood," Casimir interrupted, his words carrying through the room with ease. He held up my injured hand high. As one, everyone's eyes went to my hand, which still bore remnants of my blood, despite being fully healed. I was prepared to open the wound again, but it didn't appear necessary. There were gasps, murmured declarations, and several people making hurried gestures that probably bore some religious significance, but which meant nothing to me.

Beatrice, though, took a single step backwards. Her gaze went to my face, which was still burned, then back to my hand. "H-how..." she faltered.

I'd never seen Beatrice at a loss for words, as she was careful enough for every situation, and cunning enough to manoeuvre herself into a world that was prepared for her. I would admit to a certain small satisfaction at seeing her dismay. I wished Devereux could see it, too.

"I didn't know what I was before," I said, making sure my voice carried even to the vaulted ceiling. "But in pushing back the void, I came into my own. I am Calanthe. I am here to warn you that the other gods are returning, and they are hungry for devotion. For blood."

Voices broke out, shouting and proclaiming and talking over one another so that it was impossible to make out what was being said. One woman started laughing, the sound so jarring in the midst of chaos, that everyone fell quiet and turned to her. I recognised her, a woman with silvery white hair and piercing eyes, perhaps not quite as studied in her appearance. Dame Winters, the seer for the court. Devereux had introduced us shortly before we left for Ynysfawr, and the seer had told me that her arcane magic was not for me.

Had she known what I was?

"I warned you," she said, jabbing a finger in the direction of the Council, the queen, even Beatrice. She wore her smile with manic glee. "I warned you all that the ages past should not be forgotten, yet you worshipped your precious Fallen Star. Now she is gone and you have a goddess standing before you! The gods from beyond the veil will devour you and feel no remorse."

Winters strode over to me, eyes glittering, smile widening. She stepped past Casimir as if he wasn't there, then lifted my chin with a finger, studying me. She clicked her tongue. "And what of you, Calanthe? Will you feel remorse?"

I swallowed, my mouth dry. Before I had a chance to answer, the seer's expression softened.

"Yes, I think you will," she murmured. "If you are not careful, it will be your undoing."

"Enough!" Queen Raya snarled. She glowered down at us from her spot on the dais. Dame Winters flinched just enough to waken the fire in my veins. "Astraea or Calanthe or whoever you are, we will not be party to your machinations! Baldarskiel defended against the void for centuries, and just because the void is gone does not mean that we will bow to the first power to covet our throne. We will hold off the invaders, just as—"

"Invaders?" Ilar laughed. "The only invaders you have to fear are those that come from the realm of the gods."

"You foolish brute. Do you think we are ignorant of the forces amassing beyond our borders? The ships sent by Craigsmuir to test our defences? The *delegations* sent by Llyn Rhosalwyd or Amontys that even now ride for Altier? Baldarskiel has been the pinnacle of hope for generations, pitting ourself against the void for the sake of all Adhor. And now that the void is gone, those who cowered beyond our void-touched borders now seek to take us. To invade us. To capture us for their own. I will not stand for it!"

The queen's speech was fiery, impassioned, just the sort of thing to rally desperate people to her. But the Council was afraid, not desperate. The Void Runners were angry. And I was not the cowering shell I had been.

"The people of Craigsmuir have no wish to invade," I said, gesturing to Rietta and Lionel. "They wish to learn what happened at Ynysfawr, to understand. Did you think that the void disappearing would bring no questions?"

"Of course I knew that there would be questions," Raya sneered. "I am not the one with no memories, no knowledge of the world."

That stung, for the barb was true. I didn't understand the politics of the situation, not like she would. I could only guess at certain things and hope I was right. The fire in me flared brighter, begging to be let out. To show this arrogant woman who I truly was.

"Then why did you not wait for me to return?" I asked, voice cold. "Why did you not wait for me to answer your questions? Why did you close the gates to the palace, leaving your people in ignorance, your guards claiming that the star would be returning to awaken a reckoning?"

Here, the queen faltered.

Beatrice stepped into her place, gown shimmering in a beam of sunlight, making her radiant, her expression serene. "We had no way of knowing whether you would return, my lady."

"The guards at the gate and the people in the streets say otherwise," Casimir snapped. "They say that the Temple was counting on the star's return—Calanthe's return—to weed out the unbelievers, the sinners."

Beatrice lifted her chin. "What would you know of Temple beliefs, Void Runner? You and others like you were well known to have no faith in such things."

I held up a hand. "I do not want to get into an argument about your Temple's politics, High Priestess. I am here, as I said, to warn you. The gods—whom you pushed aside at the star's behest—are returning. If we do not stand against them, they will lay waste to this world in their desire to regain the devotion that they have been without for so long. Progress, civilisation, it will be lost to their whims."

"What of your whims?" Beatrice demanded. "You claim to be a goddess, after all."

"I am not them. I was sent here to bind the void in its own realm, not to rule over you." I wanted none of their worship. I wanted only to see them safe.

The queen stepped off the dais and walked up to me, a fire in her eyes burning bright enough to match my own magic. She lifted her chin and looked down at me, sneering. "And yet, you in your benevolence, your great power, you return without my son."

CHAPTER 7

The light in the room seemed to dim for a moment, like shadows had reached out and devoured the light. Out of the corner of my eye, I saw Casimir with hands clenched into fists, those ink-dark marks on his fingers growing. He was furious, but it was on my behalf. I frowned; did he really see me as so incapable?

Perhaps. I certainly had done little to prove my spine.

I lifted my chin and stared the queen straight in the eye, enough that she took a step backwards. The shadows slipped away and the daylight shone as brightly as ever, with no one the wiser as to who caused such a thing. Perhaps to them, it was nothing more than a cloud covering the sun. I knew better, and while Casimir was exceptional at pretending to be human, he wasn't.

"You ask me why I return without Devereux?" I asked. "I'm shocked, Majesty, since it was you who sent him to Ynysfawr with me. Oh, did you expect that he would go out into the void-touched lands, where voidlings and those who hunt them roamed and he would return home unscathed? Unscratched? Unchanged?"

"Is he dead?" Queen Raya asked. I half-expected a note of true grief, true concern to touch her words, but there was only the same starkness with which she always spoke. She had hidden her true feelings for too long, and now they were gone. Or perhaps she didn't have them to begin with.

"No," I said, shrugging one shoulder. Then, turning slightly to address the room as well as the queen, I said louder, "As my role was to seal the void beyond the borders of this realm, so was Devereux's to become its king."

The Council of Nobles gasped, almost as one. The Void Runners put their hands to their weapons. Dame Winters chuckled.

"You speak blasphemy," Beatrice snarled from her position on the dais. "My brother would not profane this world so much as to betray it entirely!"

"Betray it?" Casimir laughed. "High Priestess, your brother helped *save* it. Did you think that the void would go quietly? That even bound in another realm, it would not seek out the people here who hurt it for so long? Without a king, a ruler, the void is a lawless, fey land, where creatures who have so long been driven insane by being here roam free. *King* Devereux has claimed his throne. He has bounds its people. And he controls its magic."

"What protections do we have against such a force?" a Council member asked, fairly trembling as she pulled her sleeves of her silk gown over her hands to hide her anxiety. The feathers in her hair wobbled as she shook.

"Protections? Do you have so little faith in your former Crown Prince?" I asked, disgusted. She flinched. "The void is bound, yes, but there are still tears in the veil where its magic can seep through. Therefore, you should know these things: Do not wish at a crossroads. Do not ask for help from the midnight wood. Do not offer your name freely. And do not bargain with anything you cannot bear to lose. Abide by these rules, and you will be safe."

Raya shook her head almost violently. "You come barging in here, declaring yourself a goddess, telling us that the old gods are returning and want our very world. You tell us that my son is bound to the void as its king, but that we're only safe should we follow certain rules. You tell us all of this! Why should we believe you? You only come to claim power, to...to..."

"We believe you." A man stepped forwards from the ranks of the Void Runners, his ivory armour brushed with gold. He was older than many of the Runners, his olive skin hardened by years of fighting.

He had a thick, neatly trimmed beard and a scar on his right cheek that looked like it had come from a voidling. His hand rested casually on the hilt of the sword.

At his words, the queen took a step back, alarm painting her every feature.

"Master Garwith," Casimir said, bowing his head. To me, he murmured, "Leader of the Void Runners."

Garwith inclined his head deeply to Casimir. He smiled in my direction. "We believe you, Lady Calanthe," he repeated. Other Void Runners nodded their heads in agreement. "We will stand with you against whatever foes come our way."

"You believe *her*?" Beatrice snapped. "But she—"

"Saved us all from the void. We were there when the battle of the wall took place. You, in all your finery, hid in the palace. Very well; you are not trained to fight voidlings. But when you did not even check on us the next day? When you did not go amongst the people and ask to their wellbeing?" Garwith pointed a finger at me. "She went amongst the people. She asked after their wellbeing. And was punished for it."

I'd been restricted to the palace, yes, but because I was weak after expending so much magic. Surely he knew that. As I watched Beatrice and the queen, though, I saw otherwise. I might have been recovering, but even had I regained my strength I wouldn't have been allowed to walk the streets.

"A man even brought her ring, an emerald ring, to the palace in the hopes that he might be granted the ability to speak with her. As was promised," Garwith growled. "What became of him? No one has seen him since. Nor the ring, bearing the promise of our protector."

I'd given the ring to a man who tried to help me the first time I went into Altier. My magic had been overwhelmed by the sights, the sounds, and the stories people were telling me. It had become a fight between the guards and the people, each trying to protect me. I'd stopped it with magic.

The man. He'd told me his name. What was it?

"Thomas Key," I said. "He asked after me?"

Beatrice looked away. The queen said nothing. Garwith snorted, shaking his head.

"For so long, we let you rule without question. We had the void to fight, and you managed to keep the people alive, to hold their loyalty with the promise of your religious preachings, with the promise of the Chosen One. But now the void is gone, Majesty, and all you worry about is who may try to seize your power?" Garwith shook his head again. "You should be concerned with the lives of your citizens. You should be concerned with making alliances with the world beyond Baldarskiel, not keeping everyone away. Instead, you wish to keep the Void Runners as your elite army. We are not yours to command, as we have never been yours to command. We fight for the people. Always. And as *she* fights for the people, we follow her."

He pointed at me again. The other Runners clanked their swords in their sheaths, or banged against their breastplates, a discordant sound that somehow signified harmony.

Ilar took a step closer to me, grinning widely. "I knew you could do it. People need only hear you speak to know you care, my lady. You have their hearts."

I wanted to shrug him off, shrug them all off and go off on my own. I wanted to find Dancer and Tali and Whisper. I wanted to live my life, not fight battles for the sake of the mortal realm. Instead, I looked again at the queen.

"I do not wish to argue with you, Your Majesty. You were kind to me when I was here. You gave me shelter, training. You obviously care about your people, with all the plans you made to help them survive through the darkest nights of the void. Please, trust me now when I tell you what things may stalk this way. Stand with me, *help* me."

For all her coldness, for all her love of power, Queen Raya was not a foolish woman. She knew that if she crossed me, when I had a riot of her own citizens at my back and the Void Runners at my side, that there would be potentially dangerous consequences. She had already alienated the Runners. Her power was weakened with the Council now that

Devereux was gone; who would be her heir? Beatrice? I did not think that priestesses could rule. If she sided with me, then she delayed any action against her.

I hated that I had such influence.

She lowered her chin a fraction, her eyes gazing downwards for a brief moment. A show of respect, even if only surface-deep. "I apologise, my lady. There have been so many changes to the world that I find it difficult to adapt. And to learn that my son—though he still lives—may be lost to me forever...well, I fear that it has affected me more than I thought."

Lies, and we both knew it.

"Of course, Your Majesty," I said, smiling. "I understand completely."

"You will, naturally, have my full support. We must draw up plans and send out messengers to the rest of Adhor to garner their support. I will have the clerks draft a message to be sent out as soon as possible. For now, we must find quarters for your people, and see to getting everyone something to eat, a bath, a change of clothes. It is always better to strategise when well rested."

She took command naturally, and everyone listened to her, though I had more than a few glances thrown my way as people scrambled to follow the queen's orders.

"What of the citizens of Altier?" Casimir asked, his sharp question jolting Raya as she turned towards the dais. "Someone should explain away the false-hoods they've been told."

Without a moment's hesitation, Raya turned to Beatrice, still standing by the throne, resplendent in her finery. "Indeed, someone should do just that. As it was your Temple who allowed such rumours to spread, dear daughter, surely you wouldn't mind clearing up such misconceptions?"

Beatrice paled. She looked past her mother to me, mouth tightening. Then, smiling gracefully, she lowered herself into a curtsey. "Of course. It would be my honour to speak on Lady Calanthe's behalf."

Casimir, with deliberate motion, put his hand on the hilt of his sword. "You do not speak for the Lady Calanthe."

Beatrice recoiled as if he'd struck her. The queen all but gaped. Even the Council of Nobles seemed astonished. The Void Runners, though, all took their cues from Casimir, and why not; he had been well regarded amongst their number for years.

"If the High Priestess does not speak for a goddess, then who does?" Raya laughed nervously, eyes darting to me as though waiting for me to inter-rupt, to demure, to look down and acquiesce.

"I can speak for myself, surely," I said smoothly. A bath, some food, a rest—it would all have to wait just a little longer. "I'll go address them now, and then we can see to finding space for my people."

"They can stay with us," Garwith said, bowing low to me. "We have space in our barracks."

I nodded my agreement, then turned from the room and left. Conversation broke out as soon as I reached the threshold. I ignored it all and kept my head high.

* * *

The people of Altier were waiting outside the palace gates, far more patiently than I would have expected, given how agitated they were earlier. Upon my appearance, still flanked by Casimir and Ilar, the others milling about somewhere behind me, a hush fell over the people.

"I am not the Fallen Star," I started, and immediately there were shocked gasps. "I am Calanthe, a goddess sent to bind the void to its own realm. The only way to do so was to create a doorway between the realms to balance the flow of energy. This realm, the land of mortals; the void, land of magic; and the realm of the gods."

People stared at me, their expressions almost uniform, despite the variation in face and age and colour and gender. Confusion.

"The gods have been forgotten for an age," I said, trying to channel Tali and her ability to speak of things that were myth and legend to everyone else.

"And now, they can access this realm again through that door. They will want for all that was taken from them those many years ago. The devotion. The blood. They will come forth and destroy this world in their eagerness to reclaim it. Unless we stand in their way."

It was all my fault. The doorway was all my fault, and standing there now, before these people staring at me with desperate eyes, I wanted to turn and hide. To reverse time. Instead, I gestured to the Hunters and the Void Runners behind me.

"These people were bound to protect you from the void, and now they have sworn to help me in protecting you from the vengeful gods. But they cannot do it alone. We will need all the help we can get. Will you help me?"

A man, bent and old, his expression hard and bitter, a cane clutched in his hands, stepped forwards without hesitation. "We will help you, Burned One, in any way that we can."

Burned One. My hand lifted to my face, touching the whorls of scars that lingered there. I rarely thought about the scars, given that I didn't look at myself and was so used to how they felt. But now, I realised that they identified me. Marked me. A small part of me stumbled away and curled up, weeping for that truth, that I would never be insignificant and invisible, my identity borne out in indelible scars. The rest of me drew on the fire that lived in my veins and set myself alight, burning so all could see.

The Burned One indeed.

"Then we stand together! Or all of Adhor will fall."

They cheered. For me, for my words, they cheered. It was horrifying, enough to make me want to shrink back and flee, to bury my feet in the earth and turn my head to the sky. I promised them war, and they cheered for me. Instinctively, I took a step backwards, and then another as people moved forwards.

"Come," Casimir murmured, his hand gentle on my back. Louder, enough so that the people could hear, he said, "We must rest. Recover from our travels. Then, we will plan."

As if his words bore a sort of magic of their own, the Altians started to disperse. Most cast lingering glances in my direction, while others bent their heads together and talked fervently. I allowed myself to be shepherded back through the gates towards the palace, where Garwith was already talking to the Hunters and moving them to be quartered. Ilar gave me a few parting words that I barely comprehended before moving to help with his people. Rietta and Lionel reported in as well, then went off with a clerk, one of the queen's diplomatic corps, to discuss the state of Adhor at large.

Somehow, in a blur of motion and words and endless parades of people, I found myself walking up familiar stairs, Casimir at my side. We were heading to the room I'd occupied in the palace, the one where I had tried to devise some sort of identity for myself, where I'd spent time with my hands splayed in Dancer's fur, wracked with guilt for being unable to kill him and yet glad that I hadn't. It was the closest place I had to a home, a place of my own, and yet I couldn't bring myself to see it now.

Not yet.

I paused, my foot poised on the step. Casimir had walked to the landing before he realised I wasn't following. He turned, frowning.

"I can't," I breathed. "There's something I have to do first."

"Whatever it is can surely wait until you've rested." As if he didn't also need rest. "You may be a goddess, but you are new to your magic, to your immortality. You will tire easily for a while. As easily as any human."

I closed my eyes. I was tired, so bone weary that I wanted to collapse and sleep for a week. Even so, this had to be done. "Someone has to tell Tali's grandmother of...before word spreads around the city that I returned with an army at my back, and no Tali to speak of."

Casimir faltered. Pain, brief and intense, shuttered his features. "Yes, of course. I should have thought of that."

I hadn't realised that he, too, had come to think of the wandering poet as a friend. He seemed to reserved, so aloof from the rest of the world that it was hard to imagine him relaxing, sharing a drink with a friend, sharing words and hopes and dreams. Yet, I knew that Devereux had considered Casimir one of his greatest friends. Now he stood there, eyes cast to the stone steps beneath our feet, shadows wrapped around his hands and his throat in delicate, precise patterns.. A mixture of darkness and light. The guardian of a star, bound for generations to walk this world with no one the wiser to his identity except for the beacon of light that this world loved.

Alone but for her.

Watching any friends he might have made amongst the humans—so frail and mortal and impossibly bright—die of old age, illness, worse.

In the absence of his star, he had bound himself to me. I vowed to the heavens that had exiled him that I would not fail him. He whom I loved, who loved the Fallen Star.

"Come with me," I said, holding out my hand. Casimir hesitated. I smiled as best I could manage. "I don't even know if I remember the way back to her shop. We were in the carriage, and then there were so many people and..."

Casimir nodded, still looking distracted but perhaps a bit more at ease. "That was not a particularly calm day. Of course I'll go with you."

Pleasure burned its way through me, making the

light of the torches flicker. I hid a wince and reined in my magic, hoping that Casimir hadn't noticed.

"We can't go through the palace gates, though." He frowned, thoughtful.

"Why not?" I blurted before thinking it through. "Oh. Right. The people. If they see me, they'll swarm." I brushed a hand over my scars. "I wish I were not so easily recognised."

"Don't ever wish to be other than what you are," Casimir growled, taking the few steps down to where I was. He placed a hand against my ruined skin, brushing the whorls there. I barely felt his touch, the nerves deadened. He opened his mouth, eyes darkened with a shadow that I once knew as well as my own. A hitch of breath. A blink. Then, as though a jolt shot through us both, he lowered his hand.

"Should I have her brought here?" I asked, lowering my gaze. "I'd hate to put her out of her way, and for bad news at that, but..."

"No, I know of a way." Casimir ran a hand through his hair, the white strands framing his face. "It's not particularly pleasant, but it will get us where we need to go."

"Not particularly pleasant? Are we stealing a ride on the back of Beatrice's carriage?"

"That would be unpleasant, indeed. No, this path requires walking, but it's not going to be an easy journey. And we're both tired. In need of a bath. Perhaps..."

I took his hand. "I can do it," I assured him. "Please."

He swallowed, eyes closed. "Very well. This way."

I was led back down the stairs and on a merry chase through the palace, avoiding the glances of servants, guards, and nobles alike. Every corner we took, every staircase we descended, brought us further beneath the ground. I could feel the earth above our heads, the roots of this stone fortress that were older than the fortifying wall. Finally, in the corner of a forgotten store room lined with cobwebs, the only illumination a torch Casimir had snatched from two levels up, we came to a door.

Casimir hunched his shoulders. "Here we are," he said, curling his lip in distaste. "The only other path out of the palace. Besides going over the wall, at least."

I reached for the handle—a rusted, ancient thing of iron—and nearly staggered back in shock when I felt my magic surge up. The earth sang to me, deep and slow. It told me of a heart that beat, fathoms beneath the surface, in a pocket of magic at the centre of a dead volcano. A heart that beat in a dead god's domain.

I cast a desperate look at Casimir, who was still staring at the door. Then, tightening my panic into resolve, I said nothing about what I had sensed and pushed my way through the door.

CHAPTER 8

The tunnel was damp, dripping with moisture that gathered from years of rain seeping into the ground. Moss blanketed the walls and floors, muffling our steps and absorbing the torchlight as we passed by. Casimir muttered at each drip of water on his head, and each time the passage grew narrow enough to scrape at our skin.

"Are you well?" I asked after the third such string of curses. He turned to me, and even in the reddish light of the fire, he looked pale.

"I...don't much care for being underground. I'm a creature of the sky, and this feels too much like being cut off from everything." He hunched his shoulders and hissed as a protruding rock brushed his hair.

"What was it like, the sky?" I asked, trying to distract him. I seemed able to anticipate every divot in the ground, every twist in the tunnel. The moss hummed as I walked by and the earth sang when I brushed my fingers over the wall. I felt alive down here, just as much as I did walking through a field of grass or a garden. I wondered how foolish I had to be, a goddess of earth and fire, to fall in love with a being who had been formed in the heavens to guard a star.

"Open," Casimir said, a note of wistfulness there. "Even if you stretched your power out as far as it would go, there was always space. No one crowded you unless you wished it, and then you could become something more. Something bigger. Stars gathered into nebulae, guardians like me swam in black holes. Everywhere you went, the sky touched the earth, but it could never quite reach back." He laughed, a small sound, but genuine. "I remember once, when I was young, a bunch of us would go and dance just out of reach of the earth, taunting the creatures below. They made songs about us, you know."

"It sounds beautiful," I murmured.

"Beautiful beyond anything you've ever seen," Casimir agreed. "And lonely."

"Lonely? Surely not. There are so many stars, so many things to explore!"

"Guardians are the servants of the stars, crafted so that we might exist in between their resplendence, keeping them from being dimmed by proximity to another. They danced their way across the sky in constellations, never touching. Guardians were bound to one star and were taught to jealously keep them safe. Centuries of speaking only to beings who thought themselves above us, unless we were warning others away. It was open and vast and beautiful. Our cities were built on the northern lights, and everything was magnificent. But I would see how much closer the people of the earth were, forming families that weren't built on power and radiance, coming together out of sheer joy. I wanted that."

"And Astraea did, too?" I winced; I shouldn't have brought her up. The heartbeat had faded since I removed my hand from the door, but if I searched for it, I knew I would find it. I didn't know if it was Astraea or the remnants of my mother, but something lived deep beneath the earth and if I said as much to Casimir, he would hope for her. Long for her in a way that would only push him away from me.

Foolish. Jealous. Selfish.

I curled my fingers into fists, ashamed.

"Not at first," Casimir said, and he didn't sound hurt, merely reminiscent. "She didn't understand my fascination in the beginning, not until she saw the devotion that people gave away freely. To the gods, especially. She saw love that burned, and passion that started wars and devoured people whole. And she wanted that."

"Surely she didn't need to come here for that. She had you, after all." They were the wrong words. I knew it as soon as I spoke them, and I desperately wished I could take them back. To suggest in any way that he wasn't enough, when in truth I would not have him any other way, it felt cruel. "I'm sorry, it's none of my concern."

"No, you have a right to ask. I think..." He sighed. In the light of the torch, I could see his shadows writhing a merry dance over his skin. He was barely holding on to his control, and it was my fault. "I think that she wanted proof that my devotion was as I claimed. She was so lacking in confidence sometimes that no matter how much I told her of my love, she doubted. And she saw what the people here had, and wanted it, and so she fell, hoping that I would follow her."

"And you did."

"And I did."

My heart went out to Astraea. I understood wanting that sort of love. When I'd first awoken, I resigned myself to a marriage of politics with Devereux, but then I fell for Casimir. We'd all of us realised where things lay, where the true love lay, and that was that. Now, with Casimir a few feet in front of me, yet so far away, I understood that aching desire for passion. For a love all-encompassing. Never ending. Just out of reach.

"Casimir—" I started, ready to tell him about the heartbeat I'd heard in the earth.

"We're here." He held the torch up, revealing a narrow stair branching off from the main tunnel. It rose swiftly, the steps difficult to climb after such an arduous day. It was topped by a door set at an angle, as if halfway in the ground. Casimir set his shoulder against it and shoved. The hinges gave way with a groan, and the door swung open.

I followed Casimir out of the tunnel, blinking at the weak daylight that filtered in between the buildings of the densest part of Altier. The alley was cobbled with slick stones that obviously rarely saw the light of day. Lichens and moss grew out of the tunnel and into the alley, itself sprouting ferns and grasses. There was one window higher up that looked out on the dismal space, but otherwise it was plaster and stone on either side, blind to our entrance. A perfect place to sneak into the city.

"It's a couple of streets over. Try to keep your head down, just in case," Casimir said, tossing the torch to the ground, where it spluttered out of existence. I tugged my hair forwards, covering the burns slightly. Then, we stepped into the open streets.

After the demonstration earlier, I half-expected the streets to be buzzing with people and news, but it was relatively quiet, almost as if people were simply going about their day. A few women gathered across the way, baskets of greens on their arms. A man and donkey led a cart laden with sacks. A child laughed as it chased a dog. No one paid Casimir or I any mind, which seemed both amazing and impossible.

Then, we were slipping into the door of the dressmaker's shop, coming face to face with bundles of fabric and a myriad of colours and textures. The bell above the door gave away our presence, because a tired voice called from the back, "I'm coming! No need to get your skirts in a twist."

Casimir reached for my hand, holding it tight. I was grateful for the contact, because suddenly, telling Tali's grandmother about her disappearance seemed like an impossible task. No matter what things I'd accomplished before, this was surely worse. Then, before I could change my mind, the woman shuffled out from the back.

She looked a little frazzled, her dark skin shining with a sheen of sweat, her grey-white hair pulled back in a haphazard braid. Her dress was bright blue with green embroidery, but the sleeves were pushed up unevenly, and her hands were wet, as if they'd just been washed. Whatever Casimir and I had interrupted, Tali's grandmother did not appear as if she was pleased for it.

She took one look at us—at me—and stilled. Her eyes widened. Then, she wobbled into a curtsey. "My lady. Lord Casimir. I never thought I'd be seeing the likes of you again, not after what happened last time."

Last time, when I'd unintentionally started a battle in the square outside her shop. I flinched. "You have my sincerest apologies for that. I had no idea that, ah...I'm sorry."

"I, too," she said. "I assumed a great many things about you when you came here. Starblooded indeed.

I thought you, weak and simpering as you were, would fail us. And yet you brought an end to the void, and if the rumours floating around the streets are true, you're no Starborn, but a goddess."

I nodded, studying a bolt of deep violet cloth so I wouldn't have to meet her gaze. I took a deep breath. "I hate to bring bad news to you, Grandmother—"

"Temys," she said. I blinked. "My name is Temys. We were never properly introduced the last time, and I doubt my granddaughter, loquacious though she might be, bothered to describe her family when she was travelling with the Chosen One."

Tali hadn't told me much of anything about her family aside from the fact that she descended from a long line of *dharangui*, or Wandering Poets. Mostly, she'd asked questions and told tales of ages long past. Now I wished I'd asked more about her life.

"It is an honour to formally meet you, Temys," I said, bowing my head. "I am Calanthe."

"An old name, that one. From a time long before the rise of the void." The woman studied me, far more intently than I expected. Heat rushed to my cheeks. "It suits you better than Burned One."

"Thank you." I wasn't sure it was a complement. "Mistress Temys, I...I've come to talk with you about your granddaughter. Tali."

Her eyes softened a moment. Then, with a sigh that seemed to settle some great weight on her shoulders, she brushed past me and Casimir and went to the door, turning a key in the lock. She moved again to the back of the store. "Come along. I have someone you will want to see."

Hope blossomed in my chest. Was Tali here? Had I been mistaken in thinking her trapped within the void? She had made it to the shore a full day before Casimir and I returned from Ynysfawr, so it was certainly possible that she'd made it back to Altier before we had, especially since we'd been travelling slowly to accommodate the Hunters' speed. In my eagerness, I nearly pushed past Temys to the rooms beyond the shop.

What I saw, though, when I entered into the small kitchen area, had the embers of my magic snuffing out in shock, filling me instead with a roaring silence. My breath caught in my throat and any words of greeting I might have had died out.

"Empty night," Casimir gasped.

"Hello again." It was her voice, smooth and even, yet there was surely no possible way that the person whom I beheld was Tali. Yes, her person was there in essence, in skin and hair and eye and feature, but she looked like a mere shadow of herself. Her cheeks were hollow, her eyes sunken, her frame so thin that I thought she might blow away in a stiff wind. It had been three weeks since last I saw Tali; I didn't understand how she could have been so afflicted, so reduced.

Then, she shifted, the heavy blankets draped over

her shoulders slipping away to reveal that her left sleeve was empty. Her arm, almost entirely to her shoulder, was gone.

I don't recall moving. I only knew that I was on my knees before her a moment later, my hands running over the fabric of her skirts, afraid that if I rested my hands on her knees, she would break. Tali took her remaining hand and solved the problem for me; she brushed my cheek, then rested the limb on my hands.

"It's good to see you," she said, and there were tears in her eyes to match my own. "After what happened with the void, after I ran—" and here her eyes flicked to Casimir, with no small amount of wariness there, "—I thought that you had died. Yet here you are. And they say that you're a *goddess*!"

I managed a weak laugh. "Me? Surely it is you who is the goddess, to have survived so much. What happened? Are you alright? Your arm!"

Tali scoffed. "I am not that poorly, surely. Guardian, tell your charge that it is not as bad as she thinks."

Casimir stiffened. I had forgotten that I told Tali everything, about him being an immortal guardian, about him thinking me a star. She left Ynysfawr before my discovery about being a goddess, but it would seem she had figured that out herself, from rumour or story. I looked to Casimir, an apology on my tongue, when he, too, sank to his knees before Tali.

"I cannot do that, Poet," he murmured. "You look to be at death's doorstep."

Tali frowned. She looked to her grandmother. "What of you, hmm, do you think I'm about to die?"

"Not after all the work I've put into keeping you alive!" Temys huffed. "Tell them your tale, child, or they will pester and fuss."

Tali settled in, pulling the blanket tighter over her shoulders, and for a moment, it was like we were back on the road to Ynysfawr and she was telling us a story. Only, Devereux was gone, Dancer and the other voidling Whisper were missing, and we faced war with the gods. How could so much have changed so quickly?

"I fled the island after you told me to run, Ast—" She broke off, frowning. "That's not your name, is it?"

"Calanthe," I said, trying not to look at Casimir as I said it. "I am Calanthe, now."

"Beautiful." Tali smiled. "Anyways, I took the boat back to the mainland, Dancer and Whisper swimming beside me. I was just to the horses when the world...I don't know, it sort of broke apart. The ground shook and the sky seemed to fragment into a thousand pieces that fragmented even further until it was impossible to tell where daylight ended and void began. Darkness flew across the sky in great swaths, brushing over the land and almost pulling the vitality from it as it went. The cloud brushed over us, and the horses absolutely panicked. I managed to hang on to Titan's reins, but he was the only one. And even then, something was taken from me as I stood there. My grandmother thinks that it's because I was so close to Ynysfawr, the epicentre, that a bit of my life was drained when the void left. I don't know if that's it, but when the skies cleared and the world stopped shaking, I was so weak I could barely stand. Dancer and Whisper were gone, as were the other horses."

Tali gave me a sad smile. "I'm sorry about Dancer. I know you and he were bonded."

"Devereux is looking for him," I said with far more confidence than I felt. I could tell by Tali's expression that I would have a great deal of my own story to tell, but she kept going.

"Well, with just me and Titan left, and no indication that you or Casimir would return, I rode hard for Altier. I thought...I don't know what I thought. Everything should have been hope and beauty now that the void was gone, but I can't help feel something isn't quite right. And maybe that's to do with whatever the void took from me, and maybe it isn't." She peered at me. "You know what it is, don't you?"

"We have an idea," Casimir said. "We'll tell you all once you've finished your story. Your brush with the void explains your thinness. What of your arm?"

Tali's expression shuttered. "The country beyond Altier was empty, as empty as when we passed through. The Hunters were gone to who knows where, and people hadn't yet started returning to their villages. Or so I thought. I stopped in a place about ten miles from Altier, just for the night. I found a barn that was mostly whole and figured I would be safe enough there. So safe that I even started a fire, which I hadn't done thus far. It was a mistake. "I don't know if they were bandits, Hunters, or just starving. Whatever it was, they attacked me in the middle of the night. Took Titan, kicking and screaming, but they took him. There were three of them, and I only had a couple of daggers. I tried to fight them off, but one of them had a sword, and the others were desperate. I managed to kick logs from the fire into the face of one, and I got another in the throat when he pinned me down, but the third...at least it was a clean cut. I tied the wound off as best I could and made my way here."

Tali fell silent, as if reliving that moment of terror. I had been in fights with voidlings, and the Hunters, but never had I been so outnumbered by humans that I feared for my life, my safety. The arrow through my shoulder was my worst injury—apart from my burns, back when I was newly awakened—and even that had healed. Tali would never get her arm back. She would put on weight and grow stronger, but there would always be something missing.

"I fixed her wound as best as possible. Cauterised it, used a poultice, but it would be better if she could be seen by true Healers," Temys said. "I know no arcane spells, and even if I did, I'm not strong enough to perform a healing."

"We'll take her back with us," I promised, even though I had no idea if Tali's presence would be appreciated. Queen Raya might refuse to heal her. I had to try.

"I've told my story, now it's time for yours," Tali said, forced cheer tainting her words.

"Yours is far more interesting than ours, surely," I tried to tease, but it fell flat. My smile, false as it was, slipped from my lips. I closed my eyes, and then I told Tali everything.

I told her that the gods were returning, and would be voracious in their hunger. I told her about allying with the Hunters, about meeting the Craigsmuirians. I told her about the tentative bargain with Raya and Beatrice. I told her about my gold blood, and being able to heal. Then, trying not to wilt under the intense gaze of Casimir, I told her about the fact that I had borne Astraea's light magic, and the darkness of a guardian. About the fact that I had been made, that I was new. About swearing that we would find Astraea, find out what had happened, how it had happened. But first, we had to prepare.

"So here we are," I said. "A few hundred Hunters and former Void Runners, maybe forces from the other countries of Adhor—if we can convince them of our cause—against the forgotten gods."

"If anyone can do it, you can," Tali said firmly. She squeezed my shoulder with her remaining hand. "And I'll be right here with you."

"As will I," Temys announced. We all three of us started and turned to her. She nodded, eyes glinting. "Surely, child, you know the stories of the changing of the world?"

Tali sucked in a hiss of breath. "You can't be serious, Grandmother! That's just nonsense poems that some madman spouted centuries ago."

"Perhaps, or perhaps not." She turned her attention to me and held my eyes. "It's an old poem, not one widely shared because we can't be sure of its providence or veracity, but it is shared. They say that the man who spoke it was insane. Some claim that he was a seer, some that he only dreamt the words."

A seer. Like Dame Winters? Who was, surely, mad, yet held the truth at the tips of her fingers? I nodded, mouth dry. "I would like to hear it, if you don't mind."

Temys straightened her shoulders, spreading her feet a little wider. She drew in a breath to her belly, then lifted her chin and began to speak. To recite.

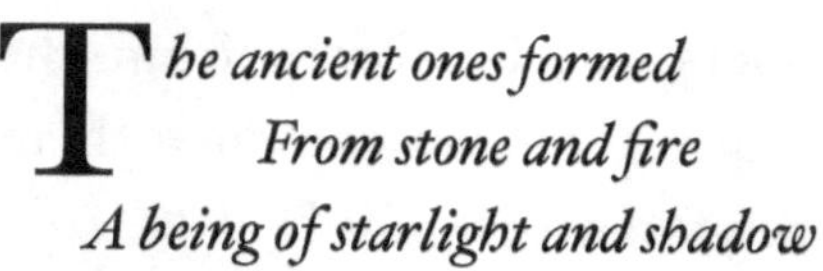

T*he ancient ones formed*
From stone and fire
A being of starlight and shadow

The world to inspire
Forgotten ones remembered
Surging forth once more
Desire in their hearts
Death in their wake
When sky and earth meet
When darkness is embraced
The changing of the worlds is nigh
Mortals shall make their fate
Stand strong and tall and broken
Before the doorway new
For faltering will mean
The world's growing doom

CHAPTER 9

"A prophecy?" Casimir scoffed. "Calanthe, pay no attention to these ramblings."

Temys straightened, puffing out her chest. "Ramblings?! I'll have you know, Guardian, that I am a *dharangui* and I do not put stock in ramblings. Not everything I gather may make immediate sense, but—"

"But nothing. Prophecies—especially prophecies given by seers—are always nonsense. People twist events around to suit the prophecy, but the words could apply to a thousand different things over the years. I could name twenty in the last two centuries alone that would work."

"Well, go ahead! In all your immortal years, surely you—"

"Enough," Tali said. She rolled her eyes at me, but there was a hint of a smile. "The two of you can argue over ancient things another time. For now, can we get moving? There aren't enough chairs to hold a debate comfortably, and surely Calanthe and her Guardian are tired."

"Hmph." Temys wrinkled her nose but didn't argue. Instead, she went to a back room and returned with a large bag, into which she stuffed various articles of clothing, as well as some powders, potions, and various items that made up a woman's things.

Casimir started spluttering again. "You cannot think to come with us!"

"Of course I can." Temys sniffed. "You're taking my granddaughter, my only family, severely injured, to the palace. I fully intend to attend to her. Besides which, I am fully qualified to provide information to our young goddess here, information which you won't find in any library tucked away by the royals. Or do you happen to have stories of the gods at your ready disposal? In any case, I would like to see you try to stop me."

Desperate, Casimir threw me a wide-eyed glance. I shrugged. Certainly *I* wasn't going to argue with the woman. She was formidable. When I didn't protest, Casimir threw his hands up. Tali chuckled.

We made our way back to the tunnel with as little fuss as possible, though we drew more attention than before. Temys was apparently well known and liked, and she waved at everyone we passed. Casimir let Tali lean on him, but her strength soon flagged, and by the time we got to the tunnel entrance, she was almost entirely being supported by him. I held up my hand, wreathed in flame, and we descended into the gloom.

The journey back to the palace seemed to take an age. Casimir carried Tali, but the walls were narrow and he already hated being underground. I tried to illuminate our way as much as possible, but my fire could only do so much against the damp and gloom. Temys, at least, seemed perfectly capable, shuffling along with only the aid of a small cane, her bag carried easily. She muttered comments about the danger of having such a tunnel and its ease of use in alternating thoughts, keeping us all entertained on the journey back. Finally, we were climbing out of the tunnel and into the palace proper.

Casimir immediately started towards the infirmary, a scowl set on his features. Temys strode after him, leaving me behind without a second glance. I considered following and decided against it. A bone-deep weariness had settled in. What was worse, though, were the words that swirled through my head.

A prophecy.

Nonsense or not, the words resonated. A doorway that was new. A being formed of stone and fire. The meeting of sky and earth. All of it felt familiar, true. And yet, it didn't actually tell me anything.

I wandered back to my room in a daze, too many

thoughts in my head. I found my chambers guarded. My heart dropped.

"Lady Calanthe!" the guard said. I recognised the voice. Tate, the guardsman who had let us into the gate. He was standing straight, an eager look in his eye. "There was some question about who should guard your chamber. I hope you don't mind that I volunteered. There will be a rotation with some of the Void Runners and the people you brought, but since I was already on duty...is everything alright?"

"Yes," I lied. "I was just surprised to see you is all. I wasn't expecting a guard."

"You're, well, *important*," Tate said, as if shocked I'd suggest anything else. And if I was so important now, then what had I been before, when I was merely the Chosen One? No, this was more than a perk of my relative status. This was political. Was the queen watching me? Were the Runners keeping an eye on my movements? Or did they truly fear for my safety?

"If you wouldn't mind." I gestured to the door. Blushing, Tate stepped aside, and I resolved to sort out the issue of a guard later. After I slept for a week, later.

The chambers were almost exactly as I had left them. Someone had been in to tidy and change the linens, but otherwise it was as cold and impersonal as it had been before. I hadn't gathered many belongings other than clothes, so there was nothing to denote that the space belonged to me. I longed for something personal. Something mine. There was nothing.

The bed was topped with a heavy quilt and two fur throws, an enticing idea. But the bathing chamber drew my attention. A bath had been laid out, and though the water was hardly hot after my detour with Casimir to the city, I didn't care. I disrobed, discarding the ill-fitting clothes in a heap. I threw the iron band around my brow on top of the pile, wanting never to see it again yet knowing I would. Then, I climbed into the water and sank.

The water smelled like roses. Even just warm, it soothed my aching muscles. It sluiced away the dirt of the road and practically remade me. For the first time in more than a month, I relaxed completely.

I pushed aside thoughts of the impending war. I pushed aside the questions about my mother, about Astraea's part in my crafting. I pushed aside my worries about Casimir, about Dancer and Whisper and Devereux. I pushed aside any thought of politics, of the schemes of Raya and Beatrice. All of it. I closed my eyes, leaned my head back against the tub, and for the first time, I simply was.

A person, maybe not human, but whole, enjoying the sensation of soaking. Of being clean. I scrubbed my hair and pulled my fingers through the wet strands, taking my time with the tangles. And when I couldn't justify being in the bath any longer, I wrapped myself in a square of linen and sat before the fire in my bedroom, brushing my hair while it dried.

Then, the world reasserted itself.

The door slammed open. I scrambled to my feet, clutching the towel tight, flames at my fingertips. They spluttered out a moment later when Casimir strode in. He was still wearing the clothes he'd travelled in, though he carried his armour in one hand. He obviously hadn't bathed, and he looked exhausted. He dropped the armour by the bed, then collapsed into a chair near the arrowslit of a window.

"Stars above," he groaned, "it feels good not to be standing."

"Is everything alright?"

An eye cracked open to stare at me, then closed again. "Perfectly fine, now that I'm not moving. Though I wouldn't mind a bath."

"Surely one's been prepared for you in your chambers."

At this, he opened both eyes and sat up. "These are my chambers."

I looked around. I was certain I had come to the right room. The wardrobe still had dresses in it. Tate guarded the door. Casimir was apparently travel-addled. Taking my silence as the confusion it was, he groaned and leaned back in the chair again.

"I forgot to tell you. We'll be sharing a chamber."

"Is there not enough space elsewhere in the

palace?" I asked, my tone hinting at frustration. I tried to rein it in; Casimir had been good to me. But I was in love with him, and there was no way I was sharing a chamber with a man who didn't love me back.

"It's not that. It's for your protection."

"As we've discovered, I can heal from a great deal. Not to mention I have magic." My frustration was building. "I don't need to be guarded at all hours of the day and night. Besides, there is already a guard outside the door, or hadn't you noticed?"

"I noticed." Casimir glared at the door, and I hoped it was thick enough to drown out our voices. Tate didn't need to hear our arguments. "It's not that you aren't...capable, it's that we are fighting against other *gods*. And the queen will certainly be doing her best to undermine your authority. The Void Runner barracks, where I used to stay, are too far. I want to be here in case anything happens. In case I am needed."

"Am I never to be left alone?" I groused. Casimir flinched.

"It's not that, Calanthe, I swear it. You are not weak, nor untrustworthy. It's just..." He sighed and shook his head. "You're right. I'll find somewhere else to sleep."

"Wait, Casimir." I held out a hand. "What is it? Why is this important to you?"

He swallowed, throat bobbing. He didn't meet my

gaze. His fingers danced over a worn patch of fabric on his left knee. "She...I..."

I understood. I sank to the stone floor before his chair and rested my hand on his, stilling his nervous fingers. "It's alright. I understand. You were Guardian to Astraea and she is missing."

"I'm your Guardian, now," he said. He still did not meet my gaze.

"Of course. And the best way to keep me safe, regardless of necessity, is to be near at hand. Right?"

He licked his lips, clenched his jaw, and nodded. "That's part of it."

"Only part?" I frowned.

"Calanthe, you know I—"

There was a knock on the door, and before either Casimir or myself could call out, it swung open. A veritable parade of maids bearing steaming pitchers hesitated in the doorway, Tate hovering behind them. They stared at the two of us, me in a towel, Casimir dishevelled. I nearly leaped backwards, tugging the linen closer around me.

"A bath, Lady Calanthe, for, ah, Lord Casimir," Tate announced. His face was flushed. "I ordered it when he, er..."

"That's perfectly alright," I said, waving the maids through. Whatever Casimir had been about to say would have to wait. They prepared the bath as quickly as possible, and before Casimir could continue the conversation, I had hurried him into the bathing room and all but slammed the door behind him.

Swiftly, I dressed in one of the garments left in the wardrobe from before my journey to Ynysfawr. It was a little loose, but fit well enough that I couldn't bring myself to mind. I was self-aware enough to admit that I had missed wearing dresses, wearing something that was made for me, even if it didn't fit quite as well anymore.

When Casimir emerged, I was sitting once more by the fire, warming my hands and feet. His hair was damp, hanging around his face in a white sheet streaked with black. His clothes were simple, and his armour had been taken away by the maids to be cleaned. He sank to the stones beside me.

"I'm sorry for not consulting you before," he said. "About the living arrangements."

"I forgive you. And I do understand. I just...wasn't expecting it."

"If it's in regards to sharing a bed—"

I straightened, shocked. "What? I mean, that's not...I wasn't—"

"Calanthe," Casimir said, and I was surprised to find him chuckling. "It's alright. Nothing untoward will happen. It just makes sense, if I am to sleep here. Besides, that bed is large enough for the both of us and Dancer, with room to spare."

I looked at the offending bed. He was right. But my heart ached, regardless, for reasons I could never tell him. "Do you think that Dancer is alright?"

"Tali's story suggests that he must have been taken by the void. He's a voidling. He'll be fine."

"He was raised with me! He's barely six months old, no matter his size. And he's fought against the other voidlings and—"

Casimir took my hand. "Breathe."

I did so, slowly. One breath in, held to the depths of my lungs, then let out. My anxiety over Dancer's fate was no less, but I felt a little less like weeping. That had to count for something.

"Dancer is one of the smartest beings I have met, including many humans, and he will be fine. If we meet Devereux again, we can tell him to be on the lookout. You have to have faith that the two of you will be reunited."

I scoffed. "Faith? In what? The gods?"

"Perhaps that wasn't the best choice of words," Casimir admitted.

I scoffed again, but didn't say anything. I had to trust that he was right, or accept that I would never see Dancer again. If I had to choose, I wanted Dancer to be alive and well, even far from me, so that was what I believed. Silence fell between us, and I was beginning to drift off with the fire so warm and soothing before us, the flames humming a lullaby as they leaped in the hearth.

"Tali is settled in well," Casimir said, breaking the

silence. He sounded almost pained, as if he wanted to say something else and couldn't. "The healers are doing their best by her. Eugenie complained loudly about some of the poultices Tali's grandmother used, but that's just Eugenie's way. Temys was all too happy to argue the point. She's been given quarters near the infirmary, so she can check on Tali."

I nodded. "I'm glad she'll be alright."

"She's lost an arm. That's a difficult thing to bear at the best of times, but in a time of war?" Casimir shook his head, strands of hair falling into his eyes. He pushed them roughly out of the way; I saw the shadows on his fingers moving about of their own accord, a likely reaction to some hidden agitation. Not that I could blame him. Nothing about this was calming.

"She is alive," I pointed out, sticking to the topic he'd chosen. "She is capable and intelligent. She will learn quickly how to adapt. I trust in Tali's strength."

"At least you trust in somebody," he muttered, then blanched. "Calanthe, I—"

"No, I think you finally said exactly what you meant to say," I said. Anger and hurt flared through me, the flames leaping up higher in a mimic to my emotions. I rose and moved away from the fire. "I have told you everything, Casimir."

Everything except the revelation about the heartbeat. And the fact that I still loved him.

"I have trusted you from the beginning, when you

started training me, when you took the time to *talk* to me. But if you wish to believe that my wanting to sleep on my own, to have time alone, to hold on to my worries for the future, any of it, is indication that I don't trust you, then you have that right. As for me, I'm going to bed."

I turned my back on him and climbed under the covers, which were a comforting weight on me. In moments, the bed was warmed from heat rising off my skin. I closed my eyes and forced the fire down, forced my temperature to normalise. The mattress sank a bit as Casimir climbed in beside me, but as he'd pointed out before, it was a large bed, more than big enough for the two of us to sleep comfortably without touching.

"That's not what I meant at all," he breathed. I thought I felt a whisper of a touch on my cheek, but when I opened my eyes to look, he was curled on his side, facing away from me.

I burrowed deeper beneath the covers, longing once more for Dancer's weight by my side, warming my feet. Instead, I had to brush tears away from my eyes. Of all the beings to make into a god, my mother had to make me. A fool who fell in love with a creature of the sky, one bound for all eternity to a Fallen Star. I was the walking example of a tragedy, my heart forever spoken for, leading the peoples of the world into a doomed battle for their future. Empty night, who did I think I was, to face down other gods who were centuries, aeons, older than me, with powers fully formed and understood, with knowledge far beyond anything I could possibly comprehend. I was ignorant, foolish, and arrogant enough to think I could lead these people into war.

I soon gave up on brushing tears away, instead letting them soak into the pillow as I brought my knees to my chest and held them tight, trying not to let my sobs shake the bed. I must have failed in that, too, though, because a few minutes later, arms strong enough to hold up the sky wrapped around me. Casimir kissed the crown of my head.

"Shhh," he breathed. "It's not as bad as all that."

Wasn't it, though?

"You doubt yourself. You have always doubted yourself. Doubted that you could be the Chosen One. And yet you saved all of Adhor from the void. You doubted that you could be worthy to bring people together to fight the gods, and yet you have not only the savage Hunters with you, but the Craigsmuirians, the Void Runners, and the people of Baldarskiel at your back. You are far stronger than you believe, my dear Astr—" he paused, then bit out the name he had given me, as if it pained him, "Calanthe. Calanthe. Never doubt yourself, not because of me, or anyone else."

I had done those things, and it was not that I doubted. It was my right to lead, when I was so ignorant, so foolish, as to give up an essential piece of myself to someone who was so obviously still in love with someone else. Would always love someone else.

No. I brushed away the last of my tears, squeezing my eyes shut until the water stopped flowing. It was time to stop crying. Time to stop feeling sorry for myself. I could not expect Casimir to stop loving Astraea; it was cruel to even consider asking. It was time I started standing on my own.

With that thought, I turned away from Casimir's warmth and fell asleep.

CHAPTER 10

"You misunderstand," Garwith said, tapping his fingers impatiently on the table. "We don't need to prepare for battle as if we are fighting against the voidlings, or even another army. We will be fighting *gods*. Individual gods. Not battalions of infantry, cavalry. The strategy for such a thing is surely to be entirely different."

"We will still need numbers vastly greater than that we possess," Raya said, all but rolling her eyes at the leader of the Void Runners. "We have, what, some hundred of the goddess's Hunters, plus two hundred of your Runners?"

"Two hundred and forty-seven," Garwith corrected. "With three hundred more still out in Adhor, not yet returned from their postings."

"Those, plus the guard, and what few fighting forces we have amongst the people—who are vastly incapable, better suited for wielding pitchforks and scythes than swords and bows—we have perhaps a thousand, fifteen hundred warriors at our behest."

I was glad to be included in the strategy session for once, having been so used to being ignored during my time as Chosen One, but the news was hardly encouraging. The nobles around the table were those from the Council who had any sense of battle at all, mostly those with estates near a void pool. They, plus Garwith, Ilar, Raya, Beatrice, and Temys—who had demanded to be included and would brook no argument—made up this strategy session, not including Casimir and myself. Mostly, though, it seemed like they were doing nothing but bickering.

"Captain Kina of Craigsmuir promised to provide support," I said.

"*If* the good Captain returns, I would be surprised if she brings more than a few ships and a few hundred fighters. Baldarskiel has been locked away from the rest of the continent for countless centuries; I doubt Adhor will come willingly to our aid." Raya leaned forwards. "Not without sufficient promise of recompense."

Garwith huffed at this. "What, do you expect the Lady Calanthe to pluck gold and jewels from the ground as she would a flower?"

I hadn't ever considered such a thing, but I imagined it would be possible. My magic would certainly bend to such a task. I met the queen's gaze evenly. "If that is what it takes, then so be it, though it seems to me unjust to judge the people of Adhor so without having met them."

Raya snorted and leaned back in her chair, regarding me cooly. "So says the woman who knows nothing of the continent at all."

I refused to flinch at that, though Casimir at my right stiffened at the insult. He had hardly said two words to me since we woke, only trailing me about to breakfast and then to this meeting like a guard dog, loyal and silent. Before he could open his mouth to defend my supposed knowledge, Temys spoke.

"It seems to me that Baldarskiel, who hasn't engaged in a war for a thousand years, is probably the wrong country to ask regarding strategy," she said, ignoring the indignant gasp from Beatrice and the queen's hiss. "What this country *does* have is one of the greatest archives in all of Adhor. Let the other countries worry about the army—once their delegates come, of course—while we focus on the face of the enemy. Or do any of you remember the names of all the gods with whom we are to battle?"

She had a point. Not only were we not facing down an army of humans, we were to fight with beings who were so ancient that their names had been forgotten. What sort of magic did they possess? What did they want? How would we fight them?

"Do you have any stories?" I asked her, feeling a bit useless. My contributions so far had been pitiful:

the promise of the Hunters, the Runners, and my own magic, with little else besides. But perhaps I could learn of our foe.

"Who is this woman?" Beatrice demanded, glaring at Temys. "What right is granted to her to be at this table?"

"I am a dressmaker," Temys said with a wily grin. Beatrice recoiled.

"A *dressmaker*? Surely you cannot—"

"She, like her granddaughter, Tali, is *dharangui*," Casimir interrupted, cutting across Beatrice without even bothering to glance her way. "And if you don't know what that is, then I would suggest your own education is sorely deficient."

"*Dharangui*," Garwith said, rolling the word around in his mouth. He chuckled. "Well, there's a title I haven't heard in decades. I thought you lot had vanished."

Temys smiled wider, showing her teeth. "We are exactly where we want to be. Hidden. To better watch 'you lot' without people falling on their faces to try and impress us. Not that your efforts have been all that successful regardless of your awareness of us."

I snorted, then covered my mouth, cheeks warming. Temys nodded at me, eyes twinkling. Casimir just stared. Trying to cover my embarrassment, I turned to Temys. "Can you put together a list of the potential gods we might face?"

"Everyone knows that," Beatrice said, rolling her eyes. "Father Sky—"

"Bound to the heavens long before the gods were imprisoned," Temys said. "As everyone knows."

"Well, fine. The god of the ocean—"

"Won't leave the depths. By all account, he's been asleep since claiming the trenches as his home." Temys examined the table before her, buffing out some imaginary blemish with her sleeve. Beatrice, on the other hand, was fuming.

"What about the Earth Mother and the Eternal Flame? Surely you can't think that they—"

"Won't be an issue." Her smile had vanished. Temys glanced at me for a brief moment, then looked back to the former High Priestess.

"Why not? Are they bound in chains also? Do you have stories of them sleeping the centuries away?" Beatrice asked. "Or are your stories just insufficient?"

"They will not appear. On that you must simply have to trust me."

"Trust you? A dressmaker with delusions of grandeur?" Beatrice was in fine form, now, lifting her chin to show her features to their best, her figure elegant and graceful, even if her words were full of spite. A royal, expecting such things as were hers no longer. Not in this changed world.

"They are dead," I said, breaking through the tension with my bluntness. Startled silence filled the room. Wide eyes stared at me. Casimir snaked his hand out to touch mine, but as soon as our fingers brushed, I pulled away.

"Dead," Beatrice said, frowning. "How do you—"

I held out my hands, palms up. In the left one, already seared with burns, I produced a fire so hot it was almost white. In the right, I called forth motes of dust and dirt from around the room, solidifying them together until a perfectly round pebble floated in my hand. People knew I had magic—it was hardly a secret—but this display seemed to make people uneasy. I closed my hands into fists, and the magic vanished.

"They're dead," I said again. "Where else would I get such magic? How else could I be a god, formed outside the bounds of their prison? Their lives for mine, their powers given over. They're dead."

"Calanthe," Casimir breathed, my name almost too quiet for even me to hear. I refused to look his way, instead staring Beatrice down until she lowered her eyes. Then, I turned to Temys, who took up the unspoken thread of conversation.

"Of the gods that remain, most, if not all, will be offspring of the original deities. Their powers will not be so vast, so encompassing. They will occupy niches, but within those niches, they will be strong. Gods of harvest. Of fertility. Of rain. Gods of the hunt. Of the hearth. More. And not all will be immediately opposed to our cause, but they will all be hungry."

Ilar intervened, for which I was grateful. "So, do

we approach them as they appear, make our demands?"

Raya scoffed openly, shaking her head. "A foolish plan. What, shall we station our army at the door on Ynysfawr, waiting for them to appear? Then, do we ask nicely, 'Please don't hurt us. You can stay if you play well with others,' and hope that they'll just agree?"

Garwith sighed. "For once, I agree with Her Majesty. We cannot simply ask them to cease their antics before they've begun. This will be the first taste of freedom for the gods in centuries. They will, no matter how inclined towards peace, hardly want to listen to us dictating terms. We are mortals, nothing before them. And you, Lady Calanthe, are entirely unknown to them."

I inclined my head. It was the truth, after all. I was newly formed, knew nothing of the ways of gods but what I had learned from stories and Casimir's words. Why would they listen to me?

"What do we do, then?" Ilar asked.

"Make a statement," Casimir answered. He looked at me, steady and sure, and for the first time that day, I was caught up in his gaze. "Tell them our rules, and when they go to violate them, strike a decisive blow. Swift and all-encompassing."

It was certainly a better option than a long, drawn out war. I leaned back in my chair, suddenly exhausted. I would have rubbed my eyes with the heels of my palms, rested my head on the table for a moment, anything to break through the pall of weariness, but they were expecting more of me. So I sat there and nodded, as though I could manage this strategy with ease.

"That is fine, but we still have the problem of not having enough people for such a blow," Raya said. I would have sworn that I heard a tinge of exhaustion in her voice as well. "We've sent messenger birds and couriers out to all the countries of Adhor, but there is no guarantee they'll arrive with any haste. It is nearly winter, and we have been cut off from the world for a very long time."

"They'll come," Temys said with a certainty I wished I could match. "Those people from Craigsmuir came out of curiosity once the void pools vanished. They are hardly going to be the only ones willing to exercise curiosity. They'll come. The real question is how long we have until that door is opened."

"I will feel it when it is opened," I said.

"You're sure?" Raya asked.

"Yes. There has been no movement at the door. And...when I spoke with Devereux, he said that the gods would have to move through his realm before they could reach the door. He will try to send word when that happens."

At the mention of her son's name, Raya flattened her mouth into a thin line. She nodded tersely, then pushed back from the table with a scrape of her chair. "Very well, then. Poet, you do as the Lady Calanthe suggests, and the rest of us will try to prepare for war."

"Prepare how?" Garwith asked.

"However you can! Get supplies. Forge weapons. Train! I don't care, only do not let us be unprepared for when the gods actually do arrive." With that, the queen swept from the room. Beatrice followed in her wake, stumbling a little as she tried to match her mother's speed. Neither gave a backwards glance. The nobles remaining watched me, as if I might explode in fury at being so disrespected.

All I could bother doing was to stand and say, "I think I will go find a late lunch."

There seemed a collective sigh of relief as I left the room.

※

—

Tali burst out laughing as I relayed the last of the morning's strategy session with her. She was looking much better with good colour, a bit of energy, and more substance to her than before. Apparently, her condition had been bad enough that Eugenie had called in the arcane healers, and they'd spent most of the night working on her. She was still thin, almost painfully so, but no longer looked to be on the point of death.

"I can't believe you just told them you were getting lunch!" she howled, wiping tears from her eye. I nibbled on the crust of some bread, my plate nearly cleaned; I'd brought my lunch to Tali, hoping for some company that wouldn't place an impossible burden on my shoulders.

"What was I supposed to do, give them some speech to buoy their spirits?" I shrugged.

"You're a *goddess*! You're not supposed to concern yourself about lunch at all, at least not where people can speculate on it." Tali kept chuckling, shaking her head at me. "Hand me that pastry, I'm still hungry."

"I thought you were supposed to go slowly," I said, but handed her the pastry anyways. "And I was hungry. What am I supposed to do, just ignore any urges for food and water? Never discuss ordinary happenings?"

"I'm sure they expect you to be ethereal and above all such things. It's what they expect of great ladies and those of superior status, so why not you?"

"That explains why Beatrice is always in such a bad mood," I muttered, making Tali laugh again. I sighed. "I should at least try to make nice, I suppose. It just all seems so pointless when we know so little and when we can do nothing but wait and prepare."

"Firstly, you did nothing wrong. Their expectations of you in regards to needing food or water or sleep are ridiculous. If you give them too much, they'll expect you to fight this war on your own. And for all your great power, you aren't omnipotent. Secondly, wait and prepare *is* all we can do with regards to the war. From what you've described, we don't know when the gods will come, only that it is inevitable. Until then, we must gather people to fight."

"Encouraging," I said drily. I had done nothing but prepare since coming to awareness, first as the Chosen One and now to fight against the gods.

"However," Tali said, smirking at me, "that does not mean you, or anyone, should focus exclusively on this. We cannot put aside our entire lives for the sake of some future event. We have to live. To wander around the city, to have lunches and dances and gatherings with people. To enjoy music. To see art. To learn about the past and think about the nature of the world. If all we did was prepare for some distant day, then what would be the point of fighting at all, for we would not have lived."

Her words struck a chord in me, resonating through my bones like the magic I held. I hadn't truly lived, not really. During my time as the Chosen One, I'd been paraded about to the Council of Nobles, and at the Harvest ball, but none of that was for the sake of enjoyment, for the purpose of living. It was all about the queen and her illusion of control over me, the power she gained in having me at her side.

It wasn't the first time I'd wondered about life. About who I was. I wanted to know if I liked art, or if I preferred music. I wanted to know what my favourite colour was. I wanted to explore. To dance. To live.

"I'm not sure I know how," I murmured.

"Then I'll help you. As soon as I get out of this infirmary, we'll go to the city. Spend a whole day just wandering about. Midwinter is fast approaching, too. We have to celebrate Midwinter!"

At my confused expression, Tali's eagerness grew. "It's a celebration with history linked back to the darkest days of the void, the middle of winter. Legend says that the voidlings were so fierce, and the void so vast, that people were afraid all the time. Until one day, at the darkest night of winter, when people threw off the chains of fear and decided to celebrate. They handed around gifts, feasted as well they could, and spent the whole night singing and dancing around great bonfires that touched the sky. And when morning came, and the voidlings hadn't attacked once, they knew that the void could be beaten."

A legend likely rooted in the time when Astraea first called forth the void. My stomach twisted. I wondered what Casimir thought of Midwinter, then immediately banished that thought from my mind. He'd gone to the Void Runners after the meeting, securing my promise that I would stay in the palace while he was gone.

"That sounds lovely," I said rather than voicing my thoughts. "Beautiful, even."

Tali's smile grew wistful. "I remember when I was a girl, we would make this cake with spices and sultanas. It was perfect. I haven't had it since moving to Altier. Maybe my grandmother knows the recipe."

I wanted a Midwinter, I realised. One beautiful memory not tainted by war or people's desire for power. "Let's do it. We'll have Midwinter."

Tali grinned. "Perfect."

I took a moment to imagine such a celebration, with food and friends and dancing and bonfires, and it seemed like an impossible dream. A beautiful, wonderful, impossible dream. "Hopefully, the gods won't get here until afterwards," I said on a sigh. "I just want..."

"Stars above, you do turn dark swiftly." Tali huffed at me, shaking her head. "For once in your life, however short it might be, try to embrace the moment. You can't know when the gods are going to come, so plan a Midwinter. Take Casimir to dinner. Do something!"

"Take him to dinner?" I frowned.

"Yes. Take that desperately sad piece of the sky to dinner. Show him that he's not alone in this world. He's floundering, Calanthe, trying to find stable ground after everything was ripped from him. Don't you remember what it was like when you first woke, when you didn't understand what was going on?"

Of course I remembered. It had been like grasping for something that wasn't there, just out of reach. I felt like I should have known things I couldn't possibly know, and I was *still* trying to sort out my identity in the midst of everything. I knew that Casimir was trying, that he'd had his dearest love stripped away when I told him I wasn't her. That I'd never been her.

"I know," I murmured. "I just...I don't want to get his hopes up."

"Why would he need to get his hopes up? He loves you, you love him. You just need to navigate this world together and...oh. You don't love him, do you?"

"No! I do!" I straightened, appalled at her suggestion. Then, just as quickly, I deflated, sinking into the chair. "He doesn't love me, though. He loves Astraea. Has always loved her. And, as we've discovered, I am not her."

Tali shook her head again. "The both of you. You're ridiculous."

I didn't probe that thought. Couldn't probe that thought. Instead, I looked around to make certain that we were absolutely alone, even though I already knew we were. Then, "I think I heard her heartbeat. Beneath the earth."

"Her heartbeat? Whose?" Tali sucked in a breath. "You don't mean..."

I nodded. "I think she's trapped wherever it was

that I was first made. Where Lady Earth stole her magic and gave it to me."

The door opened. Tali and I both jumped.

"Sorry," Casimir said, unflinchingly polite. Had he heard? What would he think if he knew I'd kept this from him?

I stared, wide-eyed, at Tali and shook my head as subtly as I could. She nodded her agreement, then smiled brightly at Casimir. "Calanthe and I have decided to plan a Midwinter celebration! You should help us."

I nearly sagged in relief, but I was certain I failed in trying to throw myself into planning. I was too distracted by the fear that Casimir might have heard. Or worse, that he hadn't.

CHAPTER 11

As much as I wanted to take Tal's advice and spend the day wandering around Altier, or doing something that was purely enjoyable, or even planning a Midwinter celebration, the next few weeks were spent alternating between the library to talk with Temys about what she'd found, and venturing to the training ground with Casimir and the others who wanted to fight. Strategy sessions took place every couple of days in the evenings, with people trying to make plans for something that seemed to me impossible to plan.

I spent most of my time at the training grounds, working with Casimir while the others looked on. Before, when I'd trained to be the Chosen One, there had been more of a focus on my magic than any physical fighting skills. Now, Casimir drilled me over and over again, trying to improve my ability with a sword, with a knife, with no weapons at all. But the truth was that I was very nearly hopeless at such things. I wielded weapons with little grace, tripping over them almost as often as I dropped them. No matter how I practised the drills, I could barely manage to keep up with the newest of trainees. Even the young Runner recruit, Eloise, with whom I'd become friends before, was so much better at fighting than me that I felt particularly useless.

And when the training switched from combat to trying arcane magic, I was entirely hopeless. I could memorise the patterns of movement, the spells, with ease, but the moment I tried to perform them, they fell apart, usually producing a blast of flame or, once, a flower crown. Casimir surmised that there was something inherently contradictory about my magic and arcane magic, but all I knew was that once more I was being excluded and left out of any useful thing I could be doing.

I practised my own magic alone in a courtyard of the palace that was rarely used by anyone but kitchen staff. At least there I could produce wonders.

In the library, it was almost worse. The strange ability that granted me the understanding of other languages spread quickly to my ability to read as well. Any text in the library, no matter how old or how different the language, was easy to decipher. *Writing*, on the other hand, was truly an embarrassing task. I'd never had occasion to do it before, and my muscles were wholly unused to such fine tasks. My words were wide and looping, the letters clumsy, and any finished product was nearly unreadable. It was bad enough that I'd been assigned a clerk to take down any notes I wanted. There were three of them that changed from day to day, and they at least ignored my illegible efforts.

By the time three weeks were up, I was ready to cry with frustration. I was never left alone except for the hour in the morning when I practised my magic, and even then, Casimir was often nearby. Tali did her best to soothe my worries, and helped me practise my letters every evening, but she was taken up with her own recovery as well as being conscripted by her grandmother to go through the vast oral history of the Wandering Poets for any meaningful information. There were always people watching me during training, and eyes never left me during the strategy sessions. Every day, people from the city ventured to the palace to approach me, often with a small gift—a loaf of bread, an apple, a quilt—so that they might exchange a word with their goddess.

I belonged to so many people, pulling me in different directions, doing *useless* tasks, that I never had any time for me.

On this particular day, the wind was high, bringing with it a biting cold from off the river, the first real sign that winter was in full effect. I'd felt it when frost came the night before, deep enough to kill off any living thing in the ground that was not already dormant for the winter. It had left me achy and grumbling for most of the day, though I tried not to let it show.

I'd just left the training yards and was heading to the library when a noise in the main courtyard caught my attention. Casimir, normally at my side at all times, had been called away earlier to attend some matter of organisation between the Runners and Hunters, who were now nearly fully co-mingled. I knew he would have wanted me to call for him before I investigated what sounded like a massive affair, but instead, I turned in the direction of the noise.

Fairly streaming through the palace gates on horses dark enough to blend into the night with ease, was a group of about fifty people. To a person, they all wore armour as black as their horses. Two standard bearers led the way, a flag of dark purple with a wyvern curled over a sword flapping in the wind. A steward from the palace was standing before them, nervously wringing her hands as she tried communicating in a halting language. As soon as she saw me, she relaxed.

"The Lady Calanthe," she said by way of introduction, bowing to me and then gesturing to the riders. "Representatives from Amontys."

The rider directly behind the standard bearers dismounted, stepping up to me. My magic bristled, fire blooming in my veins but going no further, ready to strike when necessary. I stood perfectly still, waiting. The rider pulled off his helmet and knelt, bowing before me.

"My goddess," he said in his own tongue. Then, looking up at me, he said, "I have waited my whole life for you."

He was fine featured, prettier than many court ladies who preened over their appearance. He had a long, angular nose and sharp cheekbones, both streaked with dirt from travel. His hair was a chestnut brown, long enough to skim his chin, and his eyes were a sharp, vibrant blue, piercing, as though he saw right through any facade I might want to prepare.

"Welcome to Baldarskiel," I managed.

He bowed again, hand pressed to his chest. "I am Jedrek, second son of Nimo, Sovereign of Amontys. I and my riders were on our way here as soon as the void had vanished. The messenger birds that met us halfway through Craigsmuir were only confirmation of what we knew; you have saved us. I am, and will be always, at your command, my goddess."

Immediate, undying devotion, just because I was a goddess. What a foolish thing. This man did not know me, nor did I know him. He knew that I had removed the void from this realm, but the messages given to the birds were necessarily truncated. To swear so swiftly to my side was, at the least, unnerving. If Dancer were here—empty night, I missed him more and more—then his hackles would be up. I settled for trying to remain regal and tall.

"Rise," I said. Jedrek did so. "It would seem that you have quite the tale to tell. You are most welcome. If you'll go with the steward here, she will get your people and horses settled. And, of course, you are invited to dine with myself, the current representatives of Craigsmuir, and Her Majesty, Queen Raya of Baldarskiel."

Before I could react, Jedrek bent over my hand and kissed it. "For you, anything. I care not for royalty. Only you."

Trying to maintain my polite smile, I called the steward back over and explained the situation. She seemed more than pleased to get the imposing warriors and their horses out of the yard and into quarters. Jedrek followed behind, though he kept turning to look at me. I remained where I was until they were out of sight, then all but collapsed against the walls of the palace.

Was that what things would be like in the future? People fawning over me like I was something kept on a pedestal? Or perhaps it was just the way of people in Amontys, a cultural difference that I didn't understand. It seemed so pointless, given how useless I was at helping at all for this war effort.

A wave of exhaustion swept over me. I wanted to return to my chambers and sleep for the rest of the day, but no matter how silly it seemed to keep training when it was obvious I had no skill, no matter how little I knew of strategy or battle or organising large numbers of people, I knew I would feel worse for wasting an entire afternoon on nothing but sleep. Even taking Tali's edict that we spend time living life to the fullest, I knew the guilt would remain.

There was nothing else for it but to head to the library where Temys was waiting with a pile of old manuscripts she wanted me to translate for her. Perhaps I was of use to scholars, at least. Still frustrated, I was expecting the calm silence of the archives when I entered. The sound of a cheerful laugh brought me up short.

"Calanthe!" Tali waved me over to the long table where she and her grandmother were sitting, books and papers piled around them. She was dressed in clothing that actually fit her: a pair of trousers and a sweater over a long tunic, the left arm pinned up. Her hair was piled in a mass of braids on her head. She had brightness in her eyes. "They let me out of the infirmary!"

"Finally." I couldn't help but wrap her in a swift hug. "I'm so glad you're doing better."

"Better," Temys snorted. "She was practically clawing the walls down with boredom. She's perfectly fine. Now, tell me about the Black Riders from Amontys. Has their leader proposed marriage yet?"

I recoiled and gaped. Temys and Tali started laughing at my expression, exchanging a knowing look that only had Tali laughing the harder. "I know news travels quickly in the palace, especially with so many new people here, but I only learned of their arrival not ten minutes past!"

"Oh, I saw them out the window." Temys waved a dismissive hand. "Even isolated as we were here in Baldarskiel, everyone knows about the Amontyan Black Riders. Their elite guard, trained from childhood to protect the Sovereign in case of danger. They only go to battle in the most dire of circumstances, but their opponents are always defeated."

"They certainly were intimidating," I said. "Though their leader, Jedrek, seemed a little eager to pledge his allegiance."

Temys stifled a snort, barely. "What fool does *not* wist to pledge their allegiance to you? You are the first god returned after an age of darkness. They will pledge their firstborn child if it means that you will show them any favour."

I recoiled, stumbling backwards. "What?"

Tali reached out and took my hand, but the pity in her expression had me pulling away, taking another step backwards. "Calanthe, you had to know this was going to happen sooner or later. You're not the Chosen One any longer. Human, even if with the power of a star. You're a *goddess*. A fundamental force of the world. A power beyond anything we mortals can comprehend. Even if you are not responsible for determining the path of our fates, then people are going to flock to you because you hold such power."

"Determining the path of your fates?" I was horrified and disgusted. "Is that what the gods did? Before?"

Temys shrugged. "Some. Others were responsible only for the morning breeze. Or the safety of hearths. Some gave their gifts freely while others gave only to those who prayed to them or offered sacrifices. Surely you've heard the prayers of people?"

I shook my head, hair falling from my braid and getting in my eyes. I brushed it away, blinking away the sting of its touch. I was not crying, surely. "I've heard no prayers."

"You are still young," Temys said, regarding me. "As your golden blood took time to develop, I imagine that particular skill will as well."

A hand pressed to my stomach, I asked, "And people are expecting me to...to..."

"To guide them. To help them in their fortunes. To bring them blessings. To ensure bountiful harvests. Did you think that the gifts brought to the palace gates every day were just that? No, they're sacrifices. Offerings. To buy your good will."

Nausea churned my stomach. Bile rose in my throat. I took a third step back. "That's not...I'm not..."

"You would not be the first to baulk from your

duty," Temys said, shaking her head. Tali watched me with wide eyes, a frown marring her features.

"Baulk from my duty?" That frustration I'd felt earlier flared, mixing with my fire to erupt in the flames of fury. "Is that what you think I'm doing?"

The air around me began to wobble with heat shimmer and it took all the concentration I had to keep from exploding into fire in the middle of all these books. I pulled up vines of my earth magic, trying to bury the volatile fire in the steady strength of the ancient stone beneath my feet. Heat dissipated into the stones of the palace, but still there was more.

"I woke in this world with no memories. No knowledge of what or who I was. Not even a name," I hissed. "I was told that it was my duty to face the void. Alone. So I did. I stood in the middle of the crater at Ynysfawr and I faced the void. Alone. For the sake of the entire world. For people I'd never met. For people who I had met and who wanted nothing to do with me except manipulate me, control me. I stood there in that crater and I tore out a piece of my magic so that the world might be safe from the void. And the unintended consequence—no, the *unavoidable* consequence of that *duty* is that there is now a doorway between the realms. So here I am, doing my best to prepare for a war against the gods. My own kind. Why? So that this world may live in safety! Do not ever tell me that I am not doing my duty, Poet. Not ever."

Temys, to my surprise and rage, just chuckled. "Very well then. Now, if you're not busy, I have some manuscripts that look promising and—"

"Do it yourself." I couldn't be in that room a moment longer. Not with those accusations hanging in the air like spiderwebs, ready to snare me at a movement. "Tali will help you."

I spun on my heel and strode from the room, funnelling as much heat as I could through my feet and into the stone of the floor. Trying to contain my anger. My rage. My utter disappointment. Not doing my duty. Ha! Had I not bent the knee enough to these people? Had I not sworn to stand before them on the battlefield, to protect them? Now they wanted my blessing. They wanted to buy me. They wanted something from me that I didn't even know if I could give. And they thought it my duty to do so.

I stalked through the palace until I reached the stairs, and then I climbed and climbed and climbed until there was nowhere left to go. This part of the palace looked unused, dusty, with a faint mustiness to the air that told me people rarely bothered to come all this way. And why should they, when there was plenty of more accessible space further down? I was glad for the disuse. It meant I could finally be alone.

I went to the nearest window and put my hands on the stone. It protested at first, then realising who and what I was, gave way without a second thought, widening from the narrow arrowslit to a hole big enough to fit my arm, then my torso, then my entire body. I went to the roof, and from there, I kept climbing. The roof was slate beneath my feet; I was grateful it wasn't thatch or I would have burned the whole place down. Finally, after scrabbling and scraping over the roof, there was nowhere left to go.

I could go no higher. The sky, wide and empty and open, stretched before me in endless glory, revealing the world of the humans so far below. My hands started to glow, fingers of flame rising off of them. I could contain it no longer. With a roar, I tilted my head back and sent my fire leaping into the heavens. I heard shouts and screams from a distance, but I ignored them. Let them wonder why *their* goddess was on the tallest peak of the palace, burning. Let them wonder if they had angered me. Let them wonder.

Finally, my magic sputtered. My anger flickered. I collapsed to the roof, leaning against a spire. My body shook. My tears flowed freely. I was suddenly cold.

"Could you not have found a better place to burn?"

I jerked, grabbing onto the flimsy metal spire and staring. Casimir, scowling, was clambering up the roof, placing his hands and feet far more carefully than I had. Finally, he sat next to me, apparently quite at ease so high up. And why wouldn't he be? He was a creature of the sky.

"How did you find me?" I asked, rubbing tears

from my eyes with the sleeve of my dress and not caring about the fabric.

"The burning beacon wasn't a giveaway?" He sighed when I did not smile. "I was coming to the library to meet with you. Temys and Tali told me you'd left. Temys seemed offended, but Tali explained what happened."

"Temys was offended?" I scoffed. Was I not allowed to be offended, now that I was a primal power of the world?

"Why did you not come to me?" Casimir inched closer, pressing his arm to mine.

"I had too much fire in me to think clearly," I answered, though it was only a half-truth. I wasn't sure I would have gone to him, even if I hadn't been burning with anger. "I had to get clear of anyone I could hurt."

"So you came to the roof? Well, it does afford a nice view."

He sighed at my silence. His hand found mine and he threaded our fingers together.

"You are not duty bound to anyone but yourself, Calanthe."

"Really?" I snapped. "Standing between the mortals and the gods seems like quite the duty."

"It was your choice."

I flinched at that, nearly pulling my hand away. Casimir held it tightly.

"I do not condemn you for your choice. I think

you one of the strongest people I know, not in power but character, for being willing to take on such a burden when it is not your responsibility." He wiped a tear from my burned cheek, his touch dancing tingles across my skin. "All those people who wish to exchange goods for your affection, for your blessing, they are not owed anything from you. You are not obligated to give of yourself until there is nothing left. Why do you think some of the gods so desperately want to be back here? They want the adoration and sacrifice that comes with their power, not because they wish to give to their people, but because they do not know how to live without that devotion."

"You sound like Tali," I murmured.

"She's quite intelligent. And far more reasonable than her grandmother. Frankly, that woman frightens me a bit."

I did laugh at that. "Thank you," I said. "For being here with me."

"Always, Calanthe. No matter what. Though, perhaps we should find a better place for any future outbursts. I wouldn't want people to get overly excited at your magical displays."

I elbowed him in the ribs. He laughed, tossing back his head.

"That's much better. Perhaps you should explode into a brilliant flame more often."

"Perhaps not."

Casimir leaned a little closer. He rubbed his

thumb in circles over the back of my hand. "Was it only Temys's words that had you upset?"

"No," I admitted. "I'm useless at training. Even before going to Ynysfawr, we knew I was useless at training. Between that, and the way that Jedrek from Amontys practically swore himself to me, I was just—"

"Amontys," Casimir growled, suddenly alert, tense. "Jedrek? Second son of the Sovereign? Leader of the Black Riders?"

"He arrived not an hour ago."

"Well, then, I had better go pay my respects." From the darkness in his tone, I gathered that was not a good thing.

Casimir moved through the palace like a breath of wind, swift and sure and impossible to tame. I tried to get him to stop, to explain things to me, to tell me *something*, but to no avail. He found the room where Jedrek was quartered, pausing only to ask a servant for directions, and burst through the door with a single shove.

Jedrek, standing by the fire with a glass of some sort of liquor, turned at our entrance, wearing an easy smile. He caught sight of Casimir and went pale, eyes wide. He threw up his hand, but it was too late. Casimir caught his hand, dragged it down, and rammed his fist straight into the Prince of Amontys' nose.

"Casimir!" I shouted. Shuffling in the hallway told me we would soon have company. I closed the door with a slam and leaned my back against it. "What are you doing?"

"Damn," Jedrek said, holding a hand to his nose. He dabbed at it with his finger, smearing blood. My breath hitched. The blood was *gold*.

"You," Casimir seethed. He didn't strike the man—the god—again, though it was plain that he wanted to from the way his hands trembled at his side. "How *dare* you come here. Now. After all that you've done."

"In my defense, I thought you were gone, along with your precious star," Jedrek said. He pulled a cloth from his pocket and wiped away the blood. In a movement so quick I nearly missed it, he reset his nose, hissing with pain. Then, a sniff, another clearing away of the blood, and he was healed. Like me.

"You were told to *never* return," Casimir snapped. "Regardless of whether you thought I remained."

"The void vanished. Rumours of a goddess were spreading like wildfire. No news of a star, though, or her wayward guardian." Jedrek winked at me. I was grateful for the door at my back; without its support, I would have collapsed to the ground.

"Y-you're..." I started, but the words were caught in my throat.

"Calanthe," Casimir said, as if realising that I was here for the first time. He stared at me, mouth working, but whatever explanation he was trying to concoct could wait. I wanted to hear the truth from Jedrek. From the one who had deceived me.

"You're a god," I said, my voice stronger.

He sketched a bow. "At your service, my lady."

I straightened. He was lucky that I'd burnt my fires low on the roof. Already, they were regaining energy, and I was not sure I had the control to keep them in check. My earth magic was still in full supply, and it bucked against my grip. The stone beneath my feet started to crack. Jedrek's eyes widened.

"You come here, you look me in the eye, and you *lie* to me about what you are?" I asked, my words deceptively calm, quiet.

"I wanted to take your measure before revealing myself." He shrugged. "The lie was a small one. I am Jedrek, second son of the Sovereign of Amontys, only the Sovereigns all adopt me, over and over and over again. It keeps me close to the seat of power without ever being too close, and—"

The stones splintered, shards flying through the air to ring around Jedrek's neck, points piercing his skin until golden rivulets dripped onto his black clothes. He froze.

"You lied to me," I said again.

"Calanthe," Casimir warned, taking a step closer. I threw out a hand and he stopped, looking shocked.

"My lady—" Jedrek started. The stones dug in deeper.

"A spy, perhaps? Come to see precisely how to undo any plans I might make to dissuade the others? To keep the mortals of this world safe?" More stone splinters joined the others. "How long will it take, do you think, to recover from having your head carved from your shoulders?"

Jedrek grew so still that I would have sworn he stopped breathing.

"Calanthe," Casimir said again. I glared at him.

"You did not tell me, either," I pointed out.

"Because he is no threat to you. His offenses are against me, against Astr...against me. He does not stand with the others. I promise. Ask him, if you do not believe me."

I raised my brows. Jedrek swallowed, the movement jostling the stones so they scraped against his skin. "It's true," he rasped. "I swear it on the blood spilled here that I mean you no harm, Lady Calanthe."

The golden droplets shimmered for a moment, some strange trick of the light. I was tempted to send the stone shards into his neck regardless, but stayed my hand. I pulled them back, far enough that they still ringed Jedrek, but not close enough to draw blood.

"Explain yourself." I nodded to both Jedrek and Casimir. "Both of you. You start, god who is not a spy."

Jedrek winced. "I am only a minor god, at best. Three tiers down in power from someone like you, who wields the forces of creation and destruction in equal measure. My demesne is guardianship over the children of kings, and I was only ever worshipped in Amontys and Kinbreck. When the others fell, Kinbreck abandoned me also. Amontys granted me safe harbour, and in return I devoted myself to them for generations. Then, the void fell. I felt the world change. I heard rumours of you, my lady. And, well, I was glad to no longer be alone. So I came."

"You came here, to fight a war against your own kind, so that you would no longer be alone?" I understood loneliness, but that seemed unbelievable. Another lie.

Jedrek's expression turned cold. "It may surprise you to know that you are not the only one with a fondness for the mortals of this world."

It was my turn to wince. I let my magic relax, the stone splinters lowering back to the floor, fitting into the spots where they broke free. They sealed back into place just as I grew weary enough to slide to the ground. Casimir was there in an instant, his arms strong and careful as he lifted me to a nearby chair, arranging me just so.

"I've never not felt alone," I admitted quietly. Casimir stilled, hurt flashing through his eyes. "Even when surrounded by people I care about more than I can articulate."

It was the closest I could come to telling Casimir my feelings for him, and yet he drew away. A sign that he still yearned for Astraea, that while he was here helping me, his heart would always be somewhere else. Before I could explain, Jedrek sat in a second chair, nodding. "You can love as deeply as the seas, yet it's not always the same thing as being of a kind with someone else."

I had so many questions, so many thoughts on the tip of my tongue. I wanted to know what immortality tasted like, if it was bitter ash watching the world around you change so dramatically, or if it was something beautiful to watch. I wanted to ask about the others. I wanted to ask about the extent of our powers, our obligations. What our role truly was in the world of humans. I wanted to know everything. Yet I said nothing.

"As for the reason why the good guardian there reacted to violently to me," Jedrek said, any hint of vulnerability gone, his poise and surety back in place like an implacable mask, "that I fear is my own fault. I grew...restless during the long years of the void. So I sought out any hint of light, any hint of someone who might understand my life. Which turned out to be the Fallen Star—"

"Please," I said, shaking my head. "I don't want to know. Some things are fine to stay private."

I could guess what had happened, though, and a story of jealousy, of making Casimir hurt for Astraea's actions, sincere or otherwise, was the farthest thing from what I wanted. Casimir let out a low sigh and looked away from me. Jedrek just frowned, studying me. He looked at Casimir, then me, then nodded.

"I see." He settled deeper into his chair. "Perhaps you are right. The past is gone, even for those of us with long memories. It is time to forge the future."

"Indeed," Casimir said, still not looking at either of us.

"Lord Jedrek—"

"Prince," he corrected wryly. "I am only a second son, and an adopted one at that, but I am still a prince."

"Very well. Prince Jedrek, I hope to see you at tonight's dinner. If you'll excuse me, I have some tasks to attend to." I rose, my legs still wobbly, though whether from using so much magic in such a short period of time or the shock of discovering that I was not the only one here, not the only god on this side of the door, I didn't know. I hesitated at the threshold. "You...You're sure you wish to stand against the others?"

He met my gaze evenly. "I was not lying when I swore myself to your service earlier, my lady. What power, what skill, what influence I have, it is yours to command."

I bowed my head. "Thank you."

Casimir offered his arm. I accepted. Then, we both left, a heavy silence between us. We were well away from earshot of Jedrek's chambers when Casimir spoke, voice quiet. "It was her choice, to go with him."

"You don't have to—"

"She was bored with me, or so she said. Wanted to try something different. Wanted to see if my jealousy was more enticing than my devotion." The muscles of his arm tensed where I held them. "I nearly destroyed Altier in my anger. I haven't been that out of control of my shadows for years."

What was I meant to say to that? "I'm sorry," was all I could manage.

"I thought she was so perfect. My Star. Mine to protect and love. But I don't...I don't know if she loved me back. Not really."

I jerked him to a halt. Casimir looked at me, liquid silver limning his eyes. "You can't say that."

"It's the truth, Calanthe. It just took mistaking you for her to realise it. To understand."

"But you love her!"

He shook his head even as he shrugged. "And I did. For so long. Hopelessly. Without thought or question. But that's the thing. I should have thought. I should have questioned. Should have questioned why the one person who swore they loved me didn't want me to think, to ask. Who wanted only blind devotion."

Before I could stop myself, I lifted my hand and cupped Casimir's cheek, brushing away a stray tear. He grabbed my hand, holding it against his face. "Empty night, I feel so alone sometimes."

"You're not alone," I insisted, though I had just admitted to feeling the same thing only minutes before. I was a goddess, not a guardian. How could I possibly hope to understand? Still, I believed it. I had to. "You have me."

All of me. If he wanted it.

The world stopped in one impossible moment. Casimir pressed his mouth to my palm, a gentle kiss. One that spoke volumes. More than either one of us could possibly say. Then, our lips were on each other, our arms were scrabbling for hold. We devoured. We yearned. We held on for dear life.

I couldn't think. Could barely grasp what was happening. He didn't love me. He loved Astraea. I wasn't her. I had never been her. So how...why...I couldn't bring myself to care. I cared only that I was there in Casimir's arms, and he in mine, and I would do my best to prove that I loved him just as he was.

No. That wasn't fair. Not to him.

I pulled back. My breath was heavy. My lips tingled from where we'd kissed. His skin was flushed, the tiny shadows along his neck shifting pattern in a beautiful dance. His eyes, well, they were full of starlight. That alone solidified my decision.

"I heard her heartbeat," I said.

He gaped at me. "I don't understand."

"When we went into the tunnels, to go talk with Temys. I'd never been that far underground before, which is why I hadn't heard it, but then we were surrounded by earth and my magic took hold and... and...I heard her heartbeat. A heartbeat. I think it was hers. Deep beneath the earth, in a pocket of emptiness, where fire lives. A cavern, maybe. I think it was where I was made. I think...I think she's still there. Alive."

I expected hope. Joy. Surprise. Something. Instead, he shut down. His expression flattened. He looked almost bored, carved from impersonal marble. Stone. Once again, he offered his arm. I took it more tentatively this time. Then, he led me back to our chambers. When we reached the door, he bowed.

"If you'll excuse me, I forgot I have something yet to do with the Runners. I'll see you tonight at dinner."

Then, he was gone.

✦

I almost wished that I could skip the formality of another dinner comprised of the queen, Beatrice, the various nobles, strategists, and participants in this foolish war. They were held once a week or so, to serve as another means of discussing the situation, as well as a supposed break from the usual war planning. For me, they usually resulted in people staring at me, making veiled comments, or pretending to ignore me completely. Tonight, at least, Jedrek would be attending, so I might have someone new to talk with.

Provided I wasn't too busy trying to figure out what to do about Casimir.

He hadn't reappeared since leaving me at our chambers. I'd rested, weighed down by exhaustion from failing at training and dealing with people all the time. Then, I'd dressed myself in the simplest gown I had, a piece of blue and black that I could do up without assistance. I kept my hair down, too weary to even attempt containing it.

My exhaustion must have shown, because the guard outside the throne room, where these dinners were held, gave me a sympathetic smile before letting me in. The room was busy with a smattering of people, most holding a drink and talking quietly with one another. As always, my entrance had people falling silent, staring at me. I brushed past the people and was reaching to take a drink for myself when a hand snatched up the glass first.

Jedrek, decked in black silk, took a sip of the golden honey wine. He winced. "Too sweet for my liking, but it should be safe to drink."

I snatched the glass from him, taking a long swallow. "Since when do I need taste testers? Won't I just heal from a poisoning?"

"Only the true gods, the original ones, can survive anything. The rest of us will heal from most injuries, but we can still be killed," Jedrek murmured. I winced. My threat with the stones, then, had been more potent than I thought.

"I'm sorry," I said. "I didn't know."

"How could you have?" Jedrek smiled. "Even so.

While your power is significant, you are not truly immortal. Unless…"

"Unless?" I quirked a brow.

"Your parentage?" he asked, as if he didn't know. I was about to answer when Dame Winters swept up to us. She'd attended every strategy session, every dinner, and still I wasn't certain why she bothered. Her contributions seemed steeped in half-formed poems and predictions combined with stares sharp enough to cut stone. I liked her, but I gathered that few others did.

Tonight, she was adorned in white feathers sewn into her gown, onto a small capelet, woven through her hair. She looked like a bird that had been caught in some horrible trap, feathers sticking in so many directions. The glass of honey wine in her hand was nearly empty.

"Ah, the beautiful Lady Calanthe," Dame Winters said, bowing. She wavered slightly. "I offered that *poet* Temys the use of my personal archives—I have quite the collection of ancient books, you know—and she turned me down. As if I were wasting her time! I knew that you would be more discerning, though, so perhaps you will come and view my collection tomorrow?"

I nodded. It was better than failing at training once again. "I would be happy to do so. Dame Winters, may I present Prince Jedrek of Amontys?"

The wobble in the Seer's step vanished, as did the

slightly tipsy look. Her shoulders straightened. Her chin lifted. The visage of a weak, doddering old woman disappeared entirely. The transformation was extreme. She eyed Jedrek with open interest, and I wasn't certain it was benevolent.

"My ancestors come from a great many places. Wanderers, they were, the lot of them. Except my grandmother, who could trace her ancestry back to the days when Kinbreck had a monarchy. She was a third daughter of a minor noble, but she managed to betroth herself to the prince. The heir. Until he died in a hunting accident."

Jedrek winced, closing his eyes.

"You bear a cursed name, Prince. All of Kinbreck knows that name, and their progeny also. Jedrek, god of the children of Kings. Oathbreaker."

I started to say something, but Dame Winters shook her head, what I now knew to be her facade slipping back into place. "You keep strange company, Lady Calanthe. Be careful that such company does not baulk at the first sign of danger."

She sauntered off, waving her hands in the face of a particularly rotund noblewoman. Jedrek remained silent at my side.

"She is the court Seer," I offered, though it felt like ash to speak.

"It was an accident," Jedrek said. "What happened to the prince. He had tasked me with watching his sisters that day. I thought...I thought he wished to go and have a tryst with his betrothed. Instead, he broke his neck trying to jump his horse after a deer. I wasn't banished, not then. But the void came, and the monarchy dissolved and..."

I put a hand on his arm, the only comfort I knew how to offer.

"I loved him," Jedrek breathed. He snatched up a glass of honey wine and downed the whole thing in one desperate gulp. "I loved him."

"I believe you." And I did. "We all make mistakes, even the immortals. Now, come, let me introduce you to Lionel and Rietta. They're from Craigsmuir."

I went to do just that when one more guest slipped into the room. Casimir. He looked just as he always did, and yet there was something wrong. Something fundamental that had shifted. My breath caught in my throat as I realised what it was.

"I guess the pretense is up," Jedrek murmured, then slipped away from me.

Casimir no longer looked human. The guise he wore, the one that dulled his beauty, his power, that made him look human, was gone. He hadn't worn it during our travels back from Ynysfawr, but here in Altier, surrounded by people, he'd worn it once again. Until now. Instead, he wore his shadows proudly, etched into impossible designs over his skin. His eyes gleamed with power. He walked up to me, expression set.

"Cas—"

With one look, I was silenced. He took my hand and my heart lurched. I could feel the stares of curious eyes on my face, but all I could do was lock my eyes with his. He swallowed, throat bobbing, eyes fluttering closed.

"Cas," I tried again, gentler. My heart was cracking, and one word from him could heal it or shatter it into thousands of shards. He squeezed my fingers and hope swelled. Only to vanish a moment later.

"Can you get there? To her? Can you..." *Save her*. The unspoken words I knew he could not bring himself to utter.

I smiled, though inside I was falling to pieces. I knew it was inevitable. I had known it from the moment I realised that I wasn't her. I would never be her. But Casimir—sensitive, protective Casimir—would never wish to cause me hurt, even if he wasn't truly my guardian. And this was what he wanted. This was something I could give him to repay all the times he'd been there for me. Something I could give him that would make him happy. So I smiled. I nodded.

"I can certainly try. My magic may not be strong enough at the moment, but it's growing. I'll train. Maybe Jedrek knows some methods to improve. I'll do anything I can, and I promise, Cas, that we'll get her back. We'll—"

"Thank you," he said, and looked away from me. I blinked, my breath stolen from my lungs. It took him leading me to the table, holding my chair for me, then walking to sit across from me before I could regain my breath. I barely noticed Jedrek sitting beside me, barely noticed the intense stares of Raya and Beatrice.

"Are you alright?" Jedrek murmured. I nodded. "Liar."

"I will be well," I assured him. "I just...There is no other option but for me to be well."

He gave me a sympathetic look, then launched into a story that had everyone's attention on him rather than me. Leaving me to silently collect the pieces of my heart that had been scattered about me.

Later that night, after a dinner I barely tasted and conversation I barely remembered, I found myself knocking on a door not my own. I waited. A few moments later, Tali opened it, looking so tired after her first full day out of the infirmary. I remembered that feeling, when I was first released from the infirmary, yet still felt too weak to take on the world. I felt like that, now.

"I think..." I took a deep breath. "That thing you talked about? Living despite—no. Living *in* spite of everything else that's going on. Carving out an identity for yourself, regardless of what everyone else needs from you? I think I need that."

Tali didn't say a word. She just held her arms open and I collapsed into them, my smile falling away and tears taking its place.

CHAPTER 13

"**E**mpty night, that's *awful*." I held a hand in front of my mouth, trying to find a place to discreetly spit the bite of food. My face was hot from spice and my eyes were watering. The entire restaurant was laughing, pointing at me or trying to hide their amusement. There was no polite way to dispose of the food, so I swallowed it and nearly gagged.

Tali had her head buried in her hands, shoulders shaking so hard I thought she might be crying. "Stars above, I can't believe you actually *ate* it!"

I shoved the plate away and the owner of the restaurant scooped it up with a knowing grin. "Maybe something less spicy?" he offered, setting down what looked like rice with raisins. I eyed him warily and he grinned wider.

Tali and I had been at this restaurant for several

hours, now, having snuck out from training to come into the city. Well, it was less sneaking out and more announcing firmly that I was going into Altier with Tali and didn't want to be followed around by an entourage. Casimir had been off with the Runners—he appeared to be actively avoiding me—and I assumed he would be told of my plans at some point. When he hadn't immediately come running after me, relief settled in and I set about enjoying my day with Tali.

She'd insisted that we try and discover my favourite food, so we picked a restaurant and settled in. The owner, a short, stocky man with rich brown skin and a smile that was more than a little mischievous, had at first bowed and tugged at his forelock at me. It was inevitable that I'd be recognised; my burns were distinctive and people stared wherever I went. Tali, though, quickly convinced the man that we just wanted to find my favourite food.

The games had started soon after.

People had trickled into the restaurant, filling it to the brim. Some brought dishes from home, others suggested recipes to the owner. They all laughed uproariously when I didn't like a food, and when I found something I did like, the person who suggested it preened like a songbird. So far, I'd discovered that I liked dumplings, didn't like crustaceans, and really, really hated whatever that spiced dish was he just gave me.

I wasn't any closer to finding my favourite food, but I was having a great time. And, for the first time, people weren't treating me like some precious object of power. I wasn't the Chosen One, I wasn't their goddess. I was just Calanthe, trying all sorts of different foods and listening to stories of their origins.

No prayers. No talk of battles. No discussion of the dark past. Just the history of food and having a good time.

I was taking a bite of the rice dish—pleasantly sweet and creamy, which immediately cooled the heat in my mouth—when the door opened. A gust of cold air followed the newcomer. I stiffened, half-expecting Casimir to be there, looking at me with that horrible mix of hope and sadness which had my heart pounding in my ears. Instead, Jedrek shook off his cloak and wove through the crowd until he slid onto the bench at the table where Tali and I sat. A hush fell over the crowd as people stared, indignant at the supposed liberties Jedrek was taking.

Even with all the games, no one had tried sitting at my table.

I ignored the sudden discomfort and pushed the bowl of rice towards Jedrek. "You have to try this. It's some sort of sweetened rice with raisins."

He made a face. "Raisins. No thank you. How about some roasted potatoes and a meat pie? The weather is cold enough to call for it."

I looked to the owner. "Would you mind?"

"Any friend of the lady," he said, hand across his chest as he bowed and shuffled off. I'd tried meat pie earlier in the day and found it good, but too filling.

"So, have you come to drag us back to the palace?" Tali asked, eyes bright and curious as she studied Jedrek. The two hadn't yet met, given that Tali wasn't at the dinner last night, but I had told her about him. The truth. She knew so much already that I didn't really see much point in hiding anything from her.

"Tali, this is Prince Jedrek. Jedrek, this is Tali, a *dharangui* and my friend. She's been helping me find my favourite food."

"A Wandering Poet?" Jedrek raised his brows. "I wasn't aware your order survived in Baldarskiel during the void."

"Most died out," Tali said with a shrug, though her jaw was tight. "My family managed to survive." She looked at me with a sad smile. "It turns out that in times of fear, people don't want poems and scholarly debates. They want answers. And when you can't provide...well."

The tragedies that happened during the generations of the void were not my fault or my doing and yet a slash of pain made its way across my chest. "I'm sorry."

"We'll survive and thrive again," she promised.

"Now, why don't you tell us how you found us, Jedrek. And why."

"The why is simple: I heard you'd taken a day to spend in the city, and I didn't much feel like spending hours training when I already know I can fight just fine. So I decided to join you. As to how, well, that one was ridiculously easy. I just followed the whispers and eager looks." He nodded to some of the other people who were watching, wide-eyed.

I sighed, my enjoyment in the quest for a favourite food wearing thin. "I should be training," I muttered.

Tali shook her head. "You're allowed to take a day off, Calanthe."

"I need all the practise I can get," I argued, though half-heartedly. "Especially now that I need to refine my magic to go...help Casimir."

"Oh?" Jedrek raised his brows and leaned in, then immediately jumped back as the owner appeared and dropped a plate of potatoes and meat pie before us. I stabbed a golden potato with a fork and let the buttery vegetable melt on my tongue. Wonderful.

"Our Lady Calanthe is determined to spread herself too thin," Tali said, rolling her eyes. "Casimir has, ah, a task for her that requires her to dig deep into the earth. Not to mention everyone is expecting her to fight on the front lines in this war with the gods and she can barely hold a sword."

I flushed, cheeks warming as though I'd eaten

more spicy food. "I can *hold* a sword," I grumbled. "Just not much else."

Jedrek shrugged, popping a potato in his mouth with his fingers. "Of course you can't. Do you expect a wolf to hunt as soon as it's born? You are a new god, Calanthe, so new that your blood is barely gold and your magic has yet to finish growing. You must learn to master your limbs before you can fight."

That didn't make me feel any better. "How, exactly, am I meant to do that?"

Jedrek grinned wickedly. "By dancing, of course."

He'd barely spoken the words before excited murmurs broke out across the restaurant. Within seconds, people were clearing tables out of the way and making room. Some people rushed out, only to return a few minutes later with instruments in hand. A woman pulled a pipe from her pocket and joined the musicians. Food was cleared away and replaced with large pints of ale to slake thirst.

The music was lively and exciting, so unlike the music that I'd heard at the ball officially announcing me as the Chosen One. People moved across the floor in swift, eager turns, laughing and grinning and changing partners often. I remembered the sensation of dancing with Casimir, close and warm and magical. This was different. So different.

Perhaps it was exactly what I needed.

When Jedrek stood and pulled me into a dance whose steps I didn't know, I didn't hesitate. I stumbled at first, but the other god didn't seem to mind, gently guiding me into the correct movements until I was spinning and stomping and laughing with just as much ease as the others.

Stars above, had I ever laughed this much before?

The music changed and people breathlessly settled into a slower number, holding on to their partners as though they could barely stand from running and jumping about. I let myself relax into Jedrek's grip.

"See? Isn't this much better than fighting?"

"I still need to learn," I pointed out.

"I won't disagree. But look at how much better you've got in just a few minutes. You're a natural."

It felt natural. So easy, so smooth, as though I'd been doing it my whole life. Like flames leaping into the sky, or flowers blowing on the wind. Natural. And so, I danced. I danced with Jedrek, then with the restaurant owner, with a boy with spots on his face and a blush on his cheeks, with a woman who had grey streaked in her hair, with a man whose beard nearly reached his belt, with anyone and everyone who asked. I stopped only to take large mouthfuls of ale and catch my breath before throwing myself right back into dancing.

Then, the door opened again.

Cold air blew across the floor, making candles sputter. When had they been lit? I couldn't remember. The musicians faltered, but only for an instant.

The people kept dancing, so desperately alive. I, on the other hand, froze.

Casimir stood in the doorway, wearing his Void Runner ivory armour, his hair tied back. Sweat beaded across his face; he looked like he'd been running. He stared at me with so much intensity that the rest of the world seemed to fall away. The broken heart I'd been fleeing all day roared to life, each beat splintering its way into my body.

Casimir took a step forward, closing the door. I shivered as the last of the cold air was cut off. He had to have crossed the makeshift dance floor to me, but all I knew was that he was suddenly impossibly close. His breath mingled with mine. I could pick out the flecks of light in his shadowy eyes. Starlight, though they flickered like the candles.

"I was worried," he breathed, bringing a hand up as if to brush against my face. He never touched me, lowering his hand. "You left without telling me."

"I sent Eloise with a message." And purposefully had not told him myself. Casimir flinched as though I'd struck him. A bead of sweat dripped down his cheek.

"Did you run here?" I asked. "From the palace?"

He didn't look at me. "I'm glad you're okay."

"I'm sorry for worrying you." I was, too. But I'd needed time for me. To even learn who I was. "Tali and I came to figure out my favourite food."

Something like surprise crossed his features. "Your favourite food?"

I nodded. "I haven't had a chance to try many different things, what with the restrictions placed on me as Chosen One, and then now with the...the war. So Tali suggested I find out, before war consumes my time."

"And? What did you discover?"

I hesitated. I wanted to tell him. I wanted to discuss the wonderful things I'd tasted and the terrible. I wanted to tell him some of the more outlandish stories that people had told me regarding the origin of the recipes. I wanted to describe the whole afternoon to the man I loved. But the knowledge that he didn't love me back stayed my tongue. Instead, I nodded at the dancers, who were still moving, though they watched Casimir and me with a hint of unease.

"I like dancing," I said.

"Dancing." Said in such a tone that suggested he was shocked. Confused. I frowned. Dancing was one thing that was mine. It wasn't training. It wasn't planning. It wasn't translating old documents for a hint of information we might use to fight our war. It was *mine*. My choice. I wouldn't let him judge me for that.

"Yes, dancing," I said. "It's fun."

Before I could turn and go back to Jedrek, who was waiting patiently by Tali, Casimir held out a hand. "Then...would you care to dance, Calanthe?"

I blinked. "What?"

"Would you care to dance with me?"

"You want to dance with me?" I didn't understand. He wanted Astraea. He was only by my side until she returned, until I brought her back. He may have been supportive and kind, if a bit single-minded on my training, but he didn't owe me anything. Not dancing, not anything.

"I do," he said. I studied his face, not sure if I was looking for signs of deception or just trying to understand his thoughts. "Please. It would bring me great pleasure to dance with you."

How could I say no to that? I would do so many things to bring him even a moment of happiness in a world that had treated him so cruelly. So I nodded, put my hand in his, and let myself fall into the rhythm of the music again so that my broken heart could stay well away from the dance floor.

The last time Casimir and I had danced, he had been my refuge. Steady as the earth beneath my feet when the world around me had been demanding so very much more than I understood. His arms had been safe. His smile reserved for me. I had been happy, then, dancing with him. Now, though the music was faster and required switching partners, spinning around the room and more, I felt that same thing.

His hands, when they clasped mine between partner changes, were steady as stone. His eyes never strayed from me. His arms were a safe haven when I fell into them, breath heaving from movement. I was, in the rhythm of that dance, happy. More than I could describe. When he smiled, when the sadness fell away for a brief instant as we spun in a circle around each other, I felt incandescent.

Then, the music stopped. The dancers stopped, turning to clap. Calls for more food or ale were thrown. A brief respite was declared by the musicians. Conversation filled the place where the song had been. Yet Casimir and I just stood there, staring at each other.

"Calan—"

"I need some air." I pushed past people as politely as I could; they grinned at me and murmured my name. Then, I was at the door, pulling it open and racing into the darkness of the winter night. Snow fell in bright, puffy flakes, sticking to my clothes and hair and doing absolutely nothing to cool the fire beneath my skin. I strode into the night, away from lights, away from people, away, away, away.

I stopped abruptly when the buildings vanished entirely, leaving a vast meadow in their place. A meadow stricken through with a scar of charred plants where a fire had once burned.

"Calanthe!" Casimir grabbed my arm and spun me around to face him. He put his hands on my shoulders as if to hold me still, keep me from running again. "Don't run out on me like that!"

I looked over my shoulder, at that slash across the meadow. "Is this where they found me?"

I'd never been to Starfall Meadow, to the place where seven Void Runners had died in a battle against some voidlings while the Chosen One had supposedly fought with her magic. My memories of that night were shrouded in mist, and I was certain that most of them were dreams made to feel real. I hadn't been the one to fight the voidlings; that much I knew. Nor, I surmised, had Astraea, as she'd been below the earth, trapped to strip her of her light and make me. Had there been a third Chosen One, an unsuspecting girl with wild magic of light who thought she was blessed by a Fallen Star? One who had tried to fight and failed, dying without anyone remembering her? Or had something else happened at Starfall Meadow, something my dreams couldn't piece together?

"Yes," Casimir said. "This is where they found you."

He was angry. I could hear it. Feel it in the way the night crackled around me. What right did he have to be angry with me?

"What do you want, Casimir?" I asked, ready to collapse on the ground and pull the earth over my head. Ready to be alone. The life I'd felt while dancing, the joy, had been leeched away by the empty streets and quiet night. Snow continued to fall, finally cooling me down.

"What do I want?" he repeated, incredulous. "Empty night, Calanthe, how can you ask me that?"

"How can I—" I whirled to face him.

"Yes! How can you, of all people, ask me what I want? How can you *not know?*"

I barked out a sharp laugh. "How can I not know? Because you don't tell me what you want, Casimir, except to go and rescue Astraea. That's the only thing you've ever asked from me, apart from always letting you know where I am, what I'm doing, who I'm with. And that can hardly be called something you want, can it, not when you're a guardian born and bred. Not when you must have something to guard, even though I'm not what you want. Even when I'm not her."

He frowned, a sharpness in his gaze. "What does that have to do with anything?"

"It has *everything* to do with anything!" I threw up my hands. Behind me, I heard the ground shift, reacting to my emotions. I was too worked up to even consider trying to tamp down my magic, though. The words were too necessary. So I let them out. "Gods, Casimir, you don't see it, do you?"

"See what?" he snapped.

"That I am so desperately in love with you. More than I know what to do with. And you, you who only look at me when you are angry. Who only talks with me when it's absolutely necessary. You claimed to love me, before, and I fell for you, too, but then everything changed."

He didn't say anything, only clenched his jaw. Fine. I could fill in the silence well enough for the both of us.

"We learned that I'm not her. I'll never be her. Your destiny. Your soul mate. The Star that you Fell for! The one who you devoted *centuries* to loving. No matter how much you want it, Casimir, I'm never going to be Astraea. I'm me, Calanthe, whom you named so casually, and proceeded to ignore so thoroughly. And it shatters me, because I love you, and you will always love her and I can't ever be that."

"Good."

Before I could question, before I could complain, beg for understanding as to how one word could send a knife right through me, he had moved. His hands fell to my waist. His body pressed close to mine. Then, he kissed me. He kissed me with the passion of the flames in my blood, the steadiness of the earth in my bones. He kissed me like the world had died and we were the only two that remained. And I, Stars help me, kissed him back.

"I don't care about her," he whispered in my ear as he pulled away. "I care about *you*."

Casimir brushed his thumb across my cheek and looked at me with an expression so tender that I nearly melted. "Don't cry," he said on a laugh. I shoved against his chest, but it was half-hearted and weak. Before he could release me, I buried my face in his shoulder. He hugged me firmly, and I felt safe again.

"I thought you hated me," he said at last. "For what I did at Ynysfawr, for the things I said. For...for loving her."

"I could never hate you." Despite the pain he'd caused. "But you love her."

"I did. In the past. But it wasn't until I met you, and you were so different from her, so much better, that I understood how...how toxic loving Astraea was. She was beautiful and powerful and she was so damn unsure of herself. She always needed the assurance of love. She always needed more devotion. From me. From strangers. She wanted the whole world to love her, and when I disagreed with her, when I wanted to craft a world that was better, not just another iteration of the same game she always played, she lashed out." He tightened his arms reflexively, as if protecting me from his past. "She could be cruel. Like taking Jedrek as a lover to see if she liked me better jealous. I was cast as the villain so many times in her games. So many times the hero, too. But never did she try to give love, to me or to anyone. Always she took it."

I said nothing. How could I? I'd never met Astraea, and I was jealous of her for having Casimir's heart. Except now he claimed that wasn't the case. The world was spinning too quickly for me to comprehend.

"I loved her with everything I had, and it wasn't enough. It would never be enough. Then, you appeared. And I thought you were her, only without your memories. I was so relieved when you didn't act like her. I thought, *this is it. This is a new beginning for both of us.*" He rested his head against mine. "I fell so deeply in love with you, with the new Astraea, perhaps more than I'd ever loved her before. Then, we went to Ynysfawr."

Where we discovered the truth.

"I was hurt, yes. Confused. I felt like I'd

betrayed Astraea," he admitted. "Like loving you was a forfeiture of all my previous vows. Because I did still love you, Calanthe, even when I knew the truth. But the fact is, Astraea...she broke any vows long before I did. A part of me will always love the beautiful creature that she was. But not what she became."

I wanted desperately to hear this, to hear it all. To dissect every moment of his love for me and to do the same with mine for him. I also wanted to run away and hide, because surely this could not be real. Surely I would wake at any moment, and I didn't want the world to see my humiliation when it all came apart. Instead, I stayed exactly where I was, wrapped in Casimir's arms.

"I'm sorry for hurting you," he breathed, brushing back a strand of my hair. "That is the last thing that I would want."

"And...I'm sorry for hurting you. No, don't argue. I did. You wouldn't have come after me like you did if I hadn't. And I'm sorry for it." I rested my head against his chest again. The wind picked up, blowing flurries of snow around us, nearly burying that scar of earth. "We still need to find her, don't we?"

She was out there, buried deep beneath the ground. Alone. No matter my fears, no matter how much I wanted her to stay gone from our lives, leaving her alone would be cruel.

"I am still her guardian, despite everything,"

Casimir said. "I do not love her any longer, but I still owe her a duty, until I am released."

"Then I will help you, and gladly," I promised.

He looked at me with a tender smile. "I know you—"

The world trembled. It wasn't the earth, for that was steady beneath my feet and strong in my magic. It wasn't the sky, for that was as silent as ever it had been. No, this was like someone had picked at a thread of the universe and tried to unravel it. Casimir and I broke apart, turning to find the threat, find the cause.

I found the point where the scar in the earth began. It was vibrant in contrast to the snow, but only because it was so dark as to be blinding. A familiar, darkness, too, with specks of starlight and magic pulsating at its centre. A living being, almost. The void.

"A god?" Casimir asked, as if I would know. Somehow, though, I did know. Perhaps because I had been the one to split the realms to begin with.

"The void. Someone has opened a tear to the void. There was a void pool here, right?" Already I was moving closer, knowing I would need to seal that tear before something could come through.

"Calanthe, wait!" Casimir hissed, grabbing my wrist. We'd drawn close enough to see the tear clearly, and it became immediately obvious that it wasn't a natural occurrence. Someone had opened it.

Someone had violated the rules that Devereux set forth to protect our realm from the wildness of his.

Standing before the opening between realms was Beatrice. Garbed in her finery, she practically glittered against the snow. Her back was straight, her head held high, and an expression of pure determination gleamed from her eyes. She faced the void unafraid, despite what was looking down on her. Because there was something on the other side of that veil, and I could feel its hunger from here.

Hunger for life. Hunger for power. Hunger for the realm that I'd banished it from.

It looked vaguely human, with long, spindly limbs and features that were somehow plant-like, reminiscent of an ancient tree. Antlers stood proud on its forehead, holding back a crown of hair that flowed like grass. It looked nothing like any voidling I'd ever faced. Had the magic of the void shifted enough that its beings were now different? Or had this sort of creature always existed there, deep within the shadows?

"Mortal." The creature licked its lips, revealing sharpened teeth.

"I have summoned you," Beatrice said. "I have asked for a boon from the midnight woods."

The thing smiled wider. "This is a field, mortal. Your boon is irrelevant."

"This is where your world meets mine. Surely that is sufficient for a bargain?" Beatrice snapped, tossing her head. The creature followed the movement, its eyes latched onto her throat. It licked its lips again.

"What boon would you ask?" it rasped.

"I would—"

"No." I spoke before I could gather my thoughts. Beatrice spun around, eyes widening as she saw Casimir and myself marching towards her. She flinched for a moment, then straightened again, ever the regal High Priestess and Princess. The creature hissed.

"Do not interfere," it said. "She summoned me. She spoke the words to call me. We will bargain."

"Does your king know that you are here?" Casimir asked, drawing a dagger from his belt. The creature looked at the knife and hissed, moving back towards the tear in the veil.

"My king is busy with other matters. Internal matters. I, who guard the borders, am free to do as I wish. Including make bargains with mortals."

"Go back to the palace," I said to Beatrice. She drew in a breath, affronted. I let a little of my fire flare, wrapping around my fingers. "Do you truly wish to argue with me?"

"I was only doing this to help," she said, locking eyes with me as if hoping to do battle, as if hoping to win such a ridiculous challenge of authority. I didn't care about such things; I looked back to the creature.

"You are not wanted here," Casimir said, holding the dagger up. It looked pathetic against such a thing, and yet the creature continued to move away, keeping a healthy distance between it and the dagger.

"You interfere in things which are none of your concern," the creature said, baring its teeth at us.

"None of our concern? Well, it is certainly the concern of your king," Casimir said. Then, before I could do anything, he spoke one word three times, breaking the very rules we had been set. "Devereux, Devereux, Devereux, I summon you."

The tear in the void widened for a moment, showing a forest of lush life, so intoxicatingly beautiful that even I felt its pull. The starlight of the void flitted between the trees. Vines that gleamed silver grew up the trunks of impossibly large trees. Fungi and ferns were everywhere, full of some unfamiliar magic that sang out to my own. Then, a shadow passed in front of that vision and a figure stepped out of the tear.

Devereux.

He looked almost as he had during our last meeting, with a few subtle differences. His skin was void-dark, showing golden in only a few places where his natural colour remained, such as on the tips of his fingers, his ears, in a broad stroke across his cheeks. His hair was longer, darker, wild. His eyes were bright, glowing orange. The changes, though, were harder to identify. There was a wolfishness to him, now. And I could have sworn that his fingers were tipped with claws.

Most stunning, though, was the crown he bore. Ivory white, it was simple in its design, with a point every so often in a simple circle around his head. It was only when I looked closer that I realised that each piece of the crown was carved from bone.

He spared a glance for Casimir and myself, then turned his attention to Beatrice, who was staring at him, bloodless and silent. "Well, Sister, not going to greet me?" Devereux purred.

The creature scraped into a bow, making noises—excuses—in the voidling language that grated my ears to hear. Devereux snarled at it, indeed like a wolf, and the creature backed away slowly, still bowing.

"You are not my brother," Beatrice said at last. But her facade of strength was cracking, and her fear showed through.

"Perhaps not as you knew me. Waiting for people to acknowledge me, to tell me how useful I was. To give me a purpose." Devereux stepped closer, moving fully out of the void. Tiny pricks of light followed him, settling on the points of his crown. "Now I know I am being useful. Doing good. Serving a people who need me. Unlike some, who much prefer it the other way around."

Beatrice scoffed, though she said nothing. Devereux smiled softly, sadly. "No, you never did see it that way, did you?" he murmured. Then, louder, with a frown, he asked, "Why are you here? What *idiotic* reason do you have for coming here, attempting to bargain with my people?"

Beatrice must have found some of her composure in talking with her brother, because she slipped on a humble smile. "I came to bargain for assistance. Have you not heard? Our benevolent saviour, the Lady Calanthe, has declared war on the gods for the sake of the mortal realm. She will need all the help she can get."

Such simple words, spoken with conviction, and yet I barely restrained the urge to roll my eyes. Beatrice was not one to do something for the greater good. She wanted whatever power the magic of the void could offer her. She wanted what Devereux had been given freely. I was just an excuse.

"Oh, I am fully aware of the war to be waged," Devereux said. He grinned at the creature. "My forces have already begun to prepare, haven't they?"

The creature snickered, a violent sound. "We will tear their skin from their bones and seed our fields with their blood. Gods are fertile beings, after all, so full of magic." It looked at me and smiled. "Some more than others. Significantly so."

"That's enough," Casimir barked, raising his dagger again. Even Devereux seemed to move away from the weapon, though not nearly as much as the creature, who hissed.

"Regardless of the impending war, Sister, I very

much doubt you came here with benevolent intentions," Devereux said. Beatrice bristled.

"I have nothing but benevolent intentions! Have I not guided the people of Baldarskiel as their High Priestess? Have I not done my best by them, using Temple resources to help them in times of need? Yet when the goddess returned from Ynysfawr, I was unceremoniously stripped of my position. How am I to help now?"

"Use your significant training and fight alongside the soldiers," Devereux suggested blandly. Beatrice sucked in a gasp. "Yes, I would have you stand beside the people you so claim to love. To act as one of them, not their better. Go find a different means to power, Beatrice, for you'll find none here. Void magic is not for you."

"And it's for you?" Beatrice snarled. "Look at you! You've become monstrous!"

Devereux tossed his head back and laughed. "A true compliment coming from you."

Beatrice looked as though she would launch herself at Devereux and tear him to shreds. I'd seen the two of them fight with swords once, though they hadn't known I was watching. Beatrice was strong and fast, and possessed of a ruthlessness that served her well in the circles of politics. She would happily tear into Devereux. But he was not the hesitating, questioning man I'd known before the void. He stood with surety, now, and poise. As soon as Beatrice raised her hand to strike him, his own magic lashed out. Bands of star-flecked shadow wrapped around her wrist like living plants, the leaves serrated and cutting into her flesh with ease. Beatrice gasped with pain, falling to her knees.

"This magic is not for you," Devereux said again. He knelt in the snow and leaned close to her. "Do not think that I deny you out of some petty cruelty, dear Sister. I love you, and I always shall. But this is a magic that burns away all pretence and amplifies what lies at the centre. It is a sharp magic. A dangerous magic. And it would consume you until there was nothing left but raw ambition. Let me tell you, you are not prepared to face what you would become if that were to happen. What you would lose."

Beatrice clutched her wrists close to her chest, getting droplets of blood on her skirts. "What, exactly, have you lost, Brother?"

Devereux smiled, sadly, and brushed a hand against her shoulder. "Too much."

He straightened and looked to me, bowing his head. "My forces stand ready. Call upon us when the need arises."

Beatrice scoffed. "Just like that, you offer your army, your people, to *her*? To someone whose memories only go back, what, seven, eight months? You would entrust the future of this world to her?"

Devereux sighed. Where once before he might

have said something to placate his sister, to let her preen and pretend, now he spoke without hesitation, clearly knowing the effect his words would have. "I would rather leave the world to her hands than yours."

With a bark in the voidling language, he turned back to the tear between realms. The antlered creature bowed again and followed after him, looking back at Beatrice with a distinct hunger in its gaze. Devereux paused as he passed Casimir. "Take care," he said.

"And you."

In those simple words, I caught a hint of the weight that lay between the two. Years of friendship, of being there for one another, and yet secrets still managed to drive them apart. Managed to drive them to two different realms, with momentous tasks before them. Still, somehow, they remained friends.

"Fare well, Devereux," I said, reaching for him and squeezing his hand. He grinned at me, a feral, wild look.

"I intend to." With that, he slipped away and disappeared into the realm of the void, the creature only an instant behind. Once they were gone, the tear shrank until it was nothing more than a pinprick of darkness. Then, it vanished entirely.

I rounded on Beatrice, finally letting my anger flare to life. "What were you thinking?"

"As I said, I wished to help and—"

"Liar!" I hissed. "You have had no desire to assist me, not since I came back from Ynysfawr as anything other than your submissive Chosen One. You have been trying to manipulate things in your favour. Or do you think I am a fool? Do you think that I didn't see what you have been trying to do with the Temple."

"Temple? What Temple?" Beatrice pulled herself off the ground, shaking away Casimir's offered hand. She brushed snow off of her and tossed her hair back, glaring. "You practically disbanded the Temple with one word. No one worships there. Everyone thinks that we—that *I*—am the byproduct of a failure. The star didn't come to save us, not like was promised. *You* did. A new goddess of earth and fire. Creation and destruction. I have been sneered at in every corridor, scoffed at in every street. Everywhere I go, people think that I was nothing more than a power-hungry royal child, desperate to seek some influence, even if I could not have the throne."

Casimir snorted. "That is exactly what you were. You played the part of a fanatic well, so well that the Temple made you their High Priestess. But you forget, Beatrice, that I have been around for a very long time. I have seen your rise to power."

She curled her lip. "And you, goddess. Do you even feel a moment's regret for destroying an entire religion? A way of life that sought to guide people? To improve their lives?"

"I am sorry that you have lost your purpose. I think you would have followed the tenets of your chosen religion, regardless of how well you believed them, for nothing more than presenting an image. My return and subsequent actions have taken that purpose from you. I understand that. However, I will not tolerate disloyalty. If you choose to part ways with me, if you choose not to support me, then so be it. I will not stop you, nor try to persuade me. But do not pretend to be my friend if you are going to turn around and seek power for your own gain. I will not tolerate it."

My words felt cruel, felt sharp. It was the most unforgiving speech I had made and I wished that it had been under different circumstances. I wanted to be friendly with Beatrice, if for no other reason than she was Devereux's sister and important to him. She was not like her mother, though. She did not see the benefit of entering into an alliance. She did not put aside her own pride for the sake of the future.

No, she said nothing at all as she spun away from Casimir and me and stalked back to the palace.

"She's going to be trouble," Casimir murmured, wrapping his arm around my shoulders.

"I know. But what else can we do? She has a right to her decision."

He sighed and kissed my head. "That is why you are the right person to lead this venture. Why I love you."

"Flatterer. Now come on. I've been dancing all evening and my feet are sore." True, my feet were sore. I was tired. But I also bore a worrying knot in my stomach that had nothing to do with dancing, and everything to do with how easily things could go wrong when you had impetuous humans on one side of a war, and fickle gods on the other.

CHAPTER 15

"Deeper. You have to dig deeper. Make the metal pure *before* you pull it from the ground." Jedrek wandered in a slow circle around me while I knelt on the ground. We were a half-day's ride from Altier, with only Casimir, Jedrek, and myself present to protect any mortals while I practised my magic. Jedrek's power might have been minute compared to the raging storms that my magic contained, but he was an exacting teacher and I could barely keep up with his lessons. My hair was damp from sweat, my head ached, and my fingers tingled.

I closed my eyes and tried to dive deeper into my earth magic. Jedrek was having me extract different metals and stones from the ground without bringing anything else with them. It was an exercise in precision, and I was terrible at it. My fire magic kept interfering with my earth magic, melting the ores before I could even extract them. The deeper I went into one side, the harder the other tried to rise to the surface.

This time, I used a needle-thin strand of earth magic, pulled from the deepest parts of my body. I sent that spearing into the ground and called forth the gold that Jedrek had demanded. Tiny fragments burrowed through the earth, coming together and inevitably trapping other elements within the larger piece. I coaxed those pieces out, taking a deep breath when my magic faltered, trying to expand, to grow, to perform monumental tasks that seemed now as easy as waving my hand.

Precision, as it would happen, was much more difficult.

The ground around me rumbled as I focused. I could feel sweat dripping down my back, despite the sharp bite of the winter day. The gold resisted my demands, resisted that call of earth magic tenuously under my control.

"You're trying too hard," Jedrek said, breaking my concentration for a moment. My fire magic broke free of my control, leaping for the god. I reined it in at the last moment, my fingers digging deep into the earth to ground myself.

"Breathe, Calanthe," Casimir said from where he was watching. It was far enough away that he wouldn't be in the direct line of my magic, though the edge of a crater came nearly to his feet—the result of my first attempt to extract ore. "Try not to control it so much. The tighter you hold on to the magic, the harder it will fight you. It's a part of you. Let it *be* a part of you."

I tried to do as he asked, truly, but as soon as I loosened my grip on the magic, relaxing into it, the fires in my blood leaped forth once more, and the earth started to split, flecks of gold making their way to the surface. Growling in frustration, I cut off my magic entirely, slumping to the ground as I did. The relief from not trying to wield the magic was immediate. I groaned.

"This isn't working," I said, spitting out a mouthful of snow.

"Indeed it is not," Jedrek agreed. He sat on the ground beside me, frowning at the bits of gold lying strewn over the field. "It should be easier for you to do small things rather than large, but the opposite seems to be true."

I looked to Casimir in desperation. He picked his way through debris until he, too, sat on the ground beside me. "I still think that the problem is you fighting to control your magic."

"When I try to relax, I can't hold on to just one side of things. And I certainly can't control where both sides end up." I sat upright, brushing snow from my fur-lined cloak.

"The problem is that your magic is so...odd," Jedrek said. That earned him a glare from Casimir, though I wasn't inclined to disagree. "Don't mistake me, you are extremely powerful. But typically, earth and fire are opposing forces. That you can, and do, use both in equal measure is…Who are your parents? Do you know your lineage?"

I flinched. Somehow, telling the Council of Nobles, the Void Runners, all those people who had been in the initial strategy meeting, about my background was far easier than telling a fellow god. One who might actually understand what it meant. Still, if he could give me answers, help me control things, then so be it.

"I *think* that my mother was Lady Earth," I started. Jedrek sucked in a harsh breath. "And that I was also born of the Eternal Flame."

"That's not possible."

I winced at the certainty in his tone. He sighed.

"I don't mean to contradict you, but Lady Earth hasn't taken a mate since Father Sky was bound to the heavens. And the Eternal Flame? She and her sister feuded constantly. Equal and opposite in power, they rarely agreed on anything."

"I have a memory." I licked my lips, tasting the coolness of snow there. "It's…it's the only one I have. From before waking in this world, I mean. I'm in a cavern. It's warm, barely lit with some sort of fire. There is a woman standing over me. Her skin is like the richest soil and she has flowers in her hair. She is reciting something, like an arcane spell, except…

different. *One part earth, one part the fire beneath, one part stolen light, one part shadow complete. With this touch, life I give, and where once was I, now you remain."*

My words seemed to ring in the clearing for several moments after I had finished speaking. Jedrek had his mouth pressed closed. Casimir just reached out and squeezed my hand, lending his silent support.

"Well?" I prompted. Jedrek winced.

"It's, ah, a recipe."

"A *recipe?*" Casimir sounded indignant.

"Gods have a very particular magic. Theirs is the beginning of all wild magic. They are bound within a particular set of skills, a particular demesne. Mine, for example, is protection, but only of a certain subset of people: the children of Kings. Yours, Calanthe, is earth and fire. Father Sky controls the heavens: storms, wind, day, night. You see?"

I nodded, though I didn't really understand where Jedrek was going with this.

"Right. Well. The thing is, gods like to do things that aren't always within their realm of power. Creating new life is one of those things, yet most of the gods have bred. It's not as simple as, er, coupling. It requires a spell. A recipe."

"Like arcane magic," I supplied. Jedrek let out a slow sigh of relief, shoulders slumping.

"Exactly like arcane magic. Only, instead of relying on symbols and rote spells, they have to have ingredients. A recipe. One part earth, one of fire, one of light, one of shadow. A touch to bestow life, resulting in death. It's...it's a powerful recipe, not one I imagine any but Lady Earth and the Eternal Flame could even manage. The result would be catastrophic."

I reared back, stifling a laugh. "Catastrophic? I can barely manage to pull gold from the ground!"

"I mean no offense. It's just that four different, disparate things had to come together to make you, and they were powerful enough to cause the death of not one but *two* goddesses. Primal goddesses. First goddesses. You are made up of equal and opposite powers. Earth and fire. Light and dark."

"The light and dark vanished when I bound the void beyond this realm," I said, a twinge of guilt fluttering in my chest. That light had belonged to Astraea. And though I might still feel her heartbeat, trapped beneath the surface, I had no idea what sort of state she would be in. If she would even be herself after her light was stolen.

"You may not be able to use them, but they're still within you. They're foundational pieces of you and can't just be removed. Not without killing you. Which, frankly, I'm not even sure is possible to do." Jedrek stood in a rush, pacing away from me. "You're the created offspring of the two most powerful goddesses to exist. You contain *all* of their power, so much so that they no longer exist. I don't think you can die."

"That's encouraging," Casimir said drily, but I caught a gleam in his eye. One that told me a burden had been lifted from his shoulders. One that seemed to remove some of his worry. Had I appeared so weak that he had worried about me constantly? I tried not to consider it, for fear I might discover it true.

Jedrek waved his hand dismissively. "Regardless of that, this means we've been going about this all wrong. It explains why you're having such trouble with your magic. Firstly, it's not done growing. I don't know if it ever will be. Secondly, you can't just cut off one side of you at a time. You are made up of equal pieces, opposite pieces, that will always pull you in different directions. Focus on one and the other becomes stronger. You can use earth and fire at the same time, but individually, there will always be contention."

It sounded to me like he was providing explanations but no answers. "Does that mean I always have to use both magics?" That would be frustrating and unhelpful. No I needed to be able to use one or the other at any given time.

"Sort of." Jedrek fixed me with a wide grin. "How do you feel about becoming ambidextrous?"

His solution was to focus each branch of magic to a specific hand. My left hand already bore the scars of fire, so it would wield the flames. My right hand would control the earth. From there, it was simply a matter of cementing that concept in my mind so firmly that it became instinct.

"Light the torch."

I lifted my hands, only to hiss in annoyance and drop my right hand. The fire leaped willingly to the makeshift torch we'd set up, which was nothing more than a large branch stuck into the ground.

"Good. Now douse it and bring forth a...sapphire."

I closed my eyes and raised both hands, focusing on the flames with the left and trying to call a sapphire with the right. My magic wobbled, the torch flaring bright enough to be a beacon. The ground rumbled, causing Jedrek to stumble. I took a deep breath and closed my eyes again, letting the magic flow in the intended direction. It took a minute, two, but eventually the flames died and a sapphire the size of a pin's head emerged from the soil to float over my palm.

An hour's worth of practising with each hand, and I could barely pull forth something tangible, but I *could* do it.

I beamed at Jedrek and Casimir.

"Well done, Calanthe," Casimir said, approaching. He plucked the tiny sapphire from the air and examined it. "Flawless."

"Tiny," Jedrek scoffed. Then, softening, he put a hand on my shoulder and squeezed gently. "Well done. I've not seen such swift improvement in centuries."

I wanted to preen. To blush and smile. To be proud of my accomplishment, no matter how small it might seem. I even went so far as to open my mouth to express my thanks when the world trembled.

It wasn't anything like an earthquake that shook the trees and buildings. Nor did it seem to make a sound that reverberated through the air. I wasn't even certain that Jedrek and Casimir felt it. I only know that the world trembled, turning my bones to water and my mind to agony. I collapsed to the ground, unable to do more than gasp for breath. My limbs seemed so far away, yet they throbbed in pain. My tongue was impossible to control, yet I babbled, insensate.

"Calanthe?" Casimir was immediately beside me, lifting my head so that it rested on his lap. He looked accusingly at Jedrek, who stared at me with wide-eyed fear.

A moment later and the sensation passed. My babbling stopped. The agony in my head subsided. I could breathe normally once more. I shivered, and not from the cold.

"The door," I rasped. "It opened."

"What?" Jedrek said, barely a breath on the air.

"How many? Do you know? Is it still open?" No longer was Casimir praising me, smiling, acting the lover. Now he was the guardian, the warrior, the Void

Runner. I pressed my palms to my eyes, trying to gather my thoughts.

"It was only open for a moment." Or so it felt. "It's closed again now."

"That's not enough time for more than one to get through," Casimir said, though I couldn't be sure if he was trying to reassure me or himself.

"Don't be so sure." Jedrek was frowning. "Some are quite swift. But yes, I don't think more than one, maybe two, could have made it through that quickly."

"And they had to pass through the void. Devereux gave no indication that he was fending them off, so maybe it was just one, who managed to sneak through?" It was more hope than logic, yet I still thought it might be sound.

"Let's hope so. The scouts that we posted there should be sending a messenger bird." Casimir helped me stand, keeping a hand ready should I wobble. My moment of distress was over, though, and despite feeling tired from the concentrated magic practise, I was fine.

"If they survive," Jedrek said, also moving toward the horses. "If the gods encountered the scouts, then—"

"They were instructed to be well hidden," I snapped. My heart was beating swiftly. The mortals would be fine. Surely. They had volunteered, all of them. Scouts who were well practised in remaining hidden from voidlings, drawn from the Runners and Hunters alike. They knew what they were doing.

"We just need to wait for the messenger bird," Casimir said.

At that, we mounted the horses and rode straight for Altier. After ten minutes of hard galloping, I cursed myself for wanting to be well away from people for practising my magic. What if the god was as swift as Jedrek insinuated? What if they made it to Altier before we could return? No. That was foolish. They would surely come upon us before then. Even so, I leaned closer to my horse's neck, patting it and silently urging the beast faster.

The sun was beyond the horizon by the time we rode to the gate of the palace. Our horses were spent, their sides flecked with foam and their heads drooping from exhaustion. The stable hands looked at us in consternation, only to freeze when they saw our expressions. The young boy who took the reins of my horse gulped audibly.

"Lady?" he asked. "Is everything...it's going to be alright, isn't it?"

Stars above, he was just a child, yet the fear I saw on his face was so all-encompassing that I knew it would shake him to the very core. He would never be the same for having felt this fear. I smiled and put my hand to his shoulder.

"It will be well," I promised, and I was surprised to find that I meant it. I couldn't possibly know, but for the sake of this child and so many others, I would swear to it.

The boy staggered as if I had struck him, then bowed deeply. His eyes, when he looked up, shone with some sort of light that had not been there before. Then, he took the horse and was gone. I wanted to run inside, demand any news, but I faltered.

"It's dangerous to give blessings to mortals like that," Jedrek murmured.

"Is that what I did?"

He blinked. "You've never done it before?"

I shook my head, cradling my hands close to my chest. "I've only ever wielded magic. Not...blessings. Not answered prayers. Nothing like that."

Jedrek let out a long breath and ran a hand through his hair. "I forget how *young* you are. Yes, Calanthe, that was a blessing. You gave a mortal a tiny splinter of your essence. It will grow back for you, but for him, it will...influence his life. He might become a great warrior. Or a leader. Or he might simply become the most successful tamer or horses. Either way, with a god's essence, mortals are always destined for greatness. Where do you think heroes come from?"

I winced at that. Tali had, on our journey to Ynys-fawr, told me many stories of heroes. I'd thought the tales outlandish, sometimes frightening, but rarely had I thought them to be fact. A fictionalised account of some long-ago event, perhaps, but nothing more than that. Now I was responsible for the creation of another of those stories.

"Should I take it back?" I asked hurriedly. Jedrek shook his head.

"No. The essence is a part of him now. You could remove it, but he would be diminished. Some heroes who fell out of favour with their patrons went insane when their blessing was removed. Leave it. We could maybe use a hero these days."

"Have you ever blessed someone?" *Had it turned out alright?*

"Once. I was at the height of my power. I blessed a governess to the princess. She went on to teach two more generations."

"That's not so bad. Right?"

Jedrek gave a quiet shake of his head. "Her influence became so great that she inadvertently brought about policy change that kept the monarchy in tyrannical power for nearly fifty years. But they don't all end that way. I promise."

I watched the spot where the boy had disappeared and wished that I could undo it. Wished that I could have at least asked his name before I changed his life so thoroughly. Guilt tightened around my throat. I swallowed it back before jogging into the palace after Casimir, who had already gone inside to seek news. Jedrek followed after me, sparing me no more than a sympathetic look.

CHAPTER 16

Despite our frenzied pace back to the palace, the messenger bird didn't arrive until nearly dawn. It was a pigeon, ragged and weary, but the message attached to its claw was whole, despite the night flying. The entire strategy council, including Tali, Temys, Lionel and Rietta from Craigsmuir, two others from Amontys, as well as Garwith, Ilar, Raya, and most of the Council of Nobles, was waiting with bated breath while the clerk unrolled the message and read out the encoded symbols.

"One came through. Female. Dark skin. Gold tattoos. Bearing a spear. Were not seen. Door secure."

As one, we all relaxed slightly. Jedrek frowned, but said nothing. His identity as a god was still unknown to the rest of the people; he wanted to keep quiet in case some conspired against him. The slight shake of his head could have been an indication that he didn't know who this was, or that it wasn't good.

Temys shuffled some of her papers and consulted with Tali, who shook her head and pointed to a different passage. Finally, the older *dharangui* nodded. "We think it is Myr. Goddess of the hunt. She is old, one of the more powerful beings."

"Well?" Raya asked, leaning on the table. "Is that good for us? Could she be an ally?"

Tali rubbed the stump of her lost arm absently, face furrowed in a frown. "Frankly, the stories surrounding her are not good. She...is fond of traps, of catching mortals in them and then letting them go, only to hunt them down for sport. She functioned as the patroness of hunters, but if they didn't pay proper respect, or weren't successful enough in their hunts, or even acted slightly contrary to her whims, then they could easily become her prey."

"So, not likely to be an ally," Ilar said. Tali shook her head. "Well, then we'll have to catch her. Face her."

"And how would you suggest doing that?" Jedrek drawled, sounding ever the arrogant prince. "If this goddess is as you say, then any trap we might lay would be obvious to her."

"Not necessarily." Temys sniffed, lifting her chin. "The gods have been gone from this world a long time. She might be over eager to settle back in. Might be susceptible to being caught."

"Lady Calanthe?" Raya asked expectantly. "Any thoughts?"

Meaning, of course, that I was to provide a solution immediately, seeing as I had stormed in here and declared that we were at war with the gods of the past. I wanted to pinch the bridge of my nose, to take several deep breaths, to pace around the room, anything to try and soothe the myriad of thoughts in my head. Instead, I sat calmly, my shoulders squared, and tried to run through the potential ramifications of any ideas.

Eventually, I sighed and shook my head. "The fact of the matter is, if we ambush Myr, if we catch her and then demand that she cooperate with our dictates—that is, the protection of the mortals of this realm—then I doubt very much she will agree. We must offer her the option to comply willingly."

"And do you plan on doing this with every god who steps through that door?" one of the Council asked, curling his lip at me. "Pretty please, don't harm the defenceless creatures you see before you."

Casimir snorted. "Hardly. We present our argument to those who step through first, then if—when—they refuse, we prove that we are not without teeth. Eventually, the message will disseminate and we will face less opposition."

How I desperately wanted to believe in his idea of events.

"Or—" Ilar looked at me with sympathy. "—we will find ourself facing a battle that will determine the fate of this world."

That, I feared, would be the more likely option.

"I still say we try and catch Myr," Temys said.

"I would agree," Raya said. She looked at me with all the sharpness of steel. "Any solution that ends the risk to mortal lives sooner is one worth pursuing."

Insinuating that if I left things until I could confront Myr personally, people would be at her mercy.

"You're not wrong," I murmured. "Leaving Myr to wander freely is dangerous. But even setting a trap would take time. I propose...I propose that I ride out with a hundred warriors. That will leave you with plenty, as well as time to gather more allies from the other countries of Adhor, those who have farther to travel. We still await news of Craigsmuir, and Prince Jedrek assures me that those beyond Amontys are on their way."

"A hundred warriors?" Raya scoffed. "That is a large portion of our ready fighting force, or had you forgotten that Baldarskiel has had no standing army since before the void fell upon us."

"A hundred seems reasonable to me," Garwith said. "The Lady Calanthe brought that many in Hunters alone when she returned to Altier. We have more than that in Runners, and volunteers from the city, as well as the Black Riders of Amontys."

The queen said nothing, a muscle ticking in her jaw. She tapped a finger on the table. Then, as if it were a struggle. "Very well. Prepare. You will ride on the morrow."

She swept from the room with her head held high and frustrated murmurs at her back. Ilar nearly rose from his chair as he glared at the queen's back. "As if *she* could think to command you, my lady," he snarled.

"Be at peace, Ilar. I take no offense." Frankly, I was grateful someone even had the strength to try and lead without my input. I was still unused to all the people looking at me with awe and expectation, wanting me to guide them. Lead them. "Let's go prepare. It's been a long night of waiting, and we have supplies and people to gather. Oh...and before you go, there's a stable hand. I would like him to come as a message runner, should we need to communicate with those who remain. You'll know him when you find him."

I had no doubt that he would, too. Now that he had my blessing on his shoulders. Jedrek fixed a steady gaze on me and raised his brows. I turned my head away from the unasked question.

"Let's get some food and then rest a bit," Casimir suggested, putting his frame between Jedrek and myself. "You're surely tired from all the magic of yesterday, as well as waiting last night."

I was tired. Desperately so. I allowed myself to be led from the hall and away.

*

Dawn came too soon. Gathering supplies for a hundred warriors, all of us on horseback, was no small feat. Thankfully, the Void Runners and Hunters had been preparing for such an eventuality, putting together as many packs as they could for quick movement. The people seemed so many, waiting for me on the edge of Altier, dressed in various armours and with various states of nervousness. I spotted Eloise and the stable hand mingling amongst the crowd and wondered if I had made a terrible mistake. They both seemed so young.

Jedrek remained with his Black Riders while the rest of us formed ranks. Casimir and Ilar did most of the organising, everyone—including myself—taking orders from them. Just as we were about to leave, though, a rider on a scruffy horse raced towards us, looking unsteady in the saddle. As the rider drew closer, I recognised Tali.

"That's twice you've tried to leave me behind," she panted as she came to a stop beside my own horse. She was dressed for bear, with borrowed armour and a short sword at her side. More than that, though, she looked as though she would fall from her mount at any moment. Her hand was weak and shaky, there was a slight sheen of sweat on her brow.

"You shouldn't be here," I hissed to her, careful not to talk too loudly. She didn't need the entire force to hear our conversation.

"This is exactly where I should be. Or have you forgotten what I am? I need to be there to keep this story for the future." Tali glared at me, a hint of uncertainty in the hunch of her shoulders.

"You have barely been out of the infirmary for a week!" I snapped. "You can hardly hold on to the reins of your horse and—"

"And what? I have only one arm? Therefore I will be useless in a fight?" Tali scoffed darkly.

"No." I turned my horse so I was closer, close enough to whisper to her. "I don't care about whether you have one arm, though if you cannot fight then you had better stay back. No, I was going to say that I have already lost so much in Dancer and Whisper and Devereux...and you have been burdened beyond compare. I...I couldn't bear to see you hurt. Selfish though it might be."

Tali's expression softened. She graced me with a smile, though the cheer of it did not reach her eyes. "Calanthe, no. I'll be fine. I'm *grateful* that you worry for me. Do not think yourself selfish for it. Regardless, I will be accompanying you. It is my duty, and I think you understand that."

I recalled Temys's scornful looks, her derisive

comments that I had shirked my duty because I hadn't been answering any prayers, because I didn't want anyone's prayers. Tali, though, was before me now, claiming duty as her motivator, and I wasn't sure whether to smile and nod or turn away. I settled for moving my horse into position, Tali's steed easily slipping in beside me.

"Ready?" Casimir asked as he rode up. He tilted his head at me, brows furrowing in Tali's direction. I shook my head and gave a shrug. He nodded. "Everyone is prepared if you are."

"I am as prepared as I can be, I think," I murmured, half to myself. To the rest of the warriors who followed me so willingly, so easily, I raised my hand in the air and gave the shouted command to move out. The march began.

My knowledge of organised battle—disregarding my experience with the voidlings and bandits—was limited only to stories told to me by Tali, and a few that came from Casimir's tongue. They were swiftly spoken and swiftly over, the events supposedly happening so quickly that even days' long affairs were simmered down to mere minutes. None of these stories could possibly have prepared me for the sheer frustration of marching into the unknown.

Time dragged by, wearing on everyone's nerves. At first, there was excitement. Anticipation. The knowledge—or at least, the hope—that we were moving towards a worthy goal. Then came the realisation that we wouldn't meet this Myr immediately, or even likely within the day. It would take time to find her, time to even figure out where she had been. And in that time, we had to manage the needs of a hundred people and a hundred horses. We stopped at midday for food and rest, and already, I could see fracture lines forming between groups. Hunters and Void Runners and Black Riders all started mingling with their own people. The easy camaraderie we'd had that morning was waning. The longer we moved without progress, though, the more people's conversations bore an edge of fear.

After the second day of riding, everyone was starting to get fidgety. Casimir had already diffused several arguments over such things as who was taking care of the horses, who was responsible for cooking, who got the better campsite. By the time he came to sit beside me at the campfire, he was scowling and the sky was completely dark.

"I would have helped," I said, handing him a bowl of soup.

"As much as I appreciate the thought, these people are already under pressure. To have their goddess see them in less than ideal circumstances— arguing, complaining—would only have made them more upset."

"Their goddess." The words felt like ash on my tongue. I shook my head; now was not the time to argue semantics, not when I knew that I was technically leading this charge. Instead, I changed the subject. "Why is everyone so upset? I don't remember travelling with the Hunters being so difficult."

"That's because we Hunters know what we're about," Ilar said around a mouthful of soup. Casimir scoffed.

"It's because we're travelling with warriors who are unused to fighting with each other, to head off a goddess that had all but been forgotten. A power beyond comprehension. And the only thing keeping them from panicking entirely is the fact that we have a goddess of our own."

Maybe I should just go to bed instead of trying to converse. I didn't really want to discuss everyone's expectations for me. The rest of the evening was spent in terse silence, one that spread across the camp. Eventually, all but the people on watch fell into a fitful sleep, including myself, with the hope that things would be different tomorrow weaving through our dreams.

The first warriors disappeared just before dawn.

The cry of alarm came when a young Runner—this was her first mission—got up to relieve herself and found that the entirety of the last watch was missing. A total of seven warriors had disappeared, and despite the efforts of best trackers of Ilar's people, and the most experienced Runners, no trace of them was found.

The camp was abuzz with movement. People strapped on armour that had only been loosely worn the day before. Fires and tents were packed faster than I'd ever seen, and despite the chill and the snow, few donned their fur-lined cloaks, in case fighting became an immediate need. I did my best to keep everyone calm, relaying Casimir's suggestions—orders—in as soothing a voice as possible. He thought that it would be better coming from me, and given the relief on people's faces as I gave them tasks, it would seem he was right.

Again.

We didn't move from our spot until nearly midday, and even then it was only to venture forth in well-organised groups to see if any sign of Myr could be found. We saw no tracks, found no obvious signs of her passage, but given how jittery Jedrek was, how alert Casimir remained despite finding nothing, I had no doubt she was nearby.

Once my powers developed more, I wondered if I would be able to sense other gods. I certainly wished for it then, ducking through the twisted, scraggly trees and brush that made up this part of the country. I wished for a clear path, for land that did not squelch under my boots, having not yet frozen through, despite the snow. I wished for my bed back in the palace, though I think that was more a desire to be well away from the problems of this place than anything. I wished for Devereux to talk with, Dancer to hunt with. I wished for—

A woman's scream broke out, echoing across the hills. I froze. Casimir cursed, then drew his sword. "This way!"

In an instant, he was off, haring across the hills with speed that wasn't quite human. Jedrek was close in his wake, leaving Ilar and me staring after them. I grimaced at the Hunter. "Shall we?"

"Indeed," he said, patting the handle of his battle axe. "Let's go kill ourselves a god."

We ran after Casimir and Jedrek. My magic seemed as eager to be doing something as I was, so I smoothed out the ground as we ran, trying to make it easier to move through the uneven bracken and grasses. The earth eagerly raced to meet my steps and fire danced at the tips of my burned fingers. Soon, Ilar was falling behind, keeping just ahead of the other warriors. My feet were fleet, my steps sure, as I ducked into the divot between two hills where Casimir had vanished but moments ago.

Before I could get a good glimpse of my surroundings, a knife blurred through the air towards my head. I ducked ungracefully and the earth rose up to steady me. The knife sank into the trunk of a tree just beyond my shoulder. The owner of the knife let out a dark chuckle as I turned to face her.

"Well, well, what have we here?" she purred.

Myr was, in a word, beautiful. Her dark skin was

glossy and unblemished. Her features were sharp enough to be predatory and soft enough to invite the eye. Her hair was cropped close to her head and she bore a colourful band across her brow. She wore furs of animals I had never seen, nor considered. She had an unstrung bow in one hand and another knife in the other. A hunter, indeed. I wondered if she had missed on purpose, or if I had just been supremely lucky in avoiding that knife.

Casimir and Jedrek faced Myr, swords raised. Shadows writhed over Casimir's skin, and I could have sworn that Jedrek's eyes shimmered with golden power. More concerning, though, was what lay just behind Myr. What had produced the scream.

"Beatrice," I ground out.

"Is that its name?" Myr asked, flashing teeth that were filed to points. She gave Beatrice a kick and the princess whimpered. Her foot was caught in a snare, one likely meant for one of my warriors as we hunted Myr. She wore a dull green, ill-fitting dress, likely pilfered from an unsuspecting servant. Her hair was bound in a braid and she had a bow in her hand, though the arrows were scattered everywhere. With Myr so close, none of us could strike the goddess without harming Beatrice.

"What an interesting day this has turned out to be. Did you know that I found a door in the middle of an island? A fascinating door, one that didn't exist a short while ago. But I felt it when that door was created. We all did." Myr shifted her grip on her knife. Casimir's shadows grew more agitated, spilling onto the ground around him. Jedrek stayed perfectly still, blade poised to attack.

"I am aware of the door," I said.

Myr inhaled deeply, her eyes fluttering closed. She let out the breath in a long laugh. "You have such an *intriguing* scent. Scorched earth and ancient trees. Shadows and starlight. What are you? Who are you?"

"You don't know?" Jedrek asked. The surprise in his voice was cutting, cruel, false.

"I didn't ask you, little god. Leave this place and I won't skin you alive." With a flick of her wrist, the knife flew from Myr's hand and landed squarely in Jedrek's shoulder. He let out a grunt of pain, his sword arm collapsing with the blow. Casimir took a step to the side, putting himself in front of me.

"You should bow," Jedrek rasped, drawing a growl from Myr. "You face the daughter of Lady Earth, the daughter of the Eternal Flame. You face their daughter, and their killer. Calanthe, Wielder of Creation and Destruction in equal measure. Queen of the gods."

I nearly staggered back at Jedrek's words. They pierced me almost as surely as that knife would have, opening up a wound I didn't know I had. I screamed silently in denial, yet could do nothing to argue against the accusation. Daughter and killer, yes. But *queen*? Surely not.

"Bow," Jedrek snarled. He pulled the knife from his shoulder, golden blood dripping down the blade. Behind me, I heard the movement of my warriors, humans come to face down a being that was so terrible, so much more powerful than them.

Myr curled her lip. She stepped back, deliberately placing her foot on the snare around Beatrice's ankle. Beatrice screamed again. Her eyes rolled with pain and her hands spasmed.

"I don't think so," Myr said, leaning over Beatrice. She dipped her fingers in the blood around Beatrice's ankle, then brought them to her mouth, licking up the drops. A light kindled in her eyes, one of pleasure. Rapture. "I think I would much rather *be* queen than bow to one."

Casimir didn't hesitate. He leapt forwards with a snarl on his lips and the shadows of the void in his wake. He'd been a guardian, a fighter, for more centuries than I knew, yet he barely managed to slice through some of the furs on Myr's chest before she had shoved him back, drawn and strung her bow, and nocked an arrow. It pointed directly at his heart.

"Don't interfere, star fodder," she said with a wicked grin.

She released the arrow just as I released my magic.

CHAPTER 17

The arrow flew true, but my fire was the faster. A spear of flame so bright as to be blinding engulfed the arrow, rendering it to ash. Casimir avoided the flames and raised his sword again, shadows dancing along the edge. Jedrek, now healed, picked his sword up off the ground. The humans at my back let out a roar.

Myr just smiled wider.

Jedrek had been right about dancing. It was the perfect way for me to gain control over my body, to be able to use my limbs to their best ability. It was also an effective means of funnelling my magic. Because when Myr drew another arrow, I lifted my arms to direct my magic at her. And together, we started dancing.

It was clumsy at first, her firing as I used earth to pin her shoes down, to cast her off balance. Fire ate through each arrow she aimed in my direction. With Beatrice so close, with Casimir and Jedrek at my side, the human warriors at my back, it was difficult to move properly, to give in to the raging, massive magic that could level mountains. I wanted to smother her in the ground, bury her until dirt filled her lungs. I wanted to burn her limbs from her body. I wanted her to pay for threatening what was mine.

A knife flew from behind me, landing a solid blow to Myr's abdomen. She grunted and bared her teeth at whoever had thrown it. Some sort of barrier broke, then, because the humans no longer stood back. They surged forwards, pressing close enough to Myr that she couldn't use her bow effectively. They swung with sword and knife and shield, countering her own rapid-fire blows.

It was nearly a hundred people against one. It should have been over so quickly. But they were human and Myr was a god. In attacking her outright, the warriors—*my* warriors—had invited their death knell. Every blow to Myr drew golden droplets of blood that hissed on the ground as they fell. Every blow signalled the death of a human, her fists breaking sternums, her hands crushing throats, her knives disembowelling. Bodies of the injured and dead piled up, their moans and gasps a symphony that should never have been played.

Myr bled, yes, but she also healed. She was so much stronger than the humans, so much faster.

What's more, she seemed to delight in the violence. The human blood that ran down her arms only made her fight harder. The cuts and slices she earned made her toss her head back and laugh.

Jedrek and Casimir tried to restore order, tried to push their way through the waves of humans that bore down on the once-forgotten god, but they made little progress. They couldn't do much without hurting their own, and the humans were taking their chance to fight for their future.

I, too, tried to push forwards. My magic had a long reach, but I couldn't react fast enough. More than one human was accidentally burned by my flames before I pulled back and reined them in. If I didn't do something now, something soon, then this would be a massacre and Myr would escape. I couldn't allow that.

A hand on my arm startled me. It was the stable boy, dressed in armour that barely fit him, the makeshift banner of our forces held tightly in one hand. On the other arm, he bore a round shield, big enough that he could barely lift it. It was with this trembling hand that he touched me. He smiled up at me.

"Don't worry, my lady," he said, beaming with the glow of my blessing. "Let me."

Before I could stop him, he turned from me, lowered the banner like a lance, raised the shield, and charged. As if by magic, Hunters and Runners and

Black Riders all moved from his path. A yell, full of youthful optimism and determination, rang from his throat. The stable hand, the one I'd inadvertently blessed, charged straight for Myr. She didn't move fast enough, the banner impaling her with impossible ease.

Rivulets of golden blood pooled at the corner of her mouth. It should have been done. It should have been complete. The stable hand—whose name I didn't even know—should have been able to ride home victorious, the hero of the day. Instead, Myr grinned a bloody grin, broke the banner in the centre, pulled the ends out of her middle, and with her entrails exposed, she lashed out and grabbed the stable hand by that round shield. With a wrench, she dislocated his shoulder. He cried out, a sound that was cut short as Myr wrapped her fingers around his throat and squeezed.

The only sound on the battlefield then was the unmistakable crunch of the boy's spine being shattered into a thousand pieces.

In one blow, my blessing was snuffed out.

"No," I breathed. My heart pounded so fast and I could barely get enough air. "No more. Not one more."

Myr looked directly at me as I spoke, and for the first time, I caught a glimmer of fear in her eyes. Then, it didn't matter what I saw in her eyes, because I bent the world to my whims.

A tidal wave of earth speared towards Myr, pushing my warriors aside with little worry about any potential injuries. She staggered back, already pressing her innards back in, the skin knitting together before my eyes. She tried to run, but it was too late for her. The earth split and she fell, landing on shards of rock that were enough to break bones. I moved for her, then, fire blooming around me like the petals of a flower. In what felt like a single bound, I landed beside her, the earth rippling where I stood.

"M-majesty," Myr said, holding up her hands. Her bow had snapped in the fall and her knives were strewn about the divot in the ground. Her blood spilled freely, the earth drinking it up, absorbing her power. Lending it to me.

"This world is under my protection," I said, reaching out with my fire to caress Myr's face. She screamed as her skin bubbled, golden blisters bursting.

Panting, she tried to prostrate herself. Tried to bow. "Of course, Majesty. You have my sincerest apologies. I never should have doubted your power. I never should have doubted your heritage. I will do whatever you demand to prove my loyalty. I will—"

"What must I do to tell the other gods, those who have not yet come through the door, of this fact?" I knelt before Myr, the heat of my flames making her shy away as much as she could manage. Vines burst from the ground and wrapped around her limbs, lashing her in place. She made a sound in the back of her throat, a whimper. Before this battle, maybe I would have capitulated at that sound. Shown mercy. But she killed that stable hand—a *child*—with genuine pleasure.

Mercy was no longer an option.

"I don't...that is, maybe I could tell them. Maybe I could...er...with your benevolent permission of course, go and be your messenger?" Myr was pleading, now, eyes darting about as if searching for any escape. But as a goddess of the hunt, she should have known when she was caught in a trap. My trap.

"A messenger?" My flames grew brighter, glowing white-hot. Burns started blistering on her arms, neck, her face, almost matching my own. I knew precisely how painful they were, and yet I did not wish to pull back. Maybe it was the magic compelling me, the power in my veins singing an enthralling song. Or maybe I had reached my limit and I was done with doubting myself, doubting the path I'd chosen. Maybe, even, it was the gaping hole that the death that day had carved.

Myr licked her cracked lips, wincing with the pain, though she was already healing. Already looking at me with relief. I raised my right hand and called forth the obsidian in the earth, formed by the pressure of my fire, of the fire beneath the surface. It came to me without hesitation, forming the shape I wanted without qualm. By the time Myr realised what I was doing, it was too late.

The obsidian knife cut through her neck with ease.

I took hold of her head by the short hair, struggling to get a good grip. Her body went limp, her golden blood draining to the ground. There would be no healing from that, no return from that. I looked at the head. "A messenger indeed," I hissed. "Your head will lay before the door on Ynysfawr to serve as a warning. This world is not unprotected."

A raucous cheer went up, splitting the sky. Startled, I nearly dropped the head, even as Jedrek took it from me, expression grim. He nodded, once. That was all. That was enough. It was over.

The human warriors, what remained of them, were streaked with blood more red than gold. But they cheered, raising their weapons to the sky, proclaiming victory for all to hear. My fires dimmed. The earth smoothed over. Weariness set in.

"I'm here," Casimir breathed in my ear, wrapping his arm around mine before I realised that I was about to fall. "You did it."

I said nothing at all, not as I was led from the crater in the ground, not as I was led past the bodies that were already being collected, not as I was led past the wounded who saw to their own injuries or helped others as best they could. For the remainder of the day, I found myself unable to say anything at all. People came up to me and bowed hesitantly, but all I could manage was a small smile. Camp was set up not far from the battlefield, the mood much more celebratory than the night before. The food was better, the voices brighter, the arguments fewer.

And still, I sat there, feeling the bite of my blade through the skin and bone of Myr. A fellow goddess. Yes, she'd killed those I'd sworn to protect. I didn't regret her death, not when I hoped it would prevent future ones. But some part of me wondered if it was cruel to expect the other gods to conform to a world that had long since left them behind. If they would be better off remaining where they were. That wasn't up to me, though. The door was there, for good or ill.

"I'm sorry about the boy." Jedrek sank to the ground beside me, holding out a bowl of stew. "The one you blessed."

I jerked, looking about instinctively for Casimir. He was across the camp, talking and smiling with some of the Runners and Hunters. Even as I spotted him, he turned to look at me, ready to instantly come to my side. I shook my head and dug into the stew, despite having no appetite.

"I didn't even know his name," I said, swallowing down the mouthful. "I thought blessings were supposed to help. Supposed to give them the power to be great."

"And he was. His was the only blow that did damage beyond a scratch."

"He died so easily." My throat was too tight to try and force down any more food. "They all died so easily."

"It's not your fault," Jedrek said. He sounded so desperately weary. "It would almost be easier if it were. Trust me, I know. But this battle, this war between the mortals and the gods, it's been building for a long time. The star's intervention only delayed it. The fact of the matter is that the mortals are not meant to be yoked to anyone but themselves. And even those we bless are not immortal."

I heard the words he wasn't saying. *Maybe they were always the first to die.* It was why he seemed so distressed when I first blessed the boy. It was why he hadn't done it for so long. Why he had looked at me with such sadness.

"Does it ever get easier?" I asked, poking at the stew with my spoon. "Watching the mortals die when you have immortality stretching before you?"

"I used to scoff at the weak, fragile humans. Their lives were nothing but a dream to me. One moment there, then snuffed out like a candle. But in those brief lives, do you know what they achieve? They create music. They tell stories that last for generations. They craft beautiful cities. They establish justice. They build societies that stretch beyond the memory of the gods. They forge bonds between each other that are nearly unbreakable. They love so deeply and they hurt loudly enough to rattle the skies. They rail against the inevitability of death every day, but they also live such full, magnificent lives. Even the weakest, the sickest, the humblest of them strive to live." Jedrek sighed, laying flat on the ground and staring at the expanse of stars twinkling coldly above us.

"Gods, though…They get stuck in their ways. They expect a thing to always remain true and cannot understand why it changed. They do not feel as deeply about others because there is no need. Time stretches onwards, forever, so why spare your passion now? Yet they—*we*—watch the humans living remarkable lives around us, and we want that. Desperately. So desperately that it hurts. That's why some demand worship. Devotion. Because that desperation is not selfless at all."

Around us, people laughed and talked, the sadness of the day already transformed into celebration. The dead would be honoured when we returned to Altier, but for those who had survived, those who had lived, they wasted no time at all. Casimir moved among them, a beacon in his ivory Runner armour. At some fires he stopped and talked. At others, he just slapped a few shoulders and moved on. All things that maybe I should be doing, yet couldn't. Not when they stared at me with such open devotion, admiration. Hope.

"I think you are different, though," Jedrek said, making me jump. He was still laying flat, but he had his head propped in his hand as he watched me, a slight frown marring his features. "I've never met a god so...mortal. Even the young ones have all been missing something. Even me, though it pains me to admit it. But you, Calanthe, you seem to feel things as deeply as the humans. You love passionately. You hurt deeply. You care for the nameless boy whose death might have saved everyone here. I've never seen that from a god before."

Anxiety fluttered in my belly. Nausea rolled over me. I thrust the stew aside and rose. "I think I need some space," I gasped, and staggered away. Jedrek remained behind as I slipped into the night.

I had thought to go to the place where Myr's body remained. No one had been brave enough to try and cart it off with the rest of our honoured dead. Ilar had gone so far as to spit on the corpse, condemning her to rot there forever. But as I drew closer, I couldn't even bring myself to look on the results of the day. I wrapped my arms tightly around myself and turned in a different direction. I turned towards the wounded.

This part of the camp was considerably quieter than the rest, with the injured mostly sleeping or laying quietly while they succumbed to their wounds. There weren't many fatally injured, for which I was grateful. Apparently the crush of humans had been as much a detriment to Myr as it had been to me, since most of the injuries seemed superficial. The ones who were awake brightened as I approached, reaching out for me. I smiled at them as sincerely as I could, but I did not touch for fear I would accidentally bestow my blessing again. I wasn't sure I could bear that.

One bedroll was arranged slightly farther away from the others, a small fire illuminating its occupant as she glared into the fire, furs wrapped around her shoulders. At my approach, Beatrice winced, drawing her wounded leg beneath her. "I'll not thank you for saving my life," she snapped. There was so much hurt in her voice, so much anger. "I would not owe you anything."

"You don't owe me, Beatrice," I said. "Though I am curious as to what you were doing there."

She curled her lip and flinched away when I sat on the other side of the fire. She fiddled with her dress, running the fabric through her fingers. Finally, she blurted, "I'm not beholden to you. I don't need to tell you of my movements. I can go out if I want."

"All of this is true. And I don't care to pretend that we ever were friends. But I imagine your mother is worried. Your father. Not to mention that you managed to get caught in the clutches of a god who was more than happy to skin you like some prize catch."

Beatrice, once a proud High Priestess who was always composed, always standing with shoulders back and chin high, always prepared with a plan or a comment, hunched in on herself. Her stolen dress was torn and bloody. Her hair was a mess. Her skin, gold like Devereux's had been before the void claimed him, was streaked with dirt. She looked horrible. It was the emptiness in her eyes, the despair, that struck me, though.

"I thought," Beatrice said at last, "that maybe I could find...purpose again as the High Priestess of a different god. You do not want me, and the Temple of the Fallen Star is all but dust. I've been reviled for worshipping a star, when everyone else worshipped her, too. Maybe...maybe I wasn't the kindest or most forgiving, but I was a *good* High Priestess. Now what am I? I cannot inherit my family's throne because of what I was. My brother was meant to take that role, but he turned aside. So who will inherit it, now? My mother says—"

Beatrice shook her head, clenching her hands in her lap.

"My mother says not to worry about it, that a purpose will come, but I know the fate of royalty without rights to inherit, and I will not be relegated to a loveless marriage."

Like the marriage that she and her mother had once tried to foist on me with Devereux? The former prince and I were friends, certainly, but nothing more; the scheme had quickly fallen apart. Still, I understood Beatrice's fear. She had less power than I had, less choice. Her path would not be easy to forge, certainly not with her family's resources lost to her.

"We can find something for you," I said, not sure

if it was a promise or just an attempt at comforting words. "There's no reason for you to marry unless you wish to do so."

Beatrice scoffed. She tossed a stick into the fire, watching it catch, then burn. "You made it quite plain that you want nothing to do with me as your High Priestess. And as I've learned, the other gods are crueller even than you, though they don't hide it behind pretty smiles."

I recoiled. Anger had the fire flaring, making both Beatrice and I lean away. I closed my eyes and controlled my magic, though it was an effort. When I opened my eyes, Beatrice was sneering at me, daring me to push further. "I will have no temple, no priesthood. Ever. Neither you nor anyone else will speak for me when I am perfectly capable of speaking for myself."

"And your worshippers?" Beatrice asked.

I wanted none of them, either. Though, at this point, I doubted I could escape that fate. "A thought to take under serious consideration when we are not facing a war."

"There will always be a crisis. You're just too cowardly to take what is yours, to make it something great." Beatrice pulled the furs closer, hunching her shoulders and holding her hands close to the fire. A fairly clear indication that this conversation was over. Fine. But I would take the last word, this time.

"Your ambition will get you into trouble, Beatrice.

You don't desire a purpose, you desire power. Power over others, power to tell people how to think, how to act. You want people looking to you, begging for your direction. You want accolades singing your name. But power is dangerous, and the pursuit of power even more so. If you do not abandon it, I fear it will be your end." I stood, brushing off dirt and snow. Beatrice glared up at me.

"Will you be the one to end me?" she asked as I turned away. I froze.

"If it is necessary, then yes." I walked away.

CHAPTER 18

"You need to see this." Casimir's voice woke me from a sleep that was far deeper than I ever expected, given the events of the day before. He barely gave me time to blink blearily and wrap my cloak tighter around me before pulling me up by the hand. We snuck through the camp—most were still sleeping off their exhaustion—and one of the pre-dawn watch nodded at us.

"Where are we going?" I whispered after we were far enough away from the camp. Jedrek waited for the two of us at the divide in the hills where the battle had taken place. Fresh snow had fallen, a scattering of white that completely obliterated any sign of battle. Except...

I raised my left hand, wreathing it in fire like a torch. A second thought had flame surging forwards, melting the snow to reveal the remnants of the day before.

"Empty night," I breathed.

Myr's head was in a bag at the camp, guarded over by Ilar and Rietta and several others. I'd protested, but they insisted. No one had bothered with her body, though, content to let it rot in the wilderness. Only, it hadn't rotted. It had skeletonised over night. Where skin and blood had once been, now only bleached white skeleton remained. The ground around the body was pocked, as though acid had dropped on it, and I could have sworn that I saw the beginnings of green peeking through the soil, despite it being winter. When I reached out with my earth magic, there was such an abundance of life—of power —that I nearly staggered back.

"What happened?" I asked.

"I thought scavengers at first," Casimir said grimly, kicking at the dirt with his boot, revealing a toadstool that was already growing larger. "There are reports of animals moving into the area that the humans abandoned and have yet to reclaim. With the voidlings gone, there is a surprising amount of life that chose to return. It would make sense that foxes or wolves or vultures or something would have got to her corpse. But—" He looked at me, obviously perturbed. "There are no bite marks. No tracks. Nothing."

Jedrek shifted back, shaking his head. "Frankly, I

don't know what to make of it. There is certainly power in god blood and god bones, but wielding it, extracting it, is nearly impossible, even for other gods. Their power ends when they are killed, rare as that might be. This? This is something else entirely. It's like her power leeched into the ground."

As it had done during our fight. When her magic flowed into mine. Did that mean I now possessed Myr's magic? Was I bound to the hunt as well as fire and earth? When I reached for any new, mysterious power that might have been bestowed on me, there was thankfully nothing. Still, something about the place unnerved me.

"I'll seal this grove off," I said, already raising my hand to do just that. The earth rumbled, walls of solid granite forming around the body and the pocket of magically charged earth. "If people learn of this, the plants there, the magic, then there's no telling what will happen."

"A graveyard of the gods," Casimir said, shaking his head. "It would be plundered in an instant. Talismans and relics spread across Adhor, claiming to hold the power of a god. Who knows what the actual effects might be."

Bad, surely. It was the sort of thing that people like Beatrice would happily use to their advantage. It was better to seal it away, far from the prying eyes of mortals. I turned my back to the granite-sealed tomb and shivered. A whisper floated to me on the wind, words flowing together, a prophecy, a taunt of the future. Yes, there was surely too much power in the bones of a dead god.

I twined my fingers with Casimir's and we went back to camp. Though I never once looked back, I could feel the watchful, eager magic of those bones focusing on my back long after we rode away from camp.

The head of Myr I sent away with three riders as soon as I could, sending it to Ynysfawr to serve as a warning. I felt its presence, too, though I did not mention it to Casimir or Jedrek.

✦

✦

Altier looked much like we had left it, but in our week's absence, it turned out that many things had changed. For one, the fleet from Craigsmuir had arrived.

Led by Captain Kina, who had been granted leadership over the war fleet, nearly twenty ships were anchored off shore. Boats carrying crew and supplies passed between shore and ship every day. There was not enough accommodation in town to even consider quartering everyone. The palace was quickly overrun with officers, and the throne room was now a constant area of activity, strategy and politics and diplomacy discussions going at all hours.

More than the Craigsmuirians, a veritable caravan of people had begun to arrive from the rest of Adhor, beginning with people from Great Ashmar, Llyn Rhosalwyd, Mellaig and more. Some had sent warriors, other had sent diplomats and courtiers. All learned of our battle with Myr almost immediately upon our return.

Barely had we made it to the courtyard of the palace before I could hear the gossip of the servants, guards, soldiers, Runners, Hunters, more. They stared blatantly at those who had gone with us, and more than a few eyes landed on me. I kept hearing "Burned One" whispered in reverent tones, but whenever I turned to see who had spoken, people looked away. My neck prickled. This had to be contained.

"Tali," I said, grabbing her arm before she could go to her grandmother and relay the official account. "I'd like to talk with you later, if you have time. If any of us have time."

"Oh?" Tali hesitated. I could see that her feelings of uselessness hadn't changed. She hadn't participated at all in the battle, and now she was being relegated to messenger, relaying news to her grandmother. That, and she looked simply weary. Off balance. Weak.

"It's...it's about..." I sighed. "I don't really want to talk about it here."

I winced as another person murmured "Burned One" behind me. Tali's eyes widened. She nodded. "I'll be happy to help. Maybe over supper?"

"Yes. I'll see you then."

Then, before I could even offer my thanks, I was swept away by people. I was taken almost immediately to the throne room, despite being dirt-and-blood-stained from travel. Upon my arrival, I was met with various greetings, some familiar, others formal. A few even bowed to me, which I ignored as best I could. Casimir managed to push through the crowd to get to the table, where I sat. Everyone scrambled to do the same.

"Well?" Queen Raya asked, seating herself at the head of the table. "Give us the news. There are rumours already circulating, and it's only been, what, half-an-hour since your return. We must get the proper information to plan and strategise for the future. What sort of fight did she put up? How was she subdued? How many people did it take to kill her?"

Too many, I wanted to say, but that wasn't what Raya had asked. She wanted to know how many blows it took to subdue a goddess. She didn't want to know how many died. How many were injured.

"Truthfully?" I slumped back in my chair, not

caring who saw and judged me for it. "It was very nearly a slaughter."

Casimir jumped in, smoothing over my words before panic set in. And with this many fragile, foolish humans, it would easily set it. "What Lady Calanthe means is that the warriors were eager to attack, and that proved difficult when the target was a single person. That, coupled with the fact that Myr possessed the remarkable healing properties of all gods, meant that our efforts were more of a bottleneck than an ambush. As such, a good many were caught in the crossfire. More than we had anticipated. More than we had hoped. However, we prevailed."

Jedrek snorted. "You mean we won because the Lady Calanthe unleashed her fury upon Myr. Without that, it would have taken a remarkably lucky blow to kill her."

I hadn't even noticed that he was there with us. I thought he would go off with his Black Riders to tend to their wounds or horses or something. Frankly, I had thought that of all of us. I hadn't thought we would be called into a strategy session immediately. I was perhaps as foolish as anybody. Or as weary.

"That is disappointing news indeed." This was from a rich voiced woman with a remarkable resemblance to Captain Kina, from her deep Black skin to the shaved head. Only, she wore garb that could be mistaken as nothing short of ornamental: a red dress with wide sleeves and layers of gold jewellery heaped about her neck. "Forgive me, Lady Calanthe, we have not been introduced. I am Matriarch Varess, leader of Craigsmuir. You met my niece, Kina, I believe."

"A pleasure." I nodded vaguely. "Please, continue."

"If a sizeable force such as yours cannot easily combat a single god, then we must dissemble into smaller teams. Ten, fifteen, perhaps? The exact numbers can be discussed later. However, if the gods can all heal so easily from wounds, then those teams may not be enough to take that 'lucky' blow, as you put it." Her accent was mild compared to her niece's, her voice musical and soothing. I was ready to close my eyes and drift off to sleep there until the reality of what she was saying hit me.

"The teams will have to be made up of elite warriors," Garwith said, smiling weakly at me. Judging by the ink stains on his fingers, he had been spending most of his time with the politicians and diplomats, and not much with the Runners. I wondered if that was the reason for the circles under his eyes. "But, yes, even that may not be enough."

"Especially once you consider that the other gods will not be so easy to kill." This was from Temys, who presided over her corner of the table like a queen. Her simple dressmaker's clothes had been exchanged for something finer, and there were baubles at her fingers. She looked alive, more so than I'd seen before. Palace life obviously suited her.

"Not so easy to kill?" Raya clenched her fist, resting it on the table. "You, yourself, told us that this Myr was a goddess who was of the first generation. Old. Powerful. One of the oldest, even."

Jedrek muttered something under his breath. He shook his head when I raised my brows at him. "Not now," he mouthed.

"She was," Temys said sagely. "But she was a goddess of the hunt, only. Crafty. Difficult to catch. Good at snares. Archery, perhaps. Capable with a hunting knife. But what magic did she possess besides that?"

This was directed to me. I frowned, thinking back. "Very little," I admitted. In my anger during the battle, I'd hardly noticed, thinking it bad enough that her weapons had slain so many of the people I was trying to protect. Aside from her healing and prowess in close-quarters fighting, though, she hadn't shown remarkable power.

"What of those who come after her? A god of winter may show remarkably more magic than one of the hunt. Or a god of storms? What of that?"

"Poet, you would resign us all to death the way you talk," Jedrek snapped. "There are very few gods of the first generation, and while those with a larger demesne, with potentially more magic, they can be subdued with a skilled force."

"Subdued. But not killed?" Varess leaned forwards. Jedrek sighed.

"I think," Casimir interrupted, "that this is a conversation to be had another day. After everyone has bathed and eaten and rested. All you need to know for the moment is that Lady Calanthe defeated Myr, removing her head and sending it to Ynysfawr to serve as a message for any other gods that come through the door. By all accounts, a victory."

He didn't wait for a response, just pushed back from the table and helped me to my feet. I nodded to the assembled people, ready with a polite platitude on my tongue as an apology for leaving halfway through the session. Several people I'd never met before—presumably representatives of other countries—tried to get my attention, blurting out their names and titles in a cacophony of noise that threatened a headache. Casimir shook his head and pulled me away. We left without another word.

"Empty night, I hate those things," he grumbled to me as we walked back to our chambers. "Strategy sessions that go around and around in circles without achieving anything useful."

"It seemed useful to me to decide upon smaller groups for attack," I offered, rubbing my temples.

"I'll grant you that, but not much more. If we could actually sit down and *talk* with our opponents, lay out our terms, then maybe we could get a reasonable lay of the land. Figure out who would stand against us, and who with us."

I perked up. "*Can* we do that? It would—"

"No."

"Surely the door—"

"No. Trust me on this, Calanthe, the realm of the gods is not one easily entered or abandoned. Why do you think that it has taken this long for even *one* god to come through the door? That, and we would not be able to take any mortals with us on this mission of diplomacy; they would die instantly. You, me, Jedrek, and no one else, would have to fight potentially dozens of gods. Alone. You would survive, as you cannot die. But the cost?"

The cost would be Casimir and Jedrek. And whatever damage was done to me. I recalled Myr's expression through the battle, one of sheer glee, no matter what pain was dealt to her. What had happened to her to produce such joy? I shuddered.

"No, you're right. I just wish..."

We stopped walking. Casimir wrapped his arms around my waist, resting his head on my shoulder, nose buried in my hair. "I know. I wish it, too. I wish that we could stand at the door to Ynysfawr and make our case. I wish that the gods would hear us. I wish for a peaceful end to this."

"It won't be peaceful, will it?" I hugged Casimir back, trying to lose myself in his arms.

"Very likely not." He sighed, squeezing me tighter. "I'm so damn tired of fighting, my love. For centuries, it's been me and Astraea against the void, against whatever enemies were dredged up, against...against each other. For once, I would love to sit and watch the moon rise and know I am not bound to bear a sword again. I want to travel without risk of war. I want…"

"I know," I breathed. "I want it, too. And I swear to you, Casimir, Guardian of Renown, Keeper of my Heart, that one day, we will have that peace. That freedom."

Somehow. I would make it happen.

"Careful," he chuckled, pulling back. "Vows by the gods are not easily broken."

"Good. Now, come, I desperately want a bath."

"Then a bath you shall have."

✦

The rest of the day was spent in relative quiet. I received several messages delivered by harried servants. Most were invitations from the visiting diplomats and warriors to meet with them, to dine with them, to grace them with my presence. Any invitations of the last sort I tossed wilfully into the fire. The rest I stacked on a table to be dealt with later.

A couple of invitations were offered in person. Knocks at the door sounded every hour or so, indicating another diplomat or their personal staff was there, ready to bow and offer me a gift, then beg for my blessing or the honour of my meeting, or other such nonsense. After the third one of these, Casimir refused to open the door at all.

We ate, bathed, and managed to catch a few hours of sleep, which was enough to restore me. I knew there were hundreds of things I needed to do, but it was nice to just enjoy a quiet afternoon where I didn't have to do more than venture from bed to put another log on the fire. Finally, though, responsibility weighed heavily enough on my shoulders that I dressed, did my hair in a quick braid, and ventured out once more.

Tali was just outside the door to her quarters when I found her, trying to balance a load of books in her one arm while also simultaneously open the door with...

"Are you using your foot to open that?" I asked, frowning.

At once, the books spilled from her grasp, Tali windmilled her arm and stump through the air, and nearly fell to the floor. Casimir and I caught her, setting her upright.

Tali let out a string of truly impressive curses, ones that likely hadn't been used for a very long time, and promptly burst into tears. Casimir stared at me wide-eyed while I held Tali's shoulders.

"Go. Perhaps you could fetch us something to eat? And drink?"

He nodded and was gone.

"Stars above, Calanthe, I'm such a mess," Tali

managed through her sobs. I opened the door and gathered the books, ushering her inside before we could draw attention. Tali didn't need any more humiliation.

"Listen to me," I said, all but shoving Tali into a chair. "You are *not* a mess. You have lost your arm. That takes a lot of adjustment. Not to mention being magically depleted by the loss of the void. You have pushed yourself massively over the last few days, and if I were you, I would be passed out."

"You would not."

"Do you know how long it took me to recover after...after Starfall Meadow?" After being made, I realised. "With burns on half my torso and face, broken bones from who knows what magic that forced me through the earth? I was unable to move properly for *weeks*. And that was after the healers had used all their arcane spells on me. Then, when the voidlings breached the palace walls, I managed to give myself magic sickness. That had me unconscious for nearly two days! Trust me, Tali, you're doing spectacularly well."

She rubbed tears from her eyes. "I just feel so useless. I mean, what can a one-armed person even do?"

"Your power comes from your knowledge and intellect, not your arm." I sniffed. Then, softening, I sat in the chair beside her. "I've discovered that even having all the power in the world does not reduce the feeling of uselessness."

She straightened, eyes flashing with indignation. "You're not useless! You just slew a *goddess*! Do you honestly think—oh. I see your point."

"I thought you might." I looked at the stack of books and papers strewn about the room. More research, likely, for whatever we could possibly face in the future. Just the thought of it exhausted me. "I wanted your advice."

"Anything," Tali promised.

"I was talking with Beatrice the other night—"

Tali snorted, shaking her head. "That woman is trouble. You shouldn't listen to anything she has to say."

"She may be trouble, but she is not a fool. She was discussing wanting to be a priestess for another god, any god, so that she might have a purpose again."

"Search for power, more likely."

I smiled wryly. "Indeed. In any case, I explained to her that I had no intention of ever having a priesthood. But...I don't know how to go about preventing people from speaking in my name, without my knowledge or consent. A priesthood would go a long ways towards eliminating that risk."

Tali studied me for a moment, expression serious. "What brought this about?"

"The rumours that flew as soon as we returned. I cannot even begin to imagine the stories that must be spreading around Altier right now. How many of them will take what I did, what I said, and twist them to paint a different picture. One that I didn't intend?" I pulled my sleeves over my hands, studying the stretch in the fabric. Slowly, I released it. "I think I may need a priesthood, no matter how much I don't necessarily want one."

"You want to know how to go about establishing such a thing," Tali said, nodding. "Well, I don't know a great deal about the establishment of a priesthood for any of the gods, considering that was pre-void by a great many years, but—"

"No, you misunderstand me." I pressed my mouth together and caught her eyes, holding them. "I want *you* to lead the priesthood. To establish it. To...speak in my name."

The door opened, letting Casimir slip in with a tray of food enough for the three of us, a bottle of wine tucked under one arm. Before he could close the door behind him, Tali let out another string of curses, ones that I'm sure echoed through the palace.

"Ah," Casimir said. "What did I miss?"

Tali spent the next week asking me my thoughts on everything from food to complicated philosophical questions that had me confused and irritated. Between her incessant questions and the almost constant stories about gods from the past and their requirements for worship, I was increasingly sure that my asking her had been a mistake. Thankfully, she'd kept my request quiet, not so much because I had asked, but because she hadn't yet said yes.

After a long day of training with my magic, juggling questions from Tali, and dancing politely around the various diplomats, I very nearly stumbled back to my rooms with the intent of eating large amounts of food and collapsing into sleep. Casimir was off trying to put small fighting forces together in a complementary way without angering the diplomats who wanted prestige and glory for their people. He had taken on the task at Garwith's behest, though I privately thought he was just as glad to be away from Tali's questions as I would have been.

Even so, I imagined he needed a large meal and a rest just as much as I did. We hadn't spent a great deal of time together over the last week, with everything being so busy. Our moments were stolen, whispered affairs in stairwells or tucked around corners. Our kisses were swift and fierce, each touch a brand upon our skin. It was all we could manage. Even the evenings, late at night, when we were alone in our chambers, we were often too tired for more than a quiet caress. I began to look forward to the day that this war was over for more selfish reasons than the liberation of the mortals.

A hand grabbed mine just as I reached for the door. My magic flared instinctively. Tiny bits of stone broke off from the wall and flew towards my attacker while flames flared in the torches along the wall. I called everything to a halt when I realised that it was only Raya who had grabbed me, not someone else. Not the headless body of Myr that sometimes haunted my nights.

"You frightened me," I said on a breathless huff. Raya had her back to the wall, her chin up. She stared at the torches, then looked to me. Her lip curled.

"How *dare* you," she hissed.

"I beg your pardon? You grabbed me. I only reacted."

"Not for that. For...for the insult that you have delivered my family. For the cruelty you payed my daughter. We who took you in, who cared for you. Who have supported you thought all of this... this...*nonsense* even though our country has become overrun with foreign visitors. I have put up with this circus for you, and this is how you repay me? Betrayal?" Raya was seething, her voice quiet enough that no one in the passing corridors would hear, though it appeared that was all the control she had left to offer.

"Betrayal?" I had done no such thing. In fact, I had tried my best to be gracious to her and Beatrice, despite what had happened with Myr.

"You offered your priesthood, your influence and power, to a one-armed fool who spends her time lost in the past. A Wandering Poet! Not to Beatrice? Who has been High Priestess of the Temple of the Fallen Star? Who has trained for this role her whole life?" Raya stepped forwards, perhaps trying to intimidate me with her stature and poise, honed into a weapon during her time as queen.

Tali *had* told someone, then. Probably Temys, who would likely be incapable of not bragging about it. Fine. That was her right. But for Raya to come after me for it?

I did not move either to shrink away or intimidate Raya in return. I remained exactly where I was, steady and unflinching. "I believe, Your Majesty, that the choice of who will speak for me as my High Priest or Priestess is entirely up to me."

"Beatrice claimed you did not even want a priesthood!" Raya seethed.

"I thought about it, and changed my mind," I replied evenly.

"Then change your mind again!"

"No."

Her face grew wan. She took a step back. "No? After all that we have done for you? After all the support that we have provided for your war?"

"If you wish to rescind your support, then so be it. I will take everyone into the countryside closer to Ynysfawr, so that we may be there when the door opens again. Altier and Baldarskiel will be as safe as I can make them, though once this is over, do not expect for me to have anything to do with this place ever again." I took a step forward, matching her movements. "As for my priesthood, I offered it to Tali, who is far more intelligent than you give her credit for, so that no one else may speak in my name. Twist my words to their purpose. Mislead people to their ambitions."

"You dare suggest that my—"

"I appreciate that Beatrice has studied for her role, but the fact of the matter is that the Temple of the Fallen Star is not mine, nor will it ever be. Now, I am tired. Hungry. I wish to be alone. However, if you wish to pull your support, then I will leave. Immediately."

Raya licked her lips. "There's no need for haste—"

"I am in no mood to play games, Majesty. I know you desire my influence. I know you only support me because you have the prestige of being the first. I am not as blind nor as foolish as you think. I am, though, perfectly capable of speaking for myself, making my own thoughts clear without your assistance or interpretation. So. What will you choose? To support me? Or for me to leave?"

The queen of Baldarskiel was silent for a minute. I got the impression that she was taking in every detail of me, from the burns on my face to the mud splattered on my shoes. Finally, she inclined her head. "You are not what I ever thought you would be. I don't know if that's good or bad, only that it is. If you were...human...I would say that you could not possibly make it in this world, that it would eat you up and spit you out without caring for the end result at all. But you are not human, and I sincerely hope that you can make the world into the image you try to present."

"Why? Why say that when you obviously do not like or care for my ideas?" I did not understand at all. The queen had only been friendly to me if she thought it suited her needs, but her words then felt like honesty. At last, the truth from her.

"Because I think that a world you forged would be

far kinder than one forged by humanity. And, little as I might personally think of you, that future…maybe we need it more than we think." She sighed. "I will deal with Beatrice. And I will continue to provide your support, even if only for the selfish reasons you named. And one day, Lady Calanthe, I will call in that support, that influence, and use it to build up my family's name until we are one that rivals the legends your poet so dearly likes to discuss. I am not nearly as kind or merciful as you, but I hope that your world wins over mine."

The queen started to walk away, that regal stature diminished somehow. I didn't understand. How could she exist in such a contradictory world? Perhaps that was the difference between humanity and the gods, and I was only just realising it. They could exist with oppositions as their core, and we could not. Then again, I commanded fire and earth, and they were very much in opposition. Was this what Jedrek meant when he said I was more human than any other god he'd known?

I closed my eyes and leaned against the door, weary to the bone. Maybe if I thought about it, I could use my magic to open the door so I wouldn't have to open it physically. Though, that would likely take just as much effort. Perhaps if I just leaned there for a minute, I would be able to—

"Rough day?" Casimir's voice had me cracking open an eye. His hair was dishevelled and there was a smudge of dirt on his cheek. His clothes were old and worn, but I could have sworn that the rip on the left sleeve was new.

"No worse than yours, I imagine," I said, mustering enough energy to go into the chambers. I immediately collapsed on the bed and let out a groan. "I thought that one of the perks of immortality would be not getting so tired. I thought I would only need rest every week or so."

"Ah, yes, reality. Sorry that it's such a disappointment to you." Casimir shucked off his shirt. I turned my head to watch, making no secret of hiding my interest. Even weary, the planes of his muscles, the writhing shadows along his spine, had my heart beating faster. And when he caught me eye, *knew* that I was watching, well I was glad that my earthy skin didn't easily show my blushing, especially through the burns.

"Calanthe?" Casimir smiled, the look languid. "Are you enjoying the view?"

"Very much."

He snorted a laugh and I could have sworn that he put extra effort into stretching as he donned a new shirt. He lay on the bed next to me and let out a sound that was half groan and half sigh of relief. "Empty night, that feels good."

I turned onto my side. "Do you mind if I ask a question?"

"As long as I don't have to move, then you can ask me anything." His eyes slipped closed.

"What will happen to us after all of this?"

"We'll find a nice, quiet estate somewhere—I know several people who owe me favours on the continent—and live quietly for a few years while you taste every food that's on offer and discover if you have a preference for drawing or singing or whatever else it is you want to try. I will do something ridiculously indulgent, like take up carving, and we'll travel around whenever we want."

I traced a finger over the blanket. "That sounds... lovely." And it did. "But...I meant...will we have a family?"

Casimir sat bolt upright, gaping at me. "*What?*"

I winced and lay on my back again. Studying the ceiling was better than looking at the shock in Casimir's eyes. "It's just that you never mentioned whether you and Astraea had children, and I know that gods only reproduce with magic or, according to Jedrek, great difficulty—"

"You talked to *Jedrek* about this?" Casimir's voice jumped high.

"I asked Tali first, but she didn't have any helpful information." I put my hands over my eyes. "Forget I asked. It's not important."

A gentle touch had me lowering my hands. Casimir smiled at me with such tenderness that my heart started racing again. "It *is* important, love, I promise. And it's certainly a conversation worth having, but as you and I aren't even coupling, then perhaps it's one that can wait. At least until there's peace?"

I blushed again, and this time there was no doubt that he saw it. He brushed a hand across my brow. "What is it?"

"Nothing," I blurted. He merely quirked a brow. "It's just...*why* aren't we coupling? I assure you I'm interested and—"

Casimir collapsed beside me, chest shaking. I realised a moment later that he was *laughing*. Indignant, I thwacked him on the shoulder. "Please believe me, love, I am absolutely interested in that. It's only that we come to this room every day, exhausted, and I can guarantee that it's better when we aren't tripping over our own feet."

"You may have a point." It didn't mean I had to like it.

"Be patient, dear Calanthe. We have centuries laid out before us. It will not hurt if we take our time."

I bit my lip. "I understand that, truly. But with everything that's going on, I feel...With Myr and the other gods and the humans and everything, I don't know how much time we have. I don't want to lose you."

"You won't." He moved closer and wrapped his arms around me. Immediately, I relaxed. "Even if I am killed, I swear that I will keep watch over you from the Endless Beyond. I will be by your side, always. And coupling, making love, it can be a beautiful thing, but it's not the *only* thing. You have my heart. You always will. That's what matters."

"And you have mine." I put my head to his chest, listening to that wonderful heart. It beat strongly with no sign of faltering, unlike mine which seemed to jump at every moment these days. I stifled a frown; though my feet weren't touching the earth, I could have sworn I heard another heartbeat, a third, coming steadily through the stones. Steady, but slower than the day before. Slower still than the day before that. I thought that we would have time to rescue Astraea after this impending war with the gods. That we would have time to consider how best to bring her to the surface, how best to tell her about Casimir and myself.

If her heartbeat was slowing, though, then that eternity Casimir talked about might be shorter than we both thought.

"I know we have no way of knowing when the other gods will come through the door, but you don't think they'll be here before Midwinter, do you?"

"Tali has been talking to you about celebrations again, hasn't she?" Casimir said on a sigh.

She had, but that was besides the point. "She wants to throw the biggest Midwinter celebration in years. That's not why I was asking, though."

"Oh?"

I stared at my hand on his chest, at the burns that swirled over my skin in artful designs that revealed nothing of the pain they'd caused, of the still-deadened nerves that lingered there. "I think we need to go rescue Astraea, and I think we need to do it soon."

The light in the room suddenly dimmed, as if a cloud had passed over the sun. It wasn't the sun, though, it was shadows, there in an instant where before there had been none. I held my breath as they hung in the air, an ominous stillness.

"Her heart is still..." Casimir whispered.

"It still beats, but it is slowing."

The air itself seemed to relax, and the shadows were once again gone. Casimir took a deep breath, then another, then a third. "Tomorrow. We can start tomorrow?"

I knew he wasn't asking if I was available, if the war effort would put itself on hold, if I had to make arrangements for things to be done in my absence. He wasn't asking about any of that. He was asking if I could do it. If I could control my magic enough to rescue her.

"I've been practising. Ever since the battle with Myr, I've had a bit more control over my precision. I can't promise that I'll be able to carve a tunnel in one go, but we can certainly try."

A swallow, then a nod. "Don't let Jedrek come."

"I may need to consult with him about—"

"Then do it before. But please, Calanthe, don't let

him come. I don't want him to see Astraea like that. I don't know what condition she'll be in, but I don't think I could bear it if he were there. Not when he... when she..."

When he had come between them once before. Even if Casimir wasn't in love with Astraea, he had been for centuries. He had given himself to her wholly, no matter how she treated him. To have Jedrek, who had caused such pain before, there when we found Astraea, would be too much.

My heart broke just a little then. I knew that he had loved Astraea with every fibre of his being. I didn't doubt his love for me, either. I had no cause to be jealous, no cause to fear. Never had he given me any, and I doubted that he would. It just wasn't his nature. Seeing him so concerned for her, though, was heart wrenching. He *had* loved her, and he didn't want her to be in pain.

Neither, for that matter, did I.

"I'll tell Tali that we'll be away for a few days. She can manage everyone well enough in my absence." I went back to studying the burns on my hand, not certain I could bring myself to witness his anguish.

"If she cannot, then Temys certainly will," he said, voice rough like he was fighting back tears.

"Don't hide yourself for my sake. Cry, if you like. Shout, if it will make you feel better. Do what you need to do."

His hold on me tightened. "I need to be here. I

need you to be here. I need to hold on to one good thing, and that thing is you."

I curled in closer. "Very well then, so long as you don't mind if I fall asleep."

He pressed a kiss to my head. "Sleep well and deep, my love. I don't mind."

I started to drift off, started to slip away into the sleep of exhaustion. I heard, moments before I lost consciousness, "I need you to be rested for tomorrow. To save her."

A tiny thread of jealousy wound its way around my heart. And squeezed.

CHAPTER 20

Getting away from the palace—and Altier—was a mess. Almost immediately upon stepping outside my door the next morning, dressed in a practical wool dress over wool hose, a fur-lined cape over my shoulders, I ran into Ilar. He took one look at me and started smiling.

"Are we going somewhere? Finally! Being stuck with this many people around is starting to grate on my nerves."

"Actually, I need you to stay here." I tried to sound confident in my statement, but the truth was that I was still poor at giving orders. So poor, it turned out, that Ilar immediately narrowed his eyes in suspicion.

"What's going on, my lady?" He looked around the corridor. No one was nearby. "Is it to do with the queen? I heard that she was very upset yesterday, threatening about coming to talk with you. I know that you don't want to get involved in human politics, but everyone here and in the city would support you if you were to assume the throne and—"

I reared back. "What? No! I'm not trying to assume the throne. Stars above, Ilar, what could have possibly given you that idea. No. Never mind, don't tell me, I don't want to know." I pinched the bridge of my nose. "I am just going to be away for a few days. You don't need to know the details why, only that it's important."

"And you want me to stay here," Ilar said. He scowled. "I'm no good with this politicking. I am better served with *doing* something. And I haven't even been assigned to a god killer unit yet."

Was that what they were calling them? I supposed I shouldn't have been surprised. I suppressed a shudder.

"I know that this is sudden, and I know that all this waiting and preparation is getting on everyone's nerves. I cannot predict when the doors will next open, only that we must be prepared for it when the time comes. And part of that is why I will have to be gone for a few days. I'm leaving Tali in charge; she can speak for me, and her decisions will be final. Understand?"

Ilar shuffled his feet and made a face, but he nodded. "As you command, my lady. Only...what if the door opens before you get back?"

I would have to hope that it did not. "Then I will do my utmost to return as swiftly as possible. But you are surrounded by formidable warriors. You are a formidable warrior. We learned a lesson with Myr: too many people get in the way. You must rely on your instincts, alright?"

"Rely on my instincts?" Ilar scoffed. It did sound a bit thin, but what else could I offer? I would be deep in the bowels of the earth if the door opened. I would not be in a position to help. The mortals would be on their own, and they would have to learn to fight their own battles. My mouth went dry.

"I can offer you some assistance, but you must swear to me that you will *only* use it if the door opens and I am not here."

Eyes gleaming, Ilar nodded. "I swear."

"If the door opens and you find yourself in dire need, find the site of a former void pool. They're like...empty scars on trees or in swamps."

"I know the spots," Ilar growled. His hand went to the hilt of a knife at his belt.

"Go there and ask for King Devereux. If you cannot reach a void pool, then find a crossroads. Offer to make a bargain."

"You want me to *bargain* with the monsters we spent years fighting?" Ilar snarled. "Those things beyond the void do not deserve to still exist. You should have wiped them from reality altogether, not—"

"Do you dare question my actions?" I asked in a low voice. Ilar froze, face paling. "I know full well how dangerous the beings beyond the veil are, but that does not make them any less worthy of life. Some might say the same about Hunters."

"I-I apologise, Lady Calanthe." He sank to his knees in a bow so deep that his head nearly touched the floor. "I did not mean to question you. I hadn't realised how deeply my past experiences have affected me regarding the void. I swear that if the time comes, I will be prepared to open the veil, release the void upon those who come to do us harm."

"Good. I hope it does not come to that." Then, glancing out one of the arrowslit windows, I saw that the sun was starting to rise and paint the sky in pinks and yellows. "I have to go, Ilar. Be well. Take care. And hope that the door doesn't open while I'm gone."

He rose, his head still bowed. He looked up enough for me to see a gleam in his eyes, one I didn't quite comprehend. "I have more than hope, my lady. I have faith."

Something deep in my gut felt like it was being torn asunder. I tried to smile a polite farewell, then I fled. Thankfully, the rest of the palace was quieter, given that it was barely dawn. The servants were up and about, bustling around doing chores and carrying linens, trays of food, cleaning supplies. There were a few clerks delivering missives as well, and once I even thought I saw Dame Winters striding through the hallways, looking lost. I gave polite nods to those who greeted me and did my best to stay out of the way. I doubted very much that my absence would be discreet for long.

Thankfully, it was a short jaunt through the outskirts of Altier to reach Starfall Meadow, and the people in the city were hardly awake yet. I managed to make it to the scar in the earth without any more unexpected conversations. Casimir waited for me, a pack slung over his shoulder. He'd slipped out of our room some time in the early hours of the morning to gather supplies, and looking at him now, I wondered if he'd slept at all.

His eyes were clouded and weary. The circles under his eyes were darker than before. His jaw was tense and he fidgeted as he stood. His shoulders relaxed slightly as I approached.

"You made it." He wrapped me in a hug, nearly bruising me with the hard edges of his armour. It wasn't the normal Void Runner ivory with the running hound, but a dark metal. No, not metal, I realised as I brushed my hand against it. *Stone.*

"What is this?" The edges were carefully bevelled, but I knew that one wrong move and they would cut open my skin with ease. Casimir took a careful step back, removing my hand from the armour.

"It's, ah, meteor shards."

Meteor shards? "You have armour made from a...a..."

"Falling star? Yes. The pieces that the humans didn't claim as their precious gems. Though this piece is old. Centuries old." He shrugged, shouldering a pack. "It didn't seem right to wear the Void Runner armour for this."

Unease settled in my chest, right behind my breastbone. I rubbed it absently. Why would he think he needed armour where we were going? There was nothing in the earth. Except Astraea. I shook my head, shifting my weight.

"Right, so, I'd like to start the tunnel near where I emerged. This scar should do well enough. And I don't think anyone will come here, so hopefully we shouldn't be followed. And I made sure that Jedrek doesn't know. And Ilar—"

Casimir captured my hands in his, pressing a kiss to my fingertips. "It's okay, Calanthe. I'm nervous, too. It will be well."

I nodded my head, though I wasn't sure how well I believed it. After a moment, Casimir dropped my hands. He took a step back, then another. I turned to the slash of bare earth that had been razed when I emerged. I focused on the faint heartbeat far beneath my feet. Then, I raised my arms and bade the earth to part.

Starting the tunnel was easy. The earth was eager to please, and a smooth path downwards carved itself into being. I took the first step into the tunnel and let out a breath as the ground kept carving itself away, kept moving, kept creating a path. I took another step, then another, and before I knew it, I was leading us into the depths of the earth.

The light was first to go, the entrance of the tunnel diminishing until it was no more than a pinprick of light behind us, then nothing at all. Casimir stumbled once, nearly falling into me.

"I can light a flame, if you want," I offered. Even without light, I instinctively knew where to go, my earthsense strong and steady.

"It's not the darkness that bothers me," he muttered. "It's...it's being separated from the sky. Don't worry about me. Keep going. I can manage in the darkness. We don't want to use up our air."

I didn't question him, not because I believed him, but because I knew that he was going to do this no matter what. So we kept walking. Every so often, I angled the tunnel in a new direction as I followed the heartbeat. It was nearly straight below us so I ended up carving a corkscrew shape into the earth, spiralling ever downwards, ever deeper.

The earth became stone, harder to carve and pass through. It was still eager to obey, but it did not change its shape easily. And as I didn't want to set off an earthquake that would shatter Altier above, I had to be careful. Coaxing. Gentle. With all that time, though, came a different problem.

The air was growing thin. Some air followed us down the tunnel from above, but a single point of entrance was not going to be enough, not for both Casimir and myself. "We need to stop," I said, brushing sweat from my eyes and leaning against a wall to catch my breath.

"We keep going," Casimir growled, though it sounded as though he was just as tired as I.

"No. I have to make an air vent or we'll suffocate."

"We won't die from suffocation." He stubbornly pushed forward, only to reach bare rock where I hadn't pushed through. My earthsense told me he was kicking the stone.

"Stop. It will only take a little bit." I pressed my hands against the wall and reached upwards, a tiny burrow straight through the rock, the stone, the earth, until there was nothing above me but sky, clear and open. Almost immediately, the air grew sweeter. Fresher.

Casimir paced in the narrow tunnel, his footsteps reverberating through the earth with impatience. I couldn't see him given the darkness, but I knew where he stepped, knew when he pushed against the end of the tunnel, waiting for it to move again. "Cas," I said.

Immediately, he flinched back from the bare wall and came to me, wrapping his arms tight around me. "Are you tired? Do you need rest? I'm sorry, I didn't mean to push—"

"Casimir, hush." I pulled out of his grasp, albeit reluctantly. "I'm fine. My magic is fine. Everything is fine. You, on the other hand, are making me nervous."

"I'm sorry," he murmured again. "I don't...it's just...I want to get to her so badly, and yet I am afraid of what I'll find."

"Surely knowing is better than not knowing." Even if it did cause hurt, I wanted to know. "I don't mind your eagerness, truly. I know how much this means to you. I just worry that you're not going to like what you find."

"Her heart—"

"Beats. Steadily," I said. It wasn't a lie, though her heart beat so slowly. "If you are not calm, though, it could make things worse for her."

He took a breath, loud enough that I could hear the deep inhale. Then he let it out again. Finally, he stood still. "I'm ready to continue, if you are."

I reached out my hand, brushing it against his arm. He took it, and we continued onwards. Without the sun marking the passage of time, I lost all sense of how long we had been beneath the surface. Twice more we stopped so I could open air shafts to the surface, taking longer and longer with each effort the farther we descended. Eventually, despite the fact that I could sense the earth around me in all directions, despite the fact that I knew exactly where I was going, the darkness began to wear on me. I tried to keep my movements steady and sure, but my fire magic began to interfere with my earth magic. Every third step, a spark would flare as I pushed the tunnel onwards. I tried to control it, but the fire leaped within my blood, begging for freedom to burn, to dance.

I started sweating, my breaths coming in quicker bursts. I took breaks, only a few seconds at a time, but the farther we went, the more I had to rest until I was leaning against the wall of the tunnel, fire twining its way through my body, overriding all my earth magic, desperate.

"Calanthe," Casimir whispered, brushing his hand against my cheek. "What's wrong? Do you need to sleep?"

"M-my fire," I said through chattering teeth, though I wasn't cold. I was anything but cold. I wished I had worn anything but wool. I wished I could burn the fabric away. I wished I could return to the surface and roll in the snow. I would even consider swimming in the freezing river for any relief to the inferno that raged inside me.

"Let it out," Casimir said.

"I c-can't. It will destroy you and all our air."

He guided me to the ground until we were both sitting, facing each other, the impossible darkness closing in around us. "Just a thread, Calanthe. A single thread. Can you do that?"

I didn't know. I was ready to combust, and I

didn't think I had that sort of control just then. But I closed my eyes, despite the darkness, and reached into that fire. *One thread*, I thought. Holding an image of a spool of thread in my mind, I unravelled it, turning it into white-hot flame that wove through the air, laying itself over rock like a spider web, impossibly hot. I opened my eyes and flinched back at the brightness. Just as I'd thought, webs of burning threads lined the ceiling of the tunnel, illuminating the stone with devastating light. Casimir sat before me, features painted in red and gold firelight. I could see the tension in his features, but there was relief there, too.

"Good. Is that better?"

"Yes." I still felt too hot, too combustible, but the pressure had simmered down enough where I could feel the draw of the earth again. I pushed onwards, only this time I left threads of fire burning in my wake. It meant I needed more air shafts, and now that I was using both halves of my magic, the progress forwards was slower, but at least I wasn't about to destroy Casimir or consume all of our air.

Then, I felt something that made me stumble. The fires extinguished in a single breath. The tunnel stopped progressing. The air became still and heavy and hot.

"What is it?"

I could almost feel Casimir drawing his sword, though there was nothing down here that could possibly be a danger to us. We had left the life of the surface behind so very long ago. There was only stone around us. Stone, and a single pocket of air and fire and rock, just before us. I raised my unburned hand and coaxed the rock apart, slowly, so I wouldn't disperse the pressure before us too quickly. Air hissed through the tiny hole. A trickle, then a breeze, then a sudden gust of wind as the hole grew bigger and bigger and finally was big enough to fit through. The air stopped as the pressure equalised.

"I...I can see," Casimir said, voice suddenly hoarse.

"There's liquid fire here. Magma." I knew he didn't care, not as he pushed past me, sword forgotten on the ground at my feet. I picked up the blade and slid it through my belt until it sat neatly at my hip. I lingered at the entrance to the tunnel, sensing the magma, the edges of the cavern, the space that was so alien to me, yet so familiar.

This was, I knew without a shadow of a doubt, the place where I'd been made. Where I'd been born. This was the place where life had been breathed into me and where my mothers had died. Lady Earth, whose image I knew from the memory she'd left for me at Ynysfawr, earth-skinned and gowned in flowers with kind, forgiving eyes. And the Eternal Flame, who I knew only from stories. Without thinking about it, I brushed my hands over the burns on my face.

I knew that if I took three steps forwards and turned to my left, there would be an outcropping that hung over the pool of magma below, upon which a stone bier was carved. The place where my body had been crafted. I knew that I had lain there for three days before the star's power had been imbued into my very being. I knew that someone had loved me before sending me away. One of them? Both?

Wrapping my arms around my waist, I took a tentative step into the cavern. The ground smoothed beneath my feet, creating a walkable path without my asking, glittering with obsidian and diamond. It led to the bier. I turned my back on my birthplace and instead looked to the right.

The ground there was rough and sharp, almost deliberately so, as if someone hadn't wanted the smoothing effect of the magma to touch that part of the cavern. I stepped forwards and the ground rippled, another path spreading out before me, though it was more reluctant than the first. This time, I followed it.

It rounded a corner, leading me to a slight depression in the wall, a place of comparative safety from the heat and danger that the magma posed. In this space, Casimir knelt over a pile of rags. No, not rags. Silks, once brilliant white, now stained with soot and torn. I recognised the shine. And it wasn't a pile, either, it was a person.

My steps slowed as I approached, until I was

standing still, unable to move closer. She was sooty and bleeding from many shallow cuts, likely delivered by her crawling over the sharp stones. Beneath that, though, I saw pale skin, pale hair, a face of statuesque beauty, and a quiet vulnerability that many likely found impossible to resist.

"Astraea, wake up," Casimir begged, pouring water over a cloth and dabbing at her forehead. He trickled a few drops past her cracked lips, but she barely stirred.

Something inside me that had been dormant since Ynysfawr flickered to life. A spark of light, not crafted from fire, that twined with a speck of darkness. So small as to be nearly dead, so quiet as to be nearly forgotten. I took a step forward. The magic flickered brighter, stronger. Another step. The magic flared again.

Her eyes snapped open. They were grey, so light and pale that they reflected everything around them. They reflected me, and the dismay written plainly on my features.

"Thief," Astraea hissed, barely able to lift her head. "Murderer."

"Astraea," Casimir sobbed, reaching to touch her, comfort her. "You're alive."

"Kill her!" she cried.

CHAPTER 21

The star lurched forwards as much as she could, but she was too weak to come anywhere near me. Chest heaving, she bared her teeth in a snarl. Casimir held her tightly, though I didn't know if it was to keep her still for my sake or hers.

"Come to finish the task?" Astraea hissed.

"Astraea, no, she—"

The star cut through Casimir's words as though he hadn't spoken at all. "You stole my light. *My* light."

"I am not responsible for the actions of those who created me." If it had been up to me, I would not have touched her light. I would have found a different way to bind the realms apart. Even now, that tiny fragment of a spark that somehow still existed in me felt wrong. It was not mine. It did not belong.

"Astraea, she brought me here. To save you."

Casimir brushed his thumb over a smudge of dirt on her cheek. Astraea pulled away. It was only a tiny movement, but I could see the pain flash across Casimir's features like lightning.

"You always come to save me," Astraea murmured. The words themselves were soft, spoken in a murmur that drew people in, but there was something bitter about them. Something that told me her gratitude towards Casimir wasn't genuine. Still, they obviously soothed that hurt. He brushed a strand of hair back from her face, then stood, carrying her in his arms.

"Let us go. We have a long walk back to the surface."

"The surface." Astraea's eyes fluttered, then closed. She rested her head on Casimir's shoulders, and the two of them vanished into the tunnel, leaving the cavern behind. Not one of them looked back.

I turned away from the tunnel, moving to the bier where I had been born. Running my fingers over the stone, I tried to feel for any hint of magic, any remnant of my mothers. Perhaps they had left another memory for me like the one on Ynysfawr. Or perhaps I would be able to feel the ghost of their presence written in the stone. There was nothing, only the interminable heat from the magma and the smooth stone bed beneath my fingers. No magic. No life. Nothing.

I wanted to hunch my shoulders and cry. I wanted

to wrap my knees to my chest and bask in this empty, burning place. I wanted to be selfish and mourn a life I hadn't ever known, just for a minute. My earth-sense, though, told me that Casimir was continuing up the tunnel, his steps steady and sure, never once hesitating. I should follow him. Instead, I was the one who hesitated.

Before my hesitation could turn into full-blown jealousy or heart wrenching sadness, the world trembled. The ground shook and the magma quaked and I fell to my knees, head spinning. The door had opened again. Longer this time. A full minute. How many had come through? How many would see the message that I'd left and understand it? How many would I lose trying to convince the others?

I staggered to my feet, the world as still as it had ever been. I was the one who had trembled, not the ground, not the liquid fire beneath my feet. Not the guardian to a star who walked steadily away from me. Dashing tears from my eyes, I turned my back on the place of my birth and went into the tunnel, closing the passage behind me.

Catching up to Casimir was easy, even in the darkness. I wasn't using my magic to seal the entire tunnel behind me. My fire and earth magics were both silent as I climbed, somehow sensing the urgency. When I caught up to Casimir, though, I hesitated again. I could feel his steps as he walked, unfaltering, despite the extra weight. He kept moving, saying nothing, only pausing when Astraea shifted or made a sound.

It was only a couple of hours later, as we passed under one of the air shafts and were greeted with a cool breath of fresh air that he paused.

"Calanthe?"

"I'm here." Even to my ears, I sounded tired. "Is she well?"

"She's sleeping." He shifted his weight.

"Do you need to rest? I don't think I can carry her, but I can keep watch over her while you sleep." Though if she woke while he slept, I didn't know what I would do. I didn't know how to address the star and judging from her earlier words, she had a large amount of vitriol for me.

"No. I'm...well, I'd rather get her to the surface as quickly as possible. She's been cut off from the sky for too long, and that can be dangerous. I was wondering if there were some way for you to manipulate the earth to get us to the surface faster." There was an edge to his voice that sounded like a plea. Even with me, who he claimed to love, was it so difficult to ask for help? Or was it because Astraea was here, now, and he didn't know how to act around us both.

There were too many possibilities for me to consider. Instead, I turned my attention inwards and probed my magic. I was weary; carving out the tunnel had been precise, exacting work that took a great deal more concentration than I'd expected. Moving the earth to the degree that Casimir asked—an eruption of sorts—would be a much larger task than carving the tunnel, but less exacting. I could do it, I thought, if I didn't much care about the destruction I would wreak.

"It can be done," I said at last, and I heard Casimir exhale in relief. "There will be a crater in our wake, and I cannot promise that Starfall Meadow will be able to grow anything for a considerable amount of time, but it can be done."

"Do it." No hesitation. "The Meadow isn't much used for growing food anyways."

"Now, perhaps. But for generations to come?" I asked a bit sharply. I winced at my own tone. "I'm sorry. I know you want to get her to the surface as quickly as you can. I'm just tired."

He took a step closer to me, but he was still holding Astraea and could make no further move with her between us. In that moment, I wished the darkness would lift so I could see his face, see his expression. I kept my fire magic tamped down, not letting a single spark escape.

"If it's too much, then we can keep walking," Casimir murmured. "I don't want you to wear yourself out."

I bit my tongue to keep from snapping at him that it was exactly what he asked of me. That was unfair. We'd dealt with this. He didn't love Astraea anymore, not like that. So why did my heart burn with jealousy? Why did I doubt him? Knowing that he could see me, even if I was drowning in darkness, I smiled as best I could.

"It's fine. I'll just need to sleep for a while." Not nearly long enough, surely, with what had come through the door. That thought sealed my decision. We needed to get to the surface as quickly as we could, and if that meant leaving a bit of destruction in my wake, then so be it. The gods would not wait for me to walk slowly up the tunnel. They would come for the mortals here, the innocent and unaware. Exhausted or not, I needed to be there for it.

I spread my hands out, pressing them against the walls of the tunnel. I closed my eyes and opened myself entirely to the earthsense. Immediately, I was overwhelmed with the pulse of the earth, full of life and death and the cycle of stone. Instead of directing my power into something so small as a tunnel, I simply commanded one word: *up*.

The ground rumbled.

Up.

The rumble became a roar. The stone beneath our feet rippled and then erupted. The magma from the chamber answered my call as surely as the stone and twined with my fire magic. It devoured my birthplace with ease, reaching for me. I was too far gone into the depths to pull back now. All I could do was wrap Casimir, Astraea and myself into a sphere of granite, thick enough to withstand the pressure that now boiled beneath us. The world turned and churned and shattered, and then we rose.

Up!

With a scream that tore my throat ragged, we emerged at the surface. The granite sphere collapsed as I turned my focus to the lava that now spewed from the ground, hissing as it devoured the ice and snow that had fallen in our absence. Shards of rock flew through the air, moving towards Altier. I lifted my arms and called them back.

Sweat poured down my back. My muscles trembled. But the rocks, the lava, all of it obeyed.

It went back to the earth, filling in the tunnel I'd carefully carved, littered over the surface of the ground, leaving scars of fire and rock in its wake. The roaring stopped, the world grew silent, and I fell to my knees.

The sky above was dark and mostly clear, though there were a few clouds obscuring the moon. I couldn't be sure, but I thought the stars might have twinkled a little brighter just then. No, surely not. My head swam. I was barely conscious from exhaustion. That was all.

"Astraea?" Casimir's voice cut through the deafening silence. He seemed oblivious to the wanton destruction that covered the ground around him. All his attention was on the star, laying on her back, face tilted to the sky. Her eyes were open, reflecting the starlight. She was still pale, but she had a bit more colour than before. "Astraea, are you alright?"

"I'll be fine, Guardian," Astraea said, pushing Casimir away. He turned to me, and I was almost relieved to see the worry there. Before he could move in my direction, though, she reached out and grabbed his arm.

"Don't leave me, Casimir." She stared straight at me as she spoke. "Please."

"I won't. I promise." Casimir settled in at her side. "Can you stand? We should get you to the palace so you can be seen to by healers."

"No human healers can fix what was taken from me," Astraea growled. She studied me. That spark of her magic I'd felt in the cavern was silent, not that I could have transferred it to her even if I'd wanted to. I didn't know how.

"But they can help you regain some of your strength." Casimir stood, helping her to her feet. She hissed at the sharp stones that bit into her bare soles, glaring at me again as if it were my fault. Perhaps it was, but there wasn't anything I could do about it now. I was tapped out. My body screamed in agony. I couldn't keep my eyes open for more than a second. I certainly couldn't stand.

Casimir started towards Altier, Astraea on his arm, already looking much stronger. He paused a moment later. "Calanthe?"

"Lady Calanthe!" Someone called for me. A voice

I recognised. Tali? Yes, she was moving towards me on horseback, her horse snorting with distress as she coaxed it through the field of stone and cooling lava. There were two more horses beside her, one entirely black with a black-clad rider on its back, the other without a rider. Jedrek.

"Casimir," Astraea whimpered, pulling him closer. He looked at me with a torn expression, but didn't even try to move away from her. The horses stopped and Jedrek dismounted, crouching by my side within seconds.

"Are you well?" he asked in a low voice. "We heard the commotion and came as quickly as we could, just in time to see you emerge from the earth."

"I've never seen anything like it!" Tali said. "I haven't even heard about it in stories, not control like that. The stones and debris and fire would have hit the entire western edge of Altier, but you pulled it back. Stars above, Calanthe, that will be a ballad for the ages!"

I managed a twitch that I hoped looked like a smile. Jedrek frowned, reaching out to brush my forehead. He hissed and pulled back. "We need to cool her off. *Now!*"

Casimir took half a step towards me again. His star held him back. "They have her, Casimir. Let them take care of her."

Jedrek was scooping whatever snow he could find over my body. I didn't know why I wasn't shivering, didn't know why I couldn't move. I was tired. So tired. I managed to flick my eyes to Jedrek's, hoping that he could read my questions there. "It's magic sickness," he said grimly. "Gods rarely get it, but when they do, it's bad. Really bad."

"How bad is really bad?" Tali asked, handing him a chunk of ice. He settled it against my abdomen where it started melting almost immediately. "She's immortal, right? She can't be killed."

"She is a young immortal, not even fully grown into her magic and bloodline. If anything *could* kill her, magic sickness would be it. She used too much; her body is essentially eating itself to sustain her."

"Calanthe!" Casimir cried.

"They'll take care of her," Astraea hissed.

I didn't see whether Casimir broke free of the star's hold, or whether he turned and went to the palace with her. I didn't hear what Jedrek or Tali did next. I only closed my eyes and found myself in the embrace of soothing, comforting darkness.

*

"*So you're the one.*"

I blinked and found myself in an unfamiliar landscape. There were mountains all around, a lake shrouded in mist before me, trees taller than any I'd ever seen. It was a place full of growth and life, yet I heard no bird sing, nor no crickets chirping. I felt no life in the ground. In fact, my magic was non-existent.

Panic caught in my throat and I spun around, trying to figure out where I was. A person dressed in silver from head to toe watched me. I froze. They had silver hair tied back in a short tail, silver eyes, silver silk clothes finer than any I'd ever seen in the palace of Altier. There were diamonds at their throat and ears, studded over their jacket and shoes.

"Who are you?" I asked, taking a step backwards. I tried to reach for the earth, but there was nothing there. My fire, too, was similarly quenched. I'd not felt so powerless since first waking.

"I am Emyna, god of dreams. And you are Calanthe, daughter of dead queens, goddess of earth and fire." Emyna swept into a deep bow, diamonds twinkling eagerly at their ears. They were suddenly right before me, their hand taking mine. They kissed the burned skin as though in reverence. I reached again for my fire, for anything, wishing at least that I had a knife. A sword. Something. But this was a dream. It had to be. In a dream, I was completely at this god's mercy.

"What do you want from me?" I asked, pulling back. Emyna sighed and turned to the lake.

"It has been an age since I have stepped into a dream. Gods do not dream, my queen. Yet you, a god, are dreaming. A conundrum for another time. I am glad only to taste dreams again. Centuries, trapped in a realm where I could not exercise my power." They smiled weakly at me. "Those in power can be cruel to those who have none."

I said nothing, instead looking about, trying to find a seam to rip open the dream. The landscape revealed nothing, just trees and mountains and the lake, fog slowly rolling over the water's surface. Inside my mind, too, there seemed to be no way out. My attention was captivated here, for whatever purpose.

"I belong with the mortals. Coaxing their sleeping dreams into being. Supporting their waking dreams that they ever strive to achieve."

"Mortals have dreamed just fine without your assistance for centuries," I said. Emyna nodded.

"Yes. Beautiful dreams, I would imagine. Yet with me at their sides, perhaps their dreams can mean something more. Portents for the future? Those seers that still walk the land can regain the truth of their abilities. Hopes never realised? I can coax in the night, helping mortals to realise their own capabilities."

They looked at me, beseeching, and I realised that they were asking for something. For permission to stay with the mortals. I frowned, bemused. "You wish to, what, join me?"

"I saw the head of Myr as I exited the door to this plane of existence. It was an effective message. One I, nor many others, will soon forget. You have laid claim to this world and all that lies within it. Many will fight you for it. Most, actually. Mortals provide such...sweetness. I, though, have endured enough cruelty at the hands of the other gods to know where my loyalties lie." Emyna bowed their head, hands clasped behind their back.

I shifted my weight. A spark of fire flared in my blood and I seized it with relief. "Do you swear not to harm those who do not harm you? To keep faith with those under your care?"

"As ever. Always. My queen." Emyna bowed, fog swirling around their feet.

"Then you are welcome." My spark of fire grew. Heat began to gather around me, burning off the fog. Emyna blinked, taking a step back.

"Your magic," they breathed.

"It's volatile, I know," I panted, hunching my shoulders as I tried to control my fire in this dreamscape.

"There are pieces that do not belong to you. That are not natural. They...they will devour you, if you are not careful."

I thought to the flare of light and shadow that awoke in the cavern. I'd thought all traces of Astraea's magic gone from me when I sealed the void away and balanced the realms. I'd obviously been wrong. "It's just a spark," I said, not sure if I was reassuring the god of dreams, or myself.

"Sparks can grow and spread. Then they blaze and burn all in their path. Be wary, my queen."

I was about to respond when my fire flared bright and burned through my skin, engulfing the dream world until it was no more. Instead, I lay in bed, weak, trembling, not a drop of magic responding to my call, as the serene face of the Fallen Star leaned over me, knife in hand.

CHAPTER 22

Acting on instinct, I moved out of the way of the knife as much as I could. Instead of meeting my throat, it sank deep into my shoulder. I let out a gasp of pain and thrashed as Astraea pulled the blade from my shoulder and tried again. This time, I managed to kick a foot out from beneath the bedclothes, catching her in the knee. She doubled over and the knife fell to the floor.

The door slammed open and people rushed in, moving too quickly for me to get a good look. I pulled myself upright, breathing heavily, while Astraea was restrained. Casimir held her tightly, arms pinned to her sides.

"Calm down!" he snapped as she struggled against him.

"Are you alright?" Jedrek was suddenly at my side,

pressing a cloth to my shoulder to staunch the bleeding. "Did she injure you anywhere else?"

"No." I took the cloth and held it myself; already, the pain was diminishing and the blood lessening. In another minute, it would be as if it never happened.

"Astraea, you have to stop," Casimir said, pleading. She delivered an elbow to his nose with a decisive *crack*. He hissed in pain but did not let her go.

"She stole my magic! She stole my light!" Astraea cried, still struggling, trying to reach me.

"She *saved* you!" Jedrek snarled. "You ungrateful star. You owe your life to Calanthe and you dare to act against her for something that her makers did? No wonder you fell."

Immediately, Astraea stilled. Her expression was stricken, as if Jedrek had struck her. "What gives you the right to say such things of me?" Astraea breathed. "Have I not defended against the void for countless centuries?"

"You also brought it to bear," Casimir said. She flinched as if struck. Then, looking around at all of us, she sneered.

"You all know this?"

"We do," Jedrek said. "Though it is thanks to Calanthe that the entire mortal realm does not know of your treachery. She seemed to think that you deserved to have your legacy preserved rather than destroyed."

Astraea curled her lip. "Such a benevolent

goddess, to show kindness to the likes of me. So good, it would seem, that she has twisted every heart to her, even that of my guardian, the one who swore to love me for all eternity."

Casimir released her. She scrambled away from him, curling in on herself as if she were the one being attacked. "Empty night, Astraea," Casimir said. "Do you honestly thing that what we shared was love? Pure, true love?"

Her lower lip wobbled and tears sprang to her eyes as if she'd summoned them. "You swore. Through light and dark, through all the realms. You *swore.*"

"So did you, and yet I never complained when you broke our bond over and over and over. Perhaps I should have."

I didn't want to be witness to this. I didn't want to see the pain, both manufactured and genuine, that passed between them. I didn't want to see Jedrek's scorn, Casimir's desperation. I wanted to know what happened. I wanted to clean my bloody shoulder. I wanted to go back to when things felt so much less complicated. But no matter what I did, which was I turned, how I fought, another battle sprang up before me.

I didn't need my heart to be one of those battles.

Astraea turned her ire to me again. "You've corrupted him."

No, that was you. I kept my thoughts to myself.

Without someone to engage her, Astraea scoffed and turned on her heel, gliding from the room like royalty. I wasn't entirely certain that the tears which graced her cheeks weren't for show.

"I'm so sorry," Casimir said, already rising and moving towards me. "Are you alright? Did she get more than your shoulder? I should have kept a better eye on her, but I never thought—"

"Yes, you should have," Jedrek snapped. "Did you think that two days would somehow magically cure her of her desire to see her rival dead?"

Casimir paled. "She wouldn't—"

"Wouldn't she?" Jedrek moved to stand slightly in front of me. "She went after Calanthe with a *knife*. If she hadn't woken up, that could have been fatal. She was recovering from magic sickness, or don't you remember what happened when she used up all her magic trying to get you and your lover to the surface faster?"

Hand drifting to the hilt of his sword, Casimir growled, "How dare you suggest that I was negligent in my duties. I would happily do whatever it took to protect Calanthe. She said she was fine. She—"

"Enough," I said. I stood and pushed my way between the two, going to the narrow window.

"Calanthe, I—"

"I said enough." I stared at the cloudless winter day out the window. It wasn't wide enough for me to see much, but the slice of life I could behold was so normal that it nearly broke my heart. "I know this is difficult for you, Casimir. You were duty bound to her long before you met me. If you feel like you need to remain with her to uphold that duty, then you are free to do so. I want only your happiness."

He let out a strangled sound. I didn't turn to face him. "I love *you*, Calanthe."

"And I, you. Love is not the same as duty." I understood that. Truly. "I do not wish to break your bond of duty simply because you love me. That would be unfair."

"I—" He broke off, making that same strangled sound. For a brief instant, I felt the brush of his lips against my cheek. Before I could turn around and bury my head in his chest, he had pulled away. The door clicked shut a moment later.

I whirled around, but he was gone.

Jedrek moved to my side, catching me before my weak legs gave out. He bore my weight to the bed and let me sink against him. "I'm sorry, my queen."

I brushed a tear from my eye, though I didn't know why I was crying. "Don't be. I didn't lie. Love and duty are not the same."

"Is it truly duty that keeps him by her side?" Jedrek asked, mouth twisting into a frown. He flinched at his own words. "I'm sorry. I don't doubt that he loves you, but habit—"

"The door opened again, when we were in the

cavern." I couldn't bear to talk about that any longer. My heart was too heavy. "A full minute, this time."

I told him about my dream, about Emyna, about his warning. Jedrek listened intently, eyes darkening the longer I spoke. "The god of dreams was always more popular with mortals than other gods. They don't dream. Well, all but you, apparently. But a full minute? Did he say anything about who else came through?"

"Only that they were prepared to fight me for my claim."

"And the spark...?"

I shook my head, shrugging. I had a suspicion, but without being able to access that mote of light magic and its mirror of shadows, then I couldn't confirm anything, I could only speculate. That felt too dangerous with so much at stake.

Jedrek rubbed his eyes and I wondered when he had last slept. "You've been asleep for two days and gone for a full day before that. Even with all that time, though, I fear that we're not remotely prepared for facing what came through the door. There are maybe seven teams to stand against individual gods. Many, many more are unassigned or refuse to work with members of other nations."

"Then why are they here?" My head pounded; I'd pushed myself too soon after waking, but there was no time to recover, to feel sorry for myself. "Why come all this way? Why answer my summons?"

"To fight in your army, not at the side of their enemies." Jedrek sighed, shrugging. "I don't have a good answer for you, Calanthe. Mortals are capable of great and terrible things when their lives are at stake—and they most definitely are—but they are also extraordinarily good at making things more difficult than they need to be."

I huffed. I'd seen enough of politics over the last few weeks to know he was speaking truth. "We cannot simply wait for them to come to us. They could slip around Altier and we would never find them."

"Emyna said that they saw your message. They'll come to challenge you directly. Myr was one of the few who would fight you indirectly."

"So, what, we wait here and stand with our army at the gates when the gods come for us with magic blazing?" It didn't feel right. Who knew what they would do to the countryside in the interim? Yes, it had been abandoned during the darkest time of the void, but life was returning.

"I hate to say it, but yes," Jedrek said. He held up a placating hand at my scowl. "We'll send out the teams we have in the hopes that they can take down a few of those who march for us, but you are barely recovered from magic sickness. Even with your immortality fully active, it will take—"

"No." I stood again, ignoring the trembling in my legs. "We ride to meet them. I will not stand by and *wait* for them to find me. I will not risk that they might harm people before we can stop them. I will not wait for a battle that is inevitable."

Jedrek said nothing, only watched me as I paced the room, wincing when my steps sent tingles up my legs. "You truly are like no god I've ever known."

"In what way? Are they all so content to wait for the world to come to them?"

"When you hold the power, why bother going out to declare it? Those who want will come to you. But you...you don't care about power. Only that the people you protect are safe." Jedrek shook his head. "No wonder Emyna could commune with you. You have dreams, my queen. Vast ones. Great ones. Ones that you will fight to maintain."

My cheeks grew warm. I turned back to the window. "Can it be done?"

"If you will it, the entirety of Altier will mobilise on the morrow."

I looked out at the picturesque image before me, the roofs of the city peeking up over the wall of the palace, decorating the sky with plumes of smoke from the fires in the homes. A dusting of snow capped the buildings and a few flakes fell, adding to the serenity of the scene. People had made their lives here, despite the threat of the void. They were happy. I would not risk that by bringing gods to their doorstep.

"Then tomorrow, we ride for Ynysfawr. Those

gods we meet on the way? Well, they will obey, or they will be buried beside Myr."

+

—

+

I snuck from the palace just before midnight, listening for the ripple of people's steps on the stones to keep well and truly unseen. There was a remarkable amount of activity for such a time of night, but my command to ride had been taken in truth. Already, the small teams had been sent off to see what could be done about the gods, but I counted on none of them for success. How could I, when I saw what destruction a singular goddess could reap?

Though I could have gone to the site of the void pool in Starfall Meadow to do my task, I found myself baulking at the thought of passing by the crater I'd left behind after rescuing Astraea. I didn't know what destruction lay there in full—I'd been near unconsciousness when we emerged—but whispered stories told me it was vast. I hoped that the price was worth the reward. My heart twisted at the thought of Casimir so easily walking away from me.

My steps instead lead me through the streets of Altier, ducking into shadows and turning my head away, hood of my cloak pulled forward, when anyone passed. Despite the snow and the cold, even the city was full of activity; those who had pledged themselves to my cause were gathering supplies, saying goodbyes to families. I saw more than one mother and father hugging their children as they lifted a pack or makeshift weapons to their shoulder.

How many of them would not return?

At last, I came to a place that would suit. The buildings on either side of the street were without light, empty, quiet. The snow here was untouched, showing no signs that anyone had been in this dilapidated part of the city for at least the last twelve hours. An icy wind blew at the crossroads.

I knelt at the centre of the crossroads, looking into the darkness that crept up on me. For an instant, so brief I barely noticed it, there was a tug near my heart, like some invisible thread had been pulled taut.

Dancer.

I pressed a hand to my side, gasping. I hadn't felt even the remotest hint of my connection with the shadow tiger for weeks, now. I'd begun to lose hope, to think my companion lost. I ground my teeth and reached for that connection, that thread. In my mind's eye, I saw a brief flash of fur and claw that dripped shadows. There was anger, *rage*. And fear.

In another heartbeat, the image was gone. I pressed a hand to my mouth to keep from crying out. My tears turned to ice, the wind caressing my face.

Dancer was alive. Furious and afraid, but alive. My companion, my best friend, who so easily understood me, even without words. Alive. Not lost.

I wanted to jump up and follow that thread to wherever Dancer was, but I could not. I had a duty to fulfil. So, blinking away tears, I brushed the snow from the ground and pressed my hands to the rough cobbles.

"Devereux, King of the Void and Keeper of its People, I would bargain with you."

The shadows coalesced into a figure. Devereux. Cloaked in darkness threaded with crimson, that crown of bones upon his brow, he wore a sword at his waist and held a bow in his hands. He took one look at me and broke out into a grin. "My lady Calanthe. Has the time come?"

"The door opened. I don't know how many came through, but they search for me. I don't intend to let them get this far without a fight." I rose from the ground and held out my hands to Devereux. He slung the bow over his shoulder and grasped my hands. Shadows danced between us, weaving threads through our fingers.

"My forces are ready," he said. "Impatient, actually, but such is the way of the fell void when faced with a battle."

I smiled, the first one in what felt like ages. "Are you sure they're not just taking after their king?"

He chuckled. "It's possible. I haven't exactly

become renown for my patience." Devereux looked around, frowning at the ramshackle buildings. "It's a bit narrow for a crossing, but we can make do. Casimir can organise the groupings, direct them where to go. Where is he?"

I bit my tongue to keep from saying exactly what was on my mind. That twist of bitterness jabbed deep into my side. "He is...otherwise engaged."

"He doesn't know you're out here, does he?" Devereux frowned. He released my hands and scoffed. "I thought you were going to be more careful about your safety!"

"I cannot be killed, Devereux. How dangerous can it be to come to a crossroads in Altier when you take that into consideration?" I brushed snow from my skirts in a huff.

"Dangerous enough when there are *gods* on the loose. Damn it, Astr——" he broke off, his shadows freezing in mid air. Carefully, he turned to me. "Calanthe. I'm sorry. Calanthe."

I snorted. "It's been nearly a whole moon since anyone has called me by that name. I guess some habits are difficult to break, even when they're little more than lies."

"You know that I didn't mean to hurt you when I named you thus. When I proclaimed you the Chosen One. There was little choice, and——" Devereux broke off. He narrowed his eyes, the pupils glowing orange in the darkness. "I heard a...shift in the world two days ago. What did you do? Where is Casimir?"

I wished so desperately that Dancer were here, so I could bury my head in his fur and take comfort from his strength. Instead, I held my shoulders back, my head high, and borrowed my strength from the earth. "Casimir is performing his duty, as is required of him."

"His duty is to you. It has been since...Stars above, Calanthe, you're not saying that you...you *found* her?" Devereux ran a hand through his hair, knocking his crown askew. For a moment, he glared at he straightened the object, but concern won out in the play of emotions. He took a step towards me. "Where was she? Alive?"

"Alive. In the chamber beneath the earth where I was made." I shrugged, though I wanted to shrink away and hide. "She is recovering, though the loss of her magic has been a blow."

Devereux let out a string of curses that all but echoed through the crossroads. I shook my head. "It's fine. Really. I know what it is to do one's duty, and I do not begrudge Casimir that."

"But—"

I held a up a hand and Devereux fell silent. "I came here to request aid. Will you now renege on your bargain, Majesty?"

Devereux tightened his jaw. "A bargain made is bound in chains. My forces are yours to command."

"Then, if you please, lead them to the eastern slopes beyond Altier. We ride from there tomorrow."

Devereux bowed, the move practised and graceful, reminding me that he had been born to a crown, even if it was not the one he currently bore. Whereas I was taking one by force. What gave me that right? To claim dominion over the other gods?

I hid my hands in the folds of my skirt so Devereux wouldn't see them shake. Instead, I kept my head held high and watched as the shadows around the crossroads began to move and take the shape of creatures born not of dreams, but nightmares.

<h1 style="text-align:center">CHAPTER 23</h1>

Needless to say, the next day held quite a bit of chaos. No one from Altier expected the mass of shadowy monsters that waited for them. I had stayed the night with Devereux and his forces, wandering among them and saying very little. Part of me had been looking for Dancer, for that tenuous connection that occasionally fluttered beneath my ribs. Mostly, though, I had been thinking with very little result. My presence with the collection of voidlings and worse was the only thing that reduced panic, though it was difficult to dispel all fear.

"What is this?" Jedrek asked, riding up to me with Casimir and Astraea by his side. Tali was in a nearby group with her grandmother and Kina. And beside them, to my utter surprise, was Beatrice, bedecked in armour that looked tailor made for her, a razor thin sword at her hip.

"What are you doing here?" I asked, ignoring Jedrek.

"I am here to fight. To make my own name." She didn't look directly at me, her eyes fixed somewhere off in the distance. I glanced over my shoulder and found Devereux staring back at her, frowning. "Or am I not allowed a second chance."

This was far more than a second chance, but I just bowed my head. "Welcome, Lady Beatrice."

Without a word, she spurred her horse forwards, riding straight towards her brother. It seemed the sort of reunion that was meant for private spaces, but there was little privacy to be found on the eve of war, so I simply turned away and let them have a moment unobserved. Instead, I found Casimir watching me with an intensity that sent shivers up my spine. I flinched.

"What is this? These are voidlings," Jedrek said, staring openly at a Malgrwm—a creature of horse, crow, and cat—that stalked by. A trio of unicorns knocked horns together, sparks flying. These were creatures made of shadow and starlight, wisps of fog, drapes of greenery. Many of them were voidlings familiar to this realm, and the humans who had battled them for centuries. But others, those that stalked through on two legs, antlers decorating their brows, wings at their backs, some perfectly beautiful, others horrifying and grotesque, those were far more than mere voidlings. I could feel their ancient magic roiling off of them in waves.

"You summoned him," Casimir said in a whisper. *Without me*, I filled in silently. Astraea, on her horse beside him, stiffened at the rawness of his words.

"Yes. King Devereux pledged his assistance when the time came. The time has come, so I called him—and his forces—forth."

"The voidlings have no king," Astraea said. "They are nothing but disorganised, mindless beasts who hid in a world of beauty while attacking the world of humans out of fear."

"Such it was during your reign, Star." Devereux approached, mist draped over his shoulders like a cloak. He tilted his head in acknowledgement of me, the spires of his bone crown glistening with what looked like blood. "Things change."

Astraea straightened her shoulders. "Do you think I am unaware of that? I have watched the turn of the heavens for longer than you have dreamt of a free world. I fell because I *wanted* change."

Devereux quirked his lips in a courtier's smile. "Then why play saviour over and over and over again?"

The star flinched, a gasp escaping her lips. Her eyes filled with tears and she bit her lip to stop the trembling. "Is it too much to believe that I just wanted to help people? That maybe I didn't know how else to do that than by doing what I did?"

"You had us build an entire religion around something that was a farce. A game." Beatrice was suddenly there at her brother's elbow. For someone who had been groomed for the role of High Priestess to the Temple of the Fallen Star, she stared at her idol with undisguised loathing. "You manipulated people into begging for your presence, for your assistance, when in the mean time we were dying in our attempts to push back the darkness, and the darkness was attempting to push us back. You appeared just when hope was running low and people *loved* you for it. Then, you vanished only to repeat the cycle again and again. You were cruel, toying with our lives. Yet you claim to have come to *help* people?"

Astraea let a tear fall down her cheek before she dashed it away with the back of her hand. "That was all I ever wanted," she said.

"Tell that to the dead." Beatrice spat on the ground and strode away to where her horse waited, bitterness weighing her shoulders low. Perhaps, now that she knew the truth, now that she had seen the consequences of her own actions, she could make her own name. Could carve out an existence of her own.

Astraea tossed her head. "Does she know what I have done? What I have sacrificed? My magic—"

"Was taken from you to fix the tear in the worlds that you caused," Devereux said with a casual air.

"Casimir, you know it's not true! I didn't do those things maliciously. I didn't know!" She turned to the silent guardian beside her. He tightened his grip on the reins of his horse so that his knuckles showed white through the living shadows that danced across his skin. His armour was that of the fallen star stone, dark and gleaming with some unidentifiable cosmic light. The only hint of his life as I'd known him—dressed in ivory and black, living fully amongst the humans—was the sword at his belt, the hilt wrapped in plain leather. Except for that, he looked almost unfamiliar to me. Stoic, empty. Present only to bow his head at the star's words and say nothing, eyes fixed on his horse's back.

For an instant, he looked at me. My heart stuttered. My breath caught. My throat grew tight. Then, he looked away and the moment shattered.

"I think, Astraea, that you have been too long basking in your own glory." Jedrek's words were cruel, sharp. "Perhaps ask yourself what you really meant to do all those years ago. Perhaps—"

"Enough." I lifted my hand and silence fell. "The past is over and done with, regardless of motivations. There is no need to inflict pain over something that cannot be undone."

Jedrek inclined his head. Astraea looked as though she wanted to say something, but I ignored her. "Devereux, are your people ready?"

"They move at your command," he said with a

sweeping bow, looking positively gleeful at what was to come.

"Jedrek, can you explain to the humans what the voidlings and, er, fey creatures are doing here? Just to those most likely to spread the word that they are not our enemies?" Still, the two forces, magical and human, lingered apart. The voidlings looked curious, but the hands on weapons stayed their progress.

"I'll find the appropriate gossips," Jedrek said. "We'll be ready to ride in half an hour."

It felt too long and yet too soon. I nodded and he rode off. That left me to get ready myself. I found Tali and started towards her.

"Calanthe—" Casimir cut off with a strangled sound. I looked over my shoulder. "I just...I..."

I waited, but no more words were forthcoming, perhaps due to the star sitting by his side, gaping. So I held onto the tatters of my broken heart and walked away to war.

They crowned my in an iron band and put me on a horse in borrowed armour. The sword at my side was mostly for show, since everyone seemed to know that I couldn't do more than draw it from its sheath successfully. At my left rode Tali, holding tightly to the reins with her one arm, expression forged of steel. At my right was Beatrice, who refused to look at me and who I had no doubt would carve her name in the annals of history. Behind me were a mix of humans from all over the continent, some trained warriors, others who held pitchforks as if they were a lifeline. Threaded throughout the humans were creatures described best in legends and poems.

Without a word, we marched.

I didn't know how far we would have to travel before we came upon one or all of the gods, or whether we would come across the seven small parties of people who had gone ahead to try and fell immortals themselves. I hoped that we would meet them soon, if only to get this over with. I also hoped that the gods were long gone from this place, that we would never find them.

"Hey," Tali said after about an hour of riding. "I wanted to ask you—"

"I'm fine." I was not fine. "We'll face the gods and win this world its freedom."

My priestess snorted. "I was going to ask you about Casimir, but if you'd rather talk about the chances of us coming out of this, then fine. I'm here for you."

I flushed. "Ah."

"I know that things have been a little chaotic, what with the end of the world riding towards us, but the tension between you is palpable." Tali tossed a look over her shoulder to where I knew Casimir and

Astraea rode not that far behind, but I couldn't bear to see. Was he watching me? Talking with her?

"Even I have noticed it," Beatrice cut in. "And if I have, then there is no doubt that the rest have. Lord Casimir is...a powerful warrior, a constant sign of strength. It is why the Void Runners follow him so easily, though Garwith ostensibly gave his blessing. But now, to have him at odds with you, well, do not be surprised if there are questions."

I glared at the back of my horse's neck. I didn't want to talk about this at all, let alone with Beatrice, but Tali's concerned expression had me giving in. I glossed over what had happened with Astraea trying to kill me by saying, "He was always duty bound to the star. That is why he rides with her."

Tali snorted. "That's ridiculous."

"I'm inclined to agree," Beatrice said. "That man, or whatever he is, was besotted with you. It was impossible not to notice. And you, in return..."

"Yes," I said on a sigh, not entirely sure why we were having this conversation. "I love him."

"Clearly," the princess scoffed. Then, in a more serious tone, "For him to turn his back on you, even if it was for some duty to that treacherous star, is the height of folly."

"Folly? It's idiotic!" Tali said. "Casimir's duty to Astraea should have *ended* when she fell. They're no longer bound by the rules of the heavens, and yet he still follows her around like a kicked dog."

I winced. Surely, that wasn't fair to Casimir. He was a good man, one who valued honour. One who did not renege on his promises, no matter what got in the way. As I tried to speak those arguments, though, all I could do was feel the hurt that his turning his back on me had caused, no matter how well I understood why he did it. So I said nothing at all.

"I'm sorry," Tali murmured. "You deserve a love that—"

"Please. Just...he's doing his duty. I understand it. I support it."

"That doesn't mean it doesn't hurt," Beatrice said quietly. "Like your heart is being carved out of your chest."

I flinched. "It sounds like you know from experience."

She shrugged and sighed. "It doesn't matter, not anymore. Let's change the topic. Such as why your *grandmother* is accompanying this war party, poet."

Tali groaned and heaved a dramatic sigh. "Don't remind me. Apparently it's something about this event being so significant that one *dharangui* is not enough, and..."

I listened to their chatter in silence for a while, following along as much as I could. Some of it was inane, some of it poignant, but above all it felt normal. Human. I found myself enjoying spending time with caustic, manipulative Beatrice more than I ever had before. She was less sharp like this. Less bound by ambition. And Tali seemed more than eager to have a female friend to talk with that actually wanted to natter about anything and everything.

I'd been a poor friend to her, I thought. I was constantly bringing her my problems and rarely taking hers on in exchange. She had struggled with losing an arm, and I had only given it a cursory thought. Had the healers helped her with balancing exercises? She seemed more able to keep her seat while riding, now. I hadn't even thought to ask, only assumed that she would find the strength to succeed, even when I tasked her with my priesthood.

"Hey," Tali said, drawing her horse near enough to mine that her knee brushed against mine. "You alright?"

"Shouldn't I be asking you that?" I nodded towards her missing arm. "I've hardly asked about you at all in all of this."

"Frankly, you're the only person who hasn't treated me like some sort of breakable piece of porcelain. It's refreshing. And don't you dare start feeling guilty for being busy." Tali glared at me. "You have been dealing with battling *gods* who want us all dead. You rescued the star from underground. You've had...You've had Casimir walk away from you. All of this while only having memories that stretch back six months?"

I hunched my shoulders. She was making this sound worse than it was. Making it seem like the world lay upon my back, when really all I did was warn people and try to organise them against what was coming. Hardly worth the sort of admiration that shone in people's eyes when I passed.

"You're doing it again," Tali said, using the end of her reins to strike my leg, jolting me back to reality. She was frowning in earnest, now, her displeasure plain. "Seeing yourself as anything but worthy of what you've accomplished. You can't take all the blame for the wrongs on your shoulders without also acknowledging the things that you've done right. You *saved* us from the void! You killed Myr. You *rescued that damned star*."

I flinched. "That was just—"

"I agree with your angry priestess," Beatrice said, riding closer. She studied me. "You show remarkable backbone when the situation calls for it, but you seem to think that everything is your fault. It's foolish. And I know you don't like me much, but if you take my advice on anything, you should take it on this. You are worthy of good things. Act like it."

Then, with a toss of her hair, she rode off, heading towards a patch of nightmarish creatures who parted at her approach. Devereux, crowned in bone and followed by two enormous wolf-like beasts with horns, tipped his head at his sister and even laughed at something she said.

"She's right. I never thought I'd find myself agreeing with anything she said, but she is right." Tali shook her head. "Now, come on, let's go find my grandmother before she talks the ear off of everyone in hearing range."

The rest of the day's ride was spent in a similar manner, moving from one group of people to the next, offering my ear when they wished to talk and giving encouragement where I could. People asked questions about our destination, about who we searched for, and I tried to fill in the answers as best I could. Unfortunately, I was as lacking in information as everyone else. Emyna hadn't told me who else came through; I knew only that they would come for me.

We settled into a slight valley that first night, the camp feeling cramped with so many people. The land was open enough that we could have easily spread out, but no one wanted to risk being too far away from others. Much like camping out when the void still loomed over the land, safety lay in numbers and fire. Devereux's people lingered on the outskirts of the firelight, a sort of perimeter of shadowy monsters that seemed to both make people nervous and provide comfort.

I found myself with a bowl of stew at a fire near the centre of the camp without quite knowing how I got there. Jedrek sank down beside me, and Devereux sat on my other side. Tali was already asleep, her head turned towards the fire.

Devereux stretched out his hands, hissing as the

fire seemed to leap for him. I contained the flames with a thought, but the damage had been done. The king of the void leaned away from the light.

"There are things I miss about this world," he said. "And things I do not. The warmth of a fire is one I miss, though apparently the natural tendency of the void to be at odds with fire remains."

"I can douse it, if you like," I said, holding out my hand to call the flames to me. Devereux shook his head.

"No, I'll happily just enjoy the memory. Fires don't burn the same way in the void. They're like... ghosts. Providing illumination but little warmth."

"No wonder your people look so disgruntled all the time," Jedrek said on a yawn. "I'd complain, too, if my fires provided no warmth."

Devereux kicked dirt at the god, getting some on my clothes. I sighed and brushed it off, then tilted my head back. The sky was dim, the light from the fires making it hard to see the stars with no moon.

"Do you think they're watching all of this?" I asked.

Jedrek snorted. "The stars? I doubt it. Astraea was the most worldly of them all, and she fell because of it. The rest? They might watch us for entertainment, but they're probably far more wrapped up in their own politicking and battles."

"Battles?" Devereux craned his neck. "What could

they possibly have to fight over? The gods aren't there."

"They have warring families who vie for power. It's been going on for centuries." Jedrek nudged me, bringing my attention back down to earth. "Don't concern yourself with the heavens, Calanthe. They are distant for a reason."

I turned—just for an instant—to a fire that was somewhat near to ours, but far enough away that we couldn't hear what was being discussed. Only two sat beside it: Casimir and Astraea. For that brief moment I turned, Casimir's eyes found mine like a beacon in the darkness. I felt that familiar spark of power that flowed between us. On a breath, I turned away.

"He's a fool," Devereux growled, glaring at their fire. "After all she's done, to turn his back on *you* in favour of—"

"I told him to," I said. "I told him that if he needed to fulfil his duty, then I understood. It wasn't a question of whether he...whether he..." I couldn't bring myself to say any more, the words caught in my throat.

"He loves you," Jedrek said. "I saw what he was like with her. Before, I mean. Compared to what he was like with you? It was completely different. He was jealous and had a razor thin temper, yet he was fine to bow and scrape for her every whim. With you? He is at ease. At peace. As though all is right with the world."

I stood in a rush. "I am going to go walk the boundary of the camp, see if everyone is alright."

"I'll go with you—" Devereux started to stand.

"No, that's alright. I'll be fine." Without waiting for him to protest, I stepped away from the fire and into the darkness. The camp was relatively quiet; most were sleeping already, and those that weren't had their heads bent together in conversation or were polishing weapons that would soon be stained with blood. Gold blood, I hoped. Some gave me a wave as I passed, but thankfully, no one stopped my progress. Even Devereux's forces did little more than bow their heads as I passed.

All save one.

I knew you were not what they claimed. The unicorn who had almost fatally injured Dancer. I flinched as it thrust its nose at me and took a sniff. It snorted and shook its head, shadowy mane flying. Its horn gleamed in the dim light.

"You were the only one who told me as such," I said, pulling my cloak tighter around me. "Though maybe you could have told me the whole truth."

The unicorn snorted a laugh, pawing at the ground. *It is not my place to tell godlings their business. But, you gave us our king, so I owe you thanks for that.*

"You're welcome."

The night was quiet beyond the perimeter of the camp. Any animals that had returned to the area after the void was sealed away were now quiet. Too many people, perhaps. Or perhaps, they sensed that things were about to fall to pieces.

Where is your tiger? The cub seemed remarkably devoted to you.

Dancer. I stiffened. The earth beneath my feet crackled at my alarm. I closed my eyes and soothed the magic roiling within me. "Vanished when the void fell. I...I think he's still alive." I rubbed my chest where our tether was.

The unicorn nudged me again with its nose, right where my fingers lay. *Your bond remains. The tiger lives.*

Relief swept through me in a wave. I nearly fell to the ground at the news, my body releasing all its tension at once. I didn't, though. Arms—familiar, comforting, cruel arms—caught me, holding me close.

"Can we talk?" Casimir asked, breath warm against my cheek. "Please?"

CHAPTER 24

I gathered myself and pulled away—gently—from Casimir's arms. The unicorn tossed its head and wandered a short distance away, far enough to not catch our immediate conversation, but close enough that there could be no mistaking its watching us. Casimir's expression was pained, his eyes shrouded by shadow that had nothing to do with the night.

"Certainly," I said in answer to his question. "What's wrong? Is Astraea well? I know you said that her connection to the sky had been severed while underground; is she recovered?"

Casimir winced. "She's perfectly well. Her magic remains gone but for the bare essence of what makes her a star, but that is hardly life threatening."

"I'm glad to hear it."

"Look, I…" He paused, then groaned in frustration. "This is so much more difficult, more complicated than I thought."

More complicated? More difficult? It was not I who professed love and then walked away. I froze. No, he hadn't walked away. He was fulfilling his duty. Wasn't he? Maybe Beatrice and Tali and Devereux and everyone else was right. Maybe he had walked away. Splinters of pain pierced my heart so that I could barely breathe.

Casimir hardly seemed to notice my distress, so concerned was he with his own. I could not fault him for that. "I wanted to apologise for how...strained things have been over the last few days. Astraea, well, she is set against you given what your mothers did to her. And she is not used to being powerless. I just want her to feel safe and well and—"

"Casimir," I cut in. "Please. I know full well of your devotion to her. You *fell* from the heavens for her. That sort of love doesn't just fade with absence."

He flinched. "I thought we'd talked about this before. What I had with Astraea, what she had with me, that wasn't love. Not really. It was obsession, maybe. Or need. Hers to be admired and mine to, well, be wanted in that way. But it wasn't love. Not like what I feel for you."

I wanted his words to sway me, to make me swoon as they had done. I wanted to fall in his arms and take comfort in an enduring love that would last the centuries that my immortality promised. I wanted all of this. Standing there, watching him, though, after all that had transpired, all that had happened, I found I couldn't move.

"You claim you love me. No, don't interrupt, let me finish. You claim that you love me, and I love you in return. Desperately. But I am finding it exceedingly difficult to explain away your actions over the last few days. Trying to explain things to Devereux, to Tali, to *Beatrice*? Perhaps I'm too wrapped up in this, because they all say the same thing." I shook my head, wrapping my cloak tighter. "That I am the fool for holding onto this when you have your heart's desire right beside you again."

Casimir was suddenly inches away from me, his hands—cold and snow-brushed—cupping my face. He looked at me with tears in his eyes, despair written across his face. "Astraea wanted nothing from me but my undying devotion, admiration, passion, love. She wanted me to stare after her as if she were the centre of the universe. And when I did not agree with her over the void, over her treatment of people, she *walked away* from me. With ease."

I tore myself away, a snarl building in my chest. "And you did not walk away from me?"

He recoiled as though I'd physically struck him. He was stricken, eyes wide and jaw slack, breath a harsh cloud against the winter night. Before I could say another word, whether in apology or anger I didn't know, he stumbled backwards then turned and fled back to the fires of the camp.

He hurts for you. The guardian's heart is not easily won, and when it is won, it remains steadfast and true. The unicorn returned to my side, pressing its shoulder against me, as if to ward off a cold that I would never feel, not with the fire in my veins.

"Yet now, he is in turmoil. You wish to put the blame at my feet?" I rubbed the spot where my connection with Dancer lay, hoping I would feel something. Anything.

The blame lies in many places, never in one. I merely wished to point out that it seems to me that he cares for you. Deeply.

As if that were meant to make me feel better. I sighed. "Thank you for your company. I think I had better head back to—"

A noise, like a stick cracking or a rock falling and splitting, sounded from the darkness beyond the camp. Immediately, the unicorn stepped in front of me, nostrils flaring, horn aimed at whatever would emerge, be it animal, human, or god.

Would they attack at night?

The humans, certainly, were more vulnerable in the darkness.

A silvery shape took form, streaked with dirt and grime. It moved closer. The unicorn reared back, flailing its dangerous hooves. The shape hesitated, then collapsed. A moment later, I realised that I recognised the shape, though it was wildly different from the form in my dreams.

"Emyna," I said, pushing past the unicorn and rushing to the god's side. The silvery god of dreams shared the same features as the one in my own dream, but that was where the similarity ended. The neat silver hair was lank and greasy. The shining silver skin was dim and bruised, covered in grime and tinged with frostbite. Their clothes were ragged and thin, hardly suitable for such frigid weather. Their feet were bare and streaks of gold told me where they'd stepped and bled.

"Lady," the god said, smiling up at me. "You're here."

"I'm here," I promised, brushing back a strand of their hair. I turned to the unicorn. "Fetch—"

Devereux appeared a moment later, as though he'd stepped from the shadows themselves. "What happened? Who is that?"

"The god of dreams. Emyna. They've pledged themselves to our cause. I don't know why they're so…"

"Gods do not dream," Emyna whispered, voice growing faint. They smiled. "They have little need for me."

Devereux let out a string of curses, then turned to the unicorn and issued orders in a low, furious voice. A moment later and two other creatures of the void, much like that beast which Beatrice met, antlered and with skin of tree bark, appeared. They carefully moved me aside and picked up Emyna, carrying the god to our fire. I followed, not quite certain what to do with myself.

Jedrek sprang up as we approached, and even Tali was startled awake as Emyna was laid by the fire. Jedrek hissed. "What happened?"

I explained Emyna's appearance in a few words, then found myself stumbling back, once again being caught in familiar arms. Casimir watched, Astraea by his side. Her mouth was tight and her brows furrowed, but I could not tell if it was in disdain or confusion. She nodded towards the silvery god. "A recruit, I presume?"

"Proof of what the gods will do to those who disagree with them," Casimir answered, squeezing my arms. I thought about pulling away, but in that moment, I settled in, letting myself be held. Letting some of the stress of the last few days melt away. For a moment, all was well between us, as it should be. Astraea scoffed, and the spell was broken.

"Come, Casimir. We do not need to watch the healing of a god. Morning will tell us soon enough if they lived." She turned away without looking back, expecting Casimir to follow.

Jedrek paused in his ministrations, looking up at Casimir. He glared, eyes narrowing. "Well? Are you going to stay and help, or will you walk away from this as well?"

Casimir flinched. He released me and staggered back a step, indecision warring in his expression. He closed his eyes. The shadows on his skin danced in the firelight, hinting at the chaos of what lay beneath. He shuddered. "I will fetch some water and a cloth."

He was gone.

Jedrek scoffed. "Coward. Forgive me, Calanthe, but you are better off for his going, if he cannot even muster enough strength to stand by you in the face of that star."

I bit my tongue to keep from arguing. There was no point. I loved Casimir. Perhaps I always would. Perhaps I had been made by my mothers with the capacity to love like this only once. Or, perhaps, I would find a new love in the centuries to come. No, contemplating that was too much to bear. I only knew that in that moment, I both yearned and ached. I hurt. And no amount of arguing on either side would prove a salve for that wound.

"Will Emyna live?" I asked, kneeling next to the god, laying their head in my lap.

Jedrek winced. He pulled back the god's shirt, revealing wounds that were nasty, and likely deep. The blood the poured from there was a bright gold, but the skin around was puckered and red, as though it were infected. "They must have tortured them. The other gods, I mean. Emyna...well, they were never a very powerful god away from mortals. Even here, in the mortal realm they are hardly a god of the first order, given that their power lies in the insubstantial nature of dreams."

"They're dying, aren't they?" I brushed aside a lock of silver hair. Emyna's eyes fluttered and they looked up at me, gaze full of hope.

"You're still here," they murmured. I clasped the god's hand, squeezing tightly.

"I'm still here. I'll be here until..." I couldn't bring myself to say it.

"I do not fear death," Emyna said, squeezing my hand weakly. "I have dreamed of what it would be like so very many times. If it would be like the dreams I commanded, or something not even I could dream. I am glad, though, that I lived long enough to meet a goddess who could dream. Who would dream."

A body knelt beside me. I flinched, prepared to defend Emyna with earth and fire so that they might have a peaceful end. My magic calmed in an instant and I let out a cry of relief. Casimir knelt there, sleeves rolled up, a basin of water and several cloths beside him.

"You came back," I breathed.

"Always." He smiled at me, one of pain and sorrow and regret, but a smile nonetheless. Casimir settled into his work, washing Emyna's wounds with great care, though they would never truly heal. Jedrek caught my eye, but said nothing. I wished I could interpret that arch look.

Emyna murmured a few more things to us in

those last hours before dawn, words often drowned out by a cough or a breath that never seemed full enough. Jedrek cursed once, but otherwise kept silent. Casimir said nothing at all. I sat there, running a damp cloth over Emyna's forehead and wished I had soothing words that would follow them into the Beyond.

Tali rested her hand on my shoulder shortly after the sun's rays crested the horizon. I craned my neck, muscles stiff. She offered me a sad smile. "They're gone, Calanthe."

It was true. I'd felt them go minutes past, like an exhalation on the wind. Somehow, I could not quite bring myself to leave their body.

"I don't know if it's better or worse that I hardly knew them," I said at last.

"Death is a natural part of the order. There is no shame in grieving those who have gone, but you needn't dwell. They are in the Beyond." Tali offered her hand to pull me up and I took it, the both of us stumbling a bit. I looked around the fire, but found only Jedrek, already wrapping Emyna in a spare blanket, as there was no winding sheet to be had.

"Where is Casimir?"

"He was with Astraea when I saw him a few minutes ago," Tali said. Indeed, when I turned towards their fire, I saw Casimir there, head bent together with the star's. I turned away before he could know I was looking at him.

"What do you want to do, my lady?" Jedrek asked, the words formal. An adviser asking his queen. The mantle of power settled on my shoulders, heavier than before now that this new death lay fresh at my feet. I lifted my chin, facing the sunrise.

"We force them to take responsibility for what they have done."

*

An hour later and I sat astride a horse while all the others looked on. My plain iron band sat across my brow, and for once I was glad of its presence. I spoke loudly enough that all could hear. "Last night, Emyna, the god of dreams came to us. Not as an enemy, but as an ally. The other gods who came through the door tortured them. Gave them wounds so deep that there was no recovering. This morning, Emyna died in my arms."

The people muttered between themselves, but apart from caring for my sake, I doubted this bothered them much at all. After all, they were here to kill gods. What was one more?

"The other gods have crossed their last line. I will permit no more of their cruel whims. No more of their thirst for power. No more taking from us. This world is *ours*! It's time they learned that lesson once and for all."

They started cheering, some drawing swords to

lift to the heavens. Some beat a tattoo on theirs chests. Others chanted. Each according to their custom and culture, lending their voice to the whole. The fire in me roared in agreement, thrumming through my veins even as the earth sang in my bones.

I held up a hand and silence fell in an instant.

"Before Emyna died, they gave us crucial information. They told us *who* came through the door before it sealed again. Who we face today. Arcturus, the god of winter. Lalruk, the goddess of thieves. Aza, the goddess of memories. Cerlas, the god of fools. And Talorsa, the god of war."

It was the last one who worried me most. I didn't dare let that worry show on my face.

"We have not heard from the bands who went forth, but do not fear. Five gods can hide easily from a few people in this vast country. From us, though? From *me*? They cannot hide." I let a little magic loose, enough for the ground to rumble but not shake. The warriors cheered again, and this time, I joined them. Only Jedrek, Tali, Astraea and Casimir did not cheer.

Without further preamble, without thinking of the body I'd buried where they died, without looking back over my shoulder at he who held my heart, I turned my horse and rode forth, knowing that my quarry lay before me. And would most likely be seeking me out, just as I sought them.

The initial rush of energy lasted nearly until

midday, the humans keeping up tirelessly, grim determination plain in their mien. However, the weather grew colder, snow spitting in furious flurries from the sky. With sharp winds to bolster them, icy patches formed anywhere the snow did not drift too high. The horses began to struggle, slipping on the ice or floundering in the drifts. We had to dismount and push forward on foot, but that was slow going. The energy of my people began to wane.

I cleared the way as best I could with my magic, but unless I burned away the ice with open flame, it remained solid and stubborn. After we stopped for a rest, huddled around a few scant fires that we managed to shelter from the wind, Jedrek came up to me.

"They're faltering," he said, tugging his own fur cloak tighter around his shoulders. "The humans, I mean. They cannot keep up this pace for much longer."

"This is Arcturus, then? The weather, I mean."

"Likely. He'll try to wear us down with the snow and ice and wind. It's harder to fight in this sort of cold. Fingers lose hold of weapons. Muscles falter. Some will succumb to frostbite. Others to exhaustion from pushing through the snow." Jedrek shivered. I used a little more of my energy to fan the flames of the fires and tried not to listen too closely to the sighs of relief.

"Should we..." I looked around at the many miserable forms pressing as close to the fires as possible. "Should we turn back?"

"No." Tali stepped forward, almost flagging with exhaustion. Her cheek was frostbitten. I reached up and brushed the ice away, my inner warmth reducing the bite. Tali flinched, then sagged. "Thank you. No, we should not turn back now. It's miserable, yes, and it's likely to get worse, but not one of us wishes to turn away. We will not flee."

"I was afraid you would say that," I muttered. I gave her my cloak, since I hardly needed it; my internal fires kept me warm with ease. "Then we shouldn't linger here. We need to find them. Put a stop to this."

"I agree," Jedrek said. "They obviously know we— you—are coming. Waiting to draw them out will do no one any good in this weather."

"We press on?" Tali asked. I nodded. "Good. I'll go tell everyone."

It only got worse from there. The snow turned to a blizzard, the conditions so bad that all I could see in any direction was white. Even with my fire burning, I couldn't attempt to clear away the snow without accidentally harming the humans who followed me. Within an hour, it became impossible to move at more than a snail's pace. Within ten minutes of that, I heard shouts through the storm that people were beginning to fall from the cold.

We called a halt to the travel. I carved a scoop out

of the side of a hill with my earth magic, building up a half wall to keep the snow out. People crowded together and wind still howled through the hollow, but at least we were out of the worst of it.

"Calanthe," Jedrek called from the wall. "We need someone on watch, but it's too cold for a human. Would you...?"

"Of course." I stepped out into the snow, my warriors at my back. This was a mistake. A huge mistake. I should have just brought Jedrek with me. Maybe Casimir, if he would come. No one else. I shouldn't have risked the lives of the mortals. Yes, this was their world, but it was my doing that the door was open. I was to blame for any deaths. I should have faced down the gods on my own, using my considerable power to destroy them before they fully emerged into this world.

I should have done so many things.

I had been a fool. More than a fool.

My thoughts grew muddied, spiralling into a mire of all the things that I had done wrong since emerging from this world. By the time I realised that there was something wrong, something not quite myself in the recollection of fire and earth that surrounded me, it was too late.

Hands grabbed me, rough and fierce. Snow filled my mouth as I tried to scream. Ice covered my eyes. I pulled on my fire, melting through the bindings; they were replaced as quickly as I could burn through them.

Then, I fell into an abyss. One that was so familiar. So *desperately* familiar, full of magma and carved earth, heat licking gently at my face.

"Hello, Daughter."

CHAPTER 25

"Mother." It was impossible. The woman standing before me, wreathed in flowers and vines and with skin of rich, life-giving earth, was dead. Destroyed. She had given all of herself to make me, and we'd never exchanged words except in one memory left at Ynysfawr.

Yet here she was, standing before me with arms spread wide. I let out a little whimper and threw myself into those arms, an act so natural that I wanted to cry for it. She held me close and I breathed in the loamy scent of her hair.

"Hush, Daughter," my mother purred in my ear. "There is nothing to worry yourself with."

"Nothing to worry—" I pulled back in surprise. "Then do you not know?"

"Know what?" Lady Earth asked with a gentle smile.

"The gods. The ones that Astraea bound beyond the void. They're returning and they want to take what was theirs. Only, the world has changed and the mortals are not eager to be subjugated again. We're at war."

"War! What a thought. There is no need for war, my child. The realms are merely returning to the natural order of things." As she spoke, she waved a hand and a flower bloomed, climbing her skirts and twining with her fingers, now draped in tiny pink bells. It was incongruous to have blooming things this deep in the earth, surrounded by fire. My own magic was drawn towards the strangeness; the fire to burn it and the earth to quell its growth.

"The natural order of things?" I dampened my magic, holding tightly to it while it struggled, desperate to surge forth. "Things have changed, Mother, since the gods were away. This land is for the humans, now that I've bound the void in its own realm. This land is for the mortals, that for the magic, and then there is the realm of the gods. Separate."

The ground beneath my feet rumbled as I lost hold of a tiny thread of my magic. The magma surged, spilling over the edge of its lake. My mother looked unconcerned.

"Fear not, Daughter. Things will go back to how they were. There must be balance in all things, and that cannot be achieved without the gods. Surely you know that what the star did was blasphemy?" She paced the ledge of the cave, her feet moving through the magma. She did not wince, did not flinch, did not even seem to notice it was there.

What else was not there was my bier, the place I'd been crafted and born. The place that was swallowed up in fire when I'd turned my back on it and followed after Casimir.

"Blasphemy," I murmured. "Surely she has paid for her sins. There is no need to punish the mortals."

"Daughter, you must understand that—"

"My name. What is it?" My words were even, soft. Just a question from a daughter who had never spoken with her mother. Beneath my skirts, though, my hands were clenched into fists.

Lady Earth chuckled. "What? It's Calanthe, of course. I named you after the ancient flower that—"

"You didn't name me that," I growled, pulling my hands out, threads of fire twining around my left fist, vines around my right. "Casimir did."

"C-Casimir?" My mother waved a dismissive hand. "Don't be ridiculous, Daughter."

"Yes, Casimir, guardian to the Fallen Star, named me. Not you." I called to the magma, to the stalactites and stalagmites that littered the cavern. "And this place? I destroyed it in saving the star."

The magma rose high, a wave of liquid fire that descended upon the false Lady Earth. She didn't scream, only vanished into the abyss that now filled my vision. I squeezed my eyes shut and held onto my magic, ready to burn all that stood in my path.

"I can't hold her," a female voice said, deep and soothing, with an edge of darkness. "She knows it's not a real memory."

"Release her, then, and let her look upon the face of the victors in her little war." This one was masculine, gravelly, rough, promising of violence.

Something was pulled from my head—a sack, most likely—and suddenly I was blinking away the brilliant white of a snow-covered clearing. There were drifts of snow between the trees so deep that it would be nearly impossible to ford them. The trees themselves were covered in a layer of ice, reflecting the sunlight. Spread about at even intervals were five figures, whom I assumed to be the gods we sought.

On the left was a man, slender to the point of emaciation, clothed in white furs, his white hair bound in a multitude of tiny braids, skin a pale, frosty blue. Arcturus, god of winter. Beside him was a cowering, simpering man dressed in gaudy colours, a hat with points and bells perched jauntily on his head. He had the slack-jawed face of a dumb man, and the clever eyes of a fox. Cerlas, god of fools.

On the right were two women, one dressed in black, a hood up and nearly obscuring her face. Lalruk, goddess of thieves. The other was dressed in gauzy, ephemeral fabric, which draped over her like a shroud, hiding her face but for her eyes, which were a bright amber. Aza, goddess of memories.

In the centre, however, was the very image of a warrior. Dressed in armour that was neither too finely polished nor left to rust, he wore a short sword at his left hip, a long dagger on his right, and a bow across his back. A shield lay propped against him, ready for battle at a moment's notice. It was his face, though, which showed the threat: cunning, scarred, intelligent. Talorsa, god of war. Who had proclaimed himself the victor before the battle had even begun.

They'd bound my hands and feet in ice, which I quickly melted away. I called forth the earth magic, also, and commanded the trees to grow. Despite it being the height of winter, they obeyed readily, cracking through their sheaths of ice and curling in to loom over my captors.

Talorsa let out a laugh and spread his hands. "Is that meant to make us surrender, dear *Calanthe?*"

I didn't deign to answer his question. "You think to end this war by my capture? You may have the god of fools with you, but you are more foolish than even I thought."

The smile dropped from Talorsa's face. Cerlas winced, then let out a high-pitched giggle. The god of war growled something and the fool slipped into silence. "We know all about your supposed claim on this land. We know that you think to keep it all for yourself, that you intend to keep the mortals' worship for your own. Do you think that slaying Myr will sway us? Sway *me*?"

"My *claim* on this land?" I scoffed. Fire warmed my blood enough that I could feel the pressure within me rising. I expelled the heat through the ground to keep from exploding. The snow began to melt, enough that Arcturus closed his eyes in concentration to keep it present. I rose to my feet and brushed off the snow, ignoring the looks of the other gods. "I hold no claim to this land."

"No claim?" Aza took a step back. "Then what—"

"This land belongs to the mortals," I snapped. "As you saw when you tried to hold my mind."

"The mortals?" Cerlas asked with a giggle. "You cannot be serious."

"She looks perfectly serious to me," Lalruk said. The thief grinned from beneath her deep hood, revealing a flash of teeth. "Delusional, perhaps, but what can you expect from one such as she. I can practically *smell* how young she is. How unaware of how the world truly works."

Talorsa rested a hand on his hip, close to his dagger, and smiled benevolently at me. "Indeed, child, you have been isolated from your own kind. Perhaps you would be better served by staying amongst us, learning from us. You cannot have had much taste of worship, being so, ah, new."

"New?" The trees shifted their roots in the ground, pulling themselves closer around us, leaving little space for the gods to escape between their trunks. They were trapped with me, whether they knew it or not. I let out a laugh to hide my magic's movements. "You think I do this because I am *new*? Because I haven't tasted the fruits of human devotion? I am daughter of Lady Earth and the Eternal Flame, their heir apparent. I hold their power within me, complete and entire. I saved this world from the void brought down by the Fallen Star Astraea. I have all of this, and you think that the humans do not worship me?"

"If you hold such devotion, such power, then you know the sweetness it brings. To be seen as so bright in the eyes of the humans. To be made more powerful by their adoration. To reach greater heights than ever before." Lalruk shuddered, her cloak shedding snow with the movement. At her feet, tiny tendrils began to emerge from the ground, slowly growing around her legs. I kept my eyes up.

"It means nothing to me," I said.

"All the more reason to leave it for us," Cerlas said. "If you do not want it, then—"

"This world belongs to the mortals."

"The mortals need something to worship. Did they not follow that putrid star after we were banished?" Talorsa growled. "Who will guide them? Who will check their impulses, which we all know are vast and terrible. Who will direct their growth? Be patron to their kings? Who will manage them?"

I lifted my chin. "They will. They are capable beings, after all. They made cities, developed languages. They have music and stories and communities. They have built empires and settled the wilderness."

"Without help!" Talorsa banged on his armoured chest plate, face twisted with fury.

"Not for centuries," I countered. "And if you think the star was the one guiding them during your absence, then you are sorely mistaken. She was selfish, greedy, as *you* are. She wanted none of their politicking and cultural development. She wanted only their adoration. As you do, to fill some hole that you cannot manage to fill yourself."

"You go too far, child," Aza snapped. With a flick of her hand, my head snapped back, vision taken by the abyss. This time, though, I knew what she was about and refused to take part in any memory she showed me. Devereux, in pain as he became taken by the void. Casimir, fighting the voidlings at my side, swearing his undying love. Both gone, now.

"No," I said through gritted teeth, forcing my mind back to the clearing, back to the trees whose roots were now tangled over the ground, whose boughs leaned in closer. I forced myself back to the heat of my fire, streaming through my blood with a dragon's infernal rage. I pulled that fire into my thoughts and sent it through that empty abyss.

Aza screamed.

My vision returned, bright and terrible. Aza's skin was blistering, dripping gold blood as she burned from the inside out. Her hair caught fire and she clawed at her own eyes as they melted from the heat that now consumed her. In another instant, a heart-beat too swift to count, she collapsed to her knees, body a mess of burns and blood. If she started to heal, I did not see it. I only saw death.

"You bitch!" Cerlas lunged for me, only to be held back by Arcturus, his gaze flinty and sharp. Cerlas collapsed, weeping. "You killed her!"

I said nothing, instead looking to Talorsa, daring him to defy me further. He snarled and drew his dagger. "All that power, and you use it to kill your own kind. Perhaps you are the one who should be killed."

"I cannot be killed," I said cooly. "My parentage deemed it thus."

"Then I will tear your arms from your body and watch with glee as you bleed for eternity," Talorsa retorted. He moved for me in a movement so fluid that I, who had barely learned to dance, could never counter it. A step, a flex of muscle, and he was before me, one hand on my shoulder, the other driving his dagger deep into my left eye.

I gasped in pain, and then I could do nothing at all. I was engulfed with pain, bright and blinding. If I could scream, it would have torn the earth asunder. As it was, my magic screamed for me. The trees broke through the ground, their roots reaching to strangle the gods, their limbs aiming for heart and head. My fire exploded outward in a blast that should have levelled forests. Instead, it threw Talorsa back into Lalruk, the two of them falling to the ground in a heap of tangled limbs. Arcturus managed to erect a wall of ice before my fire reached him and the cowering Cerlas. Aza's body disintegrated to ash.

Groaning, taking shallow breaths and with little control over my muscles, I lifted my arms and, fumbling, grabbed the hilt of the dagger. It slid from my eye in a rough motion, releasing another burst of blinding, burning pain. I screamed and curled over, clutching at the ground.

When I could move again, see again, I lifted my hands to the ruined place where my eye had been. Gold blood still flowed there, slowing, healing. Somehow, though, I knew the injury—made by a god's weapon—would be permanent. My eye now matched the burned half of my face: ruined.

"You may not be able to die," Talorsa said, climbing slowly to his feet, right arm cradled uselessly against his side, "but you bleed perfectly well."

"If that is what it takes to keep this world safe, to keep the humans safe, from your appetites, then so be it. I will bleed." I couldn't stand. I was too weak. My magic was shaky after that burst. I could probably manage to pull together one more large attack, but any fine magic was beyond me.

Talorsa staggered towards me, wrenching his arm back into socket as he did. Grimacing, he towered above me. He did not reach for his dagger, discarded on the snow, nor for the sword at his waist. No, he was going to tear into me with his bare hands. "This world belongs to *me*," he hissed.

"Never," I vowed.

The god of war raised his hand to strike. In a blur of shadows, teeth, and claws, something slammed into him, snarling. Talorsa cried out, rolling to the ground to do battle with this new foe. I nearly let out a sigh of relief. Devereux's army had found me. The voidlings and the nightmares he commanded had come.

But, no. There was only one and was nothing so ferocious and capable as the creatures that stalked by Devereux's side. As it pulled away from Talorsa to circle and attack again, my heartbeat filled my ears.

Dancer.

His fur, dark as a starless night with stripes of grey, was ragged and matted. His left ear was shredded and his right was missing entirely. His tail was bent in the middle and hanging low to the ground. He had raw wounds along his flank, bleeding shadows. He limped, his back right paw twisted.

"What is this?" the god of war asked, laughing. "A pitiful Walker Between, come to fight for its mistress? I thought I had done away with you on the other side of the door."

"Dancer," I breathed. The shadow tiger looked at me over his shoulder, and instant only, yet it was enough. The connection, the bond, between us flared to life and I felt every ounce of pain and fury contained within him. I sent my own magic of life and death to him, twining in a braid of rock and flame. Dancer let out a roar.

"Talorsa, Arcturus, Cerlas, Larluk, I bid you now to kneel before me as your queen. To swear to and bide by the laws which I lay down: that you shall not harm a mortal, that you shall not use them for your games, that you shall only protect and advise them. Do you swear to this?" I asked. Dancer let out a rumbling growl beside me.

I still could not stand. My ruined eye throbbed. My magic faltered. Talorsa knew I was weak in that moment, knew that he could easily best me. I would not back down. Not with Dancer beside me once again.

"You guarded the door from the other side," I breathed, sinking my fingers into his fur. He rubbed his head against my shoulder.

"What a touching reunion," Talorsa spat. He was bleeding from various wounds that Dancer inflicted, but already I could see them healing. "You shall never have my surrender."

"Just as you shall never have mine." I leaned against Dancer, using his frame to pull myself to my feet. He growled, low and deep, at the gods, claws digging into the earth.

Talorsa grinned. "Then, I fear we are at an impasse."

"I will not let you take this world."

"Oh, foolish child. You are young. You have eternity stretching before you. Can you honestly say that you will stand against me for your entire immortal existence? Alone?"

"She is not alone."

I stiffened. Beside me, Dancer let out another roar. I watched as Talorsa's easy smile faltered into a scowl. Someone stood beside me, shoulder brushing mine. Tali. Next to her was Jedrek, and beside him, Devereux. On my other side, I felt the touch of a figure so familiar that I didn't even need to turn to see him.

"Casimir," I said on a breath. "You came."

"Always, my love. *Always*."

Behind us, I heard the steps of my army. My people. Their movements had been muffled by the snow before, but on the open ground that my fire had created, they sounded of armour and stomping and impossible determination. No, not impossible determination. *Human* determination.

"This world ceased being yours long ago," I said. "It belongs to them, now. To the humans."

Arcturus stepped forward, ice at his fingertips.

Cerlas stood by his side, and Lalruk beside them both. Talorsa wiped his mouth, leaving a streak of blood there from a cut from Dancer's claws. "The humans were made to worship us. To bow to us. They don't deserve autonomy. They are weak. Finite. They will tear this world apart between them without our guidance."

"No," I said. "They won't."

The humans, lined on either side with voidlings, raised their arms and let out a cry that shook the branches of my trees. Then, they surged forwards and attacked.

CHAPTER 26

I had been in battles before. My first experience was at the battle of the wall, when voidlings breached the palace walls at Altier and I assisted the Void Runners in fighting them back. Then, I'd barely been awakened, my magic was unsteady and limited, and I was afraid of killing. Since then, I'd battled voidlings, humans, and even Myr, the goddess of the hunt. I still disliked killing, but when it came to those trying to harm my friends, my people, I discovered I had few qualms.

For all the battles I'd been in, though, this was, by far, the worst.

Even with Aza dead, four gods was enough to decimate the humans that attacked them. Cerlas happily jabbed a dagger through the throats and eyes of those who were foolish enough to attack him. Arcturus froze any who sought to fight him, or he stabbed them with icicles. Lalruk was more insidious, using the tricks of her thieving trade to appear behind her opponents, to relieve them of their arms, to slit their throats when they were distracted.

Talorsa, though, was in his element, and I doubted very much that any mortal could kill him in the midst of war. He slew with ease, disembowelling, beheading, stabbing and more, faster than I could mark. It didn't help that the clearing, which I had enclosed with trees, was made small and narrow. The humans had barely any room to manoeuvre, and the gods, though they were wrapped up in my roots and vines, were more than capable.

Dancer let out a growl and leaped towards Arcturus. I closed my eyes and forced the trees back, though it took a great deal out of me. I stumbled as the last birch pulled itself away by the roots. Casimir caught me.

"You've used too much magic," he said. A human warrior—one of the Hunters by her armour—charged forwards, only to be killed by an axe to the throat, courtesy of Talorsa, who had pulled the weapon from a dead man at his feet. I flinched at her death, shrinking back.

"This will never work," I breathed. "We learned that with Myr. We need to pull back. We need to do this differently. We—"

"You'll never get them to retreat," Jedrek said, suddenly there beside Casimir, armour splattered with gold blood mixed with red. "The gods captured *you* in the night, Calanthe. The mortals took that as a personal affront. Strategic or not, smart of not, they are here for vengeance."

"I could call a retreat." Even as I spoke, I knew it would never work. The humans were fervent with rage, with conviction. They leaped into battle without a care for the dead around them—or perhaps because they cared for the dead around them. They fought with every inch the passion that they were known for, and more often than not, they lost their lives in exchange for a few swiftly healing cuts on the enemy.

"We need to get you out of here," Casimir said, arm around my waist. "You've used too much magic. You are vulnerable."

"It's already coming back." It was, too, though at a trickle. "I'm not leaving. Not when I can *help*."

Casimir growled something under his breath, then let out a curse when Cerlas lunged for him with a dagger extended. The god of fools had slipped through the humans and come for me. And the humans, foolish, desperate humans, were none the wiser. Casimir hadn't yet drawn his sword and the blow was already aimed.

Jedrek leaped into the fray, all but slamming Cerlas to the ground. The knife meant for Casimir was buried to the hilt in Jedrek's stomach.

I sucked in a breath. "No."

My magic reared its head. Dancer roared. Time seemed to slow.

Jedrek staggered back, pulling the knife from its bloody sheath. Golden drops fell to the ground, each one resoundingly loud in my ears. He looked at me, knife in hand, and frowned.

"Heal," I whispered, clutching Casimir close even as he drew his sword to attack. "Heal, damn you."

Jedrek, god of the children of kings, opened his hand so that the knife fell to the ground. He took a single step. Another. My heart swelled.

He fell to his knees.

A shadow of confusion passed over his brow. He looked at his hands, stained now with blood of brilliant gold. In an instant where everything fell silent but for my own breath, he died.

What little magic I had left exploded outwards, reaching for Cerlas with fingers of fire and shards of earth. The god scrambled backwards, eyes wide with terror. "No, please, I don't—" My stones, my fire, met flesh and rendered it into dust.

I collapsed to the ground, spent.

"Calanthe!" Casimir knelt beside me, trying to haul me to my feet. "You need to get out of here. With no magic, you're vulnerable. Tali, get her back to the cave."

"Of course," Tali said, tugging on my arm as if she could hope to move it.

"No!" I wrenched my arm away and staggered to

my feet. Dancer broke away from Arcturus and ran to my side. Some of his fur was iced over and I saw frost on his teeth and tongue from where he must have bitten the god, but he was whole. He nudged my hand.

"Dancer will keep you safe," Casimir said. "But you can't go out there, Calanthe, not as you are."

He was probably right. Cerlas might have been dead, but the three gods who remained were the most dangerous. The humans, now that they'd been thinned a bit, were having a better time of things. They managed to deliver blows rather than just stumbling over one another. Lalruk was missing a hand and Arcturus, for all his wintery power, had a long knife through his shoulder and numerous cuts everywhere. Talorsa, too, was bleeding profusely, but he seemed only to feel more invigorated at each blow. Even with the humans pressing forward, their skill precise, the gods were healing faster than blows could be dealt.

I'd been the one to kill Aza and Cerlas, and Myr before them. I was beginning to think that only I could manage to kill these gods. I would need significant amounts of magic returned to me before I could manage such a thing.

We needed to retreat.

"Casimir," I begged, steadying myself on Dancer's shoulder. "Save these people. Help me get them out of here!"

The guardian—*my* guardian—pressed a kiss to my temple. "It will be okay, my love."

Then, shoving me away, he charged into battle.

"Calanthe," Tali said, steadying me as best she could. "We need to go. Now."

"No. I will not let them fight alone." The earth beneath me pulsed a slow, steady beat, like the beating of a heart. Beneath the crust, I knew rivers of magma flowed, ready to be released. If I couldn't draw magic from myself, perhaps I could draw it from somewhere else.

I kicked off my shoes before Tali could stop me and sank to my knees. With toes and hands in contact with the ground, I called on the magic. It responded.

Across the killing field, Talorsa met my eyes. He grinned, blood dripping down his face.

"Do you not feel the power of battle?" he asked, and somehow I heard him as though he stood right next to me. "Is it not glorious?"

Magic streamed from the earth into me, killing any living thing that lay dormant or alive in the soil. Plants that were meant to grow for centuries to come withered and died. Minuscule creatures that regulated the nutrients of the earth ceased to be. The trees that ringed this place grew brittle and rotted away until they were nothing but stumps.

The fire was harder to coax out, being so far beneath the surface. But it swam through tiny cracks in the ground and fed into my fingers, cooling the crust and letting the frost of Arcturus into the deep. Fissures of earth cracked at the sudden change in temperature. I grew hot, burning with energy that wanted to overwhelm me. I did not let it.

Talorsa pulled his short sword from the chest of a young man whose armour was more patchwork than protection. Never once did his eyes leave mine. "This power, this feeling, could be yours. *Ours*. Always. Don't you understand, child? This place was meant for us to rule. You and me. Take my hand and stand with me at my side."

I bared my teeth. Beside me, Dancer did the same. "This place belongs to the mortals."

I released my magic. The ground cracked and heaved. People fell where they stood, some pushed aside by the wave of earth, others crushed by it. I didn't have enough control to save those who stood in my way. Pools of lava broke through the ground, bubbling and streaming towards the remaining gods. Arcturus managed to freeze one pool for an instant before its heat became too much and it burst forth in a spray of sparks, engulfing him. Lalruk stumbled when the earthquake broke beneath her. In an instant, she was on the ground, being pulled apart by humans who tore her into pieces with their blades.

Talorsa, though, drew his power from war. And there was no doubt in my mind that we were at war.

He shifted his balance as the ground shook

beneath him. The lava that flowed forth wasn't fast enough to catch him. I tried to shift my magic, tried to attack him directly with fire and stone, as I had Cerlas. A blur of shadows got in my way.

Casimir struck the god of war across the face, cutting neatly into his jaw. Talorsa roared in fury and backhanded the guardian so that he stumbled into a crack in the earth, catching his leg. It twisted and snapped with a horrendous crack. Casimir cried out in a sound that rent my heart in two.

"This place belongs to the gods," Talorsa said, taking a step towards Casimir, his shield dragging on the ground. "You honestly think that the mortals can possibly rule this place alone? Do you not see how *fragile* they are?"

"They may not be long lived, but they have more strength than you could ever know," I spat. The god of war drew closer to my lover.

"They get their strength from us. The gods. They deserve only to take what we give them. We are above them in so many ways. How could they possibly thing themselves equal to the task of ruling where we ruled? This world and all its people are for the gods."

Talorsa raised his shield above Casimir, the edge glinting red. Casimir scrambled backwards, but the crack in the ground was narrow and his leg was stuck. "For daring to defy me, I will take this man from you."

Talorsa made ready to slam the shield into Casimir's neck. I screamed. Dancer leaped for the god just as my magic did, but we were both too slow.

A rock struck Talorsa in the temple. He hissed and stepped back, dropping his shield mere inches from Casimir where he lay. That brief moment of hesitation was enough; my magic, weak as it was, slammed into Talorsa. There was barely enough fire to do more than put superficial burns on his skin, and the stones that emerged from the earth were small and without much force. It was enough, though, to draw his attention.

"You're out of magic, goddess." Talorsa chuckled, wiping away some golden blood, already healing. My wave of magic earlier had pushed the humans aside, so there was no one to stand between the god of war and me. "And as young as you are, draining you of magic will still let me kill you. I think I shall enjoy this."

"You will not harm her." Devereux staggered towards Talorsa, bleeding red and trailing shadows from a deep wound to his side. He bore cuts and bruises everywhere, visible even through the darkness that wreathed him. His eyes, a vibrant, furious amber, blazed. Talorsa laughed harder.

"What's this? A human, playing king of nightmares." He struck a single blow that cracked Devereux's head back and had my friend falling back into a rock that had emerged from the ground. He let out a gasping breath, choking. "Weak."

"Don't touch my brother!" Beatrice leaped in front of Devereux, her armour splattered red, her sword stained with gold. To my surprise, she was barely wounded, the only visible signs of strain being a slight limp to her right leg.

Talorsa looked at her with glee. Like a wolf eyeing a wounded deer, he licked his lips, showing off his teeth. "I grow tired of this. Stand aside human, so that I may kill this recalcitrant goddess and take my place at the head of the world."

Beatrice lifted her sword. "No."

"Very well, then. You shall die first." The god of war lifted his short sword and gave a flourish. Beatrice didn't flinch, even when he moved from his artistic bow into a lunge. She parried, thrust forward, and launched into an attack that was vicious, precise, just as the woman herself was. Talorsa fought with a smile at first, then when Beatrice matched him, move for move, not giving an inch of ground, the smile faded. His movements became harder, more forceful. I could see Beatrice's arms quavering from where I knelt, leaning against Dancer. Still, though, her expression remained fixed and determined. Her movements remained fluid, exact. She did not once falter.

"Ah, now here is something interesting. A creature with conviction, not power. I can taste the ambition you hold. What wondrous things you could achieve with my blessing," Talorsa mused as he dealt an overhand swing which Beatrice matched, her sword shaking slightly. Her breath came in fast pants, yet still she fought.

"I have no need of your blessing," Beatrice sneered, thrusting twice in rapid succession, her sword tasting gold blood both times. "I am Beatrice Althea Rosea Valkyr Thorquan, first of her name, daughter of Queens, Lady and Keeper of the Broken Stone, High Priestess to the Temple of the Fallen Star and Sword of the goddess Calanthe. What need have I for you?"

Beatrice lunged and sank her sword in deep to Talorsa's belly, just under a chink in his armour. In any mortal, it would have been a debilitating blow, if not a fatal one. In the god of war, all he did was stumble a bit. Beatrice pulled back, gold blood dripping in the wake of her weapon. She straightened, thinking her fight was won.

"Beatrice, no!" Devereux shouted, trying to scrabble to his feet. He was too slow. We were all too slow.

Talorsa snapped his arm out and grabbed Beatrice by the throat. "What need have *you* for *me?* Oh, no, you foolish, fragile human. The real question is whether *I* have need of *you*. And I've decided that I don't."

He squeezed. Beatrice's neck snapped, the crack reverberating across the clearing.

Devereux screamed, an agonising sound that shattered my shock. He rushed Talorsa and was once again thrown aside, landing nearly on top of his sister's body. I tried to stand, tried to gather more magic, but the land around me had already been drained and my body was not replenishing the energy as it should have done. Dancer leaned against me, claws digging into the dirt and a growl reverberating in his throat. Casimir, too, tried to stand, but even with immortality healing him faster than normal, his leg had been broken and it would likely take several hours before he could move.

All this preparation, all this training and planning and gathering of forces, had come to naught. We couldn't kill the god of war and we had likely all forfeited our lives in the attempt.

"She was mine."

I jumped, craning my head to see a figure emerge from the snowy forest behind me. Dressed in white trimmed in gold and silver, she was immaculate where everything else around was strewn in blood. White-blonde hair fluttered gently in a breeze that seemed to only exist for her. She was stately and elegant and beautiful. A Star in truth in the midst of darkness.

"Astraea, no!" Casimir cried out in a strangled voice. The Star ignored him.

"Have we met?" Talorsa asked, sketching a ridiculous bow.

"I am Astraea," she said, lifting her chin, walking forwards with simple, even steps, her skirt dragging in blood and gore. The smile on her face was full of fury. "I am the Star that severed your connection from this world. I am the Star that bound you to your own realm, where you could do no more harm. I am the Star that claimed this world as my own, to protect and hold forever more."

"You," Talorsa whispered, eyes blazing. He dropped his sword. "I will kill you with my bare hands."

"She was mine," Astraea said, stopping before Beatrice's body. Devereux scrambled back, away from whatever he saw in her face.

"The human? What do humans matter to you?"

Astraea snapped her head up. "*Everything*. They are so bright, even in their brief existence. They burn with a fire like I've never seen in any star. They live with every emotion branded on their heart. They are loyal and cruel and kind and caring and impassioned. They love deeper than anything I've ever known."

"Astraea," Casimir whispered, and even from where I knelt, I could see the silver of tears in his eyes. My heart clenched, then broke, then was silent.

"Even my guardian, who loved unquestioning, who gave everything of himself, could not inspire in me the same feelings I saw in humans. I wanted that," Astraea said. She pointed to Beatrice. "I wanted that conviction that would have me throwing myself before a sword that would surely be my doom. So I took the humans for my own. Perhaps I was selfish. No, I know I was. Even in my selfishness, they were better off with me than with you. Cruel. Demanding sacrifices they could scarce afford. They were playthings to you. Toys. Easily broken, easily replaced. To me, they were *everything*."

"Stop talking, Star, and fight," Talorsa snarled. He stepped forwards and held up his hands, ready to engage. I realised in that moment, that he couldn't. Not until she did. Not until she engaged herself in war. There were limits to his power, but I would likely not see those weaknesses exploited.

I was so weak.

So tired.

My magic, even then, felt like it was draining out of me.

Astraea pointed to Beatrice. She looked ethereal, the edges of her form blurring in the light of the sun. "That human swore herself to me. My High Priestess. And you killed her."

"I did, and I would do it again," Talorsa goaded, still unable to attack first, not so long as Astraea stood there and did nothing.

"That is why you deserve this." Astraea lifted her head to the sky, closing her eyes. She spread her arms and I realised then that it wasn't the sunlight blurring her figure, illuminating it, it came from within her.

From within *me*.

I coughed, blood spattering the ground in front of me. Something was being torn out of my body, ripping through me with abandon. I screamed.

"Calanthe!" I heard Casimir scream my name, but I couldn't see him, not in the light that flooded the clearing. I wanted to call out to him, to reassure him that I was still alive, but I couldn't breathe. A piece of me—the light that I had wielded to seal off the void, which never truly belonged to me—was emerging, pulled to the surface.

It manifested in the form of a tiny ball of flame so bright that looking at it would blind. My good eye watered at the sight, but I couldn't look away. Not as it pulled itself from me, leaving shreds in its place, not as it flew across the clearing and merged with the light streaming from Astraea, not even as she turned and looked at me, her features all but gone in the light she emitted.

"Take care of him," she said. I nodded numbly. "Love him fiercely." I nodded again.

"What are you doing?" Talorsa asked, shielding his eyes. "What is this?"

"I am saving this world. One. Last. Time." Then, Astraea went nova.

CHAPTER 27

There is something magnificent about the death of a star. Something terrible, like the rending of worlds. Something achingly beautiful.

Astraea's form seemed to flare, brighter than the impossibility she'd been before. I wanted to look away, but couldn't, held in place in rapture and awe. My good eye burned and my skin grew hot. In an instant, the brightness faded as she seemed to fold in on herself. Just as my eye began to tingle in healing, the light flashed again, exploding outward. A part of me, the part of me that was made with her magic, the part of me that was made with the shadows of a guardian, cried out in horror as the world reverberated.

The ground shook. The dead trees were burned to a crisp, then gone. The pools of lava that I'd pulled from the bowels of the earth disintegrated in the heat. I heard everything, then nothing.

When I came to my senses, the clearing where this terrible battle had taken place was gone. Flattened into emptiness, smooth and still and remnant of nothing. Yet, impossibly, those humans who had yet lived at the end, still remained. They lay prone, yes, but they were alive. The dead, including Astraea and Talorsa, however, were gone.

"Calanthe!" My name rang oddly in my ears. I looked around and saw Devereux crawling towards me. He looked the same as ever, his skin the colour of the void touched, his eyes blazing amber, even the crown of bone on his brow. Unharmed.

"Devereux." I extended my hand towards him and found I couldn't stand. Some of it was surely to do with the drain in my magic that this day had caused, but I also felt...different. No less than I was, but also not the same. Whatever Astraea had torn from me was now filled in with earth and fire, yet the memory of what had been remained. I nearly fell over in my attempt to stand, only to be caught by Dancer, not a single piece of fur even singed.

"You're alright?" Devereux asked, too loudly. I winced.

"Yes. I just need to rest." I looked around, not sure what I was looking for until I spotted the form laying prone not far from where Astraea had gone nova. He still wore the armour made from a falling star. The shadows he bore had grown, writhing over his skin like words in a book. His hand stretched to the point where Astraea had died.

"Casimir!" I tried to crawl towards him, but even that seemed almost beyond me. Inch by painful inch I dragged myself to him. He wasn't dead. Astraea wouldn't kill him. He couldn't be dead.

I cradled his head in my lap, brushing back his hair. "Please," I breathed.

His eyes flickered open and settled on my face. Some indescribable emotion crossed his features until, after agonising heart beats, he twitched his lips in a smile. "Calanthe," he said, barely audible. "You're here."

"Always." I kissed his brow, wiping away my tears. "Always."

✴

I wouldn't hear them for a hundred years, but there were songs written about that day. The day the Fallen Star saved the world. All I knew in the aftermath was agony and weariness. Somehow, the survivors managed to drag themselves away from that empty place and back to the cave where we'd sheltered the night before. Winter, now that Arcturus was gone, seemed to have lost its grip and we were swiftly warmed by the fires of those who had stayed behind.

Of the several hundred humans who had ridden out with me from Altier, only a handful remained. Tali and her grandmother quickly saw to the injuries of those who lived, taking their stories as they did so. They didn't ask questions about the dead, not yet, though I heard whispers of plans for a memorial to the fallen.

I wanted to mourn for Jedrek, for Beatrice, for everyone, yet I found myself barely able to function. What little I could do was spent by Casimir's side, never once asking him about her, yet never leaving him, either. Dancer remained with me, guarding me from an enemy that did not emerge, yet who hung over my head.

"Sleep, my lady," Temys said in the quiet hours of the night. She had somehow procured a blanket without my seeing and was guiding me down. Already, my eyelids drooped. I struggled to raise my head and looked for Casimir. He lay beside me, already asleep, the sorrow he refused to show in the last hours now painted clearly on his sleeping face. I reached out and twined my hand with his, then, with Temys standing over me and Dancer at my back, I fell asleep.

I did not dream.

I did not know if I would ever dream again.

When I woke, though, an image transplanted itself into my mind, clear and impending. I sat up with a gasp, my body sore, my thoughts frantic.

"Casimir." I looked around, sure I would see him

where he had fallen asleep the night before. Instead, I saw Devereux, dozing. He started as I woke and scrambled to his feet.

"You're awake." He seemed surprised. Shocked, even. It was then that I noticed the hollows in his cheeks, the way his hair lay in unkempt strands. He also wore no crown, his clothes simple and unadorned. I looked around at the rest of the camp and found similar changes there, too. Nothing looked as it had done. There were fewer people laying to be treated for injuries. People's clothes looked ragged, their features drawn or tired. The nightmares that were Devereux's people had vanished entirely, leaving Dancer as the only remaining voidling. The tiger was prowling the edge of the camp, keeping an ever-watchful eye on things.

"What happened?" I asked, rubbing my face. My hands stilled when I felt the ruined space where my eye had been carved out. It had healed, yes, but the eye was gone. Was that why things looked so strange?

"You've been asleep for nearly two weeks," Devereux said. I gaped at him. "Tali said it was magic sickness, that you needed to recover, but some feared that you would never wake."

"I didn't...I couldn't..." I rested my elbows on my knees, cradling my head in my hands. Two weeks. "What happened?" I repeated, a command.

"After that first night, those who could returned to Altier to tell the queen and diplomats that we were successful. Those who could not be moved remained." Devereux frowned, mouth a thin line. "Three days after that, a messenger returned with a missive for you. Casimir took it. It, ah…"

"What is it?" Had more gods come through the door? The door that would taunt me until the end of time, it seemed. I felt replenished in magic, but there was no telling how many could have come through, how much destruction they could have reaped.

"My mother and the other diplomats there have declared themselves godless." Devereux winced. "They claim they will not worship any gods. Including you. If you return to Altier, or venture through the other lands with any intention of displaying who you are, then they will declare war on you."

I bit back a chuckle. Then, unable to contain it, I covered my mouth so my laughter wouldn't echo around the cavern. "Empty night, do they honestly think I *want* worship? After everything that I've done for them, after everything we've achieved against the others?"

"I know that," Devereux said. "And there are many others who know that. But my mother has declared herself the leader of this godless movement. She has said that this will usher in a new age. A human age. You are not welcome in it."

I snorted. "By that definition, neither are you."

Devereux smiled weakly.

"Oh. I see. I'm…I'm sorry. She told me that her

ambitions were vast, that I should not expect benev-olence from her. I didn't realise that—"

"That it extended to her own son?" He sank onto the ground beside me and shrugged. "It doesn't matter. I have my own kingdom. The people there need me."

"It doesn't change the hurt," I murmured, and this time when I looked, I found Casimir immediately. He was leaning over one of the injured, changing bandages and nodding at whatever words were being exchanged.

"He woke up after two days," Devereux said. "Wouldn't talk to anyone but Tali for two days after that. Dancer stayed close to him or you until yester-day. He...he hasn't stopped doing things since he woke. Cooking. Fetching firewood. Acting as healer. He even used arcane spells on some of the more seri-ously injured. But he won't talk about what happened."

He had lost Astraea. His Star. The person he was sworn to guard against the world. The person he had fallen from the heavens for. He claimed to have given me his heart long before that, but I couldn't imagine the pain of finding her again only to lose her forever. He had loved her, deeply, even if now he looked back and saw things differently.

I took a breath, absently rubbing my chest. "Thank you for all you did," I told Devereux. "I'm sorry for your sister. She was a vastly different person at the end, and I think she would have been the perfect person to lead this new age of humans."

Devereux nodded, throat bobbing. "Yeah," he said thickly. "Me, too."

"But, all that being said, I think you should go back to your kingdom."

"You...do not want me here?"

"I would love it if you were to stay. As you said, though, your people *need* you. A lot of things have changed. I think we all need time to adjust." I pushed myself to my feet and held out my hand. Devereux took it.

"Where will you go? What will you do?"

The door flashed in my mind again. "I have a few loose ends to tie up."

He nodded. Then, he bowed over my hand and kissed it. "Lady Calanthe, queen of the gods, I swear myself to your service. If ever you have need of me, call and I will come."

"As I will come to you," I promised. Devereux smiled, a hint of the cheerful, irreverent man I'd known shining through. In a blink, he was gone.

I found Tali next, arguing with her grandmother over the wording of something. She spotted me and waved me over. "Calanthe, I'm so glad you're awake. Tell my ridiculous grandmother that her prophecy is done. Please. I want no more *arguing* over the particulars."

"The prophecy?" Words spoken so long ago in the

palace. It felt like a different world, then, full of hopeful preparations and complaining about little things like not being able to train well. "I... You'll have to remind me."

Temys straightened her shoulders, shooting her granddaughter a triumphant smile. "The first bit is *The ancient ones formed/From stone and fire/A being of starlight and shadow/The world to inspire.* Which refers to you, obviously."

"Obviously," I murmured. Inspire? Hardly.

"Then," Tali said, "it talks about the old gods. *Forgotten ones remembered/Surging forth once more/Desire in their hearts/Death in their wake.*"

I nodded. That made sense.

"The part that we're having, ah, disagreements on is the next half," Temys said, sniffing. "*When sky and earth meet/When darkness is embraced/The changing of the worlds is nigh/Mortals shall make their fate.*"

I shivered, and not from cold. Tali puckered her brow, looking me up and down. "Are...are you alright? I mean, you look fully healed, and so much better than you did before, but—"

"I'm fine." I tried to smile at Tali, tried to hold on to the facade that everything was well. "Perhaps we can discuss this later. I want to talk with Casimir. See that everyone is well."

Tali blinked. "Oh. Of course. It's an ancient prophecy, anyways. No one will care if it's not solved tonight."

I laughed softly and wandered off to where Casimir still tended the injured man. Her words were too precise, like a knife to my gut. Earth and sky? Myself and Astraea. And with our actions between us, the world was never going to be the same again. But that wasn't the end of the prophecy. As I crossed the camp, the last words came to me.

Stand tall and strong and broken
*   Before the doorway new*
For faltering will mean
The world's growing doom

Casimir lifted his head as I approached. "Calanthe, you're awake." He spread his arms, and without hesitation, I fell into them. Burying my nose in his shirt, I inhaled deeply. Mist and shadow and pine, with just a hint of smoke. Casimir. Alive and well.

"I missed you," I breathed.

His arms snaked around my shoulders and waist, unfaltering, as if there had never been any space between us and never would be again. "I've been here all the time."

"Have you?" I asked the question before I could think. Casimir stiffened.

"I...I'm sorry for what happened." He tightened his grip on me. "I didn't mean to make you feel abandoned. I know that you said you were happy for me to do my duty, but that doesn't change the fact that I—"

I twined my fingers in the fabric of his collar, staring at the threads, wondering about its making. I said nothing. Not even when the words, *You walked away* lay heavy on my tongue. He had, but he had also come for me in my hour of need.

"I did release you to do your duty. I didn't want you to feel your devotion had to be split. But I also don't think that I understood what it would mean to have you by her side every day, how that would make me feel. And I'm sorry for that." I pulled back, studying his features. Still inhuman, perfect, sculpted from marble and painted with shadow. "I'm also sorry for her death."

His expression shuttered. He released me from his grasp, and for a moment I thought he was going to run away. Instead, he met my gaze, faltered, and fell to the ground, crying. "She's *gone*," he choked out. "She's been with me since the moment we were formed. I fell with her! And now, without a single backwards glance, she goes nova as if she's being noble, as if she's being benevolent and good."

I knelt beside him, this time wrapping my arms

around him. He hid himself in my cloak, sobs shaking his body. "She saved us, Cas," I said. "Surely that's worthy of—"

"You heard her," he spat. "She did it so she could save the world one last time. So that people would sing about her forever. So that her name would be a legend that lay on people's tongues when they talk about the god war. It wasn't *benevolent*. It was selfish. One last selfish act."

I said nothing. I just held him, letting him cry and rage and come to terms that one of the two loves in his life had gone.

Eventually the tears subsided and silence lay like a blanket on us. We sat there by the fire, watching the movement of the camp. The humans that remained didn't bother us; they barely even looked at us.

"Everything has changed," Casimir said. "Not just with Astraea's...death. The whole camp knows of the queen's decree. And while it only truly affects Baldarskiel, I can't imagine that the rest of Adhor would dismiss the movement."

"Devereux told me," I said. The flames of the fire leapt and danced, singing out to me. With a thought, I could have the fire expand and destroy everything in the camp. I understood Raya's fear. It was one thing to know of stories of such power, to hear of legends of the gods, whispered at night when such tales held strength. It was another entirely to see such power. To know such power actually existed. No arcane spell that the humans could perform would ever hope to compete.

"I still know places where I am owed a favour. Llyn Rhosalwyd, perhaps. We could go there. We could see the world, even if we had to do it quietly, until people forgot about what we looked like." Casimir twined his fingers into mine and held fast. "We could find a cottage in some isolated clearing and live there. Whatever you want."

I let out a long, slow breath. "I would gladly see the world with you."

"I'm sensing a 'however' in this. Is it because of Astraea? Because of...how I felt about her?"

I shook my head. "No. No, that's not it at all. I know you loved her. I know a piece of you will always love her. This doesn't have anything to do with that, with her."

"Then what?" Casimir asked, brushing some hair back from my bad eye and tucking it behind my ear. "The humans have discarded us, even after all we have done. What is stopping you from going with me? Is it Tali?"

"Tali?" I hesitated, the words of the prophecy ringing in my head. "No, it's not to do with her. Or rather, it's to do with something she said."

"What did she say?" Casimir growled, ready to leap to my defence.

"The door, Cas," I murmured, squeezing his fingers tight. "It's still there. Still unlocked. And though Talorsa was perhaps the most dangerous, there are other gods who would come through. Who would claim this world."

"The humans seem to think they don't need you—"

"It's not about what they think. It's about what's right." I sighed. "We need to go to the door. To prove to the other gods that once and for all this world belongs to the humans."

"You need to take your throne," Casimir said in dawning understanding.

I shivered. "I never wanted to be queen. But if this is the only way to ensure the humans are safe, forever, then so be it. Let them have their world. Let them have their Age of Humans. But let them do it without fear peering over their shoulders."

Casimir leaned his shoulder against mine. "Very well. Then, as soon as we can ride, we go to Ynysfawr?"

"To Ynysfawr," I agreed. And, perhaps, to my doom.

CHAPTER 28

"You keep trying to leave me behind," Tali said the next morning as Casimir and I swung into the saddles of our horses, Dancer prowling at our sides. She put her hand on her hip and raised her brows. "A lesser person than I would be offended."

I chuckled. "A lesser person than you would never have accomplished all that you have."

Tali smirked and lifted her chin. Her smile faded. Then, "You really were going to leave me behind, weren't you?"

"This time, Tali, I don't think that you can come where we're going," Casimir said. He still looked a little hollow, a little tired, but there was steel in him that I didn't think he knew about.

"Where are you going? Is this because the stupid queen made her decree about being godless? Because

I don't care about that. I'm your High Priestess, after all."

I winced. "I'm afraid that title will draw more ire to you than anything. It's...it's probably why Raya drew up that decree to begin with. I gave you the position when I told Beatrice that I wanted none of being worshipped or prayed to or any of it."

Tali shook her head, dark hair blowing into her face. She brushed the strands aside in a huff of frustration. "I don't care! You're my friend, Calanthe. That you would trust me with such a thing means so much, and I won't let you—"

"No," I said with a tone of command. Tali blinked. "Raya is right. Perhaps not in how she's going about things, but certainly in the substance. The time of the gods is in the past and it should be left there. I never wanted worship. I wanted you as my High Priestess so that people couldn't speak falsely in my name. You know that."

"I know," Tali murmured, lowering her gaze. "It was—is—still an honour."

"You will always be my friend," I said. "If ever I return, I will find you. We can finally figure out my favourite food."

"Dumplings, right?" Tali said. She tried to smile and it wobbled. Before she could break out into tears, I was off my horse and wrapping her into my arms. "I don't want you to leave me. What will I do?"

"What will you do?" I asked, smoothing out her

hair. "How can you ask that? The great Tali, *dharangui*. You have witnessed the fall of the void, the death of gods. You have the histories of ancient peoples in your head. I have no doubt that you will *lead* this new Age."

She laughed, the sound a choke of tears. "You bet I will." She hugged me tightly with her arm wrapped around my waist. "I will never forget you, Calanthe. Not you or Jedrek or Emyna or Dancer or Astraea or any of them. And I'll make sure that no one else forgets either. This may be an Age of Humans, but it was built on gods and stars."

"Thank you," I breathed, and pulled away. I remounted my horse and prepared to ride out, not sure if I could handle lingering any longer.

"Wait!" Tali cried out as I turned my horse. Dancer lifted his head, whiskers twitching. I paused. "Where are you going? I can't tell your story fully if I don't know how it ends!"

"We're going to see about getting Calanthe a proper crown," Casimir said, nodding to the iron band I wore on my brow. Strange to think that it fit so easily there, now, when at first all I had wanted to do was throw it off and leave it far behind.

"You're going to the door. To the realm of the gods." Tali gaped at us. She looked for a moment like she wanted to protest, but finally, she just smiled. "Don't let them take no for an answer, okay?"

"I won't," I promised.

"Hey, Calanthe, guess what?" Tali asked. She beamed at me. "It's Midwinter."

I left her there with a smile wide enough to bolster me for hours. It was harder than I thought to leave the humans behind. Even those whose names I didn't know, or who I had only a passing acquaintance with, I mourned their loss.

"Does it get easier?" I asked after we had ridden in silence for a while, the sound of our passing muffled in snow. "Leaving mortals behind, knowing that you may never see them again?"

"I have no doubt you *will* see Tali again. She's persistent. Keeps showing up," Casimir assured me. He sighed and part of him deflated. "No. It doesn't get easier. For a while, I never bothered getting to know any mortals at all because they seemed to be there one moment and gone the next. It was impossible not to get attached, though, and eventually I just came to accept it. It was a little easier, knowing I had...knowing that Astraea would still be there even when my human friends had gone."

"I'm sorry," I said again. He flashed me a weak smile.

"I will be well again. It will just take some time."

"We have all the time in the world," I said. I only hoped I was right.

The path to Ynysfawr was beginning to feel familiar. I recognised some of the hills, the divots in the earth. I knew the place where we had stopped when

Devereux fell to the void. I knew where we had camped on our return trip with Ilar and the Hunters. Even blanketed in snow, this place of wild hills and scraggly trees, gullies, bracken, it began to feel like home.

Somewhere during our second day of riding, Casimir and I fell into silence, each buried under the weight of our own thoughts. At night, we slept beside one another, arms and legs entangled, the fire keeping us warm and safe. Dancer prowled the edges of our camp, sometimes sleeping near, sometimes venturing off into the night and returning with a rabbit or grouse or nothing at all. He seemed wilder than before, more sure of himself and yet ready with tooth and claw at any moment. A bit like myself, I supposed.

After four days of riding, my uncertainty began to manifest in a metallic taste on my tongue. Dancer, sensing my fear, stuck close to my horse, spooking the creature more often than not, until I had to give up on riding and walk beside the shadow tiger, fingers entangled in his fur. Casimir walked a short distance away, leading the horses.

My nerves were stretched taut. I knew that I was to face the remainder of the gods on the other side of that door, but not who they were. I knew nothing of the realm of the gods apart from the few things that Emyna had told me of their treatment there. I could barely believe that I was doing this. That I could claim right of leadership after the few things that I had done. I'd killed Myr, yes. And Aza, Cerlas, Lalruk. Arcturus had been pulled apart by the humans. But Talorsa? The real threat, the true challenge? I'd failed miserably to protect the humans from him.

My hands were shaking, the tremors hidden by Dancer's dense coat. He flicked his shredded ears at me and chuffed, pressing in closer. *It will be alright.* He wasn't yet old enough by my reckoning to use the language of the voidlings, but I understood the message all the same.

I smiled, took a breath, and let it out in time with my steps.

We crested a hill just as the last of my breath left my lungs, and I froze.

Before us lay the ocean, sparkling and calm in the brisk winter air. Beyond a small strip, as innocuous as any other piece of land, lay the island of Ynysfawr.

"Are you alright?" Casimir asked in a low voice, threading his fingers through the hand not clutching Dancer's fur. "You've been quiet."

A strangled sound escaped my throat. "I don't know if I can do this."

"You *can*," Casimir insisted. I shook my head and he spun me around to face him. His teeth were bared in a snarl and he looked fiercer than I'd ever seen him, save in battle. "Don't you dare doubt yourself now. I know you, Calanthe. I have been there since your waking, and I *know* you. You are strong as the earth beneath our feet. You have fire in your blood that will let you burn brighter than even a star. You have sacrificed your own life, your own choices, to save the people of this world over and over again. You never once questioned your duty. I have seen you struggle only with thinking yourself capable, worthy. That is the last thing that you should doubt."

"I..." I couldn't find the words. Did he truly think so much of me? Heat bloomed on my cheeks. "I know I am powerful. I know I bear the legacy of two goddesses who made me. I know I will protect this world with everything I have. But I am still afraid, Casimir."

"Change is never easy, no matter how many centuries you have under your belt. That is why I think the mortals are so...astonishing. They experience—even instigate—so much change and embrace it with more courage than anyone I know. Except you." Casimir lifted my chin so I stared into those eyes shrouded with shadow. Once I had thought that they were dangerous, hiding a darkness that could devour the world. Now, I saw they held multitudes. Pools of infinite reflection. That was his talent, reflecting back what he saw in you. Perhaps that was why Astraea hadn't looked back as she died.

Before I could say more, express further doubts or turn away, Casimir kissed me. It was ferocious, hungry, as though something were racing for us and we had to make every moment count. We had eternity stretching before us and yet we still devoured each other. Sparks travelled between us. Fire roared to life in my blood. Flowers bloomed through the snow. His hands held me tightly, so tightly I could feel the pulsing of his heart in his chest, matching mine beat for beat.

My breath caught when his teeth grazed my lip, biting down. I opened for him, letting him explore what he wanted, take what he wanted. In turn, I took from him, demanding and desperate and so hopeful.

"I love you," I said on a gasp. "I don't think I was made to ever have another love, to be able to give my heart to more than one person. It's yours, Casimir. Forever."

"Damn you, Calanthe." Casimir's voice was rough, his nose against my shoulder, teeth grazing my skin. "I will love you until the end of time. Do you understand me?"

I understood. He had loved Astraea. He loved me. There would always be the two of us there in his heart and it was a war I wouldn't win. Nor did I want to. What he gave was enough.

I cupped the back of his head and pulled him to me.

We spent the day on that hilltop overlooking the ocean. My inner fires warmed the ground and melted the snow, my earth magic bringing a bed of grass and flowers to life with a thought. Then there was no room in my thoughts for anything but Casimir and myself.

Sunset touched my eyelids as I lay nestled against his side. "We can't wait any longer," I murmured.

"I know." He kissed my hair. "Whatever happens, I will be beside you. Know that."

I pulled myself up, the grass dying even as I did. Dancer lay in the snow a few metres away, keeping watch over the horses. He stirred as I rose, letting out a roar. "Yes," I agreed. "It's time."

Last time I'd been on that beach, I had been newly named, naked, and afraid of losing everything. I knew so little about myself, only that I was a goddess and that I had fulfilled my duty in sealing away the void. I didn't know what sort of future this world held for me. I didn't know if Casimir would ever love me as I loved him. I had lost Dancer. I had lost Tali. I had lost even the small surety of being the Chosen One.

Now, I was returned. My clothes were worn and dirty under the simple armour I wore. I had no sword, no shield, only a small knife and the iron band at my brow. Dancer walked at my side, scarred and battle weary, but ready for anything. Casimir stood beside me, wearing armour formed of a fallen star, sword at the ready.

"The boat should be here somewhere," he said.

"No need." I raised my arms and called forth the

earth, parting the waters of the ocean to form a small bridge. He looked at me and huffed.

"Useful trick."

I half-expected stepping back onto Ynysfawr to be momentous. To feel something. Instead, it was just land like any other. I lowered the bridge behind us so that no enterprising humans could follow with ease and faced the crumbled ruins of the temple that stood just before the doorway.

"It looks...the same," I said.

"You are the one changed, not it."

I stepped into the ruined temple. It had already been falling down when first I arrived on Ynysfawr, but after I had sealed away the void, the temple had been all but destroyed. There was a mural depicting the fall of the gods and the rise of Astraea, how she bound them away and the void was created. I don't know who made the mural, who Astraea would have trusted with the truth of what she had done, but it was a beautiful piece. Almost gone, now.

I brushed my thumb over the face of the representation of Casimir. In this mural, he was a being of shadows, without substance. The one thing the mural managed to get wrong.

"What do you think will happen to this place?" I asked.

"It will fall to the elements. Perhaps in a hundred years, or a thousand, someone will dig it up and try to piece together the past."

An inevitability, said so casually. He'd seen it happen before.

"Do the humans ever get it right? Piecing together the past, I mean."

Casimir smiled wistfully. "Sometimes. Tali and her grandmother are the most accurate keepers of the past I've encountered. But even then, things get distorted. Forgotten. Evidence is erased."

"How long before we are forgotten, do you think?"

He grabbed my wrist, turning me away from the mural so he could look at me. "Are you afraid of being forgotten?"

"The opposite," I admitted. "I welcome it. It's those looks of admiration, of desperation, that I want to escape. I want to see the world as myself, not as the goddess Calanthe."

"I fear you cannot escape one in favour of the other," Casimir said. He smiled again. "But I will be glad to help you try."

I wanted to linger there with him. Perhaps use my magic to reconstruct the temple so it would live a little longer. Explore the rest of the island with Dancer. But the fact of the matter was that I was delaying what had to be done. So I slipped my hand from Casimir's grasp and stepped through the temple to emerge on the other side.

The crater was exactly as I had left it. Smoke curled up from fissures in the ground, indicating the fires that lay beneath. It was formed of obsidian, the walls gleaming in the sunlight. There were steps that I had carved on my last journey, but they were jagged and crude. Inside the crater, though, were two pillars of black glass, and between them, a door. Wooden, worn, as though it had been standing for ages beyond count. The handle was a metal ring, rusted almost through. I knew, though, that it would not fall or fail.

The door would endure.

Before the door was a stake with the skull of Myr on it, nothing of her flesh remaining. My warning, for what little it had been worth.

"Are you sure of this?" Casimir asked, hand on the hilt of his sword. "This place is…"

"Where I need to be." I, too, could feel the magic in the air, but it didn't unsettle me. It sang to the magic in my blood, in my bones. It was, after all, my magic.

I descended into the crater, smoothing the steps as I went. Dancer and Casimir followed, all the support I would ever need. I took one step closer to the door; it began to shimmer. Another step and the door started to shake. A third step. I was an arm's length away, and as I lifted my hand to grasp the handle, the door opened for me.

I stepped through.

I don't know what I expected of the other side in the realm of the gods, but what I found was nothing short of idyllic. The door was situated in a forested grove, surrounded by tall oaks and sycamores. There was meadow grass all around, dotted with wildflowers. Birds sang beautiful melodies to each other as a breeze rustled the leaves of the trees.

The place was empty but for Casimir, Dancer, myself and the door. We moved farther into the glade and the door shut with a slam behind us. I jumped. Dancer snarled.

"Is this...it?" Casimir asked, hand still on the hilt of his sword. He looked suspicious, oddly out of place, the edges of his form tinged with an afterimage of the night sky. "I expected something more."

"Look at your hands."

He lifted them and gaped, stepping back. "No. It...it cannot be."

"Cas?" I reached for him and he staggered away.

"It's like I never fell. I can feel the shadow magic, too, stronger. Sharper. Empty night, Calanthe, it's like I never left the heavens."

"Maybe it's that the realm of the gods is closer than the realm of the mortals. Maybe—"

"You are not from here."

I spun around and came face to face with what looked to be a ghost. They were human in shape, with robes of tattered mist. I couldn't see their face. The closer they came, the colder I grew, until my inner fire flared to warm me. Dancer bared his teeth, tail twitching, but made no move to attack.

"Who are you?" I asked.

"I might ask you the same. Mortals aren't allowed here."

"I'm not mortal." I held up my hand and pulled my knife, preparing to cut myself and show off my gold blood. The ghost hissed and withdrew, flinching back from the steel of my knife.

"We won't hurt you," Casimir promised, though he looked unsettled, a cold sweat shining on his brow. "Calanthe, put the knife away. Perhaps you could use your magic instead?"

I did as he suggested, sheathing the knife and calling forth a blackberry bush from the ground. It sprouted and bloomed in an instant, and soon fat berries hung heavy from its branches. The ghost drifted for it warily, then crept forwards on silent feet and snatched a berry from the bush with a skeletal hand.

"It's true!" they said. "A true blackberry bush, not an illusion. Only Mother Earth could do that, but she's de—"

They froze, berries tumbling from their hand. "No. You killed her. Stole her powers."

I reared back. "What? No. She and the Eternal Flame made me."

"Liar! All the gods knew when they died, when their life was ripped from existence. I most of all, for the transition of the living to the dead is my domain. You murdered them!" the ghost snarled, voice a howl that set the leaves on the trees to rustling. Before I could defend myself, the ghost turned and fled, insubstantial form passing through the trees as they went.

Casimir and I exchanged a glance. Dancer let out a low growl and leaped after them, following them through the forest. We ran after him. This was going to be more complicated than I had anticipated.

CHAPTER 29

I barely had time to take in the scenery as I ran after the ghost. I knew only that the forest grove became dense wood, which then changed to mountainous forest, which then opened to a vast plateau. I could take no stock of the types of trees, nor the view; I made no note of the animals or insects that flew past. I knew only that I had to catch the ghost-god.

Had to make them understand.

"Calanthe, stop!" Casimir caught my wrist just as we emerged onto the plateau. Dancer skidded to a halt beside me, teeth bared, sides heaving. I turned to Casimir in annoyance, ready to scold him for letting them get away. Instead, he nodded to something in the distance.

I stilled.

A city. Vast and tall, with spires of silver rising from

the ground without effort. There were smaller buildings surrounding the main cluster of towers, swirls of smoke rising from chimneys, despite the mildness of the day. I saw people—tiny specs of movement at such a distance—milling about. Some were massive, others small. Some flew, circling the spires with ease.

"A city of the gods," I breathed.

"*Your* city," Casimir corrected.

No. Surely I didn't deserve this. I was made to be queen, yes, the power of my parents flooding through my veins and singing in my bones, stronger in this place. But what had I done to deserve the throne? Sealed off the void? Fighting those gods who came through the door?

"It is yours, Calanthe. Do not doubt that. You protect those who are weaker than you, without reserve or hesitation. You seek only what is best for those under your power. You were made for the throne, and you will be a magnificent queen."

"You always seem to know what to say," I murmured, taking his hand. He squeezed it, some of those glimmering shadows brushing against my skin. There were still doubts swirling in my mind, such as how I was to achieve such an impossible task, all the things that came afterwards, the sheer obstacle of my ignorance of the world, but it faded as he held my hand. I was not alone, not anymore.

An alarm roared across the plateau. It was a

piercing shriek, a tremor in the earth itself. The god-wraith had made it to the city, and they had warned the others.

An entirely different fear coiled itself in my belly that had nothing to do with whether I was deserving of the throne, but everything to do with whether I could even take it. My power had been so weak against Talorsa. I had needed Astraea to defeat him, and she was gone. I had no human armies to back me up, no Jedrek, no arcane magic users, nothing but myself, Casimir and Dancer.

I spun towards Casimir, breath suddenly caught in my throat. "I can't fight anymore," I choked out. Tears filled my eyes and the magic in my blood and my bones roiled, trying to escape. "There's been so much death already. I don't think I can stand another battle."

Casimir rested his hand on his sword and gave me a gentle look. "I know. It's not easy to bear witness to such things. But what if these gods are like the others? What if they seek to go through the door, to lay waste to the world we left behind?"

I squeezed my eyes shut and clenched my hands into fists. It was all too easy to imagine: Tali's body lying broken on the ground, eyes unstaring at a cruel god who was her death; the queen, weeping and injured, bowing to a goddess who cared nothing for her Age of Humans. All I had tried to protect, in tatters, lorded over by those who took pleasure and satisfaction from the weak.

"Would you leave the world to fend for itself? We have come this far, Calanthe, but you are not obligated to do more."

At this, I snapped my eyes open. Casimir looked calm, even, but there was a flash of something in his expression that had me relaxing. "You know as well as I that, obligation or not, I would never let them fend for themselves," I murmured.

He pressed his lips to the crown of my head, just above my iron crown. "I know. It's why I love you."

"And I, you." I leaned into the embrace for an instant longer, wanting to linger there for eternity. I pulled back. "I don't want to fight. I'm so tired of fighting. But I will," I vowed. "I will fight until all the stars grow dim if that's what it takes."

I pulled my shoulders back and lifted my chin. Then, I started across the plateau.

Instinct had me silencing the trembling of the earth caused by the alarm. It still pierced the air with its shrieks, but at least the ground was still. A few moments later and the alarm silenced as well, though I had a feeling it was more to do with the three gargantuan creatures that now stood before the city than myself.

One was a dragon, a creature I had seen depicted only in tapestries in the palace of Altier. Its scales glimmered green and blue, its claws dug furrows in the ground. Yet there was a wisdom in its gaze that nearly had me faltering again. I walked on.

The second creature was humanoid, nearly twice the size of any mortal that I'd encountered. His skin was blue brushed with gold and his golden hair was plaited in a long tail down his back. He wore a silky tunic that fluttered in the breeze like water. His eyes were dark and deep and terrible, yet calm. I knew him, even without having never met him. This was my kin, son of Mother Earth and Father Sky: the Ocean Deep. I thought he slept still on the ocean floor. Apparently, Temys' information had been wrong. What else had she been wrong about? I clenched my fists to still my trembling magic, but still I walked on.

The third being was as though a crone had twisted her shape into that of a tree. Stooped and bent, her bark-like skin creaked as she moved. Branches sprouted from her head and back, leaves rustling in the wind. Twisted fingers like roots supported her as she leaned on the ground. I didn't recognise her, but I could sense the power she held. It was similar to my connection to the earth, but different. She could not control it, only hear it. Listen to it. Exist within it. A spirit of life, rather than whatever I was.

I stopped twenty feet away from the three beings. Politeness, perhaps a purely mortal concept but not one I could easily discard, had me bowing slightly at the waist. The dragon inclined its head. The Ocean Deep blinked. The crone chortled.

"Well met, mortal," she rasped, her voice like the grating of rocks.

"I am no mortal," I responded.

"You bear the shape of a mortal," the Ocean Deep said, words beating against my ears like the crashing of waves. "You wear the clothes of mortals. You hold the weapons of mortals. You come from the world of mortals."

"Yet she shines with the powers of gods," the dragon hissed, fangs gleaming. It brought its head closer. "I can see the magic within you."

"Stolen, as the wraith said," the Ocean Deep snapped. "From my mother."

"One does not steal the power of Lady Earth," the dragon growled. It peered at me again, wide cerulean eye unblinking. I withstood the inspection with as much grace as I could muster, silencing the fire and earth warring inside me, eager to leap forth and strike. "It could not possibly have been stolen into this form, either. Woven together with the entire power of the Eternal Flame, my forbearer."

The tree-crone leaned towards me, limbs creaking, leaves rustling. "What *are* you?"

A being far younger than those that stood before me, and with terror beating a tattoo in my heart. I steeled myself, taking a deep breath. Dancer leaned against my side, lending me his solid strength.

Casimir was at my other shoulder, gazing at me with trust and hope. Believing in me, even when I had told the world so many times that I wanted no followers, no mortal awe.

I held out my left hand, burned and nerve-deadened, a flame curling around my palm. In my right hand, I conjured a flower, a rose, its thorny stem burrowing into my skin and producing droplets of golden blood. They steamed as they hit the ground, the power in them much more potent in this place. Grass and marigolds grew where the droplets fell, changing into thorny brambles before my eyes.

"I am Calanthe, daughter of Lady Earth and the Eternal Flame, queen of the gods."

Though I spoke with conviction, I half-expected these beings to break out into laughter. To mock me. To throw me off the plateau or to return me to the door. Instead, the dragon crouched on the ground and blew a breath into my face, blowing back my hair.

"You are quite sure for one so young. Even if the claim of your parentage is true—and I can see the magic within you that would give credence to that claim—then what makes you think you could be queen?"

"Indeed," the crone rasped, shifting her branches as she leaned closer to me. "You would upset centuries of order, of tradition and rule, and why? How? It takes more than magic to make the gods bow, child. It takes soul deep conviction, and a strength I doubt that you possess."

I let my flame burn brighter, my rose sprout into a bush that dug its roots into the soil, taking hold. The fire leaped from my hand to the flowers, shining like a beacon, though they did not burn. I wanted to falter, to hesitate, to claim that I didn't know why I was meant to be queen, only that it was so.

Words flew through my mind. Silly, ridiculous words that meant nothing until I gave them meaning. Until I decided that they were true.

Stand tall and strong and broken
   Before the doorway new
For faltering will mean
The world's growing doom

Only, it was not one world, it was all of them. Mortal and void and godly. Connected forever by my actions, magic flowing freely between them. *Life* flowing freely between them. And if I faltered, then that life would become death, for where there was power, there were those who wanted it for their own. As Talorsa and the others had proven.

"I am Calanthe, she who exists of both life and death. I am the protector of the mortal realm. I am the bane of Myr, the end of Arcturus, of Aza, Cerlas, Lalruk. I am the end of war. I am the goddess who dreams, and who mourns and who loves. I held the power of a star and her shadow within me and I bound the void between the realms. I am the saviour of this realm, of the mortal realm, and of the void. If you doubt my power, then I will remake this world until all who live in it are safe, until all who long for more are held to account, until the weak and the strong are equal." I lifted my chin and gestured to the rose that did not burn. "I am Calanthe, and I am your *queen*."

The tree pulled her rooted feet from the ground and bent before me, staring straight into my eye, taking in the burns and the scars, everything. "*You were the one who stabilised the realms?*"

In binding the void, I'd let the energy flow freely. "Yes," I said. "The door is my doing."

"And my mother," the Ocean Deep rumbled, "she is dead?"

"She died in the making of me. She and the Eternal Flame both. They...they gave everything they had to make me and send me to the mortal realm so I could fulfil my duty." I bowed my head. I had memories of Lady Earth, but none of the Eternal Flame.

"What of this creature?" the dragon asked,

pointing a claw at Casimir. "What of the Walker in Shadow?" Another point, this time at Dancer.

"Dancer is my friend," I said, laying a hand on his back even as he rumbled out a growl. "He won't harm you."

"He is younger even than you! To not even have a voice, yet." The dragon flicked its tongue out, tasting the air around Dancer. He hissed and hunched his shoulders, hackles rising. "Yet he has ventured to our realm, where his power is weak, without hesitation. A loyal creature indeed."

"And the other?" the tree-crone asked, looming over Casimir. He stiffened, those star-flecked shadows writhing around him in time with the ones on his skin. "You are...familiar. I know you."

Casimir's eyes flashed to mine, alarm there.

"Yes..." The Ocean Deep took in a deep breath, as if tasting the air. He let out a rumble, and the humidity in the air increased. "You are a Star guardian."

"I was bound to Astraea," Casimir said, lowering his head. "The binding is dissolved, and now I serve the queen."

"Astraea?" The dragon let out a puff of hot air, tasting of brimstone. "The star who chained us here? Who bound us to a dying realm with no way to thrive? Have you come to pay for your crimes, guardian?"

"The crimes were not his," I said, laying a hand on

the dagger at my belt, as if it would do anything against such vast and ancient gods. I reached for my magic, too, but I was still weak after only recently waking from magic sickness, and I doubted very much I could do anything against gods such as these. "They belonged to Astraea, and she has paid for them twice over."

"Astraea is dead." Casimir announced this clearly, without any hint of the anguish I knew he was feeling.

The dragon swung its head to me. Eagerness glinted in those cat-slitted eyes, and its claws dug deep into the ground. "At *your* hand?"

It might as well have been, as the fault for Talorsa being in the mortal realms was mine. Inevitable, perhaps, but still my fault. "No. She died saving the mortals from the god of war."

"We warned him and those others," the crone said, sighing as she straightened, her leaves rustling. "The mortal realm is a dangerous place. Myr went first, to test the waters, as it was. And when she— that was you? You killed Myr?"

I nodded.

The Ocean Deep let out a quiet sound, one of contemplation. "You are powerful for one so young, and I doubt your power has stopped growing."

"What would you have us do, young one?" the dragon growled. "You come here with a powerful claim, and you have the opening of the realms behind you. Assets, yes, but you must know that to take the throne, as you wish, is surely impossible. You are unknown here. We have ruled ourselves in our way for centuries since our chaining. Few will want to give that up. Your parentage may mean nothing at all in the face of those who would oppose you."

I frowned. "Will you oppose me?"

The dragon weaved its head. Its tail twitched. The Ocean Deep and the tree-crone watched the creature with interest, as if their own answers would be determined by whatever the dragon said. As if the fate of the entire realm would be determined by what the dragon said.

"If I told you I would oppose you?" it asked.

"Then I would tell you that I will continue to make my claim until this land is drowned in gold blood, and all the realms are safe from those who would take what does not belong to them."

The dragon dug its claws into the dirt and brought its face so close to mine that I could see my breath fogging on its scales. "You would dare plunge this realm into a war that might never end, simply so you could protect that which you left behind?"

"More than that," I snapped. "Any who need a voice that are voiceless. Like Emyna, who spent centuries here in pain and agony, simply because their domain was one for which the gods—*you*—had no need. I watched them die in my arms because of what was done to them and I refuse to watch it happen again. I will protect them all. Any who suffer because they are considered weaker, less powerful, not worth the effort of treating kindly."

Casimir stepped forward so he was by my side. Dancer bared his fangs at the dragon, ready to fight.

The dragon pulled back, snorting hot air through its nostrils. The tree-crone shifted, her roots digging deep into the earth, her expression unreadable through the bark. The Ocean Deep, though, gave a single nod of his head.

"You certainly have the spirit of my mother in you," he rumbled. "Oh, yes, there is the fire of the Eternal Flame, certainly, but that spirit? That enduring determination? That is entirely my mother."

I furrowed my brows, confused.

"We are the oldest of the gods, child," the crone said, brushing her root fingers over my hair. "With Father Sky bound to the heavens and Lady Earth and the Eternal Flame gone, we are the oldest. We were there when the mortal realm was born. We remember what it was like before. Before the birth of the stars, before the mortals worshipped us, before power became the ultimate goal. Times have changed, but I think...perhaps...that maybe it is time they change again."

"Change will not come easily," the Oceans Deep said in a low rumble, waves against a cliff. "That is the problem with immortality; it is easy to get set in one's ways and difficult to break out of it again."

"The rewards, though," the dragon said with a hungry glint in its eyes. "They will be vast."

I remained still. Beside me, the rose bush burned brightly, flaring with my surge of emotions, my surge of hope. Casimir threaded his hand through mine again and I held tightly. "So you will support me?"

"Yes," the Ocean Deep said. The dragon gave a nod of its head and the tree-crone bowed, her trunk creaking as she did.

Still, I hesitated, not quite certain I could trust this truth. Trust these people. The dragon chuckled. "We will not fight you, if that is what you seek. These claws are better meant for reading books than rending flesh. They have been dulled by the centuries."

"Welcome home, Sister." The Ocean Deep spread his arms, and for once, I didn't hold myself back as I threw myself into his arms. Into the touch of the only family I had left. He squeezed me tightly and spun me around, forcing a strangled laugh out of me.

My feet were barely on the ground before I broke out laughing again. Casimir came to my side, ready to hold me up should my laughter turn to hysterics. Instead, I leaned into him. "We did it," I breathed. "We did it."

"*You* did it." He kissed my hair. Dancer butted his way between us, rubbing his head against me. I knelt and buried my head in his fur.

"Now, come, let us show you the city. There is

much to be done. I'm sure you know full well that gods are stubborn creatures. Some will take a great deal of convincing. Luckily for you, you are immortal, or you would be bones and dust before anything got resolved," the dragon said, sweeping its tail towards the city.

The tree-crone made a rough sound in her throat. "I may *still* be bones and dust by then."

"You will outlive us all," the Ocean Deep said, slapping the crone on her shoulder and making her branches shed leaves. She immediately started bickering with him, the dragon punctuating the conversation with occasional remarks that told of a history long and storied between the three of them.

I had no such history. I woke a short while ago to a world on fire, no knowledge of who or what I was, no idea of my place in the world. Now, wearing the rags of mortals, stained with dirt and grim, hair tangled, scarred, broken, following behind the ancient gods, I finally felt like I was on my way to figuring that out. To crafting a history of my own. To understanding who I was.

I slipped my fingers through Casimir's, and with a smile at him, tugged him towards the city of the gods to take my place as queen.

ACKNOWLEDGMENTS

I would like to start by thanking Pip, my cat, who is currently sitting on my hand and making typing incredibly difficult. Your daily challenge to sit on me in the most inconvenient way for all things writing is endearing, and also extremely unhelpful. You're lucky you're cute.

A big thanks also to the people at Krafigs Design who helped redesign the covers for this series, taking my initial idea and making it so much more fantastic than I could have conceived. They're beautiful.

As always, there are too many individual people to thank, but they include the people who support me in my daily life, as well as those who read my books and don't think I'm (entirely) crazy for pursuing this as a dream. Readers like you make everything worthwhile and I would never have made it this far without you.

This duology has had my evolutions over the last year, from being a standalone to a series to its now, final, form. I am grateful for all the input from my fellow authors and readers who patiently listened and helped shape this story into what it has become.

You have my eternal gratitude.

ABOUT THE AUTHOR

Evelyn Grimald "E.G." Stone is an independent author, editor, and linguist who has been writing, creating and causing vast amounts of trouble since a young age. When not writing, she is off musing about the workings of languages—both real and created—or reading and sewing. E.G. reads voraciously, much to the confusion of her two dogs and two cats. Weird, nerdy, perhaps a little crazy, she is having a grand old time writing, reading, editing, musing on language, and, naturally, continuing her endeavours in causing trouble.

9 781954 865136